The Angel

of

Parliament

Harriet Bletchley

ISBN: 9781549817304

INTRODUCTION

In 2036, the death penalty has returned to Britain and the country has descended to unimaginable levels of decadence. Scientific breakthroughs and draconian new laws have jeopardised the very nature of humanity.

Evie Atherton, a young, ambitious, warm-hearted Home Secretary faces a terrifying task as she battles to survive in a corrupt Government who are using her as a sacrificial lamb.   Her destiny becomes entwined with the lives of:

- **Prema**, a midwife who has emerged from a bitter divorce and stands accused of murder, facing a barbaric death.

- **Aidan, an ex-Bishop and his wife Miriam**, caring for their bizarre extended family.

- **Oliver Bunton,** the eccentric Speaker of the House of Commons, who literally has his feathers in a twist....

Their lives become entangled, as the true extent of the darkness engulfing Britain emerges. But amidst the turmoil, a greater power is transforming their lives and none of them will ever be the same again. As Evie emerges through the refiner's fire of trauma, she is challenged to consider whether she has come to power for such a time as this......

DISCLAIMER

This is a work of fiction. Any resemblance to actual persons, living or dead, is purely coincidental. Names, characters, organisations, institutions, businesses, places, events and incidents (including medical processes and technology) are either the products of the author's imagination or used in a fictitious manner and their imagined future in 2036 is purely speculative. No parrots were harmed in the writing of this book!

ACKNOWLEDGEMENTS

Thank you to all my wonderful family, close friends and colleagues who have given me company, feedback, support, encouragement, food, coffee, the benefit of their wit and humour and relaxing home comfort away from the city to recharge my batteries during the writing process. You know who you all are!

Contents

i)   A Poisoned Chalice

Meridian Birthing Centre, South London, 9.30pm, 13th February, 2036

He was ten centimetres dilated.

Prema fought against fatigue in the icy, sterile delivery room.

"What am I doing in this vile place?"

She struggled to remain focused.

At the end of her fifteen-hour shift, her thin uniform and poor heating offered no protection against the coldest night in seventy-three years. Her numb fingers handed instruments to a surgeon who ignored her, except for an irritated rebuke when her reflexes were slower than his requests.

A dishevelled man lay on the trolley, with cold sweat mingling with his lank hair. He had a bloated, prematurely middle-aged, hormone filled torso and limp legs bulging with varicose veins, shaking arms and clenched fists. The block anaesthetic had almost eliminated the pain, but could not dull his fear. Every patient knew the risks.

She had a natural ability to calm her patients. Sustained eye contact, warmth and a quiet, intense authority.

"Nurse, I'm terrified!" I don't deserve this, it was only a driving offence."

"Harry, the Judge said you either do this or National Service.   I'm here to help you."

"My wife refused to come. She feels robbed!"

"OK, calm down and look at me. You'll be fine. Just a bit of pulling, but no pain."

The day was nearly over. She exerted her will to concentrate on the final task, shutting out the thought of three weeks holiday. Every patient deserved her full engagement.

The surgeon worked with relentless precision and the forceps slid home. Sam winced and Prema gripped his hand.

"OK, this won't hurt. You'll feel some pressure, that's all!"

The air turned blue as expletives resounded through the theatre and down the corridor.   A purple, slippery form was pulled into a cold, forbidding world.

A loud, indignant cry pierced through the theatre as a 9lb newborn expressed her outrage at the stark, bright, chilly surroundings greeting her.

"Congratulations, you have a beautiful baby girl!"

Prema clamped and cut the cord, gently wrapped the baby in a warm, white towel and handed her to Harry.

"There, meet your daddy! Can I take a picture for you?"

She repressed her inward revulsion. Everything about this screamed against her sense of right and wrong. But her patients deserved her very best. She told herself not to judge.   She reserved her anger for the system which let this happen and the man responsible....

Lewisham, South London, 13th February, 11.15pm

The fume-laden clouds above Lewisham rarely produced the right kind of snow.   They made a rare concession, when Prema had booked an 8.00am flight to Sydney for the following morning.

A ten-inch backlog of powdery flakes engulfed an eerily silent South Circular A210 road, adorning the tangle of commuter railway lines, Victorian terraces, 1990's yuppie flats and maisonettes, council blocks, cheap takeaways, barbers, car dealers and twenty-four-hour stores. The white blanket slowly stifled the sirens from fire-engines and Humanity Arrest Vans.

Prema gazed out of the window, exasperated yet half-mesmerised by flakes drifting onto her red Ford Mercury, white vans and the rusty corrugated roof of a dilapidated office. Snow, however unwelcome, has its own kind of peculiar seduction. Her ginger tom, Atrixo, emerged from a hedge, stretching his claws and gazing up at her window with green eyed pleading for a second helping of supper.

She drew back from the window and switched off News 24, bored by the pundits on global warming whom the BBC still wheeled out whenever freak weather reared its tiresome head.   She would snatch four hours of sleep, then check the travel news again. In fading hope of flying to Sydney, she zipped her case, placing it by the door.

She pulled on her dressing-gown and locked her front door, quietly confident that South East London had buried its collective head under a fifteen-mile duvet, in frustrated anticipation of closed schools and boisterous children, or the happy thought of cancelled trains, tubes, tramways and the luxury of working from home the next day.

In 2036, London was still incompetent at handling any kind of weather.

She curled into bed wearing socks, dressing-gown and cardigan over thick fleece pyjamas. As the chill yielded to warmth, she hovered fitfully between wakefulness and full sleep. To begin with, she had reassuring dreams of Atrixo as a kitten, jumping on her bed with a chewed plastic mouse and then the darker, fear filled visions of an angry face across the kitchen table, accusations, slammed cupboard doors, breaking glass, blood on her face, broken lip, begging, pleading, fear, falling…. a thud!

Suddenly she was wide awake and more alert, sharp and attuned than in her most frantic working hours. In the stillness, every shadow and shard of light stood in sharp relief. The ticking of her clock became a rousing hammering which shattered the soundproofing snow-blanket which wrapped the suburb.

Had that thud been real, or was it just part of the receding nightmare gripping her core and still strangling her with fear as waking reality reclaimed her senses? She sat up, pulling the duvet around her. Her solar heaters were not powerful enough to counter the chill from the outer wall of her bedroom. Silence. But not for sleeping. A pregnant, laden, living, crawling silence.

Her heart thudded as she heard dull footsteps along the opposite driveway. She edged the curtain open an inch, to see a tall figure in a heavy grey coat, rucksack and boots trudging towards the deserted main road.

It was only her colleague, Midwife Gregory Wilson leaving for his night shift at Meridian Birthing Centre. Wrapped for a thirty-minute trek, he would not start his car on a night like this, but faithful to duty (not to mention his public image), he would be a punctual and reassuring presence for anyone who had the misfortune to go into labour on the most treacherous night for seventy-three years.

Wilson's footfalls receded. Her breathing slowed and she curled into her pillows, desperate for sleep before her 4.30am departure, unlikely though that was becoming. But warmth and oblivion still eluded her. With an act of will she turned her mind to happier thoughts of Sydney, her twin sister Reeta, hot sun, long evenings and early-morning swimming.

Another thud!!! This time she sat up sharply and for a few seconds, panic and indecision engulfed her reasoning.   Then her mind made itself up. She slid out of bed, tightened her dressing gown and grasped a solar flashlight. It seemed to come from the direction of the lounge. Impossible! It wasn't Atrixo who had wisely entered the cat flap and now lay curled on her duvet.

Hesitating to leave the safe confines of her bedroom, she steadied her breathing, took a faltering step into the hallway and slowly edged downstairs.

She stepped into the kitchen. Strange…. there was a half-filled crystal glass of water by the sink. She never used the crystal except for visitors, why was it out of the cupboard? But a deeper instinct told her the terror lay in the dark expanse of her lounge. She moved downstairs towards the door. Fear, instead of sharpening her rational decision making, drew her relentlessly into her living room.

The dining room was pitch dark, totally still, but with a crawling presence, from this world or another? Something drew her, in sleepwalking terror, towards the table. The reflection of her heavy, gold framed mirror flashed the streetlight from the crack of open curtain. Her adrenaline levels pitched ten degrees higher. She had a split second to think: *"Why's my mirror on the chair? I was going to rehang it."*

Sudden, blinding, excruciating pain ripped through her head. She staggered, whimpered, turned her head and in the corner of her eye caught sight of a huge black figure poised to bear down again.

Concussed and sleepwalking, with no rational instinct, she grabbed the mirror and drew every ounce of muscle, sinew, lifeblood, strength into smashing it down on the intruder. She crashed the frame onto what seemed like a skull bone, shattering the glass. He fell against the chair and onto the floor.

Gasping, shaking, crying, semi-concussed.... her head swam from the blow to her temple. Her vision began to steady. She still held the mirror. She let it drop to the floor. For the first time, she felt the sharp pain of cuts, gashes and hot sticky blood on her hands...

Angelica House, Hertfordshire, 13th February, 12.30am

Angelica House was a politician's nightmare. It offered no grace and very little favour. Why they called it 'grace and favour' accommodation was anyone's guess.

The house was a cold, damp, high-ceilinged, poorly heated, grim silhouette of a building looming against the dreary, windswept fields half a mile from the twenty-four-hour droning of the M1. The threadbare Persian carpets and fittings, which had once been ornate and opulent, did nothing to compensate for the fading curtains and fraying upholstery.

The Right Honourable Evie Atherton, Home Secretary, was sprawled on a sofa in a draughty study. She was surrounded by the cold remains of a solar heated meal, research reports, papers and drafts of a speech which stubbornly refused to pull together with sufficient coherence to prevent mortification in the House of Commons at 3.30pm tomorrow.

Style Hobbs, her tall, slightly dishevelled Private Personal Secretary sat on the floor, collating papers and trying to bring order to her free-spirited chaos.

"Style, let me get you a hot chocolate!"

"If you were Margaret Thatcher, you'd offer me a double whisky!"

"If I were Margaret Thatcher, God rest her, they wouldn't dare dump me in this draughty, fungus-ridden ice box! Anyway, if you're driving me back to London, you can't drink, remember!

"Fat chance of me driving in these Arctic conditions!"

"I need to finish this Geriatric Crime Prevention speech and I must brief the PM by 8.00am!"

Energetic, chaotic Evie had been appointed Home Secretary just nine weeks ago. At thirty-five, a 'rising star' in the Government and useful PR commodity for a party still dominated by a male hierarchy.

Fifty years of equality legislation had still not fully penetrated corridors of Westminster. No-one could legislate for human nature and terms like 'lass', 'totty' and 'skirt' (to coin the politer terms) were still used at all male party booze-ups, from which she was excluded.

The right-wing tabloids adored her, maximising every photo-opportunity and anecdote on her lifestyle, while praising her entrepreneurial skills, academic genius, agile mind, intuition and vision.

Women's fashion pages devoured the colour of her nail polish, the shape of her eyebrows (1950s arched and pencilled), ample thighs, bright primary colours, long brunette hair immaculately flicked back and her trademark electric blue eyeshadow and massive earrings which had stirred yet another 1980's revival.

Evie was the antithesis of what politicians called 'middle England'. Her rounded size 14 figure endeared her to both women and men. Her northern accent, flushed complexion and genial brassy manner distanced her from Tory Independence stereotyping. 'Young, alternative and fearless' were the more flattering adjectives used to describe her. The comments of her detractors were less printable.

She sighed angrily.

"The Tory Independence party have stitched me up. My promotion to the Home Office has nothing to do with my talents. The Prime Minister and his cronies are snivelling cowards!"

"Snivelling cowards? That's a bit harsh, Evie."

"It's true! No-one wants the job, now the new Penal Reform Act is law. And since they closed the Ministry of Justice in 2035, responsibility for Prisons has reverted to the Home Office."

"Bad luck!"

"Worst of all, the Labour Socialists abandoned their principles and voted for the new law!"

"They wanted to embarrass and derail our minority Government."

"Of course, Style. They've forced us to pass a law we've publicly supported for years, while never wanting to enact it! My post is now a poisoned chalice and I'm a sacrificial lamb."

Evie knew the Prime Minister had already planned to distance himself from her. Dismissively, he had given her the worst 'grace and favour' accommodation in England. She would never live at Dorneywood, Chevening, Chequers or Admiralty House. Instead, her rural bolt hole was a dilapidated, disused Bishop's palace in the Home Counties.

She gazed at the cracked wall and shuddered.

"I hate these Victorian portraits of ancient Bishops glowering at me."

England was littered with empty Bishop's palaces. The Government decided to use them. The Church of England had finally split in 2027. In divorce terms, it would have been called irreconcilable differences. The Biblical Anglican Fellowship had drawn away 90,000 parishioners, 500 clergy and 14 Bishops.

Evie now battled fear, loneliness and suspicion in a grim house where the disillusioned echoes of the former ecclesiastical incumbent resounded in her brain. She frantically forced herself to shut out the mocking whispers calling success a cruel impostor. She could not acknowledge the taunting jab of their fingers so early in her career. She continued to force her smiles, wisecracks and down to earth charm. She drove her feisty spirit to jolly herself, as well as the world around her.

Invisible eyes bored into her, in this poison-laden gilded cage. She would laugh and joke with Style, but never mistook his camaraderie for friendship. Style was a fast-rising Cambridge educated civil servant with a master's degree in stealth which belied his geeky charm, good humour and self-effacing manner. If she fell tomorrow, he would endear himself to her successor, without a backward glance.

"Style, put the telly on, it's too quiet in here!"

She needed a distraction. The homely chuntering of the hologram TV would drown out the fear she refused to entertain.

Style stretched across the floor and flicked on the news. There were stories of holidaymakers stranded at Heathrow, Gatwick and Stanstead. The entire rail network was in meltdown as snow drifts increased. Then news coverage moved on to geriatric alcohol and drug-abuse which was rife across England, especially among over-seventy-fives who were forced to continue working.

Suddenly a news flash and picture of a missing twenty-five-year-old woman in Devon leapt onto the screen. Evie dropped her paper and sat straight amidst the crumpled notes around her. Her stomach tensed. Stories like this brought the crouching terror one step nearer. The woman had been missing for thirty-six hours. Evie glanced out of the window at the clearing moonlit skies and falling temperature. No-one could survive out in that….

"Not another one! Eighteen women have gone missing in the last three months!"

The dread of the ultimate crime rose from the knot in her stomach and poured out in an anguished cry.

"Not a murder case, please!   No!!"

Style looked at her grimly. He understood her unspoken fear, but could do nothing to help her. His support for her would be impeccable, as he scaled the heights of his own Whitehall career.

"Evie, you'll be fine. Let's cross that bridge when we come to it."

He would say all the right things to her, but any student-fanned embers of compassion were cooling as he rose in status and favour with 'the powers that be' and the poker of conscience rarely stoked his once youthful heart to life these days.

Evie struggled to regain her equilibrium.

A high-profile murder, with media coverage was her ultimate nightmare and every missing person brought it closer….

Lewisham, 13th February, 12.45am

Prema had stumbled to the light switch, as her shaking and gasping gave way to numbness at what lay before her. Unable to move, she lifted her hand to wipe away her tears and then winced in pain as the movement pulled on a gash in her forearm.

Shattered crockery, photo-frames, magazines and other personal effects were strewn upon a newly-washed carpet, which was now, smattered with blood, splattered onto the upholstery, airing laundry and suitcase.

The trail of blood flowed from a lifeless six-foot figure in a heavy black overcoat which was slumped forward, beside the shattered remains of the mirror.

It was several minutes before she could steady her frame enough to edge towards the battered form. She hesitated, crouched down and gathered enough courage to hold the limp wrist. The absence of pulse reassured her that her assailant would not renew his attack. She dropped the grey hand with a shudder.

Rational thought tentatively resumed activity in her brain. Reality began to engulf the numbness in her spirit, rising from her core into a gut-wrenching scream which echoed down the street and broke into the muffled snow outside. She screamed again, this time with a sob rising in her throat, vaguely aware of the noise and scuffle of neighbours stirring.

Her mind began to register action. She must call the Police. She reached for her phone, but before dialing, suddenly turned back to the corpse again. An unknown instinct urged her to lift the shoulder and turn the head. As she did so, the familiarity of the heavy-jawed features caused bile to rise in her stomach and a cry of anguish and terror cut across the snow-deadened landscape.

"Ralph!!"

She clasped her hand to her face, smearing blood against her brown complexion and dark, cascading hair.

Her huge dark eyes, so used to concealing her true feelings and presenting a mask to the world, reflected terror and searing loss.

The force which had generated love, passion, then in later years dread and fear, lay lifeless before her.

He was not meant to be there. She had changed the locks.

But as she registered the freezing draught for the first time in an hour, she realised the front door was open...

Peckham, South London, 13th February, 13.00am

Bishop Aidan Breakspeare huddled by his kitchen boiler, with a pint mug of Horlicks.

Lively teenagers outside welcomed the first snow in seven years as a cue for a party. Boisterous snowball fights intermingled with thudding music, raucous excitement from the nearby pub, a late-night family party in a West Indian restaurant, a hen night and banter from a group of students alighting from an intrepid, mud strewn night bus, which had somehow fought its way through the elements to convey them from Trafalgar Square to their rented flats. In this street, anything was an excuse for a celebration.

But he had fallen in love with Peckham, with its vibrant, cosmopolitan explosion of energy, colours, smells and juxtaposition of cultures. He thrived on its unpretentious vivacity, the warmth despite the all too real corners of deprivation and poverty, edged with shadows of danger.

This corner of Southwark had embraced and enfolded him, beginning to heal the raw wounds of the past two years, though he still felt battered, bruised, rejected, humiliated and emotionally drained.

He had an overwhelming urge to love the community back, not just driven by indebtedness, but from a heart expanded by the camaraderie and affection of people to whom life had dealt all manner of body blows, but who seemed to roll and bounce back.

He had arrived in Peckham as ex-Bishop, licking his wounds and had found friendship and, he hoped, the beginning of his real identity. But the healing process was slow, as he and Miriam came to terms with their status as outcasts from public life.

Miriam wandered in anxiously staring at her wrist-phone.

"Any news Miriam?"

"No, dear, she's still on the labour ward and only 5 centimetres dilated, poor love. Dave's trying to be supportive, but he just keeps winding her up, bless him."

"Amelia has a short fuse at the best of times!"

"She's getting exhausted, but still refusing an epidural. She's been there since lunchtime. I wish I could talk some sense into her. Look, I can't just sit here, I can try to drive there, if we clear the path!"

"But it will freeze over later. She'll be fine. She's in good hands"

"That midwife Gregory Wilson is looking after her!"

"Oh no, him??!!"

"Yes. Frankly, I would rather she had a vet!"

"Well, I just hope he remembers his training in conventional medicine."

Their revulsion was ideological rather than clinical, but the whole idea was no less distasteful. There was nothing to be done for now. Miriam reboiled the kettle, poured a drink and joined her husband at the narrow breakfast bar.

"This is so cramped!"

"At least it's warmer than Angelica House. Decent central heating, no damp and no mice.

The painful memories surfaced as they quietly drew comfort from their closeness and hot beverages. Angelica House had been inhospitable, with the dingy, forbidding ambience being a backdrop to the conflict, rejection and isolation which had engulfed them. The very walls in each room had seemed to glower at their presence as an unwelcome disturbance to their grim and soulless equilibrium.

"I hated that place, Miriam".

"So did I. I really feel for Evie Atherton. She must be miserable there, all on her own."

"Don't get ideas!"

"Oh, don't worry, she's too much of a trollop for our Ben!"

'Project Ben' helped Miriam to numb her own heartache. Their thirty-five-year-old social worker son was content with a South London flat and string of ill-assorted girlfriends.

Miriam absorbed the pain of others. Her well intentioned projection of her own suffering included counselling, pastoral visiting, a toddler group and adult literacy classes. Her once attractive features carried the battle scars of stress, sleepless nights and upheaval.

Her husband's anguish had been hers too. Bishop Aidan had founded the Biblical Anglican Fellowship (BAF) with thirteen other bishops, who had concluded they could not accept the national Male Pregnancy Incentive Scheme, the law against baptising babies with gender specific or Biblical names, or marriage to non-human primates.

The BAF ran a tireless national campaign to convince the public that such acts had no Biblical foundation and were clearly against the laws of nature, whether one had any faith or none.

Meanwhile, the Episcopalian Church of England had accommodated all the new laws passed by successive governments. Claiming that they reinterpreted the Scriptures in the light of changing knowledge and human experience, they declared their acceptance demonstrated their 'caring' approach.

A very 'hip' London church had funded the production of a Bafta-winning film called 'A Parking Ticket to Africa,' about a female Baboon's unrequited love for a fifty-year-old traffic warden.

Those who protested, such as Bishop Aidan had been called bigoted, fundamentalist, antediluvian nasty pieces of work by the church, media and every 'right-on' group which called itself enlightened. As Aidan and Miriam had settled into Peckham, they had struggled to forgive their vitriolic enemies, while gradually healing from every poisoned dart, backstab and insult that had been hurled at them.

There were days when anger surfaced and tears flowed. But at the age of sixty-five, despite their own vulnerability, they embraced a new-grown family of every shape, size and situation in the vibrant corner of Southwark where they had been catapulted.

Miriam downed the final dregs of her Horlicks.

"Did you apply for that job, Miriam?"

"Yes love, the Hospital Chaplain post and that Prison Chaplain role as well. I used my maiden name on both forms."

"You don't want to be tainted by association! They'll soon find out you're married to me, though!"

"I need something to keep me busy. Maybe they'll take a chance on me."

"But you're already busy, sweetheart."

"I think we should write to that Home Secretary lass, poor love. I've still got Evie Atherton's email address. I do wonder how she's settling into our old house. There's a knack to getting air out of those radiators, we should have left her a note. Yesterday, I saw her in front of those crowds of paparazzi. She's so young to face all that."

"I doubt if she'd let you mother her. She has a very old head on those sturdy young shoulders."

"But does anyone care about her? People are only interested in whether she exfoliates her knees, or whether she really will implement the October 2035 Penal Reform Act. I wouldn't want to be in her shoes."

"Neither would I, not now!"

Aidan and Miriam looked at each other. Whatever they endured, it was nothing compared to the baptism of fire awaiting Evie Atherton.

Lewisham, 13th February, 13.15am

"I've killed my husband... I've killed my husband!"

With a piercing scream, she slumped in an armchair sobbing, gasping and mangling saturated tissues in her hands. She turned away from the patch where she had vomited, as she felt bile rising in her throat again.

A cascade of tears tumbled down her face, but only partly driven by grief for the man who had tormented her life for six years and then abandoned her. She felt horror, fear and revulsion at what she had done to protect her own life. She was overwhelmed with shock that this was not an unknown rapist or murderer, but the person with whom she had once vowed to share her life.

She felt genuine sorrow for the loss of the father–figure she had married and the hope he had offered to a lonely twenty-five-year-old. But there was no grief for the monster he had become. The very smell of his hormone-infused shower gel turned her stomach.

A colossus lay at her feet. Ralph Hardcastle, Senior Consultant, Abdominal and Gynaecological Surgeon. A towering academic genius whose breakthrough had driven a scalpel, not merely into human flesh, but into the very rock and core upon which society was founded. To some people he was a pioneer, but to others he was nothing but an emissary of the darkest force endeavouring to grip the world.

She had been cut free physically, emotionally and legally and the final signing of the divorce paperwork had been accompanied with the cleaning of cupboards, filling of bags for charity shops and systematic disposal of every item that linked her to him or triggered excruciating memories.

Three precious weeks in Australia had beckoned, with a new-found self-confidence for a future without that dark spirit and toxic entanglement, with its calculated dismantling of her sense of self, breaking of her will and crushing of her spirit.

With frightening arrogance, he had called himself 'the spirit of the age and a new dawn'. Who was she to challenge a man who regarded himself as a global force?

That holiday, the longest she had booked in her working life, would have been her final step of freedom. The knowledge that she was capable, independent, and not the helpless, incompetent waif that he and his cohorts had led her to believe. Because it wasn't just him, it was the others. It had only been a few months before he had introduced her to them....

But Ralph always won. Ralph always had the last word and even in death, the mocking, lifeless eyes seemed to relish the fact that, once again, she had lost. She would not be boarding a plane, or even attempting to negotiate her way through a frozen and dysfunctional railway network.

The hysterical yapping of a Jack-Russell along the road mingled with the voices of neighbours stirring, their slumber being replaced by a realisation that there was something more dramatic afoot than severe weather. The general commotion drowned out the sound of the police car and the sudden, sharp, loud knock at the door delivered a fresh stab of fear into her stomach.

She opened the door. For many years she would torment herself with the incoherent flow of words which tumbled from her mouth.

"I've killed someone… he was an intruder. He smashed me over the head. I killed him. I didn't mean to kill my ex-husband!"

Bill Clinton Towers, Peckham, 14th February, 10.00am

Bishop Aidan pushed his spoon around the chipped, deeply stained coffee mug and allowed the remains of his drink to go cold. Before him sat a straggle-haired youth, with thin arms, grey complexion, a missing front tooth and red eyes, wrapped in a large, loose jumper which seemed his only protection against a world which had thrown every cruel taunt in its armory against his young, short life.

For the next hour, he would push aside his own euphoria at becoming a grandfather. The visit to see his granddaughter must wait, while his exhausted daughter had a well-earned sleep.

"I'm scared Aidan, mate, really scared."

"Well you know I'm here. Me and Miriam, we're always here for you."

Aidan placed an arm around the skinny, angular frame, clasped a clammy, veined, bony hand and became aware of stale breath, cold rancid sweat and a wheezing catch of breath.

"I'm frightened they'll take it away from me."

"Who?"

"The social welfare people, when they find out about my history with the Police, the drugs…"

"You must get clean, Tony, you've got to stick at it."

"I've tried. I've been on the programme, but it's so tough."

"For the sake of the baby."

"But it's hard. I'm throwin' up all the time. No-one warned me it would be like this. I'm shivering and my back really hurts."

Bishop Aidan gathered the frayed cushions on the sofa and eased them behind Tony's back, trying to make him comfortable. He reached for his parka and spread it over Tony's knees. The flat was cold, even with the solar heater the Council had provided for him.

"Why did you do it, Tony?"

"To get this council flat, of course."

Bishop Aidan sighed with exasperation which was not directed towards the frightened youth before him, but the entire system which lured the Tonys of this world into their pregnant condition.

"The benefits for pregnancy scheme?"

"Yeah."

Aidan sighed angrily.

"I'm not angry at you Tony, but I'm furious with the Government. I was shocked when they introduced male pregnancy on the NHS in 2020, with uterus implants and Caesarean delivery, especially when they started offering it to heterosexual men."

Aidan had protested alongside other Christians. Many Jews, Moslems and people of other faiths and none had also been horrified. Certain religious groups had tolerated or embraced it, however.

There had been cries of concern from many in the medical profession about the potential long-term physical and psychological health risks to a child born in this way. Many men had died during pregnancy and birth, or suffered long-term health complications.

Aidan sighed.

"Uterus implants, with Caesarean births, were pretty civilised compared with what you'll have to do, Tony."

"But what exactly will happen to me?"

"You'll have to push the baby out. You've had uterus colon interface surgery. Ralph Hardcastle pioneered it in 2031.   You have a uterus transplant, with a cervix and expandable stent grafted into your colon. The stent has the elasticity of a birth canal."

Tony's face looked blank.

"I don't understand any of this. What's my colon?"

"Have they explained nothing to you? Your colon is part of your intestine. They've put a special bionic sensor valve in your intestine, to keep your bowel closed when you're in labour."

"But how do I go into labour?"

"You'll be induced with a high-dose oxytocin injection, which stimulates contractions in your uterus. They'll shut down your digestive system, beforehand."

"I'm terrified. Other blokes have died."

There had been an aggressive media campaign to say the process was safe, but the tragic deaths of hundreds of young men had nearly ended the whole venture.   The colon was not designed to be stretched ten centimetres and the pain, without anaesthesia, was unimaginable.

The health risks (among others) included puncture, rupture and damage to internal organs, blood poisoning, internal bleeding, hemorrhaging and the side effects of hormone treatment.

But in 2034, new UN equality laws demanded a 5% quota of male colonic births from each member nation, which became condition for World Bank funding and many trade agreements. After a major recession, the British economy had been in dire straits.

Under vehement protest from some parts of the church, the Government had introduced the Male Birth Incentive Scheme, to persuade men between twenty and forty-five to undergo the dreaded process.

Tony knew the risks. Every month there was another tabloid newspaper story about the heartbreak of a mother, wife or girlfriend who had lost a son, husband, or boyfriend in a painful agony for which his anatomy had never been designed.

Some young criminals were given the choice of community service (i.e. participating in the Male Birth Incentive Scheme) or joining the Army. Most of them chose National Service, preferring to take their chances in the more turbulent areas of the Middle East.

Tony shifted on his threadbare sofa. A lethargic cat emerged from under the soiled plastic-covered table. The contemptuous expression in its eyes, made Bishop Aidan unwelcome. From the smell of the carpet, this cat also hated outdoor excursions and regarded the short stroll to the litter tray as a distasteful imposition.

Aidan and Tony jumped at the abrupt sound of the key turning in the lock. Tony sighed when he heard the familiar voice.

"Tony? Tony! Where are you? Who've you got in there?"

"Nan! Aidan's here with me."

Norma McCrief staggered into the room with bags of fruit, vegetables and fresh fish. At five feet tall, she towered over everyone by the sheer force of her presence. The hooked nose, missing front tooth, dangling cigarette and grey hair drawn severely back from her face made her all the more imposing.

Ignorant but not unintelligent, she carried her small-mindedness with a poise and authority which gave nonsense credibility. A trait which gave her the upper-hand over those she caught off-guard.

Aidan had a good rapport with her, but that acceptance had been hard-earned. She was accompanied by Ceiba, a fresh faced, feisty, seventeen-year-old with a ten-month old baby girl strapped to her front.

"I told you nana, I shop online. And the Council brings me a box of stuff!"

"I know you. You don't eat any fruit and veg. And I've brought you some cod-livin' oil!"

"It's cod liver oil."

"Don't argue with me. You got yerself in this mess! He got 'imself in this mess. You tell'im Bishop Adrian!"

"It's Aidan actually."

"And I'm inna right mess an 'all, 'cos I'll have to look after the babe, won't I! 'Cos Tony can't look after it and the forrities will take it away!"

Aidan looked puzzled.

"The forrities?"

Ceiba sighed.

"She means the authorities."

"That's what I said. The forrities! Anyway, how's he gonna give birth? I was thirty-six hours having his mother. And Ceiba had a seizure."

"I had a Caesarean," Ceiba corrected her, "and it wrecked my bikini line. But Tony you ain't fit enough to go through all that. You couldn't 'andle 'aving a splinter pulled out of your toe. You wouldn't 'andle it, Tony. I was bad enough, but at least I'm the right shape. Heaven knows what your insides are like after that surgeon messed them about."

Tony's spirit was already weakened. In silent acquiescence to their words, his eyes pleaded with Aidan for reassurance.

"They'll look after you, Tony. The Health Trust provides the best care to men who join the scheme. You've got Midwife Gregory Wilson managing you. He'll be with you right the way through. "

"Yeah," added Ceiba sarcastically, "you'll remember Gregory Wilson's got an OBE, a TV Personality of the Year award and he won that jungle celebrity reality show, so you're in expert hands."

It was clear from the expression in Tony's eyes that the insect eating exploits of Midwife Gregory Wilson offered little or no reassurance.

"Will you be there, Bishop Aidan?"

Aidan felt ashamed of his slight hesitation, but in a split second realised that there was only one reply he could decently give. And from the God he served, he sensed a quiet nudge to overcome his squeamishness.

"Er, yes…., yes, of course I will Tony."

"Promise?"

"Yes, I'll be there."

Aidan squeezed Tony's hand and could see a tear of relief welling in that weathered, life-ravaged young face.

Norma McCrief sensed she was losing her place as the centre of attention, a position in life she hated to forfeit.

"Well, you useless primagravity, are you gonna fix us a cuppa tea or not?"

At seventeen, Ceiba was a qualified life expert with combined honours in pregnancy, fake tan and nail extensions.   She could not resist the chance to correct her grandmother.

"The word's primigravida, nan."

Tony sighed and pulled himself out of the chair. Aidan gently eased him back.

"I'll make a cup for everyone, you stay there, Tony."

Aidan was used to making himself at home. He slipped into the kitchen, filled the kettle and started to wash some chipped mugs from the pile on the draining board. Norma joined him and wiped up, tutting at the lack of cleanliness. She sank into a subdued silence. Sensing the heaviness, Aidan looked at her gently. She answered the unspoken question.

"You'll be with 'im, won't ya, when his time comes?"

"Yes, of course I will."

"Well, you'd darn well better be, mate. He's got a weak institution, he has."

"You mean constitution?"

"Yeah, that's what I said!"

Norma tightened her lips and was trying to compose herself. The armour plated matriarch was showing the tiniest crack of vulnerability. Aidan was silent, pretending not to notice and he graciously allowed her to regain her self-possession.

"He doesn't know what he's doing. I blame that Job Centre. They get pregnancy commission, they do. They get some young bloke who can't get a job. They give him all this talk about a council flat, extra benefits and food parcels. They don't warn 'em what it's like. That operation nearly did him in. He could barely move for eight weeks. And he got blood poisoning."

"Norma, I feel the same way as you do, but the only thing we can do now is support Tony."

"They show them this flippin' publicity film, making it all look nice. They make those poor lads think they're doing their bit for King and country. It's brainwashing, innit!"

"Yes, Norma, I realize that."

"So why didn't he ask me first?"

"He only thought about the money. For all of you."

"He never considered what happens if he dies! I lost my daughter. I ain't gonna lose him as well!"

"I'll be here for both of you, whatever happens."

"I can't believe both my granddaughter and grandson have got themselves up the duff! He won't die, will he?"

"He'll have the best care."

"And what about that God of yours?"

"You're a bit cynical about all that, aren't you?"

"Yeah. But I'm keeping my options open. At the moment, I'll try anything. So, you'd better darn well say your prayers, you Bishopric! You're supposed to have a hot line."

ii)   Lucinda

Lewisham Police Station, 14ᵗʰ February, 11.30am

Prema sat on the floor in a cold, narrow police cell. Carefully avoiding the damp walls, the filthy bunk and bucket shared with a fellow inmate, she curled in a ball as though her own body was the only shield against reality, now that the first shock of the night's events had passed.

Her head throbbed and blood seeped through her matted dark hair, the makeshift bandage and stitches, which a paramedic had hastily applied, before the police had thrown her, sobbing and disoriented, into the icy damp hovel. Peeling brown paint mingled with graffiti and black patches of condensation.

The woman on other bunk was dishevelled and badly bruised with a broken and bleeding lip. She was tall, muscular and wearing expensive sports clothing under a thick parka, legwarmers and long scarf wrapped several times around her neck. Her face was lightly tanned, with neatly shaped eyebrows and surprisingly delicate features for such a strongly built woman.   She looked rough and ready, but there was a refinement about her.

The torment of that first Police interview replayed through her mind. She had sat eyeball to eyeball with a burly, aggressive, red-faced officer who thumped the table.

"You killed your ex-husband deliberately, fully knowing who he was! You could not have mistaken him for an intruder. If he had a key, is it not reasonable to assume he's allowed into your house?"

In the cold grey light of the morning, Prema asked herself how on earth Ralph had obtained that key?

She had answered every question with slow, careful precision, hesitating between sentences as she gathered her thoughts. To anyone who didn't know her, her quiet, studied reticence seemed like defiance. Prema refused to be rushed by anyone, a quality which could infuriate friends or enemies in equal measure. Others mistook her slowness for timidity.

"You had a packed suitcase by your door! You booked a flight to Australia didn't you! I suggest you planned to dispose of Ralph, disappear and change your identity!"

After an excruciating silence, Prema had replied:

"I would hardly have raised the alarm if that was the case."

"Your plan backfired, didn't it! There was a commotion, your neighbours woke up and you had no choice but to ring the Police and pretend it was an accident."

"That's not true."

"And the bad weather ruined your little escape plan, too! No planes, no trains!"

"But how could I have disposed of Ralph on my own? He's massive."

"Hah! You're a trained nurse and midwife, very used to carrying heavy stuff and lifting and supporting male patients."

"I've never had to carry a man, let alone dragged a dead weight."

But the officer and his quieter colleague continued to bully and cajole her in the interrogation room, twisting every word she said.

The law would allow them to detain her in this putrid cell for a whole week without charging her. She had been allowed one phone call.   She had tried to call Midwife Gregory, only to be told he was in the middle of a press conference, paying tribute to her late husband.

In desperation, she had finally phoned her frantic twin sister with the news that she would not be arriving on the 2.00am flight in Sydney or leaving England any time soon.

They had given her a solicitor during their questioning. He was the last word in low energy.

Her cellmate stirred from a concussed, morose stupor and groaned expletives at whoever had reduced her to this state.

Prema slowly lifted her head from her knees and looked across to the glassy eyes, extending a glance of empathy towards another battered creature flung into this place.

Angelica House, 12 noon

Evie was not sitting in Portcullis House in Westminster eating a hearty lunch before the afternoon Parliament session.

She was livid at being stranded at Angelica House, with roads and rail at a standstill. They would not send her a swift-chopper, the small, light, sleek vessel which had superseded the helicopter. They were a luxury enjoyed by ministers, but today, the Whitehall mandarins preferred to save money. How dare they!!

The House of Commons was virtually empty, courtesy of cancelled trains and impassable roads. Even in 2036, presence in person was mandatory and hologram appearances were not accepted.   As hundreds of MPs gave their apologies, party whips gave up the ghost. Many MPs were grateful to stay huddled in their constituencies.

Evie had been fiercely determined to travel to London. She had sat up until 3.00am finishing her speech. She had sent a copy to the PM's implant phone and snatched 3 hours sleep before their hologram meeting.

Infuriatingly, her speech had been 'bumped' in favour of the Male Employment Bill. Never mind geriatric crime, male job applicants must be given the right to avoid declaring their uterus implant surgery to potential employers!

She demolished a third bacon sandwich and a honey and cashew chocolate bar. She noticed her flushed, blotchy complexion in the mirror. A cold-sore was appearing at the side of her mouth and there were dark circles under her eyes. Her long, raven-black locks cascaded in a dishevelled tangle down her back, in serious need of attention from her stylist and her immaculately-tailored skirt pulled uncomfortably across her abdomen. She didn't care.

A morning wasted on self-pity. Miserable thoughts had hovered round her head for weeks. Now they made a bird's nest in her mind. She had fought them off, pushed them away, distracted herself and laughed with others at her own expense, making allowances for snide comments, or deflecting them with a witty remark of her own.

Her defence walls had finally crumbled. She felt slimed and the gunk from peoples' spite which seemed to make her skin crawl was in danger of mutating into self-hatred. She was in danger of absorbing the emotions of others and embedding them as her own. Her spirit was weakening, but any awareness of the invisible darkness closing in on her was eclipsed by a fiercely secular upbringing, education and working environment.

Then she panicked.

"I need to be camera-ready."

She pulled herself out of the sofa. The effort was excruciating, but Evie's early success in life had been the fruit of fierce self-discipline.

She wanted to vent her rage with a torrent of expletives and then fling herself on the sofa and sleep for 10 hours. But her enemies wanted her to break. Her tenacity, driven by a mix of pride, indignation and fear of failure was just enough to rouse her to push back. For now, she would bury the pain and vulnerability, which would bide it's time for another opportunity to surface and dislodge her.

"Hologram interview. They'll ask me for a hologram interview!?"

TV channels and websites would soon tire of the Minister of Transport's pathetic excuses, after yet another failure of his Department to cope with British weather. After the national meltdown following the October 2035 hurricane, there was little more to say about England's failure to deal with a few inches of snow.   Indignant pundits tweeted:

"We live in an age where a man can give birth, but we still can't get our trains running!"

There was still no news on the missing woman from Exeter. How many more? A serial killer? The pattern seemed too random. One was from Perth, one from Belfast, another from Hull…. yet none of them found.

"I must check my mail!"

She grabbed her plasma pad and clicked the heading of each electronic message. The voice recognition programme read out the opening line.

She shuddered. Fifty messages on the Penal Reform Act, which The House of Lords had passed by the slimmest majority. Now the Government expected her to implement it in England, Wales and Northern Ireland.

After seventy-two years, the British Government had reintroduced the death penalty for murder, as well as treason.

Lewisham Police Station, 14th February, 12.30

Lucinda Grant was an entertaining cellmate. Bruised, battered and dishevelled, she nonetheless exuded vibrancy, resilience and humour. Her accent betrayed her boarding and finishing school background, but her warm, open, accepting manner, even in these dubious circumstances was fast recommending itself to Prema.

Lucinda was svelte and her manicure and perfectly highlighted hair screamed high maintenance and if anything, her broken nails, split botoxed lip and dishevelled hair seemed to give her even greater poise. Lucinda had warmly taken to the calm, patient, diminutive and knowing creature with huge brown eyes, who had mysteriously appeared in the cell while she had been asleep, and who was clearly out of place in such grim surroundings. Prema was enjoying her anecdote, which momentarily distracted her from the horror of her situation.

"So, I screamed 'fascist swine! Tory Independence pigs OUT! OUT! OUT!' Then we lunged at the barricade on Blackheath, darling! They dragged me through the snow and I was freezing and bruised down my arm. My bike was wrecked. And look at my face! And now I'm in this wretched cell, I've missed my slot with my personal trainer!"

"But how ever did two thousand of you get there in this weather?"

"We're called Cyclists for Justice, darling! It takes more than a bit of snow to scare us lot off! We couldn't get to Westminster, so we all gathered at Blackheath. I thought I would demonstrate for a couple of hours and then nip into a bar for a brandy-and-ginger! The Police weren't ready for our barrage of icy missiles or our snow barricade!"

"So why are you demonstrating?"

"We're protesting against the Guillotine, darling! It's barbaric! Can you believe they're planning to chop people's heads off? They haven't done it in England for three hundred years! Well, they used an axe then, but even so!

It's evil! Inhumane! It's taking this country right back to the Middle Ages! If someone commits murder and we execute them, we will simply be going down to their level!"

Prema's complexion turned grey.

"But surely, no British judge will actually sentence anyone to death? They won't…. they won't go through with it, will they? Surely people won't stand for it?"

"It's the law, now, darling! A New Year present from the Government!"

"Yes, but everyone was horrified when the law was passed and they only scraped it through by two votes. There was a public outrage, even from people who used to support it!   Everyone thought the House of Lords would block it."

"Some of liberal, lefty Lords would have done, but some of that lot thought it would be a laugh to vote for it and embarrass the Government! And the Tory Independence Party recently packed the house with right-wing peers, but I bet they're regretting it now!"

"But I thought they were only bringing it back for really nasty cases like child murderers and serial killers? Like whoever's killed all those missing women?"

"Don't you believe it. The first big murder trial in England or Wales will be a test of the Government's strength. They're a minority Government and can't afford to look weak."

Prema tried to fight the nausea rising in her stomach. Lucinda was in full flow, oblivious to her new companion's discomfort.

"And if the Government does wimp out, their confidence and supply agreement will fall apart. After all, who demanded the death penalty in the first place?"

"The Meccan Party, of course. But they only have twelve MPs at the moment".

"That's enough to bring down the minority government! Anyway, they owe the Meccan Party a favour, especially after appointing a woman as Home Secretary! If the Meccan Party is campaigning to move women back into traditional roles, they don't want female ministers!"   Lucinda tried to wipe her lip as it trickled blood and Prema passed her a crumpled tissue.

"They really hurt you."

"I can handle it darling. Boarding school and an alcoholic mother taught me to cope with anything. Even when I was home at Woodley Hall, I had to fend for myself. Stuff like this is water off a duck's back. Anyway, when life's unfair, it gives you a sense of justice. At least by protesting I'm doing something."

"So, what happens now, Lucinda?"

"Oh, Magistrates Court, a fine and an electronic photo record to get me banned from the best clubs. But don't worry darling, the nightclubs know me! Anyway, enough about me, what about you? Why are you in here?"

Prema hesitated. She was enjoying the company of this entertaining madcap and did not want to lose it.

"There was an accident last night...... an intruder came into my house. I went down to investigate and he attacked me in the dark, and smashed me over the head. So, I grabbed a mirror and hit him. I saw he was dead. Then I realised he was my ex-husband."

Lucinda sat open-mouthed. Prema's stomach knotted. She was about to lose any goodwill generated in the last half hour. Finally, Lucinda spoke.

"He tried to kill you?"

"Yes, I think so."

"And you defended yourself?"

"Yes."

"Well, good for you, darling."

Angelica House, 14th February, 1.00pm

"They did this deliberately! They want to destroy me!"

Evie was on the phone to her father – the one person in the world whom she trusted. She was using a friend's old wrist phone to conceal her identity.

"They all voted for that cursed Guillotine. They didn't want to lose their seats! But none of them wanted to oversee an execution! They don't want to be in charge of the Judiciary, the Police and His Majesty's Prison Services! So, they gave it to me!"

George Atherton was probably the calmest man in England. Unfazed by any outburst from his daughter, he remained silent.

"Dad, dad, are you still there?"

"Evie, slow things down. Stall things."

"Stall things?"

"Just play for time. You're a 'doer' Evie, you deliver and that's been the secret of your success. But now you need to learn a new skill. The art of doing nothing. Delay."

"So how do I do that?"

"You're the politician, not me! Exploit loopholes. The Opposition will find plenty. So will the death penalty opponents. And the counsel of any condemned man or woman will find endless delaying tactics. Give them all the time they want. In America, prisoners sit on death row for twenty years or more. And one more thing……. make a few anonymous donations to the condemned person's defence costs. That will keep things rolling."

"The Act has a six-month appeal timescale limit."

"Then push through an amendment – at least get the appeal timescale to twelve months. You've got time. If someone is arrested for a major murder, it will take five months or more to bring it to trial. For your sake, I wish it took a year, like it used to."

"Thanks, Dad. I wish you were doing this instead of me."

"I'll stick to running my business! Remember, Evie, delaying tactics! After all, how do you think I put off marrying your dear, departed mother for ten years?"

Evie smiled for the first time that day.

"Dad, you're keeping me sane!"

"Well, good, I've got my mates in Warrington to think about. Can't have my lass going doolally, our northern reputation is at stake! Just stay strong, love, like you always do."

"Thanks Dad."

"By the way, I see your old chum nutty Lucinda's in the news again!"

"Lucinda Grant?"

"That's the one! Elegantly dishevelled as ever."

"What's she been up to now?"

"Arrested with Cyclists for Justice. I saw her being dragged away on telly."

"Oh, she'll love that. She'll be fluttering those tinted eyelashes at the police and name-dropping them into submissive puppy dogs!"

Evie felt a quiet guilt as her long-suppressed bitterness began to surface. Lucinda Grant had been her closest friend and partner in every raucous act of mischief with which two spirited, robust teenage girls could divert themselves from the academic rigours of a prestigious boarding school.

The Warrington born daughter of a company CEO, Evie had been a misfit, ridiculed for her accent, gaucheness and weight.

Lucinda was the daughter of a royal lady-in-waiting and a notorious, womanising, drug-fuelled Earl who mysteriously went missing in 2020. Gregarious, genial, energetic, comfortable in her own skin and at times dangerously uninhibited, Lucinda's social graces compensated for an average intellect which barely scraped her through the school entrance requirements.

But Lucinda was kind and unpretentious, and her self-assurance gave her no desire to impress or gain street credibility. As she befriended Evie, the bullies withdrew.

Their friendship thrived for nearly fifteen years, until Lucinda's ebullience mellowed into sensuality, with her foghorn voice developing an appealing huskiness, while her high maintenance skills crafted the ultimate, low maintenance, 'just got out of bed' look.

Evie dated a small string of ne'er do wells, or men rejected by Lucinda. They never stayed and her high octane high street fashion, black eyeliner, red lipstick, killer heels, endless diets and military hair-tonging regimes did little to help her.

With a first-class honours degree in Business Studies, capital from her father and ferocious drive, she had built a designer fashion brand 'Roxanne' with outlets in expensive high street stores. Within three years, the brand had its own glossy magazine and booming mail order industry, displacing household names and winning her a national young entrepreneur award.

On joining the Tory Independence Party, she had been selected as a candidate for a safe Northern Labour seat with little hope of success, but against overwhelming odds, she had charmed Warrington with her brusque warmth and forthright promises to regenerate the area and had stormed to victory.

But the sweetness of success was eclipsed by romantic failure. Until James appeared. A warm, drily humorous, offbeat, highly talented character actor who had recently won a Bafta award.

She made the mistake of introducing him to Lucinda.

Evie tore her thoughts away from the painful memory.

"Dad, I'd better say goodbye, I must smarten myself up."

"And I must clear the driveway of snow, before my car gets totally buried. And your Uncle Ron's calling! Talk about geriatric delinquents! 'Bye for now, love."

Evie's mood lightened as she put the phone down. Dad had that effect.

She flicked the bedroom wall television back on, turned to the mirror and began to apply a light green cream where her complexion was flushed, an expensive foundation and a slick eyebrow pencil. She had just started to paint her lips holly berry scarlet, when there was a newsflash.

The heavy-jawed face of Ralph Hardcastle appeared on the screen. The caption underneath read: *Ralph Hardcastle, pioneer Senior Consultant Surgeon found dead in Lewisham.* A reporter stood outside Hammersmith Hospital.

Evie turned up the volume.

"We are all devastated at the death of Dr Hardcastle. He was a much-loved colleague and a pioneer who changed the lives of millions of straight, gay and transgender men who can now have a natural birth and push their child into the world. It would have been unthinkable, a generation ago. Dr Hardcastle broke the final equality frontier between men and women and will be deeply mourned."

The news coverage moved to a press conference with the Metropolitan Police.

"Dr Ralph Hardcastle was found dead in a house in Lewisham in the early hours of this morning. A post mortem examination is now being carried out. A thirty-two-year-old woman is being held on suspicion of his murder. We cannot give any further information at this time. His family has been informed and I would like to express our sincere condolences to them at this time of devastating loss."

Evie felt considerably stronger after her telephone call with her father, but she still struggled to keep her hand steady, as she applied her lipstick.

Meridian Birthing Centre, 14th February, 3.00pm

It would take Armageddon to prevent most new grandparents from holding their first grandchild at the earliest opportunity. Grandmother and granddaughter gazed into each other's eyes.

Miriam stroked the tiny pink fingers and cradled the tiny 7lb 4oz frame against the thick jumpers she had donned to force the car (with the aid of a shovel, blowtorch and sheer dogged recklessness) to the maternity ward.

After sixty-five long years, this precious moment had arrived. The woman who had played grandmother to mums and toddlers' groups, babies in supermarkets and even fallen in love with Royal babies, finally had a grandchild of her own.

"Did you get some sleep this morning, Amelia?"

"No and neither did David! Because Midwife Gregory Wilson was snivelling into a mountain of loo-roll!"

"Was Wilson so moved by your happy event?"

"You must be joking! He's blubbing about the death of Ralph Hardcastle!"

"Hmm, I suppose Hardcastle helped to make him famous."

"It's pathetic. He found time to do a TV interview this morning, when he should have been monitoring me.   You tell 'em David! David!!! Wake up!"

After twenty-four sleepless hours, David's default mode was either gazing lovingly at his newborn or staring into space.

"Yeah, he left us to it."

"And he abandoned me for two whole hours during the night! He said he was going to get me another cylinder of gas and air and he just disappeared!   I will never forgive him for that! You tell 'em David!"

"Yeah, I had to put up with the swearing…. And when he came back, he looked totally distracted. Wasn't bothered about Amelia."

"Look, they're repeating the interview for the fifth time today! "

Miriam turned to the TV, where BBC News 24 was showing footage of a tearful Gregory Wilson making a statement at the front entrance of the hospital.

"…. *A giant among giants, with zeal, courage, compassion and humility, Ralph Hardcastle changed our world forever. The genius who brought true equality and after many millennia, gave men the joy of bringing new life into the world. He was truly the people's gynaecologist. He was my inspiration. I am devastated by his loss and the terrible manner of his death…. it's so wrong, it's…. it's…."* The recording showed him bursting into tears before the cameras.

"Yuck! It's pathetic!"

"Oh Amelia, don't be like that, he's just safely delivered you."

"I don't care, mum. He's a smarmy, time serving, pampered little creep who's made himself the darling of low brow media. It's happened through the mutilated bodies of young men, their untimely deaths and the sickest degeneration our world has ever seen."

"Well, that just about sums it up," sighed Aidan.

Angelica House, Friday 15th February

The world felt a better place after the luxury of six hours' sleep. She rose at 6.30 am, which was quite a lie-in!

As most MPs and ministers settled into a long weekend out of London, Evie was cocooned in Hertfordshire. In better surroundings, she would have relished the prospect, with no press conferences, interviews or official visits to distract her.

Her only appointments, today, were routine hologram calls with the Head of the Immigration Office and The Lord Chief Justice. She would then attend to her red box and review, authorise or delegate her paperwork.

She switched on her hologram TV for the news. Two more women had gone missing in Hampshire and Derbyshire. How could this possibly be a serial killer?

She shuddered at the ugliest prospect the day, the thick file of papers and processes on the new capital punishment procedures.   She would follow her father's advice and generate endless revisions, queries and amendments.

She had once despised Whitehall red tape. Now she must learn to exploit it, while concealing her true intention. This was a challenge, being rather out of character. Her strength lay in brusque dynamism, energy, drive, inventiveness and a solution focused approach to everything she tackled. While by no means naïve, Evie was not manipulative or devious by nature. Her opponents already saw this as a weakness. It was not enough to destroy her yet, however. For now, the highly capable tart with a heart was a useful commodity.

But as Evie's terror of the guillotine tightened like a vice around her mind, the spirit of cunning beckoned to her seductively. In the desolate building, it cajoled in soothing tones….

"Learn my ways and save yourself."

Saturday 16th February, Meridian Birthing Centre

They were finally leaving the hospital. As Amelia nuzzled and lovingly wrapped her newborn to face the stark, icy world beyond the sterile warmth of the maternity ward, she felt she would rather endure another twenty-four-hour labour, with or without pain relief, than see the inside of that hated building again.

As David proudly secured the baby into the car seat, Midwife Gregory Wilson arrived with a broad smile, to carry their bags and help Amelia into the passenger seat.

"I'm fine!" Snapped Amelia. Even with thirty stitches, she would lower herself into the car without his assistance. David shook his hand and thanked him for everything.

Amelia gave a civil nod, but as their car disappeared around the corner, she added a scowl and a two-finger salute.

"Amelia!! Really!"

"Don't worry Dave, he didn't see me. I'm relieved to see the back of him."

"I'm just glad I have a healthy baby and wife! We have so much to look forward to!"

"You're right. Let's forget the creep. But I keep thinking about Midwife Prema Gupta. I wanted her to deliver me. Now she's been arrested, poor woman."

"You had a lucky escape if she's a killer."

"But I've met her. She wouldn't hurt a fly."

"Don't be naïve."

"If they find her guilty, will they really execute her?"

"Suppose so."

"But beheading? Can they really do that in cold blood? It's crazy. In the US, they have lethal injection. Even when we had the death penalty in the 1960's it was hanging, which was far more humane."

"Yeah, but it's politics, innit! The Meccan party was behind this. And they're propping up Orchard Mayhew and his pathetic Tory Independence Government."

Epping Holding Centre, Thursday 21st February

Prema had been transferred to more comfortable accommodation. A plain white room with the fresh smell of newly laid carpeting, a new bed, fresh linen, ensuite toilet, hand basin, radio and a multimedia centre with hundreds of TV channels and movies.

But this was no modern hotel chain. Five electronically controlled combination locks separated her from a corridor which could only be accessed via a bionic recognition card. A grim iron door, an electrified fence and ten ferocious Alsatians guarded the deceptively plain rectangular block which lay on the edge of Epping Forest, three miles from the M11.

After a week of gruelling interrogation, they had finally charged her with first degree murder. She would appear before a magistrates' court and while awaiting trial at the Old Bailey she would be the first person to experience incarceration in the second highest security facility ever built in the British Isles.

Prema was curled on the bed in foetal position. After five hours, she had no tears left and struggled to register the shock of being remanded in custody.   She pulled herself up and grabbed the small rucksack of the possessions they had allowed her to bring. Everything had been tightly scrutinised by prison security, but being on trial for her life, they had permitted her some measure of comfort.

She gazed at the photo of her twin sister, Reeta. They were identical, but Reeta was the giggly, vivacious and adventurous one. Prema had been the quiet, thoughtful child who pondered before she spoke. Everything about her was slow, measured and meticulous. As a seven-year-old, she had given each of her parakeets a name with a meaning.

Her mother had asked:

"Darling, why are you calling your bird Hannah?"

"Because she wants a baby and she's very sad. Just like Hannah in the Bible and God gave her baby Samuel."

Twenty-five years ago, Reeta had fidgeted, whispered and pulled at her hair during Sunday School in the stiflingly hot classroom in the small Baptist Church in Mumbai. Prema had gazed thoughtfully at the colourful pictures on the wall, depicting scenes from Bible stories, until she imagined herself transported back two thousand years, to the house of Mary, Martha and Lazarus, or the Last Supper, almost tasting the Passover food...

Her teacher had shouted:

"Prema, stop daydreaming!"

But she smiled when Prema's bright brown eyes registered her attention. Prema was the one everyone adored.

Reeta was the clumsy, reckless one who had broken her ankle playing pirates in the school gym. Prema had swiftly come to the aid of her screaming sister, calmed her and put into practice her Girl Guide first aid training. For the next three months, she had been Reeta's 'extra leg', always walking with her arm around her sister's shoulder.

When Reeta had married Hardeep and left Mumbai for Australia, she had cried nonstop for a month, feeling her entire being had been torn asunder. The marriage was an extremely happy event for everyone except Prema, a love match sealing the longstanding friendship between two families. For four years Prema had lived alone, with a frustrated mother who could not understand her daughter's stubborn refusal of every marriage introduction.

Prema had become increasingly morose and depressed as her yearning for a soulmate remained unfulfilled. Some introductions had been non-starters, but a few had been kind, fanciable, intelligent and in one case there had been some mutual attraction. But they had all had a major shortcoming, their failure to be her sister. No-one offered the unique connection which only a twin can give.

Eventually, much to the anguish of her mother, Prema had travelled to London, to qualify as a midwife. But no frontier or quarantine can prevent pain from travelling across continents and time zones.

Prema's misery was compounded by the damp loneliness of South London, until she began to work with Ralph Hardcastle at Londinium Hospital Trust. He was twenty years older than her with a tall, heavy frame, piercing eyes and a formidable manner. He was neither handsome, nor well-groomed. But he was larger than life and his sheer decisiveness, force of personality and total defiance of convention had intrigued her.

She had failed to perceive his divergent thinking as amorality. Maybe she had been in denial. But his fierce vibrancy, energy, drive, passion and charm persuaded her that she had found that missing chemical ingredient to fill the void inside her. Most of all, he had seemed totally besotted with her and she had been caught up in a current of love and attention which had suddenly swirled into her dark ocean of loneliness.

Oh, how he had changed and shown his true colours....

Deptford, South London, Friday 22nd February

In a tiny café in Deptford, South London, which lay inconspicuously sandwiched between a Chinese restaurant and a barber's shop, a plump, pretty woman slowly sipped a Cappuccino. She had a clean, scrubbed face and wore a sweatshirt and scarf over a pair of leggings and trainers. Her hair was scraped into a damp ponytail. A green parka was draped over the chair.

A large half-open gym bag lay beside her table, with a child's jumper and dungarees visible at the top. With tiny stud earrings, a simple locket, clear nail polish and trace of lip balm, she looked like any other young mother who had dropped her child off at Saturday morning swimming classes, done a workout at the gym, taken a shower and was now snatching a well-deserved coffee before collecting her offspring.

But Evie Atherton was a master of disguise. As a piece of public property, this had long been her only way to duck beneath the relentless radar of zoom lens cameras and persistent, intrusive journalists seeking to twist her every word. Today, however, the camouflage was for another purpose and did not merely depend upon her own discretion, but that of another player. She glanced anxiously at her wrist phone and tried to stay composed and nonchalant. She dialed her own number, the phone rang and she pretended to answer.

"Hello love…. is she? Oh, don't worry, she's teething. She was a bit grouchy last night. I'll be back in an hour. Yes…. Yes. Please give her a couple of drops. Thank you….!"

She made a passable attempt to lose her Northern accent.   But she would not have deceived any phonetics expert.   Unlike Margaret Thatcher, she had never taken elocution lessons. Her accent was considered to be an advantage.

She was quietly relieved that the café proprietor and his staff were Italian and that the only other clientele were a very elderly, shaky gentleman spilling coffee into his saucer and a young Ghanaian woman with a two-year-old boy.

She pretended to check messages and made the coffee last as long as she could. She became quietly distracted and almost on the verge of a daydream. She nearly jumped when a tall, dark-haired woman bounded up to the table.

"Julie! Hiya!"

Evie collected herself and played the part as well as she could, kissing the woman on both cheeks.

"Laura, hi! How's the week been?"

"Great! Nearly ready for half term. We're flying to Spain tomorrow. The boys are so excited".

"I bet they are!"

The woman pulled up a chair.

"So, what time are you leaving in the morning?"

They began to lower their voices, maintaining the air of jollity, closeness and familiarity.

But it was, in reality a painfully uncomfortable meeting. This was the first time she had met Lucinda since James had disappeared into her arms. She had hoped Lucinda would look remorsefully sheepish. But the voluptuous Sloane ranger was as comfortable in her skin as ever.

"Darling, how are you doing? Sweetie, I've missed you. It's been ages."

"I know. Are you quite sure no-one followed you here?"

"Totally. I changed into this chav get-up in the Ladies at Charing Cross. I'm unrecognisable."

Lucinda giggled. Evie grimaced. Lucinda was unrecognisable apart from the pheromones, probably. Whatever sex-appeal she exuded never went away.

"You know I need your total discretion and absolutely no-one must ever know about this?"

"I understand."

Evie decided to take the driving seat. She leaned forward.

"You intend to organise major demonstrations against the guillotine at Trafalgar Square, Birmingham Bullring, then in Manchester, Liverpool, Cardiff, Newcastle and Nottingham?"

Lucinda was visibly shocked.

"I haven't even put that on my social media sites."

"MI5 have ways of finding out."

Evie quietly enjoyed her discomfiture.

"You're also planning a major blockade of North Greenwich holding unit, with smoke bombs and incendiary devices, if any condemned person is transferred there ahead of execution."

"I'm not even supposed to know about North Greenwich Unit."

"But you do know. And I know you know."

Evie's dark green eyes bored into hers. Lucinda bit her lip. Evie was taking back power after a painful humiliation.

"One phone call from me and I could have you arrested on any number of conspiracy, breach of the peace or even terrorism charges."

Lucinda held her poise and quietly nodded.

"Mercifully for you, I hate the guillotine too. Quite apart from liking my fellow human beings too much to decapitate them in cold blood, I have no wish to become a public hate figure."

"It was a real bummer when they promoted you to Home Secretary. Bad luck old thing!"

"I'll make my own luck. I'm from Warrington!"

"How?"

"Discreetly controlled obstruction, Lucinda, my dear. I want enemies I can work with. Since we rubbed along well as friends, I think we could do business together."

If Lucinda had arrived hoping all was forgiven and that past wounds could be swept under the soiled café table onto the sticky floor beneath her trainers, she was mistaken.

Evie leaned forward, sensing capitulation.

"How much money does Cyclists for Justice currently have?"

"Nothing left, I've been digging into my own account to help them out."

"How much would they need, to build an internet platform, an online donation site and advertise on radio stations and public transport?"

"At least £100,000."

"And how much would it cost them to visit every university in England and Wales, town halls, churches, community groups and build grassroot support around the country?"

"£500,000. We'd need staff."

"What would give Cyclists for Justice enough credibility to be powerful partners with the Green Party, the Labour Socialist Party, the Welsh and Scottish Nationalists, local councils and NGOs who oppose the guillotine?

"We would need £2-3 million!"

"I can give you that money, to build a serious national movement."

"Wow!"

"But under my control, Lucinda."

The steel glint was back in Evie's eyes.

"You must give me a budget. Hard figures. The money will be transferred into your private account. It won't come directly from me, but from Orchid Publications, who produce Roxanne Magazine. You will be asked to do a bit of modelling to explain your massive fees. And you will donate all that money to Cyclists for Justice."

Lucinda controlled her reaction, with the training her nanny had instilled in her since infancy. She managed a restrained inclination of her head.

"So, you'll become a highly paid supermodel and the world will see that your generous donations are driving Cyclists for Justice into the vanguard of British humanitarian campaigning. You'll be quite a national treasure, my dear!"

"And if I don't?"

"I have the Head of Scotland Yard on speed dial."

Lucinda dropped her gaze and stared down at her tepid coffee for nearly a minute. She sighed, fidgeting with her newly-manicured nails.

"OK."

"Good."

Evie relaxed, returned to her old convivial manner and turned the conversation to girl talk.

"So how is life these days?"

"Oh, still trying to build an art collection. I've been scouring the antiques. December was all parties, I went skiing a couple of weeks ago, but there's not much on the horizon now, until Easter."

"And how is James doing?"

"Fine, as far as I know."

"As far as you know?"

"Yes, we split up in November. I dumped him."

Evie went silent to digest this. Lucinda attempted sympathetic eye contact.

"So yes, he's footloose and fancy free again!"

Evie became quietly irritated at the patronising tone. The insinuation that she might be grateful for Lucinda's cast-off.

"*He's* footloose and fancy free? Don't you mean you're on the market again? But I'm sure you'll have no trouble! Do you have anyone in mind? If not, there are plenty of nice young MPs I could introduce you to. Southerners of course. I'm sure Geordies aren't your style."

Lucinda realised the friendship would never be the same again. The lame duck was now in control.

iii)   The Soldier with the Shining Sword

Angelica House, 22nd February

This evening she would forget the diet. Evie indulged in the most expensive curry on the menu from the Indian takeaway in the nearby village. The locals enjoyed her VIP patronage.

She was savouring a first glimpse of hope. No longer a victim of the Tory Independence grandees, or of Lucinda. But the cumin flavoured duck breast left an unpleasant aftertaste and in her spirit, there was some unease. A vague feeling that she had done something less than worthy…. worthy of herself?

All her life she had prided herself on being straightforward. *'What you see is what you get'* was her catchphrase, during campaigns, interviews and speeches. Now she had done something manipulative and had taken pleasure in controlling and intimidating Lucinda, under the barest veneer of courtesy. She had enjoyed the fear and discomfort in Lucinda's eyes. But now she almost felt defiled by her actions.

Had she let someone down? Herself? Her party? But they had no absolute standards. Her father, perhaps? But he would help her with this conspiracy. Who then? Was there another goalpost she had moved, or boundary she had transgressed? Was this guilt? If so, guilt against whom?

She had taken a risk, too. Her actions were not only corrupt, but detrimental to her party. Discovery would mean ruin. But the alternative would be to sign a death warrant. So, did that justify her behaviour? Even if political expediency was mixed with personal revenge?

She pushed her naan bread around her plate, mopping the rich, spicy sauce, but never quite lifting the bread to her lips. She stared at her plate mesmerized and trying to make sense of her feelings……

She jumped as her wrist phone suddenly rang on full volume. She recognised the number immediately.

"Hello Frank?"

It was Frank Southwold, Chief Commissioner of the Metropolitan Police. They had a good professional working relationship which included the occasional half pint of lager with a panini. Frank usually had the good taste not to disturb her on a Friday evening.

"This had better be something heavy. I'm enjoying a well-deserved curry."

"Sorry about this, but I'm livid!"

"Is this about the missing Hammersmith woman?"

"No, it's about the funeral of Sir Ralph Hardcastle. Have you heard the latest?"

"I know they've released his body for burial, but I assume Bishop Burstall will do the funeral in Leicester?"

"They're doing it in London. In Westminster Abbey!"

"A state funeral?! You're joking".

"A Ceremonial funeral. The King has pushed for it and given Royal permission. He's badgered the Prime Minister, who has given in to him!"

"Well, it's the first I've heard of it. Nice of them to tell the Home Secretary!"

"You haven't heard the worst bit. They're doing it on Saturday 29th February. We're having to cancel all weekend leave, at short notice, for thousands of my men and women. A Royal event's one thing. But this??!!"

"But why's the King getting involved?"

"You know Hardcastle's always mingled in Royal circles. After the knighthood, he even had a few invites to Sandringham. And don't forget he was a Royal physician, 15 years ago. The King is calling it a time of unprecedented national mourning."

"I'm sorry about this. Not fair on you or your troops."

"No fun for you either. You realise you'll have to clear your diary on February 29th. Hope you weren't planning to propose to anyone this leap year!"

"Fat chance of that!"

Westminster, 29th February

Bishop Burstall adjusted his cloak and gold and white stole, as a young, frazzled member of the TV crew powdered his face for a third time, as though a shine on his nose was the worst disaster which could blight this sombre day.

He patiently endured all the fussing with a brief grunt of thanks and reached for the small glass of port on the dresser in front of him. He had refrained from alcohol for the past six months, on the strict advice of his doctor, but given the enormity of the occasion, he felt a quick tipple would be in order.

He was a heavily built, portly man and these days he had a growing paunch. He looked older than his forty-seven years. Instantly recognisable, he was the Bishop wheeled out whenever the BBC wanted an ecclesiastical pundit for controversial news items or Sunday morning discussion shows.

He was a familiar voice on Radio 4 and regular online columnist in the left-wing media. He was the darling of the liberal great and good. Warmly avuncular in public, but closed, withdrawn and uncommunicative in private. His wife had given up on their marriage, despite all the counselling the Church had thrown at them. The Episcopalian Church of England valued him as a high-profile asset, but he was certainly not clubbable.

He had hoped today's ceremonies would be graced by the splendour of Leicester Cathedral, giving the East Midlands a rare taste of the limelight, but it was not to be. However, there had been no doubt about who should officiate at the funeral. No-one but himself was expected to proceed down the aisle before twenty-five million British viewers and a global audience. Even the Archbishop of Canterbury was content to stand aside. And in Westminster Abbey? This was his moment!

He heard the toll of the muffled bell outside and the noise of the gathering crowds. He turned to the hologram TV, which made him feel part of the huge crowd in Kensington, along The Mall and down Whitehall, ten deep against the crash barriers.

Westminster – Portcullis House, 29th February

Evie adjusted the diamond brooch on her grey designer dress, pulled on a black, faux fur jacket and tightened the clip on her black fascinator. In twenty minutes, a black limousine would transport her, the Chancellor of the Exchequer, the Foreign Secretary and their wives, the very short distance to Westminster Abbey. Evie found the whole thing irritating. It was a less than five-minute walk. But protocol was protocol.

The TV coverage was now at fever pitch, as a reporter stood outside West Kensington Hospital. The small crowd of staff and officials gathered in the driveway suddenly stood aside, as a small procession emerged and edged down the front door steps. Eight officers of the British Army transported a coffin on the gun carriage which had, not so long ago, conveyed the longest reigning monarch in British history to her state funeral. Evie quietly felt it was an insult to her memory.

At least the funeral coverage was diverting attention from the disappearance of yet another woman in Coventry and for today at least, there would be no media speculation about a serial killer and whether they would be sent to the guillotine.

The gun carriage slowly emerged into the street and the TV cameras zoomed in on the tear-stained faces of members of the public who had camped out during the cold February night and now pressed against the crash barriers with sleeping bags draped around their shoulders as a comfort blanket and to ward off the biting wind.

But as Evie scanned the faces in the crowd, she not only saw expressions of grief, but also of anger. And from the badges and flak jackets which several of the mourners were wearing, she recognised some militant Hardcastle supporters. Then she saw it. A white sheet tied to a crash barrier, with huge black letters scrawled across it: "MURDERER. GUILLOTINE HER!". Countless other banners appeared, as the cameras panned along the procession route at Barons Court. As the soldiers marched past the Brompton Oratory and Harrods, there were angry cries:

"Kill her!"

But at Admiralty Arch, a solitary middle-aged woman screamed:

"Hardcastle murdered my son!"

She let rip a stream of expletives. From nowhere, two Humanity Arrest Officers seized her by the hair and dragged her into a black van.

But it was now 10.40am and time to leave. She and her colleagues would be the last to arrive before the Prime Minister and senior members of the Royal family, followed by the arrival of the King and Queen. At 11.00am, Sir Ralph's closest family would follow the coffin down the aisle. Celebrities had arrived earlier, and among them was Midwife Gregory Wilson.

There was a knot in her stomach. Today was a litmus test. It was volatile out there.

Westminster Abbey, 29th February, 10.40am

Bishop Burstall, now fully robed and mitred, was holding court at the Great West Door of Westminster Abbey with the Dean at his side, as he extended a handshake to Evie.

It was not the easiest meeting. They were at opposite ends of the political spectrum, having had difficult exchanges in the past. Bishop Burstall had made cutting speeches in the House of Lords about her pro-business initiatives, when she had been a junior minister. Protocol required a courteous acknowledgement. Evie moved on quickly, enabling him to offer a warmer welcome to the Foreign Secretary.

To a backdrop of sombre organ music, the arriving dignitaries took their seats. Evie was ushered to sit to the left of the Prime Minister and immediately behind the Princess of Wales. She was uncomfortably close to the catafalque which would soon receive the coffin and to the TV camera which would be trained on her face, as well as those of senior Royals.

She had never prayed in her life, but now she found herself beginning to pray that nothing would be said during the service which might encourage the cameras to zoom in on her reaction. Her mind frantically raced to find the most suitable facial expression. Sadness would not do. It was too close to vulnerability. Her public image was vivacious and resilient. Besides, she felt no sorrow whatsoever for this vile butcher, idolised by the nation. She opted for a grim, purposeful demeanour and fixed her eyes on the service sheet.

Peckham, 29th February

"This funeral disgusts me!"

"I totally agree with you, Miriam. But you know how deluded people are. Would you expect anything else?"

Bishop Aidan and Miriam sat huddled under a blanket, watching the funeral coverage. Miriam winced with back pain, as she heaved herself out of the faded, sagging sofa to top up their coffee and butter some banana cake.

"Your back's really hurting, love."

"I'm OK. It's the damp, but we really can't afford to turn up the heating. Your severance pay is running out and we have to get used to living on the Anglican Fellowship stipend."

"It's infuriating that the Episcopalian Church and the Church Commissioners kept all the assets."

"Leaving folk like us to freeze!"

"Yet they waste public money giving that wretched man a ceremonial funeral! And thousands of people are camping out in the cold to watch his remains pass by? It's like they're worshipping him."

"God warned us this would happen, love. Remember, the Bible warns that there is a way that seems good, but leads to destruction."

"Well, the Episcopalian Church has degenerated almost beyond hope into total deception. Look at them all in their fancy dress, celebrating the monster who defied God's natural order."

"At least we're safely out of it, Miriam."

"I never feel safe."

"No woman feels safe these days, with all these abductions."

The funeral service was underway. The processional hymn had sounded regal, but hollow. As the choir sang an anthem to perfection, it felt more like a performance than an act of worship.

"Oh no Aidan, I can't believe that midwife Gregory Wilson is doing the eulogy."

"The people's gynaecologist?! And the man's blubbing again. I'm beginning to think Wilson is the people's waterworks!"

"Oh look! Evie Atherton is there! Fancy her having to endure all that, poor love. Oh look, I love her hat and that gorgeous outfit."

"She looks preoccupied. She's staring into middle distance."

"I really must write to her."

"And we must keep praying for her, among those vipers!"

Westminster Abbey, 29th February, 11.40am

Evie cringed inwardly as a group of twenty children sang a specially composed song about love, harmony, peace, rainbows, bluebirds, daydreams and just about every nauseating lyric which might cause her breakfast to make a hasty exit, save for her resolute public self-control.

These children were Hardcastle babies, ranging from four to ten years old. They had been birthed by men and they were now being paraded in front of the massive congregation and one billion TV viewers, to impress the world that they were happy, well-adjusted young people. The establishment was shamelessly reinforcing the political message that no emotional or physical damage befell the children brought into the world in this way.

She felt a momentary sense of relief when the song came to an end, but there was no time to enjoy the respite before Bishop Burstall came forward to give the address. Her stomach tightened.

The first three minutes were tedious, but bearable. He took, as his text, 'suffer little children to come unto me.' Even with her agnostic, almost non-existent understanding of theology, she knew this was a blatant misapplication of a Bible verse, carelessly patched to a sermon which had been crafted to sell his political agenda. His deep, resonant voice began to grow louder and then more passionate as he paid tribute to his beloved personal friend. He began to declare Sir Ralph Hardcastle to be a martyr, taken from the world before his time.

"He poured out his life for others and sacrificed his tomorrow for our today, and for men to be set free from the oppression of being banned from gestating their offspring."

Evie groaned inwardly as he shamelessly plagiarised phrases from remembrance services.

Bishop Burstall's voice rose to a crescendo, as throbbing veins showed on his reddening face.

"The murder of the greatest Briton of the 21st century was a wicked, wicked deed!!"

Evie felt her pulse quicken and tried to steady her breathing.

"I may believe in Christian forgiveness, but there can be no forgiveness or mercy for the ruthless killer who snuffed out this beacon of joy and hope. The process of British justice must take its course!"

Everything inside her pleaded with him to stop. Her stomach muscles knotted and contorted, as she sensed the cameras closing on her face and the eyes of congregation members boring into the back of her head.

"The Bible says 'an eye for an eye and a tooth for a tooth'! The killer must die! The nation must be avenged!"

His voice rose to a shriek and his fists clenched.

"I demand the death penalty! That woman must die! I demand the guillotine for Sir Ralph Hardcastle's murderer! Guillotine! Guillotine! Guillotine!!!!!!!"

Evie clutched the chair in front of her and everything seemed to sway before her eyes as a ripple of applause grew and gathered momentum in the congregation, until it was drowned out by a huge surge of noise from outside the building. A glance at a wall mounted TV coverage screen showed thousands of mourners applauding in Hyde Park, St James's Park, Whitehall….

She was cynical about prayer, but in sheer utter helplessness she suddenly found herself inwardly crying to the unknown God. She found herself begging, pleading with the invisible one she didn't believe in to make himself known and please, please do something, anything!

For a split second, it was as though time was suspended. She felt as though she was outside Westminster Abbey, beyond this horror... somewhere where nothing could ever harm her again. It was only a split second, then Bishop Burstall's hefty figure registered in her consciousness again.

Then she suddenly noticed two things. First, a very tall, dark, Army Officer stepped forward, as if to guard the coffin. He raised a sword in salute, then stood still, as a ray of sunlight pierced through the stained glass and caught the blade. Then she suddenly saw that a small trickle of water was gathering around the feet of Bishop Burstall and gradually swelling into a small pool. She glanced at the ceiling, but no rain was penetrating one of the most expensively-maintained buildings in Britain.

The pool grew larger. She noticed two of the Hardcastle children giggling and the choirmaster glaring an angry rebuke. Then Bishop Burstall looked down, with an expression of utter dismay. Evie sensed the cameras pulling away from her and some disconcerted murmuring from the front rows of the congregation.

Two sidesmen, a chaplain and a young girl from St John Ambulance stepped forward and escorted Bishop Burstall a few paces to one side as the organ boomed the opening bars of the National Anthem. In tune with the descant of the choir, the Bishop uttered a piercing scream.

As the Dean of Westminster Abbey stepped forward to give the final blessing, a few more people huddled around the ailing Bishop to hide him from camera view. But it was no use. The cameramen were smelling and indeed, very loudly hearing, a story.

Eight soldiers hoisted the coffin on their shoulders and steadfastly bore their charge to the Great West Door during the recessional hymn. But very few people were paying attention either to them, or the lyrics.

A few minutes later, a large black hearse proceeded away from the Abbey and around Parliament Square, bearing the people's gynaecologist to his final resting place. Immediately behind proceeded an ambulance, which drove over Westminster Bridge and turned right, conveying Bishop Burstall to Lambeth Paternity Unit.

iv) James and Tony

Crystal Palace, 29th February, 5.30pm

Vaughan Williams' 5th Symphony resonated through an open window, across the Victorian houses and dispersed into the wind across the parade of shops leading to Westow Road and Crystal Palace Park.

The fine music was now competing with the discordant drone of returning football fans, as red streaks of dusk crept across the South London sky. James Cardew's house stood on a hill with views of Hampstead, ten miles away on a very clear day.

The ten-mile distance suited James. He had no desire to move to The Socialist Republic of Luvvies. He preferred the view from this side of the river. He lived a comfortable stroll from the more bustling, rough and ready Penge to the south west and a fifteen-minute walk from Sydenham Hill to the southeast.

James had higher priorities than the funeral in Westminster Abbey. On his comfortable, well-worn sofa, he nursed a bundle in an old, tartan blanket. Two ginger paws and green, runny eyes peered out from the crook of his arm, framed by matted fur and broken ear.

Two weeks ago, this stray ginger tom had wandered into his garden meowing piteously. After a few scraps of fish and a bowl of milk they had become inseparable. But now this shivering bundle of fur needed medical attention.

James was unemployed or, as they said in his acting profession 'resting'. He had earned enough money from that wretched Bafta-winning film to manage for the time being. But the movie about a traffic warden's love for a baboon had been beneath him. He would not accept any more scripts like that.

He noticed a damp patch on his trousers.

"I must get you to a vet, old thing."

He grabbed a magazine to protect his lap against any further lapses of feline bladder. He glanced at the front page of the Sunday supplement. He rarely read the fashion section, but the cover girl staring back at him made him jolt and he nearly sent the ailing cat scurrying from his lap. The makeup was uncharacteristically professional, but there was no mistaking the carefully tousled hair and nonchalant smile. Since when was Lucinda a fashion model?

After several months' respite, her photo was an uncomfortable intrusion. He slid the magazine into the cat basket, placed ginger gently on top and secured the metal grill.

Ten minutes later, his precious cargo was carefully secured in the passenger seat. But as he pulled out of the parking slot, he jerked to a standstill. A gaunt football supporter vacillated in the middle of the road. He was about to vent his most choice expletives when the young man staggered and collapsed.

"Not two casualties!!"

He dashed to the crumpled form which lay on the tarmac, wrapped in a heavy parka and a Crystal Palace hat and scarf. The young man's red eyes stared pleadingly, as his wheezing lungs fought for breath. Then James saw the swollen abdomen. Not now, please!

"Hello. Can you hear me? What's your name?"

"To…. Tony…."

"OK Tony, listen. Are you getting stomach pains?"

Tony shook his head.

"Well, I'm not taking any chances. Listen, I'm taking you to the hospital. I can't stay with you, I have a moggy to sort out as well. But I'm not leaving you here."

Camden, London, 29th February, 5.30pm

In the North London drizzle and failing light, cameras and umbrellas were carefully positioned and a tall, svelte figure reluctantly removed her camel coat and took her place by Camden Lock. Lucinda had already endured a punishing schedule, after only one week of modelling for Roxanne magazine. Today the photoshoot had started at 5.30am with a rigorous hair-straightening and make up regime, before arriving on location at early dawn.

They had soon discovered she was a 'natural' and her relaxed poise, patient good humour and raucous socialite tendencies (which endured until the small hours of the morning) had endeared her to the editor and other members of the publication team. When they discovered who her father was, they even offered her a monthly column. Notoriety could only increase circulation figures.

As she stood immobile in a flimsy silk shift, the cold penetrated through to her bones. She hadn't eaten since yesterday and the effects of her 4.00am antics were taking their toll. A very powerful micropore concealer covered the dark circles under her eyes.

After half an hour, she could endure no more and as her incessant shivering reduced her ability to produce a nonchalant smile, the team and crew withdrew to the bar of a hotel ten minutes' walk away at the north side of Regents' Park. Freddy, a tanned, skinny, dishevelled photographer, handed her a double brandy. Thawing out in front of a solar heater, she gulped it back in one go and Freddy refilled the glass.

Lucinda gave him a grateful hug.

"Thanks darling, I'm exhausted. And they're doing a studio session this evening, too."

"Why d'you do this, Lucinda? You're rich. And you don't need the publicity – you're always in the gossip columns."

"I have a charity to run darling!"

"Ah, Sloane girl doing her bit for charity!"

"But it's Cyclists for Justice!

"They're just a few bikes!"

"We're going nationwide, darling, campaigning against the guillotine!"

"So, you care about that cow who murdered her husband?"

"Don't call her that. I shared a cell with her when I was arrested on a demo. She's a real sweetie. And her husband abused her."

"So, she told you, my gullible friend!"

"I'm no fool, darling. I can spot social climbers, gold diggers and psychopaths ten miles away. Being in the aristocracy, you see the worst side of human nature. But she was sweet and passive, poor love, not a natural killer."

"But she killed Ralph Hardcastle. There's no other suspect."

"But the guillotine's so brutal, darling. The pain. How ghastly, just imagine it."

"But you'd die instantaneously, because it severs the spinal cord.   The Rochdale Engineering Company has designed it to behead a person in 1/100th of a second! That's quicker than cancer, a heart attack or even a plane crash!"

"But they only tried it on an old ape from Chester Zoo last year! As an animal lover, I was utterly sickened by that and so were many other people!"

"Don't fret my love, the ape didn't feel a thing."

"The ape was in no position to comment. In the French Revolution, people's eyes and lips moved after they were beheaded."

"French Revolution, eh? The victims were all aristocrats like you, so you have a certain empathy!"

"Oh, don't be ridiculous, darling. Anyway, why did they have to go for beheading? They might have chosen lethal injection, or even hanging."

"It was the Meccan party. They wanted it. And they're propping up the Tory Independence Government. But as far as I'm concerned, they can all go tomorrow! The sooner we have a Labour Government back the better. Vernon Stack for Prime Minister!"

Lucinda yawned as fatigue overcame her.

"I can't be bothered with that creep! He's pond life."

"Well, at least he's good socialist pond life! And he's against the guillotine."

"I'm too exhausted to argue politics with you, Freddy. And I don't know how I'll keep going tonight."

Freddy leaned forward with a knowing smile.

"I've got something to help you keep going, if you're interested, that is?"

Lucinda met his gaze and paused. There was an uneasy choice to be made. For a split second the image of her late father's emaciated face flashed before her. She pushed it away and her hesitation was only slight. She needed to keep going. She thought she could handle it. She gave a half smile and nodded.

Freddy glanced up and saw the others deep in conversation. He quietly led Lucinda to a discreet corner away from their colleagues.

Meridian Birthing Centre, 29th February, 6.30pm

With the ailing cat safely deposited at the vets, James Cardew had rejoined Tony McCrief at the Meridian Birthing Centre paternity suite, where he was being examined by a young, slightly dishevelled doctor. Only twenty-eight, he looked exhausted but determined to give Tony his full attention and put him at ease.

"OK dad, you're thirty-five weeks pregnant and no contractions. The baby's position is fine and the heartbeat is nice and strong. However, your temperature and blood pressure are very high and that chest of yours is rattling."

"I had to get to the football." Groaned Tony

"They would still have won without you.   You were crazy, going to that match. You must look after yourself and the baby. Just relax and let's listen to your chest."

The doctor frowned, as Tony wheezed against the stethoscope.

"Nasty infection there. I'll send you down to X-ray. And you're asthmatic, aren't you? Breathe into this for me."

Tony's exertions produced three weak peak flow readings.

"Sorry, but we're admitting you for bed rest. And I'm prescribing stronger blood pressure tablets. Once the X-ray results come back, you'll need antibiotics and steroids on an IV drip. "

Tony protested weakly. "But it's 5th round FA Cup on Tuesday."

"We'll set up a hologram broadcast link for you. Wait here until they take you down to X-ray."

As the doctor left, James moved to the chair by Tony. "Is there anyone I should contact? Any family?"

With a shaking hand, Tony pulled an old-style smartphone, dislodging used tissues and congealed sweets from his trouser pocket.

"Mum and sister are on there, and Bishop Aidan. Cheers for bringing me here mate…. Sorry, dunno your name… but seen you somewhere before…." Tony was gasping for breath.

"Take it easy. I'm James…. James Cardew."

"That James!?"

"Yup. Guess I look better without the traffic warden uniform?"

Tony gave a wheezing laugh. "And baboon girlfriend!"

"Don't embarrass me! Do you have anyone?"

"Nah…."

"Who's the mother of your baby?"

"They never told me".

"Does it bother you?"

"Yeah. But there's no way to find out…."

Tony looked distressed. James was quietly afraid of overstepping the mark.

"Sorry, didn't mean to stress you. I won't ask you why you did it. Glad I never had to."

Had he sounded critical? He had no wish to be hauled away in a Humanity Arrest Van.

James eased a pillow against Tony's back, then sat in silence, as his heavy wheezing settled into slower, laboured breathing. He made no further comment. Careless words were lethal these days and the most innocuous looking individuals could anonymously phone the Humanity Helpline. The slightest comment or nuance could be perceived as bigotry or a 'phobia'. A grudge could be silently pursued.

In the heavy silence, Tony's senses became more attuned to the smell of disinfectant and the flurry of activity in the corridor, as another pregnant man was rushed past on a trolley, followed by ashen-faced relatives.

"I... I don't like hospitals."

"You're in the best place."

"Scared I'm gonna die."

"You won't die."

James knew that, for all his RADA training, he did not sound convincing.

"What happens when you die? Do you just conk out? And when they cremate you? Would you feel it burning?"

"No way, mate. You'd be past feeling anything."

"And where do you go? Do you float from your body into a dark place? No night or day. Just a horrible grey mist forever? Does it feel cold? Will I be transparent like a ghost? And is there a grim reaper? Frightening..."

"Don't think about it."

"I 'ave to, because whatever it's like, I'll be there forever. And what if there's a hell?"

"I really don't know."

"I've done bad things. I shouldn't be pregnant, I only wanted the dosh. I wanted to meet a girl. Now it'll never happen...."

"You'll recover and be fine. You'll meet someone."

"You were with that.... that... Lucinda bird, yeah?"

Tony slurred his speech.

"Yes. The tabloids had a field day!"

"And...... She dumped you?"

James glanced round anxiously for a doctor, as Tony's chalky, clammy complexion drained of colour.

"Don't believe all you read in the Sun!"

"But she's a hot model now, she......."
Tony's face drooped on one side.
"Tony? Tony, can you hear me?"
James reached for the red alarm cord.

v)   A divine appointment

Vauxhall, London 29th February, 7.00pm

Evie was enjoying the sanctuary of her comfortable, secure, exclusive, London apartment which towered over the Thames. In tracksuit, baggy jumper and slippers, she slumped watching the recorded funeral coverage. The trappings of high office, her designer dress, shoes and fascinator lay in a discarded heap on her bedroom floor. For tonight, the red box with sensitive documents of state remained firmly shut.

It was nothing short of a miracle. The whole event had been upstaged by the four weeks' premature labour of Bishop Burstall and the delivery of a frail 6lb baby boy at Lambeth Paternity Unit. Some commentators declared it a fitting tribute to the great surgeon. In the privacy of their homes, many people berated the incident as an insult to decency and sacrilege in a place of worship, though they did so quietly for fear or arrest.

One thing was certain. The birth had overshadowed Bishop Burstall's speech. The mention of the guillotine was either the third or fourth item on the hourly news. But something puzzled her. She repeatedly pressed the replay button to view the final five minutes of the service. She froze the recording when the cameras focused on the coffin, a minute before Bishop Burstall's frenzy had culminated in the bursting of his waters.

Where was the army officer with the glistening sword, which had caught the light from the window? Something inside her desperately cried out to see him again. Why? Why did she desperately want to relive that split second when a feeling of hope had pierced her spirit?

For a fraction of a second, something had awoken in her soul and she longed to cling to it. It had penetrated the internal walls she tried to wrap around her inner being, to ward off the hurt, fear and paranoia which always lurked just outside. She wanted to frame that moment, yet she realised this beautiful something was free flowing and blew where it wanted to. Containment was against its very nature.

She didn't know whether to laugh, cry, or pull her cardigan tighter round her shoulders and hug this new sensation to herself.

Peckham, 29th February, 7.00pm

Miriam crouched over a small electronic tablet as Aidan stood at the chopping board, practicing his low budget culinary skills.

"*Dear Evie, we hope you are happily and comfortably settled into Angelica House.*"

"Happy and comfortable? Don't make me laugh!" Muttered Aidan, as he pared and diced a pile of carrots and sweet potatoes.

"Well, what do you suggest as an opening line? *Hope you're not having nightmares?*"

"I'm only saying be normal with her. Friendships aren't built on platitudes. If she just sees us as a pair of fuddy-duddy respectable clerics, she'll only ever be superficial with us. I'm not saying we should behave like a needy pair of has-beens with a chip on our shoulders. I just want her to feel safe with us."

"Don't people always feel safe with me?"

"When they need mothering, or caring for, yes."

"But that's what I'm supposed to do."

"But you're not meant to mother everyone. Friendship is meant to be on equal terms with people, if they want our friendship."

Miriam looked hurt.

"Are you saying I patronise people?"

"No, I didn't mean that. I just think that you need to be needed."

"And you don't? So, what about Tony, then?"

"He's vulnerable. That's different."

"You father him! You've had a gap in your life since you were forced to resign from office. And look how you're filling it! So, don't call me co-dependent!"

"Look, let's not quarrel about this."

"But you're saying I can't have an equal relationship with people."

"How many friends do you have? People you're not looking after?" I go for a pint with Pastor Rebus and Jake. What about you?"

Miriam was close to tears. They rarely had disagreements.

"Friends? I've spent the last two years supporting you, Aidan. I've adjusted to living in a place with little opportunity for my kind of social life. I'm sixty-five, so where do you expect me to go, nightclubs!?"

"Darling I'm sorry, really, I am. I didn't want to sound critical. And you're right. I came to Peckham feeling utterly rejected by the Episcopal Church and needing to be needed. Probably more than you did."

"We still haven't got over that wretched business, have we?"

"Not easy, when we're eating cheap cuts of meat and vegetable casserole. And you've put up with it, because of a situation you didn't create. You deserve better."

"I wouldn't have done anything else, Aidan."

Aidan pushed the chopped vegetables to one side, cleared the chopping board and tossed the utensils into the dishwasher.

"Aidan, what are you doing?"

"Just for one night, we're doing something different. Get your coat on."

"My coat? Where are we going?"

"Mystery tour!"

"What do I bring with me?"

"Nothing but your appetite!"

Vauxhall, 29th February, 7.15pm

Cocooned in a duvet, Evie grew tired of watching the funeral coverage and switched channels for some light entertainment.

The Big Impressionists Show appealed to her raucous sense of humour. A cast of talented comedy actors lampooned the week's events and satirized current affairs, with their sharp impersonations of politicians, celebrities and sporting personalities.

She settled back into her sofa and chuckled as the idiosyncrasies of the Prime Minister, fellow Cabinet colleagues, the England football manager and a Bafta-winning actress were hilariously portrayed. She was less amused at the next sketch. Bishop Aidan was portrayed as a hellfire and brimstone mad priest, frothing at the mouth and ranting at Bishop Burstall as a sinner. It was a poor impression of Bishop Aidan and it seemed unfair, as he had not been in the news in recent weeks. Anyway, she had no love for Bishop Burstall.

Her blood ran cold at the next sketch. A viciously cruel impersonation of her. The actress wore her trademark blue eyeshadow and exaggeratedly pencilled eyebrows. Horror of horrors, she had huge, red, blotch marks painted on her skin. There were large patches of sweat under her armpits. Her tan coloured tights had coarse leg hair poking through and worst of all, the actress wore a monstrous fat suit exaggerating her larger curves to the point of obesity. The merciless sketch ended with her being decapitated by a guillotine.

When she saw the fat suit, tears pricked her eyes. The sight of that vile rubber drew out all her worst feelings about herself, which she had tried to suppress, since James had dumped her. All her self-deception collapsed. Her recent revenge on Lucinda could not heal the hurt and pain. She was left with her wounded, humiliated self as she screamed unrepeatable expletives and hurled her shoe at the grotesque parody of herself.

Where was that feeling of peace? Now another invisible entity tore at her spirit. But this felt darker and more evil than anything a mere actor in a fat suit could convey.

She had to escape this thing. Why was it breaking something inside her? Where was the armour plated stateswoman who could roll with the punches in Cabinet meetings, fire verbal Exocet missiles in the House of Commons and withstand gruelling interviews with lethal TV journalists? She frantically pulled on her tracksuit top and thick parka. She scrunched her hair into a ponytail and pulled on a baseball cap, tightened her running shoes, then scurried down ten flights of stairs. The duty porter leapt up as she dived out through the back fire-exit door and ducked behind the bins. She slipped through a gap in the fence and scurried into a dark alley.

There were no paparazzi in sight. But she still wore her wrist phone with a tracking device.   With no bodyguard or armour plated car, she sprinted into the back streets of Vauxhall towards Harleyford Street and Oval. The Head of MI5 would berate her for disregarding her personal security. She didn't care. Nothing mattered, except escaping that oppressive heaviness. She ran faster as her limbs loosened.

The biting wind and icy drizzle pounded her face and muddy water from passing cars soiled her legs as she hurtled past chicken takeaways and off-licences. In ten minutes, she had covered nearly a mile. Her head throbbed and in despair, she could not believe that for the second time that day, she was gasping:

"God, help me!"

As her professional composure crumbled, she miserably concluded that, on top of everything else, she was becoming a backsliding atheist.

Camberwell, London, 29th February

Aidan and Miriam sat in a quiet alcove in The Rose of Selly Oak restaurant, studying the menu. Newly refurbished with bright spotlights and a hologram TV screen in every alcove, it had taken over by an ambitious chef. There were new, expensive South Indian speciality dishes.

"Can we really afford this?"

"Just for tonight, I'm treating you. When did we last really enjoy ourselves?"

"Probably this morning, when Bishop Burstall was carted off in an ambulance! Sorry, I shouldn't laugh, but you know I can't abide that man!"

A grinning waiter came to the table.

"Ah, good evening, mad preacher! Are you ready to order?

"We'll wait a minute, thanks."

Aidan looked perturbed.

"Mad preacher? What did he mean?"

"Heaven knows."

They turned back to the menu, as a blast of freezing air from the front door signalled the arrival of a casually dressed, weather-beaten and breathless young woman. As she unbuttoned her rain-drenched coat and swept past, Miriam glanced up. The woman lowered her eyes, as though deciding whether to avoid them, but then, with a flicker of recognition, she gazed back. The arched eyebrows and vivacious green eyes were ummistakable.

"Bishop Aidan? Reverend Miriam?"

The Merseyside accent, even in a hoarse whisper, was even less mistakable.

"Evie? Evie Atherton?" Miriam's voice went up a few decibels.

"Shhhhhh! Please!"

The bedraggled and panting Evie flung herself into the alcove next to Miriam, who felt a damp patch seeping through her jumper.

"So the actress finally gets to meet the Bishop! I wish I was more presentable! Sorry about the mess. Can I join you? I was planning to grab a curry alone, but I may feel less conspicuous, if I plonk my bum next to you!"

Miriam was completely tongue-tied as the vivacious politician made herself at home. Evie was even more informal and down-to-earth than she had imagined. Aidan, though astounded, took the situation in his stride.

"Well, this is an unexpected pleasure!"

"I'm thrilled to meet the Angelica House survivors!" Call me Evie, please, no titles. And may I call you Aidan and Miriam?

"Of course! Be our guest!"

Behind the small talk, Aidan offered a silent prayer of thanks as the evening unfolded beyond his wildest dreams.

"So how's life after Angelica House?"

Aidan's grimace said it all.

"Let's just say we prefer the view from Peckham!"

"Enough said. So what are the charms of Peckham?"

"Oh, decent butchers, character and real people!"

"Real people? Tell me more! I'm stuck with politicians!"

"We feel part of a local community, we're building quality relationships and we can give people practical care and support."

"Is that important to you?"

Miriam finally found her voice.

"It's our ministry and what Jesus has called us to do."

Evie's mouth tightened. Miriam had crossed a boundary and at the mention of Jesus, she quickly changed the subject.

"Now let's look at this menu. Please order whatever you like. Let's go for starters, main course and dessert. Dinner is on me tonight, as my honoured guests! Now let's start with an aperitif and will you be drinking red or white?"

Aidan glanced reproachfully at Miriam for her premature attempt to talk about religion. Evie had seized control of the conversation, while establishing herself as their host, diplomatically taking power. Aidan saw the steel behind the effervescent charm.

"You're paying? Are you sure? That's incredibly generous of you."

"My pleasure."

"So what brings you to sunny Camberwell?"

"I need a change of air and they do a decent Balti here!"

Evie gave nothing away.

"So what brings you guys here?"

As Miriam opened her mouth to speak, Aidan shot her a warning glance to caution against sharing too much of their woes…..

Epping Holding Centre, 29th February

After two weeks, Prema had lost all sense of time and place, in the sterile monotony of the comfortable but pristine cell, which was her only world.

Her one link with reality was Gloria Baxter, the lawyer she had finally acquired, who this evening fidgeted angrily with her electronic recorder as Prema divulged the excruciating details of the six years of abuse from Ralph Hardcastle.

Gloria Baxter was short and immaculately dressed with a perfectly tailored dark grey suit, bobbed chestnut hair, a chalk-pale complexion with little make up, perfectly manicured nails and neat gold and diamond earrings which glistened when her sleek mane of hair was flicked back.

"So now I'm defending Hardcastle's wife and he even brutalised you!   In my early career, I pursued compensation claims for families who lost sons, brothers and dads because of his butchery. I've dealt with cases against the consultants he trained. They introduced this dreadful practice to other hospitals!"

"You may as well know I have a formidable reputation and am feared by the senior management of Hospital Trusts. I've secured life-changing sums of money for bereaved and disabled clients."

"I started to specialise in criminal law four years ago. I was determined to defend these young men who get sentenced either to join the Male Birth Incentive Scheme or do military service. They're given a terrible choice for comparatively minor offences. I have a habit of winning cases!"

Prema realised that while Gloria was a first-rate professional, she was unlikely to become a close friend. She didn't make small talk. Utterly goal driven, she focused on her principles and wider objectives. She had little emotional involvement with individual clients, preferring to view them as the collective victims of injustice. Her guard rarely dropped. The raw energy of her own personal grief was fiercely channelled into her work.

"Well Prema, my initial view is we have a strong defence case. You were defending yourself against a violent intruder in a dark room and had no way of knowing the intruder was your ex-husband, particularly as you had not seen him for four months and he did not, to your knowledge, have a key to your home."

"And there's the history of abuse too?"

"Prema, I've carefully considered that. But decided if we pursue that line of defence, it's tantamount to admitting you recognised him that night and killed him deliberately, albeit under extreme provocation. You would almost certainly go down for manslaughter, though mitigating circumstances could reduce your sentence."

"However, there's a far more serious risk."

Prema realised what was coming.

"You're on trial for first degree murder, with a secondary charge of manslaughter. If the Jury decides you recognised your ex-husband, they could find you guilty of murder. That would mean a sharp blade through your neck. I won't sugarcoat this."

"But surely not? The death sentence is only on Jury recommendation and there's an appeal process. And surely the public won't……."

"Prema, this may sound harsh, but you must face reality. There's a huge public anger at the death of your ex-husband. The media's having a field day out there. The politically correct 'great and good' are manipulating opinion everywhere from chat shows to pulpits and even the Oscars.

Social engineering is shifting everyone's assumptions, to accept your husband's uterus colon interface surgery as mainstream. The world celebrates him as a great humanitarian, whatever some of us may think."

"But I'm a woman. I'm Indian and……"

"If you really think gender or race would trump uterus colon surgery, you're even more naïve than I thought."

Prema had hidden her emotions with consummate skill, but now looked crushed and as her shoulders hunched, it was impossible to see if tears were welling. Gloria softened her tone slightly.

"I know this is a huge shock to you, which may have put you in denial.   But you'll be on trial for your life. It's my job to prepare you for that, to the best of my professional ability. You must follow my advice."

"I don't have enough money for my defence. This will cost a fortune."

"You will get legal aid. And I've also set up a website on your behalf, so supporters can donate to your costs. People out there want to help you. Activists like Cyclists for Justice!"

"But I don't want charity."

"Do you actually want to live?"

Camberwell, 29th February, 8.30pm

Evie was right. The curry was excellent and her recommendations for dishes and wine were perfect.

The conversation between her, Miriam and Aidan was convivial and entertaining, even with very little personal disclosure on either side. Mercifully the idiosyncrasies of Angelica House and Evie's drily humorous anecdotes about the House of Commons bar, meeting foreign dignitaries and being interviewed by BBC journalists were enough to entertain.

Adrian saw that she was excellent company, warm and gregarious with razor sharp wit, but she was utterly self-possessed. While refilling glasses and breaking chunks of naan bread to share, she never dropped her guard. There was a rigid iron boundary they dared not cross.

But Miriam saw something else as the laughter flowed and staring at Evie's eyeliner and mascara, she noticed black traces had streaked down onto her cheeks. And her eyes, though now laughing and dancing across the table, were slightly red. She made the mistake of staring too long and Evie caught her eye.

"Now Miriam, do try some of this duck."

Miriam turned to the subject of the funeral.

"I thought you looked beautiful at the service this morning."

"But Bishop Burstall upstaged me, didn't he!"

"I rather think the baby upstaged him!" Chuckled Aidan.

Evie remembered the sensation which had stirred the depths of her spirit, in the Abbey. She was desperate to resolve the mystery.

"Who was that Army Officer who stood by the coffin? The one who raised that huge sword, when the light flashed on it?"

"What Army Officer?"

"We only saw the eight soldiers who bore the coffin."

"But he was there, just before the Bishop's waters broke."

"You mean, when Bishop Burstall started going on about the guillotine?" Said Adrian, before realising he has strayed into sensitive territory.

"Yes, exactly at that moment. I watched a recording of the funeral this evening, but he…….."

Evie checked herself. A sacked Bishop was about to think the third highest woman in the land (after The Queen and The Princess of Wales) was losing her marbles.

A sudden realisation came over Miriam.

"But he wasn't there?"

"He didn't seem to be. But camera angles do funny things. Don't worry, I'm not cracking up!"

Miriam's face lit up, as the candles flickered between the wine glasses.

"Oh, I don't think you're cracking up. Not at all!"

Epping Holding Centre, 29th February

Prema repressed her anger at being drilled, sergeant major style, by Gloria.

If Gloria were not her main hope of keeping her head on her slender shoulders, she could have cheerfully strangled her. Not that Prema ever expressed such emotions. Everyone who met her found her sweet, gracious and calm. Those who knew her less well, thought she was unassertive. But years of self-imposed discipline had taught her to restrain her reactions as she built up a defensive wall around herself. Some of her reserve was down to her good nature, but part of it was ingrained habit, while some of it was calculated.

"Now speak slowly, clearly and try to put a bit emotion into your voice. But no! No! Don't overdo it! Keep your shoulders back and look up. If you slouch, your body language indicates you're hiding something."

Prema nodded and quietly seethed.

"And let's tie your hair back off your forehead. The more open your face appears, the better."

"Hair off my face doesn't suit me."

"Headless would suit you even less."

"This is only for Epping Magistrates Court, not the Old Bailey."

"Have you any idea how many journalists will be crowded in there? Your pictures will be beamed to every corner of the earth!"

Prema shrugged.

"Fair enough."

Prema realised that the quietest girl in the school was now the most famous woman in the world. For all the wrong reasons. Even the endless TV coverage had not prepared her to face with a baying crowd of real people.

On hologram TV she could still detach herself, with iron self-will.   But she would soon encounter the flesh and blood reality of the worst human excesses of ghoulish curiosity, self-righteous outrage, spite and malice from the public, as the press vultures descended to pick her slender bones, even while her fragile soul, spirit and flesh still clung to them.

Camberwell, 29th February, 10.15pm

Evie, Aidan and Miriam continued to bond as they demolished an aromatic Kulfi. Evie had laughingly invited them to Angelica House for dinner, if they could face the place again!

As Evie signalled to the waiter for the bill, Aidan's wristphone rang. He expected a call from his daughter, but instead a man with a deep, resonant voice introduced himself.

"Is that Bishop Aidan? Good evening, it's James Cardew here."

Aidan froze. This was the Batfa-winning star of 'A Parking Ticket to Africa.' He had vented his outrage at the ill-fated love affair between a traffic warden and baboon in the press and on social media. If James Cardew was still offended, he was in no mood to quarrel tonight.

"I'm in a restaurant. If it's about 'A Parking Ticket to Africa', can we speak another time?"

Evie's stomach tensed, as she realised who was on the phone.

"It's not about the film. It's regarding a friend of yours, Tony McCrief. I'm sorry, but he's been taken seriously ill. He's in intensive care at the Meridian Birthing Centre. I found him in the street and brought him here. His sister and grandmother are with him."

"Oh no, is he in labour?"

"He's had a stroke."

"Right. We're driving over straight away. Thanks for letting me know and see you shortly."

Aidan looked across at Miriam.

"It's Tony. We need to go, now."

Miriam looked at Evie apologetically. But Evie had a gentler expression in her eyes and it was clear that she understood only too well.

"Male pregnant friend of yours? You'd better get going. C'mon, hurry and I hope he pulls through."

Evie paid the bill, and with hasty thanks and embraces they grabbed their coats and parted company in the pouring rain.

Evie pulled up her hood and hurtled towards her Vauxhall flat, in turmoil.

The encounter with Miriam and Aidan had lifted her spirits from her earlier despair. She had enjoyed her happiest evening in months.

But the phone call had violently shattered that warmth and serenity. In a split second her emotions were torn again, with James Cardew so near and yet so far.

vi) The shadow of grief

Dulwich, 29th February, 10.30pm

Gloria's suit and blouse were neatly pressed in her wardrobe for tomorrow. Wrapped in a silk dressing gown, she carefully dried and straightened her hair. She set her alarm and did a final check of the internet.

PREMA GUPTA IS INNOCENT

Stop the Guillotine

Donate to her defence costs, please click here

She clicked the password to review the total. Unflappable though she usually was, she suppressed a small shriek.

An anonymous donor had given £3million.

This was the nearest she had come to feeling happiness, in four years. Here was concrete evidence that something good could still happen in this barren, desolate world. She allowed herself a flicker of optimism, but not joy.

The painful memory of her brother's death closed in on her. She remembered Theobald on the final day of his life. His labour pains had begun at breakfast time. She had seen the fear in his eyes and her mother's terror, as they had made the frantic drive to the hospital.

Theobald tried to be so brave, refusing to give vent to his torment in front of them. But after forty hours, her hands had been sore and bruised from his terrified grip. At midnight, the hemorrhaging and convulsions began, as she looked at her mother in despair.

Afterwards, as his lifeless body lay on the hospital bed, she had clung her mother, beyond grief.

What was £3 million compared to a precious brother?

He was Ralph Hardcastle's victim.

Then she remembered that Prema was also Hardcastle's victim, and that made her worth saving.

Camden, 29th February, 11.00pm

Lucinda's dishevelled figure was spreadeagled across the bed. Her blonde hair was matted with sweat and vomit. Mascara and eyeliner streaked down her face, turning her cover girl makeup into a gothic mask, with dark rings around her eyes and a pale, clammy complexion.

Whatever her companion had given her, had propelled her to an ecstatic high, followed by the most terrifying delirium, pain and nausea she had ever experienced. From a cauldron of horrific nightmares, the first traces of consciousness began to register in her brain.

For an hour she lay between dreaming and waking and then her eyes slowly opened and focused on an object. It was strangely comforting. Something she had seen before. Oh yes, it was called a wardrobe, and this was a bedroom.

She very slowly tried to lift her pounding head, but a huge wave of nausea and bile immediately rose in her stomach and she vomited again on the duvet, then retched until her empty stomach could produce no more.

She tried to stand and as the ground swayed beneath her, she clutched at the headboard of the bed, then balanced against a chest of drawers, in an attempt to manoeuvre herself to the ensuite bathroom.

As she clutched the sink, she attempted to splash water on the hideous apparition she saw in the mirror. Was this really her? Was this a hallucination, or had she been modelling for a glossy magazine? Another memory flashed back as she remembered being presented to the Prince of Wales at Buckingham Palace as the eighteen-year-old daughter of an Earl. She had exuded confidence, ebullience, sophistication and class. What was she now? A grey, haggard face stared back at her as thoughts whirled around her pounding, aching head.

Memories crowded in. Now she was in a school hall twenty years ago, thirteen years old and on the stage. There were upturned faces of parents and teachers. She was in A Midsummer Night's Dream. A high-waisted gown cascaded down to her ankles. Her tousled hair draped over her shoulders. She was playing the role Hermia. Demetrias and Lysander were madly in love with her. But then, wasn't every man intoxicated by her? Surely? Surely that was still true?

Where was the doubt coming from? A painful memory jabbed a sudden, sharp finger into her train of thought.

"James...."

She was back in October 2035. They had walked along by the river in Kingston-upon-Thames. The autumn sun had dappled the Thames, as a sudden breeze had tossed up a huge swirl of golden leaves into their faces. She had laughed and clutched his arm. But he had been unresponsive. His silence had deepened as they continued to stroll.

And then he'd said it.

No man had ever dumped her before. The very concept was beyond her frame of reference.

But James, chivalrous to the end, had told their friends that she had ended the relationship. Her outward dignity remained intact, but in her private humiliation there was no shoulder to cry on.

Meridian Birthing Centre, 29th February, 11.30pm

The oppressive warmth of the intensive care unit was stifling after being in the freezing air outside. As Aidan and Miriam stood by Tony's bed in their rain soaked and mud splashed clothes, they felt incongruously unhygenic as they kept vigil in the sterile room.

Tony lay attached to a drip and a maze of tubes, his face sagging and drooling from loss of muscle control. His breathing was shallow and although his eyes flickered half-open from time to time, he showed little sign of recognising them. A monitor measured his heartbeat and that of his baby.

Ceiba held Tony's hand with her eyes constantly trained on his face. She nervously pulled at her matted hair extensions and frequently talked to Tony in a desperate attempt to get a response. She occasionally swore under her breath.

"You gotta get better, Tony. We're going on holiday to Jaywick in August. We'll go on the hologram ghost train. Tony, oh why don't you just wake up, you stupid pratt!"

As a registrar stepped into the room they all glanced up nervously. She looked gently at the three of them. "Which of you is the next of kin?"

"It's me. I'm his sister. He ain't gonna die, is he?" Cried Ceiba.

"We've had a difficult choice. We've delayed surgery because Tony has had a massive stroke. His heart is weak and his lungs are badly damaged. He's not strong enough to undergo surgery. But we can't hold off any longer for the sake of the baby, who is now showing signs of distress."

Miriam placed her hand on Ceiba's shoulder.

"You're going to do a section?"

"We have no choice, but I must warn you the procedure carries an extremely high risk for Tony. But even if we don't operate, Tony will die if he continues with the pregnancy and he is unlikely to survive beyond the next forty-eight hours. I'm very sorry."

"When are you doing it?"

"The Anaesthetist will be here in ten minutes, to give him an epidural block. We can't risk a full anaesthetic."

"Tony! Tony!!" Tears rolled down Ceiba's face.

James Cardew had stood in an uncomfortable and embarrassed silence during the conversation. For the last hour he had felt unsure whether to stay or leave and he increasingly felt his presence was an intrusion.

He had exchanged uneasy glances with Bishop Aidan from time to time. Their social media exchanges in recent weeks had been unbelievably hostile. It was excruciating that, when they finally met face to face, it should at the bedside of a desperately ill pregnant man. And while Bishop Aidan hated 'A Parking Ticket to Africa', James quietly detested it himself and had come to realise his adversary was right.

And James felt guilty about his motive for staying. The truth was, he preferred to be at the deathbed of a total stranger, with this odd group of people, than attend tonight's Theatre Awards ceremony and after-party in Mayfair. The longer he stayed here 'with a sick friend', the less obliged he felt to make tedious small talk with actors and other celebrities, some of whose company would be drunkenly unbearable on champagne and cocaine.

But nonetheless, he needed some breathing space.

"Look, I think you guys need time to yourselves. I'll be downstairs in the coffee shop. I'll come back in a bit."

Ceiba grabbed his sleeve.

"No, please stay. You looked after him and brought him here."

Aidan's expression softened.

"Yes, please feel free to stay with us. If you don't mind us praying?"

James suddenly felt ten times more uncomfortable, but found himself, saying:

"Er, no, not at all"

Aidan took Tony's hand and gazed around the room at a tearful Ceiba and Miriam, whose cheeks were reddening.

"Listen everyone, I must prepare Tony."

He turned back to Tony and raised his voice slightly.

"Tony? Tony, can you hear me?"

Tony gave a faint movement of his head, but still unsure, Aidan continued:

"Tony, if you can hear me, please squeeze my hand."

Aidan felt the faintest pressure on his hand.

"Tony, in a few minutes you will have an operation. You might not make it."

Ceiba sobbed quietly. James was utterly shocked by Aidan's bluntness, which seemed out of character with his fatherly demeanour.

"I need to prepare you in case you die. Do you understand?"

Tony squeezed his hand.

"Tony, do you remember what I've told you about Jesus?"

Tony's eyes flickered.

"Before you leave this life, do you recognise that Jesus died for your sins?"

There was a long pause, where everyone froze and Aidan's own heart seemed to stand still. He began to feel somewhere outside time and space.

Then he felt a very tight squeeze of his hand. Tony's eyes flickered and the dry, cracked lips moved, with a very faint:

"Yes."

"Do you turn to Christ?"

Tony squeezed his hand.

"Do you repent of your sins?"

Tony gave a faint nod.

"Do you renounce evil?"

Tony gasped "Yes…. Yes…"

Aidan opened his top pocket and pulled out a tiny bottle of very fragrant purple-coloured oil.

He turned to everyone in the room.

"This oil is called Myrrh." He whispered.

"What?" Cried Ceiba. "You mean like the Three Wise Men and Gold, Frankenstein and Myrrh?"

James involuntarily spluttered a guffaw of laughter, then immediately reddened as he realised the total inappropriateness of his reaction. He now felt even more incongruous. This was even worse than the painful memory of forgetting his lines at the National Theatre before the Prince of Wales in 2026. What was he doing with this chavvish blonde girl, a Bishop who was his enemy and a dying pregnant man he'd only just met this afternoon?

Vauxhall, 29th February, midnight

Evie ploughed furiously through a red box of Parliamentary papers and briefings, typing notes into a small tablet.

At midnight she felt more alert. Her meeting with Aidan and Miriam had energised her and indigestion from the curry kept her awake.

But most of all, she was fighting a ferocious battle to repress the emotions which had surfaced when James had phoned Aidan and she'd heard traces of his resonant voice. Memories of his calming warmth flooded back. The strong, reassuring hand, which had gently swept her dark hair from her stressed, blotchy face when hours of backbreaking work, frantic schedules and political aggression had drawn tears she would never show in public. She was still wet, muddy and unkempt from running through Camberwell. He would have dried her hair, put an arm round her……

Grief began to rear its head and tears pricked her eyes. This would not do! She made a superhuman effort to compose herself and concentrate.

She switched on her Hologram TV.

"Three more women have gone missing, in Stroud, Chester and Newcastle."

The 3D coverage drew her into the Newcastle studio, where a tearful mother made an anguished plea. The abductions must surely be linked, but surely it must be a ring of network? It could not be the work of one killer.

She turned to a bulky file on the new Home Office procedure for arranging execution by Guillotine.

"The Home Secretary will chair the Privy Council Committee to review the capital case, but will have no discretion to offer a clemency, unless the King (on the advice of the Prime Minister) offers a Royal reprieve or pardon."

Heavy policing would include riot gear to control demonstrations. The Greenwich Holding Centre would have rigorous suicide watch procedures. There would be guarded road blocks around a 500-metre radius. Three computer-coded electronic doors would guard the route to the condemned cell. Staff would only be admitted on biometric recognition. Only four people in the country would have computer access to override or release that electronic system, The Governor of the Holding Centre, The Chief Commissioner of London Metropolitan Police, the Head of MI5……. and the Home Secretary.

"A procedural rehearsal will be carried out twenty four hours before the execution, using a bionic dummy the exact size and weight of the condemned prisoner."

"Ah, the art of science," mused Evie "unlike a real human it will shed no blood!"

"A full medical examination of the condemned prisoner will be conducted by approved practitioners, to ensure that they are of sound mind and in perfect health."

She was nauseous as she read the actual execution procedure. Then she kept re-reading the sentence:

"The target time from the prisoner leaving their cell until their death being confirmed by the prison doctor will be twenty-four seconds."

She stared at her watch as the hand moved twenty four seconds, counting the number of breaths and the number of heartbeats to eternity.

She froze as she read the section about signing the death warrant. She hated to be reminded that:

"The Home Secretary will be required to sign a death warrant before 2.00am on the morning of an execution. The document will then be couriered to the Greenwich Holding Centre.   No further reprieve or stay of execution may then be issued, except at the personal request of the Prime Minister."

Meridian Birthing Centre, 29th February, 1.00am

In the Hospital Cafeteria, they made a miserable gathering.

Norma had now arrived and her presence heavily dominated the group. She punctuated the conversation with outbursts of rage at the Government and everything which had conspired to bring Tony to this piteous state.

As a chain smoker, she mercifully left the room from time to time, giving everyone respite from her angry, oppressive, grief-laden presence. She tolerated James, apart from scathing comments about his accent and aftershave. Mercifully, she hadn't seen the film.

While Tony was undergoing surgery, they drank four rounds of bitter coffee from an overworked vending machine. Seated round a drink soiled table, they had avoided the stale pasties and greasy bacon rolls, though for Aidan and Miriam, the curry was a distant memory.

To distract Ceiba from sniffling into a mountain of tissues, James had graciously indulged her embarrassing questions, telling anecdotes about the Baftas, the Brit Awards and chat show hosts. He had shown her celebrity photos on his wrist phone and told her what toiletries and hair removal products he used. He even allowed her to try on his designer scarf. Notwithstanding the crisis, Ceiba was developing a crush.

But he felt the boundaries of familiarity were overstretched, when Ceiba squawked across the soiled benches:

"And what was it like, doing 'you know what' with a baboon?"

The customers seated nearby glanced up. James braced himself awkwardly, but was rescued by the ringing of Ceiba's wristphone.

"He's out of the theatre and in recovery. It's a boy!"

As they rushed back to the ward, an elderly lady at a corner table mused:

"He still hasn't told us."

Vauxhall, 29th February, 3.00am

Evie gulped another black coffee and scrawled her signature on Home Office Execution Procedure file, vowing to do everything in her power to make sure it would never be actioned. London would rival Texas for delays and stays of execution!

As she tossed the document aside, her eyes alighted on the next batch of papers. These were strangely unfamiliar.

They were headed Secretary of State for Health. What were these documents doing in her red box? She scanned through proposals to close more Hospital A&E Departments, a new Paternity Unit in Manchester, a new Trans-species Transition Centre in Colchester. Not for her attention, surely? Then she saw a thick brown envelope stamped 'Classified Information, Official Secrets Act'. She furtively stared around her lounge. Stupid really, who would be watching her in her own flat?

Her curiosity was overwhelming, but with presence of mind, she grabbed a pair of tweezers and some plastic gloves from her dressing table.   Avoiding fingerprints, she carefully prised out the contents; a letter to the Secretary of State for Health and a very tiny portable memory stick. Did Whitehall still use these things? She hadn't seen once since the 2020's!

The blue, metallic memory stick caught the ceiling light, giving it an eerie glow.   A childish memory surfaced. Was this what Krypton looked like? She had a peculiar feeling that something, or someone was presenting her with a gift. It felt deliberate. But if this was human error, then some driving force was delivering this into her hands.

She retrieved her old-style laptop from her bedroom. Manufactured in 2023, it was useless for modern broadband systems. But she still used it for old photos. She carefully inserted the memory stick and clicked on the one spreadsheet it contained:

Paternal Childbearing Act 2027 (Section 3) Register of egg donors and male uterus host recipients

Her heart thudded. No-one except the Prime Minister, the Secretary of State for Health and a few embryologists were supposed to have access to this information. It was the most fiercely guarded secret in the country, driven by fear of mothers seeking their offspring. Especially those who had donated eggs in desperation, then found themselves childless in later life.

She scrolled through the lists, year by year, name by name. With a thrill of terror, she realised she would be killed if anyone discovered she had read this. Not the guillotine of course, but a car bomb or convenient accident?

Her eyes alighted on names she recognised. This was terrifying knowledge.

Her stomach suddenly lurched with fear as the ringing of her wristphone broke the silence. Was her bedroom under surveillance? And why would anyone call this time of the night, except for a national or family crisis?

She frantically closed the computer screen, returned to the lounge and clicked her wristphone.

"Hello? Frank?!"

It was Chief Commissioner Frank Southwold. Surely he didn't know? Besides, they were close friends, weren't they?

"I thought you'd still be awake. You never sleep"

"Neither do you, it seems. You're the only person who gets away with calling me at midnight. And you'd better have a good reason!"

"First of all your personal safety. Please don't give my staff a headache with your late night running in darkest Camberwell! The Met has enough to do. You know the rules, you have an armour-plated chauffeur-driven car. You take your Security Officer with you."

"So MI5 told you and you've rung to scold me? You could have waited till tomorrow. Anyway, I was carefully disguised."

"Well, my men recognised you! And a second thing, my eldest daughter is desperate to meet you. She keeps pestering me. So instead of beer and panini, I was going to er....invite you for Sunday lunch, your busy schedule permitting? Sorry, a bit presumptions I know, but....."

"Hmm, I don't see why not. Who am I to refuse a seventeen-year-old? I'll check my diary."

"Very formal!"

"No, seriously, it's very kind of you."

"I'll take that as a yes, then!"

The phone went dead.

Was Frank's daughter was really desperate to meet her, or was he making an excuse to take their friendship to a new level?

She drifted asleep, pondering on whether she felt more uneasy about the possibility of his attraction to her, than the risk that he knew which documents she had read?

But as she sank into unconsciousness, her final thought was of James....

Meridian Birthing Centre, 29th February, 4.00am

In the stifling warmth of the intensive care unit, the monitoring equipment bleeped steadily and ominously. Tony was alive and semi-conscious through a haze of morphine.

Ceiba bonded with the new life cradled in her arms. A tiny baby boy, hastily wrapped in a white bloodstained towel. As soon as Ceiba had first seen and kissed him, a huge rush of maternal instinct had overwhelmed her and she already loved this baby nephew as dearly as her own child.

Miriam held Tony's hand.

"Tony, my love, you have a beautiful little boy."

Tony groaned.

"What would you like to call him, my love?"

Tony murmured something unintelligible.

"Oh, speak up, you useless primagravity." Rasped Norma, who was now venting her pain with an abrasive bedside manner.

"Mum... mother..."

"Your mother's dead! She's not here! Lost your bloomin' memory? You never were the brains of the family."

Miriam glared at Norma.

"Leave the lad alone. You can see what he's been through."

"Bit late now, when they've carved his insides out. I'll say what I like to him. He's my grandson!"

"Say something nice to him. You may not have another chance!"

Miriam glanced anxiously at the monitoring equipment which showed his dropping pulse and falling blood pressure. Tony's breathing became more shallow.

"I'm going out for a fag!"

As Norma stomped out of the room yet again, Miriam leaned closer to Tony.

"Tony, what are you trying to say?"

Tony struggled to breathe "Mum.....mum....my baby mum."

"Your baby's mother?"

Tony squeezed her hand.

"The egg donor?"

"Yes.... want to know who she is. Please find out."

The monitor bleeps became slower.

"We will find out, my love. I promise."

"Thanks. Ceiba?"

"I'm here, Tony."

Ceiba suddenly handed the baby to a totally embarrassed James and moved across to the bed, wrapping her arms around her brother's gaunt frame, carefully avoiding the wires and tubes as Miriam gently brushed her hair extensions safely away.

"I love you bruv."

"Love you, sis."

"Love you….."

"Sis….sis…."

Tony's head slipped against the pillow, Ceiba sobbed, as his plummeting pulse and blood pressure set off the alarm.

In years to come, she would only have a blurred memory as the crash team burst into the room, disentangled her from Tony and pulled him away from her arms as she screamed hysterically.

Thrashing around vainly in Miriam's arms, she knew their efforts would be useless.

Lewisham, 1st March, 2036

Midwife Gregory Wilson lived in a large Victorian terraced house in one of the more pleasant areas of Lewisham.

With a mug of green tea, he staggered into his large bay-windowed lounge, stacked to the ceiling with professional magazines, travel memorabilia, the latest fashion glass ornaments and exotic plants.

A massive hologram screen covered one wall and his room was crowded with state of the art electronic gadgets and designer lamps, uplighters and spotlights. The mantelpiece of his huge marble fireplace was adorned with TV awards and photographs of himself with celebrities.

He slumped on a huge sofa draped with ethnic throws and a strange, beaded back massage device. He was in his dressing gown, unshaven and his hair, usually immaculate and expensively cut and waxed, was dishevelled.

His eyes were red and swollen. Today he actually looked his age of forty-five. Usually, his high maintenance routine, expensive toiletries, high fashion wardrobe and perfect skin made him look considerably younger. Most people thought he was twenty-nine, or at least, that he had successfully stayed there for the last sixteen years.

On his coffee table lay a mountain of condolence cards and letters from fans who had witnessed his distress on TV. Many of them were from pregnant men, birth fathers and children who were Hardcastle babies.

Gregory opened a few envelopes, then impatiently swept them aside and snapped:

"What a load of drivel! I hate these pregnant men and birth fathers and I have no time for their wretched squalling children!"

Yes, they'd made him rich and famous. He was a celebrity midwife. But they were a means to an end. He was highly skilled, totally professional and his emotional intelligence had won the trust and confidence of men during the most terrifying ordeal of their lives.

But the process quietly filled him with revulsion.

"The men are so egotistical," he muttered, "always thinking they're heroes and the only little soldiers ever to give birth. They're much more demanding than women!"

How often his patient manner masked his irritation and disdain!

And today, he was engulfed by pain. The funeral had given him a focus. During the build-up he had been surrounded by people. But now everything seemed futile. He trusted no-one. He had a wide circle of friends, but few confidantes. He created a façade for family, friends and public, convincing them that midwifery gave his life meaning.

He flung himself onto the sofa.

"Everyone believes my lie! But now I'm completely and utterly alone…"

He buried his face in his hands, shutting out the light and staring down a dark tunnel, to the age of fifty, sixty, seventy-five, then retirement, with nothing but the drudgery of gruesome hospital procedure, the shallow existence of TV celebrity and superficial relationships.

Now he would have to carry the truth to the grave alone.   He was the prisoner of his own deception.

Today was Sunday and he would cocoon himself away.

But on Monday, there would be urgent matters to deal with…..

Bill Clinton Towers, 1st March

A forlorn group huddled in the damp, threadbare, odorous lounge where Tony McCrief had been incarcerated during the final, dread-filled weeks of his short life.

The heating barely penetrated the cold and Aidan shivered in a t-shirt, having wrapped his anorak around the shoulders of the ashen-faced Ceiba, as she gently coaxed the newborn baby to feed. The infant occasionally whimpered, but had hardly cried, either absorbing the searing grief which consumed the group around him or overwhelmed by the cold, stark world into which he had been prematurely thrust. They had been turfed out of hospital with indecent haste, at 5.00am, once the maternity unit had decided that the 5-weeks premature baby was healthy and able to feed.

Aidan glanced anxiously at the wizened, frozen figure of Norma, staring into middle distance. Apart from the slight steam of her breath in the cold air of the room, she seemed barely alive. She had neither cried nor uttered a word. Aidan's massive, heavy, jumper engulfed her birdlike form, but could not cocoon her against the cruelty of the night or the emerging reality, as dawn had broken across the leaden skies.

The silence was punctuated by a clattering from the kitchen, as Miriam frantically sterilised bottles, sanitised kitchen surfaces and tried to eliminate every health hazard which might endanger a frail infant at 36 Bill Clinton Towers.

James nursed ten-month-old Mango, who wriggled incessantly in the arms of this clumsy, inexperienced newcomer. Now more ill-at-ease than ever, he couldn't believe he was still with the traumatised family he'd only met twelve hours ago. But those grim pre-dawn hours had offered no diplomatic moment to withdraw. He was still unsure if his presence was a kindness, or whether he had long outstayed his welcome. He made awkward attempts at small talk.

"Tony told me he was a Crystal Palace supporter. I support them too."

"Oh good!" Replied Aidan, vacantly. Everyone else remained silent.

"Do you have any brothers or sisters, Ceiba?"

"Not any more." Snapped Ceiba.

Then Miriam returned to the room and broke the ice.

"You'll never guess who we met in the Indian Restaurant last night? Evie Atherton, the Home Secretary."

James jerked forward and the sudden movement made Mango cry.

"Evie Atherton?!" He gasped.

Ceiba was suddenly alert and she glanced up from feeding Tony's baby.

"She was your girlfriend. I read it it in Studio Magazine!"

James's pale complexion turned pink as he nodded.

"You dumped her, didn't you? Then you went out with that Lucinda woman and she ditched you."

It really was time to go. James passed Mango to Aidan.

"I must leave you all in peace now. I'm sure you have things to do."

Diocese of London Office, 3rd March

"I don't know how to dress for this interview." Mused Miriam.

She held the tatters of a wind-wrecked umbrella over her grey, drizzle-dampened blow-dried hair as she arrived at the Diocese of London Offices in Pimlico, which the Episcopalian Church of England still owned.

"I look very vocational, in a plain navy dress, dog collar and sensible shoes! But do I look right for the sharp, streetwise young ladies I would encounter in Holloway Prison?"

"Worse still," she pondered "I'm no longer a member of the Anglican Communion. What are my chances?"

The Receptionist offered her fresh coffee and pastries. This branch of the church still had money!

A familiar voice suddenly boomed from behind her.

"Miriam, welcome, lovely see you again!"

"Bishop Forrest!"

The Rt Reverend Forrest McCaulay, the Bishop of London who had humiliated her husband warmly clasped her hand. His manner seemed conciliatory. Miriam forced a smile as painful memories surface. Why was such a senior Bishop interviewing her for a low-profile post?

In the interview room, an even more formidable gathering awaited.

"Miriam, meet Powys Williams, a Prison Governor and Fantasy Rimmer, Consultant Psychotherapist at Hammersmith Hospital."

Miriam maintained firm eye contact as she shook hands with the trap-mouthed man and the wasp-waisted, burgundy-haired young woman with horn-rimmed glasses.

"I'm honoured to meet such a distinguished panel!"

"This post is challenging. We must assess you thoroughly."

"Of course. Holloway is a challenging place."

Bishop Forrest leaned forward and lowered his voice.

"The successful candidate will not work at Holloway. The location is strictly confidential. The chaplain will be a spiritual advisor to prisoners on death row."

Miriam frantically prayed as she absorbed this.

"Are you still interested?"

Her emotions screamed against it, but Miriam sensed a gentle voice speaking deep inside her spirit.

She found herself answering. "Yes."

There followed thirty minutes of intense psychological grilling from Fantasy Rimmer. As a trained counsellor, Miriam withstood the intrusive probing, feeling angry at having to make personal disclosures before an old enemy.

Then Bishop Forrest began to question her. As a series of missiles fired, Miriam held her nerve.

"Would you ever evangelise a condemned person?"

This could ruin everything, but Miriam could only give one answer.

"Yes, I would."

"Really? Even if it seriously offended them?"

"A man or woman is about to have their head sliced off with a vicious, electronically controlled, steel blade and you're worried about them being offended by a mild-mannered, ageing old trout like me!"

She scarcely knew where she had found the courage. Then, she realised.

As she left the interview room, she felt strangely peaceful. She had probably blown it. But who cared?

vii) The Welsh Ultimatum

Wrexham Glyndwr University, 6th March

In the new, massive Students Union block at
Wrexham University, nearly two thousand students had
gathered. An influx of sympathisers from Bangor,
Liverpool and Chester swelled the numbers.

This rally had been planned at short notice. But
social media had gone viral. It had taken just 48 hours to
assemble this young, passionate crowd and emotions ran
high.

The BBC and Welsh broadcasting channels were ready
and paparazzi were strategically positioned around the
auditorium.

Massive cheers erupted as two beautiful women
stepped onto the platform. The first was Myfanwy
Roberts, the petite, fiery curvaceous Plaid Cymru MP for
Wrexham and First Minister for Wales. The other was
Lucinda Grant.

Myfanwy Roberts moved to the microphone.

"Diolch yn Fawr! Croeso! Thank you and welcome!"

There was another massive cheer.

"We are here for one reason! To stand with the
young people of this country who represent the future and
declare that Wales opposes capital punishment! The
People of Wales voted for Plaid Cymru! There are no Tory
Independence seats this side of the border! The guillotine
is barbaric and undemocratic! We declare Wales a
guillotine-free zone!"

The house erupted. Myfanwy beamed as the
shouting, waving, denim-clad throng settled. This was her
moment.

"The British Government has chosen a different
direction to Wales on a fundamental issue of life and
death. We have a right to decide what kind of society we
want. A humane and merciful country, or one which has
reverted to the 18th century?

"I therefore announce that I will be calling for a referendum, on whether the people of Wales wish to remain in Great Britain or become an independent nation!"

Lucinda thought the roof would collapse in the deafening, jubilant mayhem which followed. She stepped to the microphone as the din subsided. There were loud cheers again, notably from the men.

"Thank you Myfanwy! And on behalf of Cyclists for Justice, thank you for coming tonight. You are wonderful people and change makers! I love you!! You will build a just and merciful future!

I have a message to the Government! Prime Minister Orchard Mayhew will you betray the young lifeblood of this nation, by shedding blood on your murder machine? Will you take us back to the dark ages?

Vauxhall, 6th March

Evie gave a satisfied half-smile as she watched the BBC News live coverage.

"Good girl, Lucinda! So you've joined forces with the First Minister of Wales. And she's threatening a referendum? Ha! Now that will terrify Orchard Mayhew and all Whitehall! That guillotine may never be used!"

But she could barely contain her jealousy as the male students cheered Lucinda. How did she do it? Why was she so utterly irresistible? She didn't have perfect features. Evie was delighted to see the shadows under her eyes. And her face was thinner and paler. Yet infuriatingly, she radiated such vibrancy.

Previously Evie had wallowed in her resentment, almost enjoying it. But now she felt a new sensation. Was it guilt? A sense of uncleanness in her heart?

Now Lucinda's speech turned into an attack on her.

"And Evie Atherton, Home Secretary, I say this to you! If you sign a death warrant, you won't only kill a person, but you'll destroy the Union between England and Wales. Do you want that on your conscience?

And would you really kill such a beautiful person as Prema Gupta, whose trial is prejudiced before it has even begun, by vile media mud-slinging?"

The tumult of shouts and applause could have been heard from Lands End. The Lucinda and Myfanwy hugged, to seal their alliance.

Evie shuddered at the words "death warrant". Yes, she desperately needed Lucinda's influence. Let her flirt and win hearts and minds, with that husky voice.

She pushed the guilt and fear aside and ploughed briskly through her red box, relieved to see routine papers on a new Police and Local Community Reform Act (her own brainchild to improve Police relations with the public – now didn't that make her a decent, caring person?)

She had almost regained her sense of self-justification by the time she had reviewed new MI5 Surveillance Regulations.

She was exhausted.

The envelope with the egg donor data microchip sat invitingly on her bedside table. But she must not touch it again yet!

She crawled into bed and tried to sleep.

With resolute self-discipline she forced James to the back of her mind. But she had a strange longing to see Miriam and Aidan again. They were real, genuine and seemed to understand about the soldier with the sword...

Wrexham Glyndwr University, 6th March

Propped up against the Student Bar at 1.00am, Lucinda laughed and joked with the young activists. With designer jeans, silk top, perfect complexion and hair rough-dried to a "just got out of bed" look, she was every student's dream, even at thirty-four.

But she battled fatigue as she joined in the banter. The campaigning week had taken her to Newcastle, Manchester, Birmingham, Stoke on Trent and finally to Wrexham.

Three Engineering students, Hywel, Spring and Gary, noticed that she was flagging.

"Hey, Lucinda, how about coffee in Hywel's room? That'll wake you up!"

Lucinda tossed her hair and laughed. "The last of the big spenders! You sure know how to romance a girl!"

Skinny, sweatshirt-clad Gary pleaded with huge brown eyes.

"Oh come on Lucinda! Coffee and no funny business!"

"OK, I've never been in a student room. Take me there!"

****

She felt free-spirited and alive in the tiny bedroom, surrounded by books, dirty washing and ill-matched crockery as rock music thudded from Hywel's wristphone.

Lucinda's education had ended at a Swiss finishing school. Having missed the experience of University, she felt like a bird that had finally flown home, as she bantered with her new friends.

But at 3.00am, she was beyond exhaustion.

"Hey, Lucinda, don't fall asleep!"

"I'm shattered, darlings. I'd love to party on, but…."

Gary grinned.

"If you want to keep going, there's something I can give you?"

She hesitated. She had vowed never to do this again, after that vile experience in Camden. But the sensation had been blissful to begin with. And would she ever be in a roomful of students again?

She nodded.

Dulwich, 9ᵗʰ March

Evie regretted accepting Frank's Sunday lunch invite. For months, they had enjoyed a beer and sandwich in Westminster, mixing business with platonic friendship. He was good company and neutral territory was fine. A home visit to meet his teenage family took things to a new level. Her massive workload was an ideal pretext avoid it.

But he had rung just as she was reading those classified Department of Health papers. Lunch might help her to gauge his motives. She chided herself for being paranoid. Was she really under such close surveillance? She was head of MI5 and yet their technological capabilities eluded her.

She would test the waters with Frank.

Her chauffeur drove her to a pleasant road near Dulwich Park.

Frank welcomed her with a hug and his expensive shirt and liberal use of aftershave put her on guard.

"Come and meet the kids."

Evie was ushered into a chaotic lounge where a tabby cat and two budgerigars rivalled a dog for attention. A morose seventeen-year-old girl and two teenage brothers sprawled across the sofas, with little intention of disturbing themselves.

"This is Starlight, the princess of this house (present company excluded!)"

Evie squirmed at the clumsy compliment. Starlight scowled and grunted.

"This is Archway."

Archway ignored Evie and focused on his wrist phone.

"And here's Linden, my youngest."

The plump adolescent with auburn curly hair, bowed and gave her hand a slobbering kiss.

"He's practicing for his school play!" Laughed Frank.

Evie discreetly wiped her hand against her skirt.

Frank gazed affectionately at his brood.

"This lot keep me sane, since my lovely Anna died, three years ago."

Frank left her to the painful company of his offspring. Starlight rebuffed her attempts at small talk and clearly had no desire to meet her.

After fifteen excruciating minutes, she joined Frank in the kitchen.

"Can I help?"

"Can we talk shop?"

Evie braced herself.

"What do you think of the Home Office execution procedures?"

"They've consulted you?"

"Hard work for my troops. Riot gear and 500 metre radius guard."

"The whole thing will be stressful."

Frank stirred the gravy pensively.

"So, what do you really think about all this, Evie?"

She hesitated. How far could she trust this man?

"Cutting a young woman's head off? Frank tell me, what _you_ think?"

"I ask myself what God thinks?"

"Oh no, please don't tell me you're in the God Squad? I thought you were cooler than that."

"It's a central part of my life."

"You've kept that well hidden. First Aidan and Miriam, now you!"

Evie groaned. This rugged man had always seemed resolutely secular and grounded. So he had invited her to lunch to convert her?

"I'm an agnostic atheist, I'm warning you!"

"You're agnostic about atheism?"

"I'm a decent person. I don't need God to tell me what's right or wrong."

"But morals can't be man made. There must be an outside reference point."

Evie pondered this silently.

"Do you think God disapproves chopping people's heads off?"

"It's not an easy one. There are differing views on capital punishment, even in the church. Personally, I'm against it. God can forgive and change people, whatever they've done, so I think we should give them a chance."

"The Government expects me to oversee the process and sign the death warrant. I feel sick at the thought."

Frank's piercing eyes met hers as he silently nodded. She noticed a familiar sensation. Through the grey irises someone else seemed to gaze compassionately at her. Where had she felt this warmth and peace? Then she remembered those few moments in Westminster Abbey……

She was suddenly afraid she would yield to the thing her heart had long resisted.   With an iron will, she snapped out of her momentary transfixation and stared at the floor, breaking a manicured nail as she fidgeted.

Evie was used to outstaring people. It was time to take control of the conversation.

"What about you? You'll be policing the event. How does that sit with your Christian conscience?"

"I protect the public and make sure no-one's killed or injured."

"Except Prema? You'll prevent people from stampeding into the Greenwich Holding Centre to rescue her."

"I appreciate it's harder on you, Evie."

"The Jury may find her not guilty. I'm extending the appeal process and she has an excellent lawyer."

"The indomitable Gloria Baxter, I hear. And you must be thrilled that Cyclists for Justice are campaigning. Their behaviour's a nightmare for my men!"

Evie's blood ran cold. Could he possibly know about her pact with Lucinda?

She quickly composed herself.

"Your gravy's burning. Time to dish up."

Her beautiful hair was roughly shorn to her neck by the executioner, to make way for the knife. In a white dress, she almost looked bridal. As the executioner tied her hands behind her back, the tight cords dug into her tender flesh.

They placed her on a rough open, wooden cart for the long journey to the guillotine. With poise, dignity and courage, she kept her eyes down to avoid looking at the jeering, spitting crowd. When she arrived at the scaffold, which overlooked her old home, her lip trembled, but she regained her composure. As she climbed the steps, she apologised to the executioner for accidentally treading on his foot.

They bound her to a plank of wood and lowered her under the knife. At 12.15, the blade fell.

Prema was watching the new Hologram movie about Marie Antoinette. There was a Marie Antoinette for every generation, this one played by an actress who infuriatingly seemed to appear in every costume drama.

The cell door buzzed as the electronic lock was released. A prison warder entered and glanced disparagingly at the video screen. Was she watching that film yet again, morbidly obsessed with her own fate?

"There's a visitor for you."

Prema was led through several electronic doors to a small, comfortably-furnished room with a long table, guarded by a warder at each corner.

"Nothing like a private conversation!" Chuckled the nonchalant, casually-dressed woman perched on the end of the table.

"Lucinda!!"

"Darling! They've given you a mansion to yourself, with your own staff! I thought you might be glad to see your old cell mate!"

Lucinda was as relaxed, jovial and carefree as she'd been in their shared prison cell four weeks ago. She was still beautiful, but Prema was shocked at how haggard her face had become. Her blonde, highlighted hair was lank and she noticed a tremor in Lucinda's hand.

"Lucinda, you've remembered me!"

Prema edged forward to embrace her, but her warden snapped "No!" She led her to the opposite side of the table.

"I see they're taking good care of you! Why, the service is nearly as good as Woodley Hall, where I grew up!"

"You were born at Woodley?"

"Well, my father was Earl Grant Woodley!"

"I never realised you were an aristocrat."

"Yes, I know you only saw me as a fellow jailbird."

"You have a title?"

"Lady Lucinda Grant, but I don't do titles! Anyway, I stopped being a lady years ago!"

"Did the Police let you off?"

"They cautioned me for having no bike lights. But they mysteriously dropped the whole matter of the Blackheath snow protest!"

"And you've been modelling! I read Roxanne magazine. You look amazing. How did you get into that?"

"I've got contacts and even an Earl's daughter needs an honest job!"

"So you're not demonstrating any more?"

"Darling, I spend 50 hours a week modelling and 50 hours campaigning for you! I won't let this wretched Government behead you! Every penny I earn goes to the cause!"

"But will it make any difference to me? The law will take its course."

"Of course campaigning works! Slavery was abolished because Wilberforce kept fighting. The Suffragettes never gave up!"

Lucinda's voice rose to a cry. The Prison Warders listened as this wild and glamorous woman railroaded their monotonous routine.

Lucinda softened her voice, but fixed her small audience with passionate eye contact.

"Unfortunately, it even works for the bad stuff and people can now be changed into animals, because trans-species activists wore the Government down."

She raised her voice to a triumphal tone.

"But historically once laws change, they never reverse, for better or worse."

"But they abolished capital punishment in 1964 and now they've brought it back. So that bit of progress has been undone."

"Prema darling, please stay positive!"

"I don't want false hope."

"But you must fight. And when you've won, then seize every second of your life!"

"It's all very well for you, Lucinda. You have a perfect life, but mine isn't worth fighting for. You're rich, charismatic and beautiful. I've always been an underdog. I attract abusers like Ralph Hardcastle. You attract gorgeous men like James Cardew."

A faint shadow fell across Lucinda's eyes and for a split second, her vibrance dimmed. But she rallied herself, determined to energise Prema.

"Prema, grasp your future and be what you want to be. Don't let your past control you."

"Sometimes the thought of dying and going to heaven just seems easier."

"Don't think like that sweetie. You're beautiful, but you hide yourself away. If you die, a wonderful man may never meet you – would you do that to him? "

"Lucinda, I'm grateful for all you've done, but you're driving yourself so hard. Are you sure I'm worth it?"

"Cyclists for Justice keeps me sane. Otherwise, I'll be just a spoiled, silly little rich girl with an empty life. I'll end up marrying a polo-playing stuffed shirt."

Suddenly pensive, Lucinda quietly sipped a black coffee.

She still smarted from that menacing exchange in Deptford and could feel Evie's eyes flashing hatred and vengeance. She would be merciless if Lucinda failed. Lucinda finally understood what drove her former friend. Her love for James Cardew was even more powerful than her unspoken ambition to become Prime Minister.

viii) Who is Sophie Hammond?

Warrington, 22nd March

In Warrington, Evie was secluded in the safety of the spare bedroom in Uncle Ron's red-brick terraced house.

In a twenty-five minute walk from her father's home, she had cut across a back yard, scuttled along a narrow, muddy lane, disappeared into a thicket of damp, tangled undergrowth to find a gap in the broken, wooden fence in her uncle's garden.

But on occasions such as today, it was a safer option. MI5 could be monitoring her beautiful house in Wilmslow and probably had a surveillance operation in her father's home, because she visited him regularly. But in this nondescript house, she felt safe and hopefully unrecognisable, wearing wellingtons, an anorak and dark-rimmed glasses. Her hair was scrunched under a beret.

Uncle Ron happily allowed her to 'rest' upstairs. At ninety, his only interest was watching Everton v Preston North End, before nodding off at half-time. She drew the curtains and carefully searched for hidden devices, checking the dusty picture frames, photos and ancient wooden wardrobe with clanging metal coat hangers.

She turned her attention to the light fittings. There was no evidence of tampering. She locked the door from the inside.

At the writing desk, she put on plastic gloves and with a pair of tweezers, pulled a thick envelope from her rucksack. She carefully eased out the contents and scanned through the document:

Register of egg donors and male uterus host recipients

Her heart thudded. The spreadsheet listed hundreds of women whose eggs and reproductive organs had been removed. Some were marked 'voluntary' but others were listed as 'plea bargain'. So these women had offered their eggs to avoid prosecution or get a reduced sentence? Anger rose within her.

As Home Secretary she was in charge of the Police and the judicial system – yet they had concealed this from her? Other women were listed as 'restraint and sedation used.' So innocent women had been forced and drugged?

She scrutinised the male birth list. 3,582 men had 'deceased' marked against their names. This was way above the published statistic of 523 deaths per annum, out of 35,000 male deliveries. How had this been hidden under the media radar?

She recognised the name of Tony McCrief. Out of curiosity, she glanced at the name of his egg donor. Sophie Hammond? That didn't ring any bells.

The House of Commons, 26th March

At 3.00pm the green benches in the House of Commons were packed with murmuring anticipation and Evie stood at the Despatch Box, face to face with Vernon Stack, the Leader of His Majesty's Opposition.

Vernon Stack was an elderly Labour warrior approaching seventy. Having held several Cabinet and Shadow Cabinet posts, the ultimate prize at Number 10 had eluded him. He was an experienced and formidable man, and his grandfatherly, slightly unkempt appearance often put opponents off their guard. After forty years in the Commons, his finely tuned instincts gave him split-second timing and he could score against adversaries on the rebound, even when his briefing team failed him.

Evie relished the opportunity to take him on, however much her Tory Independence colleagues feared him. She had shown spectacular form in the past, as her repartee and razor sharp retorts whizzed across the chamber to stun Opposition Shadow Cabinet members into bemused retreat.

Both the Prime Minister and his Deputy were absent with Avian 'Flu, so they had designated Evie to take Prime Minister's Question Time. At four hours' notice she was ill-prepared and she frantically sent Whitehall scurrying for briefing material. But she could think on her feet.

She hoped Oliver Bunton, The Speaker, would maintain strict protocol today because some MPs hovered like vultures.

The Right Honourable Oliver Bunton was a formidable presence. Draped in a cloak of green and red feathers, he wore a bright green quiff on his head and a huge yellow prosthetic beak on his face. His nails were filed into impressive claws.

Oliver Bunton was undergoing Trans-species Reassignment Therapy, courtesy of Westbourne Health Trust, convinced that he was a parrot trapped in a man's body. His transition had raised questions about his suitability as Speaker but the new Equal Opportunities legislation had won the day. He self-identified as a parrot, so everyone was legally obliged to treat him as one, (except when he demanded a pint of beer, a vindaloo curry or expensive hotel accommodation.)

His friends called him 'Olly Beak', his detractors named him 'The Squawker', but no-one dared ridicule him, for fear of contravening Humanity legislation (which had become a misnomer in its extension to non-humans). It was now an offence to call a transmutant a human.

For some MPs, the challenge of keeping a straight face in his presence was far more testing than the cross-fire of heated debate.

The dishevelled Vernon Stack grinned as he rose to fire his first question.

"I wish the Prime Minister and his Deputy a speedy recovery and I would like to thank the Right Honourable lady for stepping into the breach this afternoon. And may I say how charming and elegant she looks in her designer dress."

Evie gave a wry half-smile, knowing he was poised for attack.

"I understand that, like many outfits, the Right Honourable Lady's dress is designed for her by Roxanne, one of many companies owned by herself and her father, Mr George Atherton, MBE. Enquiries have shown that these dresses do not appear on your Tax Return and have never been declared as gifts."

Evie was ready for him.

"An examination of my expenses will show that all my outfits are fully paid for out of my clothing allowance allocated by the Prime Minister's Office, for which I pay taxes. My Right Honourable Friend should do his homework properly. Although he conspicuously failed to do that as Secretary of State for Education!"

There were hoots of laughter and cries of: "Hear, hear!"

Evie drove the dagger home:

"And if my Right Honourable Friend needs lessons in personal grooming, as the Daily Mail suggested today, I'm sure my personal stylist and indeed, Roxanne Fashions, would be very pleased to help him!"

Both sides of the House erupted in mirth and the feathered Speaker yelled: "Order! Order!"

Evie glanced at her Front Bench colleagues.   They were laughing and nodding in support. But in the corner of her eye, she clocked a smirk on face of Sir Chawton Holland, Secretary of State for Health. However robust her response was, he enjoyed seeing her under fire. She had enough information to destroy him. She salivated at the thought. Could she fire a subtle question to unsettle him this afternoon? But perhaps it would be dangerous to put him on guard.

Suddenly, Hedge Roberts, the young Shadow Secretary of State for Trade and Industry rose to his feet.

"I understand that the Right Honourable Lady was educated at Hartworth Ladies College."

"That is correct."

"And you were in the same year as Lucinda Grant."

"May I ask the point of this? We seem to be straying a long way from Government policy this afternoon."

"On the contrary, nepotism and potential breaches of Employment Law by the Home Secretary, would be a matter of concern for the House. Many of us have seen that Lucinda Grant was recently promoted, at an astronomical speed, to the coveted role of Cover Girl and Face of Roxanne. Indeed, the public could scarcely fail to miss her. She's come from nowhere and risen at a speed which would leave most struggling models green with envy. And now she even has her own magazine column!"

Evie's heart was racing. She mustered all her experience to give an assured and authoritative reply.

"Lucinda Grant is employed by Roxanne Magazine, owned by Wilmslow Publishing. I have no control or influence over their recruitment procedures and neither does my father. Like all employers, they are required to keep records of their selection processes. I'm sure they would be happy to share these with a Select Committee, if Members of the House choose to waste their valuable time on such trivia!"

"Order! Question from Harper Sykes, Tory Independence Party!"

Harper Sykes, Secretary of State for Work and Pensions, was an ally.

The Speaker had come to her rescue. He had never seemed to be her greatest fan, but at home he had a massive deluxe state of the art aviary with a swing, jacuzzi and disused church bells, provided by the Health Trust (for medicinal purposes) from taxpayers' money. He had no appetite for seeing the House delve into Evie's personal affairs, as this could lead to awkward questions about his own.

Evie steadied her breathing and responded to a friendlier question from her own side. Her enemies had been held at bay for now, but they would not go away...

She would not fire any warning shots at The Secretary of State for Health today.   Partly for her own sake, but also as a favour to the Speaker who had done her a favour today. He had his own issues with Sir Chawton Holland…..

Bill Clinton Towers, 27th March, 11.00am

A dismal group gathered in the darkened flat. Miriam had valiantly tried to clean and sanitise the threadbare lounge, but even her robust efforts could not expunge the lingering odour of cat faeces and damp.

Ceiba cuddled the babies on the sofa, struggling to keep her black dress and jacket clean. James stood awkwardly by the window, wondering why he'd accepted an invitation to the funeral of a man he'd only met on the day of his death.

Norma's three nephews and their wives huddled in the kitchen doorway.

Aidan, in a purple shirt, dog-collar and cloak sat quietly beside Norma. For today's sombre occasion he had donned his Bishop's attire.

"The hearse is here!" Called James. Ashen-faced Ceiba struggled to maintain her composure as she prepared to leave, but Norma was transfixed and refused to move.

"Nana?" Ceiba vainly tried to pull her to her feet.

"Norma, it's time to go." Whispered Aidan, gently. But Norma froze and stared into space.

"Dead son, dead women!"

"Dead women? Norma, what are you on about?"

"Abducted women!! All murdered! Dead!"

"It's Tony that's dead, nana!"

"She's confused. Let her stay here with me." Whispered Miriam.

"Norma," persisted Aidan "you must do this for Tony."

But Norma remained immovable, as the dismal party piled into the two damp, clunky lifts conveying them to the waiting cortege in the courtyard.

ix) Decadence

10 Downing Street, 28th March, 9.00pm

Champagne, canapes and carnage.

Evie felt that was an apt headline for the dishevelled, unshaven young journalists and paparazzi permitted to join the hedonistic throng.

It was the Prime Minister's fortieth Birthday. Like an over indulged schoolboy, Orchard Mayhew mingled with the 'great and good', with a beaming smile crinkling his chubby, reddened cheeks, as his sweaty palm clasped those of adoring guests and enemies paying him homage tonight.

Actors, footballers, rock stars, media controllers, politicians, members of the Royal Family and the aristocracy schmoozed, swanned, grovelled, brayed and indulged with varying levels of dignity.

Some exhibited a studied poise, as they sipped wine, mingled and targeted those they hoped to influence. Others carelessly indulged in the flow of lethal cocktails, either indifferent to their decorum and public profile or desensitised by the mix of spirits, which had been camouflaged with sweet juices. Tomorrow they would wake to the stench of congealed, vomited canapes and humiliating photographs in the right or left-wing press, depending on which detested them the most.

Style Hobbs was easy company. He didn't raise any eyebrows.

She was teasing him. "So, my lovely, what brings you here and why has the Prime Minister invited my Private Personal Secretary?"

"Maybe I bring a touch of class!"

"That's my prerogative, Style!"

But she chose not to scare him away. She needed the security blanket of his presence tonight.

The smell of perfume, aftershave, hairspray and perspiration mingled with the spicy, greasy aroma of a hot buffet now being wheeled round on trolleys by waiters.

The microphone and sound system were being tested, as Apocalypse Massacre gave a discordant foretaste of the horrors to come. Evie shuddered.   Apocalypse Massacre was a ghoulish, war-painted, leather-studded and heavily tattooed platinum disc and Brit Award-winning rock group. The grotesque musicians were personal favourites of the Prime Minister.   With prosthetic monster-shaped heads and gargled voices, they would plummet the event to even worse depths, as everyone danced the night away.

In the toilet, she checked her appearance. In her maroon, immaculately tailored dress she oozed style and class. With minimal jewellery, perfect hair and tasteful make up, tonight was about displaying the poise and gravitas to recommend her as a future Prime Minister. She would be the only dignified person in the room.

As the ghastly thudding began, she emerged into the darkened hall, where a glitterball now reflected tasteless coloured light bulbs onto the assembled throng. Her shoes stuck to the filthy floorboards soiled with beer, food and other horrors.

This shambolic party would be a PR disaster for Orchard Mayhew. Her public approval ratings were high, so let him embarrass himself!

As her eyes became accustomed to the dark, a bulky figure edged towards her. Only when the person was five feet away, did she realise it was Oliver Bunton, wearing a feathered body-suit, large wings and his prosthetic beak.

He seemed to be approaching her for a dance. Unable to face the mortification of dancing with a lycra-clad trans-species parrot, she frantically dived into the crowd and pulled Style onto the dance floor.

Paparazzi cameras flashed round her. The pleasure of outclassing the Prime Minister must wait for another day. As Oliver Bunton hovered, she clung possessively to Style.

When the torment became too much, she made an early exit.

She slid from the freezing night into the warmth of a chauffeur driven car, reflecting on Oliver Bunton's behaviour. No wonder he had tried to save her skin during Prime Minister's Question Time. Now she must keep him 'on-side', without raising his hopes.

As she reflected on the evening in her apartment, she was overwhelmed by the empty and meaningless debauchery in Downing Street.

Why were these people called the great and the good?

She thought about Sophie Hammond. The 'powers that be' had harvested the eggs of this young woman and Tony McCrief, the father of her child, was dead at 25. Had Sophie been desperate for benefits or a reduced sentence?

The world was an evil place.   Did she want to be pulled further into this cesspool? She shivered and pulled her dressing gown around her.

The pollution, darkness and sleaze began to engulf her spirit. She stared over the rooftops of Vauxhall, the Thames, the lights of Chelsea Bridge and Millbank. Centuries of corrupt humanity thronged along the black, snaking river which would ooze through the city long after she was dead.

So where was her home? Not Wilmslow, because her house there was a recent purchase.   Was it Warrington, with her father? But although she loved him dearly, George Atherton had his own form of corruption. One rule for family, another for business dealings. And after he and Uncle Ron were dead, what then?

She would not sleep tonight. With black coffee, she tackled the papers in her red box. Work would settle her, surely? But the correspondence on the new Immigration Bill could not fill the gnawing hole in her being. She was still desperate for something good, genuine and solid. She thought she'd found it in James. He was no longer with Lucinda. Long-buried emotions surfaced. Dared she contact him? No! She refused to weaken.

Could Oliver Bunton really be infatuated with her, even after months being pumped with chemicals and hormones to change his body into a very disturbing avian form?

Should she phone Frank? The look in his eyes had reminded her of that moment in Westminster Abbey. She looked at her wrist phone, then checked herself. Still uncertain of his intentions, she must not encourage him.

Suddenly Aidan and Miriam jumped into her mind. They cared about her and she felt safe with them.

She sent them an instant message.

Putney, 7th April

Crowds jostled along Putney riverside, cheered by the afternoon sun gleaming on the Thames. Evie, Aidan and Miriam (accompanied by two of Evie's security officers) were ushered to an idyllic vantage point half a mile from Putney Bridge and further from prying cameras. Evie was wary of being seen with an unpopular ex-bishop. After a pub lunch, they were set to enjoy the Boat Race.

Their second meeting had been a convivial reunion as they relaxed over carbohydrates and gravy in a homely pub. But Evie sensed an awkward silence, as lighter topics of conversation were exhausted.

As they waited for the Oxford and Cambridge crews to pass by, Miriam seemed lost in thought and Aidan shuffled uncomfortably.

Evie broke the ice.

"I'm sorry for your loss. I mean... Tony."

"Oh, thank you my love." Responded Miriam, giving her hand a squeeze.

"The funeral was last week. He was a sweet boy."

Evie sighed. "Such dreadful things are happening, every day. Not to mention the missing women. Abductions used to be headline news. Now the public is becoming desensitised to them."

"I never thought I'd live to see the world become like this." Whispered Miriam, mindful of the security officers behind them.

"Please don't think I approve of these awful events." Evie pulled her scarf over her mouth as she leaned towards Miriam's ear, wary of TV cameras, wrist phones, video devices and lipreaders. "I may be the Home Secretary, but...."

"I know, love. But wicked people are destroying the very nature of humanity."

"The reproduction process itself."

"And all this trans-species surgery."

"You mean, like Oliver Bunton?"

"Yes. Whatever will happen to him?"

"The Health Trust will surgically alter him. At the final stage, he will legally renounce his humanity and they'll do a DNA transfer. As Home Secretary, I'll then be asked to withdraw his citizenship of the United Kingdom."

"That's just horrible."

"It gets worse. He will be shipped to Australia. For the first six weeks, they'll take him to Queensland and place him in a supervised habitation unit with other new parrots. When they release him into the wild, that will be the end of all human contact."

"Worst of all, he will lose his soul. He will be eternally lost when he dies."

"Can't an animal go to heaven?"

"Oliver Bunton was created as a human being in God's image. God redeemed humanity by becoming a human being himself. In changing his DNA, he will put himself beyond God's plan of salvation. It will be an act of eternal disobedience because once he loses his human brain, he will be incapable of repenting."

Tears poured down Miriam's face.

Aidan passed a tissue to her.

"As in the days of Noah! It happened thousands of years ago. In the end times, it is happening again."

"Happening again?" Said Evie, muffled by her scarf "They didn't have trans-species technology thousands of years ago."

Aidan held his cap in front of his mouth, sensing Evie's wariness.

"But an evil mix of DNA happened more than 3,000 years ago. Before the Great Flood and Noah's ark, demonic beings intermarried with women. The human race became wicked and corrupt. It could have put the whole human race beyond the reach of redemption."

"I never believed all that Genesis stuff."

"Yet you see it happening all around you, Evie."

"Is that why God destroyed the world in a flood?"

"Yes."

"But he won't this time, surely?"

"No, but he will return soon. And people must choose whose side they're on."

Evie shuddered. She struggled to cling to her walls of reason and intellect. Was there a more infinite dimension, beyond the sun-dappled Thames, which offered more frightening choices than she could possibly imagine?

As the Oxford and Cambridge crews rowed past to raucous cheers, she could barely focus on the sporting occasion. Could there really be another world, interspersed with this one?

Lewisham, 14th April

Gregory Wilson was surprisingly agile. Wearing a white overall, scrubs and plastic gloves, he resembled the forensic scientists who had systematically scoured Prema's house.

But his visit had another purpose. Glancing over his shoulder, he grabbed the keys and slid quickly through the back door. With plastic slippers over his shoes, he tiptoed through the kitchen, lounge and hallway which had been ransacked during the investigation process.

He carefully glided up the stairs to her study and searched her desk and drawer units, before creeping over to her bedroom, where the forensic team had emptied every cupboard and overturned the bed.

About to give up, he suddenly noticed a small airing cupboard on the landing. As expected, it was stuffed with linen, which he systematically removed. There was something solid at the back and he pulled out an old-style laptop. How had the forensics been careless enough to overlook this, and why had Prema chosen such a bizarre place to store her old PC? But it was a massive stroke of luck.

Ralph had secretly buried data in her sub-folders. Until now, he and his cohorts had had no desire to retrieve it.   Why raise her suspicions? They now held the files elsewhere. And she would have soon recycled her old computer.

But now the obscure little midwife was the most notorious woman in Britain. Forensics had combed through her house and it was only a matter of time before an ambitious journalist broke in, seeking the ultimate scoop.

Gregory wrapped the laptop in a pillowcase, stuffing the parcel under his white coat. Sneaking through the back door, he checked the coast was clear and darted across the road to his house.

Honor Oak, South London, 14th April

Warm air breezed through the grass after light rainfall, as the sun worked its way through the clouds. Golden light caught the blossom and wet grass. It was as unpredictable as any Easter Monday.

Millions decided whether to dust down their BBQ, do some gardening or drive to a DIY centre. Workers enjoyed a lie-in before tomorrow's return to commuting.   Single, widowed and divorced people dreaded the emptiness and isolation which bank holidays seemed to bring and looked forward to the normality which Tuesday would restore.

Two lone figures stood in the grounds of Honor Oak Crematorium. The breeze lifted the sweetness of newly placed wreaths and floral tributes to their nostrils, mingled with the stale smell of older, wilting flowers.

A tiny, square plot of land marked where an urn had recently been interred. Bishop Aidan made the sign of the cross and laid flowers on the small slab, gently reuniting the Crystal Palace FC scarf with its owner. He draped his anorak over Norma's shoulder and held her close.

Norma's lip trembled, as she ran a saturated tissue against her grey complexion and scrunched it in her quivering hand.

"It's OK, we can stay here as long as you like."

Aidan grasped her hand and gave her more tissues. The tears fell faster and she began to quake.

The convulsed sobs erupted and grew louder, until a searing, gut wrenching howl echoed across the lawn, the memorials and to the heavens.

The hoarse screams subsided into sobs. Aidan continued to enfold her and finally allowed his own tears to fall.   She glanced up, for the first time registering his grief. With stiff knees, she slowly knelt and caressed the stone.

"He's all alone here".

"He's very loved. And he's not suffering anymore."

Tony's mangled and torn body was finally laid to rest.

Peckham, 1st May

As Miriam prepared a shepherd's pie in the kitchen, she felt her anger rising, yet again. Why had Aidan done this to her? Ceiba stood at her side, peeling potatoes, with two screaming babies. While she prattled on about her favourite celebrities and their sex lives, Norma gave a rasping cough and filled the steamy, stuffy air with her cigarette smoke.

Aidan had invited Norma, Ceiba and the babies to live with them, without even asking her. Torn between his own personal comfort and the heartbreak before him, he had felt he had no choice.

Three days ago, he had found Ceiba in floods of tears, with Norma having a foul-mouthed outburst.

"The social services told us we've lost our privileged status as the family of a pregnant bloke!" Ceiba had sobbed. "Now Tony's dead, we count for nothing! They're evicting us and we'll be homelessness!

"They offered Ceiba a dingy mother and baby hostel!" Snarled Norma.

"And I refused it! I won't be separated from nana!" Cried Ceiba.

Such was the cruelty of a benefits system which invested a fortune in pregnant men, but did little for young mothers or elderly people.

So now Ceiba and the babies were sleeping in their back bedroom, while Norma camped on a sofa bed in their lounge. In fairness, Ceiba had efficiently assumed the role of mother to Tony's little boy and was clearly a 'natural' at looking after young children. She took the feeding and nappy changing routines in her stride and never allowed Miriam or Aidan to do the night feeds.

Ceiba's company was a horrendous culture shock to Miriam, however, as the house was suddenly being subjected to daytime TV at full volume, clumps of hair and blonde dye in the sink, towels stained brown with fake tan and the permanent stench of acetone and nail varnish.

Their bathroom had become like a branch of Boots, awash with cosmetics and electronic gadgets to hone every part of Ceiba's anatomy to man pulling perfection. She had offered Miriam the use of her thigh shaping equipment, only to be curtly told:

"I have one satisfied customer, my love and that's plenty! Aidan accepts my thighs as they are."

But Norma's presence had pushed Miriam to the edge of her endurance. She and Aidan had always laughed at Norma's formidable matriarchal tendencies, from the safe distance of her own flat. After a short visit, they could escape. But now, she seemed determined to rule the roost and there was a power struggle. As Miriam and Ceiba peeled the potatoes, Norma lectured them abrasively:

"Cut'em in two-inch chunks, you useless pair! And it's one teaspoon of salt in the pan, innit!"

Baby Landscape McCrief screamed louder as the kitchen became hotter. In frustration Miriam carried him outside to the cool breeze on the tiny patio.

An angry Norma hollered:

"I know how to look after my own grandson!"

Miriam began to have very un-Christian thoughts about her various kitchen appliances and how they might be used to rearrange Norma's anatomy….

She checked herself and hastily repented. But there was no love lost.

x) The fallen ugliness

Vauxhall, 8th May

Evie was satisfied with the day's proceedings. The House of Commons had voted in favour of the Capital Punishment Appeal Bill, which was now amended to apply to existing cases.

If it passed through the House of Lords, Prema would be allowed three stages of appeal against the death sentence, if it were passed. There were now five new Tory Independence Peers in the Lords, created by a very nervous Prime Minister. Labour Peers would not be able to block the amendment, however much they wanted to embarrass the Government.

Evie began to feel invincible. Her father was right. She could draw out the process as long as she wanted. If she could protract it to the end of this Parliament, the Labour Socialist Party would be re-elected and would repeal the Capital Punishment Bill altogether.

On a hot, humid evening, as the setting sun glowed through her window across the skylines of Vauxhall and Millbank, she worked through her red box and tucked into a Chicken Jalfrezi.

Towards midnight she was spurred on a warm glow. She was saving a life. She basked in the idea that history would remember her as an honest and principled politician who encouraged enterprise and championed justice. The pride of Merseyside, alongside the more musical incumbents….

She ploughed through her paperwork until 2.00am, feeling at one with the world. Then, as sleep closed in, a wasp sailed through the window with an evil whirr on a current of cold air. She tried to evict the wasp with a wad of papers, poured a coffee and switched on the hologram TV for the news.

She was almost asleep on the sofa with a briefing paper in her hands, as the news signature tune trumpeted 3.00am. But as the headline image appeared, she jolted awake and iron fingers gripped her stomach.

Photographs of a gaunt, blonde, once-beautiful figure filled the screen, with the headline caption LUCINDA DEAD.

A presenter stood outside a block of mansion flats in Earls Court, as a body was carried out to a waiting ambulance. Photos of a drunken, drug-fuelled Lucinda in nightclubs were followed by a recent shot of her leaving Hammersmith Hospital, fragile and haggard, with no trace of the luminous glow which had seduced men and eventually the tabloid-reading public.

As the flow of tribute interviews began, every part of Evie froze, except for her manicured hands, which scrunched the briefing paper into a ball.

A weeping TV soap actress (who herself led a dissolute lifestyle) sobbed.

"All that success came too suddenly for her. She wasn't equipped to handle it. But I never thought it would end like this."

Then came the worst moment of all. The face she loved more than any other in the world filled the room in three hologrammatic dimensions. An angry and grief-stricken James.

"Lucinda was a compassionate, warm, beautiful and vibrant woman. She was a tireless campaigner for justice. She treated everyone the same. The world will be poorer without her spontaneity and capacity for joy and laughter. The tabloid images were not the real Lucinda. When I was with her, she never touched drugs. The people who exploited her beauty for advertising revenue and circulation figures have blood on their hands tonight."

Epping Holding Centre 8th May

The Central Line journey lasted forever, but as the tube emerged from darkness to daylight at Leyton, then hurtled through the greener suburbs of Snaresbrook, Woodford and Loughton, the early morning spring sun danced in the trees of Epping Forest.

Miriam had left the house at 6.00am.

"I must see Prema before anyone else does."

A blonde girl with smeared mascara was crying into her paper. She had seen the headline. Miriam gave her a knowing, compassionate look.

Miriam took a taxi to the Epping Holding Centre. The intensive security procedures no longer intimidated her. At least she was free to leave at the end of her visit.

She held her breath as she was escorted to Prema's white-walled quarters.

"Miriam! What an early bird!"

Freshly showered and dressed, Prema embraced her, with the smell of hair products wafting from her neatly towel-wrapped locks.

"What a surprise! Can I order you some breakfast?"

"No thanks. You're looking very elegant!"

"Ah, I'm trying the new hair treatment which Lucinda gave me, bless her!"

Clearly, she hadn't heard the news.

"Prema, something's happened. I'm really sorry."

St Mary's Hospital, Roehampton, 8th May

St Mary's Hospital in Roehampton had been restored to its former glory, after years of neglect.

Members of His Majesty's armed forces, who had lost limbs in recent conflicts in the Middle East received rehabilitation, physiotherapy and ongoing care, alongside elderly veterans from Iraq, Afghanistan and even the Falklands War in 1983.

But Government investment had also been poured into two new facilities.

One was a dedicated paternity unit.

The other was the trans-species physiotherapy and orientation suite. Land formerly owned by Roehampton University had been cultivated into habitats to acclimatise transitional orangutans, horses, cats and other 'safe' species. (The Government had passed 'triple lock' legislation to supposedly prohibit the creation of dangerous animals. Even the cause of liberalism must defer to the media risk posed by a fatal mauling.)

A red and green figure with an 8ft wingspan streaked across a grassy runway, rose 5ft in the air and veered to the left, crash-landing into a large pond. As the soaking-wet, dismal wreck emerged, it was greeted by an angry gaggle of trans-species geese using a torrent of expletives which betrayed their human origins.

Oliver Bunton was having flying lessons. He was an abysmal pupil.

"Bad luck mate, why don't you have another go?"

Dave Hammond helped him out of the pond, fending off the geese with a long wooden pole. Dave was a quiet, calm, patient teacher. But with a gregarious wife like Amelia he had learned to be placid.

And Dave had learned to be quiet (and even look slightly stupid) around his in-laws. He told Aidan and Miriam he worked as a vet in an animal sanctuary. A convenient half-truth. They would have disapproved of a man helping to create what they called "an abomination".

"I could murder a drink." Spluttered Oliver

"You're already having one, mate!"

"I mean a beer!"

****

In a quiet pub near Putney Heath, Oliver eagerly guzzled a pint with his prosthetic beak pushed to one side.

They had the lounge to themselves and the Landlord was deaf. Most of the locals typed their orders on a small screen, but Dave's sign language was perfect, so he was a popular customer.

"Do you really think you're ready for a DNA transfer?" Said David gently.

"Of course I am. I can't wait!"

"But have you seriously thought about what you're giving up?"

"I want to do it!"

"But you're still boozing. You've struggled with flying lessons and you're holding public office. You have so much to lose."

"You're as bad as Chawton Holland!"

"The Secretary of State for Health? What's he got to do with it?"

"He's trying to block my species reassignment process."

"Why?"

"Because I'll resign as an MP before my parrot DNA transfer, generating another by-election. The Tory Independence Party is already struggling to prop up a minority Government, which depends on a 'confidence and supply' agreement with the Meccan Party. The Labour Socialists will almost certainly win my seat. Vernon Stack will be licking his lips at the prospect of a 'no-confidence' vote and General Election!"

"So, the Prime Minister's behind this too?"

"Of course he is. He'll sack Chawton Holland, if he fails to stop me becoming a parrot and further weakening the party!"

"Sorry mate. What a bummer."

"The hospital's been withholding steroids and genetic-mutational drugs. I'm on much weaker doses than other trans-species patients. I've been blocked from going private and now they're making me pay for my own sandpaper!"

"But what can you do?"

"I'll destroy the Chawton Holland long before the Prime Minister does. Then he'll know who to more be afraid of!"

Epping Holding Centre, 8th May

Catatonic with grief, she sobbed hysterically on Miriam's shoulder, shaking, gasping and catching her breath. For two months, Prema had remained calm, composed and dignified in the face of false accusation, public vilification and the prospect of a barbaric death. But Lucinda's death ripped a chasm in her spirit.

She cried inconsolably for the charismatic beauty who could have befriended anyone, but had opened her heart to a frail nonentity like herself. Lucinda, who had championed her and urged her to fight for survival, lay dead in the hospital mortuary.

While giving motherly support, Miriam did not have the infectious, thick-skinned vivacity to stir Prema out of her pit of despair. After an hour, Prema was still hysterical.

Miriam's mind was besieged with self-doubt.

"Am I really meant to be a Prison Chaplain? I feel powerless."

Negative thoughts built a bird's nest in her head.

"Are you really called to this ministry? Were you any help to your husband! You're sixty-five and you have nothing to show for it!"

Where did these thoughts come from? The accuser continued.

"You can't connect with people. You don't have Lucinda's spirit?"

But the accuser made a fatal error, mentioning the word "spirit".

Miriam's train of thought was intercepted and changed direction.

"Spirit? What kind of spirit? I can only give human consolation. But there's a more powerful comforter. I'm just a vessel. That's it!"

She snapped out of her defeatism.

As she lifted a silent prayer, the light filling the room was hidden to human eyes. Invisible warriors with swords lined the perimeter of the room.

Prema calmed down, as Miriam gently she sensed her a battle had been won.

Peckham, 9th May

As the doorbell rang, Miriam rushed to tidy the lounge, but then shrugged and tossed a cushion aside. The chaos was beyond remedy. Anyway, Evie wouldn't mind.

Evie gave her a warm hug, stepping into the dingy hall cluttered with prams, scattered toys, shoes and spilled boxes. Her smart-casual linen shirt, chino trousers and loafers were too upmarket for the surrounding streets and her Roxanne designer sunglasses offered minimal disguise.

As Evie removed her shades, Miriam noticed her dark-ringed eyes and grey, drawn, blotchy complexion, which even an expensive colour-correcting foundation could not hide.

"Come in my love. It's awful news about your friend. Dreadful."

Tears pricked Evie's eyes and she struggled to compose herself, as Miriam cleared the sofa of laundry, bedding, nappies, feeding bottles, toiletries and cigarette boxes.

Evie was oblivious to her surroundings, including the congealed baby food and vomit trodden into a once-presentable carpet. In a sea of raw pain, she focused on maintaining some semblance of poise in front of this dishevelled, motherly woman.

She leaned back and shut her eyes, until Miriam returned with a pot of tea.

"Thanks for letting me drop by. I know you have a houseful now."

"It's crazy, my love, I won't lie to you. But we do our best."

"I think you've been wonderful, taking them in. This is the sort of community action and voluntary spirit my Government works to encourage."

"Fat choice we have, because your Government does naff-all for people like Norma and Ceiba. A young man dies in childbirth and his family are thrown on the rubbish-heap. No home, reduced benefits. It's a disgrace."

"They were made homeless? There's supposed to be a safety net, with every case reviewed."

"Well, they fell through the cracks. They'd be destitute without us."

"Look, please write to your MP about them and copy it to me. I'll forward it to the Secretary of State for Work and Pensions."

"I hope he gets off his bony backside to do something!"

"I'll try, but I have a lot on my plate at the moment."

"Our country's a right mess.   Law and order's breaking down. The Police have done nothing about those abducted women. And as for geriatric substance abuse, those drug barons make me livid. I wish your Government would get its act together and..."

Miriam sounded like a member of His Majesty's Opposition. Evie's fragile hold on self-control evaporated and tears cascaded down her face as she stifled a sob.

"I wasn't blaming you, sweetheart. I know the Home Office do their best."

"You're right to blame me."

"No, love...."

Evie stared into Miriam's eyes, as she scrunched a tissue in her hand. Could she really make herself vulnerable to this woman? But who else was there?

"Miriam, can we get some air in the garden, please?"

"It's a bit of a wilderness."

Evie pulled a notepad from her handbag and wrote: *"Your house could be bugged."*

"WHAT?! That's impossible..."

"Shh!"

Evie grabbed Miriam and moved to the door.

As they paced on the patio in the hot sunshine, Miriam could hardly contain herself.

"You think our house is bugged?"

"MI5. Humanity operations. They keep the breakaway Anglican Bishops under surveillance. I've tried to use my influence to divert them from you, but I can't guarantee your privacy."

"But Heaven knows what they've overheard!"

"I don't want to know. And keep your voice down. Now do I have your total confidence?"

"Of course. I'm an ordained Minister."

"I need to confide in someone or I'll go crazy."

"Just take your time"

"I blame myself because I messed up Lucinda's life. It's my fault she was on drugs."

"How on earth did that happen?"

"We go back a long way. We were at school together and I was badly bullied. I didn't fit it, but Lucinda looked after me. We became inseparable friends for years."

Evie bit her lip.

"It's OK my love…."

"We really fell out badly. She had this certain something about her. Charisma, sensuality, call it what you will. Men fell for her like limp puppies."

"So, your friendship broke for the oldest reason in the world?"

"Yes. I met a wonderful man and fell madly in love with him. Guys don't exactly queue up for me (unless they're dirty old men), but I thought he loved me. Then I made the mistake of introducing him to Lucinda. They were in a full relationship within two weeks."

"Oh!" A sudden realisation dawned on Miriam.

"Was it James? James Cardew?"

"Yes!"

"We know him. He played the traffic warden in that scene with a baboon.

"It was an only an actor in a baboon suit"

"We love James, but we were appalled by the film!"

"I never liked it myself."

"But Lucinda was star struck?"

"Yes, she wasted no time at all. We fell out for months, until I found a use for her…."

"How?"

"You've seen how she's campaigned against the guillotine?"

"Ferociously!"

"I made her do it, by blackmailing her. I wanted to turn public opinion against capital punishment. I've secretly sabotaged it. I raised her profile, by getting her a top modelling contract."

"Using your connections?"

"I'm not proud of it. And look what it's done to her. She embraced the clubbing, drug-taking circles she landed in. And the gruelling schedule drove her to narcotics."

"What you did was manipulative and wrong, I won't lie to you my love. But Lucinda made her own choices. You didn't give her the drugs."

"I put her in a place where her weaknesses were exploited."

"But she inherited a family weakness. Her dad went the same way. She might have still chosen that path, sooner or later."

"We'll never know. But I no longer like myself."

"You acted out of bitterness and revenge, my love, but you were hurting. And I still think, overall, you're a lovely person."

"No, I'm not. I went into politics thinking I was down-to-earth, transparent and a breath of fresh air. But I'm as polluted as the men who manipulated me into high office. And I see something hideous when I look in the mirror...."

Evie struggled again to compose herself.

"This awful feeling of ugliness, what is it?"

Miriam braced herself. Evie was a high-ranking politician. Could she say this?

"Everyone has that ugliness, whether they know it or not. It's called sin."

She had said it.

Epping Holding Centre, 23rd May

Gloria had a spring in her step, as the huge iron gate swung open. The blazing sun caught the red glint in her hair, as she sauntered across the cobbled courtyard.

She was even cheerful during the body-scan and frisking by a bad-tempered security woman with dirty fingernails, who scratched her designer handbag. She was finally escorted through three grey, formidable, electronic doors to the grim, concrete corridors of the third floor Capital Remand Wing and into Prema's sterile, though comfortable room.

Gloria rarely allowed hope to stir her emotions, but today it penetrated every self-protective wall she had constructed, through years of self-discipline.

"Good morning Prema! Great to see you!"

Gloria was struck by Prema's calmness and serenity. With smiling poise, she shook Gloria's hand.

Prema wore a silk blouse and batik-print skirt. Her hair was carefully arranged with sparkling pins which shone in the sterile artificial lighting. She wore light make up with carefully applied eyeliner and her complexion had regained its luminance, now she was eating regularly again.

"Gloria, have some mango juice. They've allowed me a small fridge!"

"So how are you feeling?"

Gloria could barely contain herself as Prema poured the drinks.

"You've heard the news?"

"Yes."

"The House of Lords have passed the Bill! If you're found guilty, you're allowed three appeals! This gives us three years, or more!"

Prema calmly drew up a white-padded chair.

"I'm glad they've passed the Bill. It will save many lives."

"But Prema, you don't sound that excited. Don't you see what this means? You can fight this till the next Election! Labour will almost certainly win and they'll repeal the death penalty! You'll live!"

Prema drew a deep breath.

"Gloria, I've thought hard about this. I appreciate all you're doing for me. But if they find me guilty and sentence me to death, I've decided I won't appeal."

"What?!"

As so often happens with major disappointment, there was a split second between hearing and registering the news. As Prema's words became a reality, Gloria felt a searing stab of pain.

Then a cocktail of anger, humiliation, betrayal erupted to the surface.

"You won't appeal?! What do you mean? Why do you think that I'm flogging my guts out seventeen hours a day, before you've even been tried or sentenced? I'm already working on the appeal because the verdict is so inevitable!"

"But if the British establishment is determined to kill me, what's the point of enduring three appeals? The process will be stressful, with only disappointment at the end. The Royal Family, the Health Trusts, the pharmaceutical firms, companies profiting from male pregnancies, the Media and even some Bishops all want me dead! Gloria, you're really good, but everything's stacked against me. Why prolong the agony?"

"But Prema, my girl, you'll feel very different once they sentence you."

"No, I won't! How long do any of us live? Look what happened to Lucinda."

"The execution has to be carried out with forty days of sentencing. This is not the USA! It's only slightly better than the 1950's when hangings were done within three weeks! If you don't appeal you'll be staring at the blade in less than six weeks!"

"I'm not afraid. I'd rather get it over with."

"Believe me, life will seem very precious when your last days are slipping away, your sister's heart is breaking and the ordeal looms closer. There's nothing like the terror of imminent death to make you want to fight it!"

"You can't stop it happening in the end! The election's three years away. The powers that be want me dead before then."

"So that's it? You have no confidence in me and our working relationship's over?"

"No, don't say that. You can still make my defence at the trial."

"Prema, if you don't believe I can take on the British establishment, what makes you think I can achieve a 'not guilty' or 'manslaughter' verdict, or persuade the Jury to recommend mercy?

"The Jury isn't part of the establishment. You can persuade them I killed Ralph in self-defence."

"The Jury will be directed by a judge who is part of the establishment"

"If I'm meant to live, I'm in God's hands."

"You're into that religious nonsense?"

"I've started believing again. Miriam has encouraged me.

"So, you're clinging to fairy tales, rather than facing reality. No wonder you've made this decision. You've escaped into a load of myths! Forget about God. The only one can help you is me!!"

"Actually, that's where you're wrong."

Peckham, 25th May

Evie had invited herself back to Aidan and Miriam's house, totally disregarding security procedures. Her suit was in a holdall and her jeans, sunglasses and hastily-scrunched ponytail were her only disguise. Frank would be livid, but she didn't care.

Like a dog with a bone, she felt an urge to continue her conversation with Miriam, even though she disagreed with every word.

"I'm a decent individual. There's just one tiny piece inside me that's ugly. Maybe I need psychotherapy to help my self-esteem."

Evie leaned against the garden fence and winced as a rose briar pricked through her immaculately-ironed shirt, drawing blood against the white linen.

She tried to control the tremor in her voice.

"I went into politics to improve people's lives. I sit up till 4.00 am answering letters from constituents."

"What attracted you to the fashion industry?"

"Making people look good. Stylish clothes made me feel better about myself. I did the same for others."

"You've always striven to make yourself good, outside and in."

"Yes."

"It doesn't work. We all have a basic problem."

She sipped her coffee, unable to look Miriam in the eyes.

"So, you're going to use the 'sin' word again? But I'm mostly good. "

Miriam looked at her gently. Best not to mention Evie's vitriolic exchanges in the House of Commons.

Miriam passed her some Victoria sponge.

"Have some cake."

Evie's sugar levels were low and she grasped it eagerly.

"Would you still grab that cake, if it had a milligram of arsenic in it?"

"No way."

"But it would still be mostly good? All that jam and cream?"

"I wouldn't risk it."

"Evie, that's what sin does. One small sin pollutes the whole person."

"I don't believe in a God to sin against!"

Evie gulped the last dregs of coffee, knowing her atheism was under siege. As her walls crumbled, every part of her felt exposed. Suppressing the memory from Westminster Abbey, she tried to regain control of the conversation.

"It's interesting to talk about these things and thank you for listening. But I must go home soon – my red box awaits!"

Miriam wasn't fooled.

BBC Broadcasting House, Central London, 15th May

Bishop Burstall shuffled in a cramped, soundproofed BBC recording studio. His battle with baby weight and lack of sleep made him irritable, but the arrival of a nanny had freed him to record his homily on Radio 4.

With avuncular, soothing tones, he would shortly launch into a monologue, to further seduce and anaesthetise the minds of 'middle England'.

He quietly laughed at the thought that listeners regarded him as a man of a God. He had long served another master.

"Seismic shifts in values have long been skillfully masterminded by the establishment."

He mused.

"What could be safer and more reassuring than Thought for the Day? There's an old saying that it you slowly boil a frog, it won't notice until it's too late. Plenty of frogs have been successfully boiled since the 1960's. Today's values and assumptions will be tomorrow's 'bigotry'.

He turned to the microphone.

"Good morning. I woke this morning to the cries of my beautiful baby boy. It reminded of another baby in the Old Testament. A child hidden in a basket in the bulrushes. A princess rescued him and saved his life. He became a great hero, portrayed in Hollywood epics and blockbusters. His name was Moses.

And today, other heroes rescue babies. Men who give birth. Thousands of children might never have lived, if courageous men had not faced surgery and pain to bring new life into the world. And as with the martyrs of old, some of them have paid the ultimate price. Tolerant people of all faiths and none must welcome these little ones. They're our future and proof that anything is possible. My son is a joy. How wonderful that we men can partake in the wonderful mystery of birth. Have a blessed day!"

Twenty minutes later, he made a swift exit from Broadcasting House, heading along Langham Place to a quiet coffee shop.

"Burstall, that was quick!"

"The professional touch, Gregory."

Gregory Wilson breathed in, as the overweight Burstall squeezed into a discreet booth. "Bad news about this Appeal Bill. Gone through the Lords."

"Only a set-back, Burstall, she'll be dead soon enough."

Bishop Burstall reddened.

"She could be alive in three years. Longer, if Labour win in 2039!"

"Relax, man. Her case is very weak. And who'd pay her legal costs?"

"It's not just Ms Gupta I worry about. Will Evie Atherton actually sign her death warrant?"

"What, fatty?"

"Fatty? She's a trim size 14. I detest her, but would admit she's decent-looking."

"Anyone's trim compared with you, Bishop! As far as I'm concerned, any woman over a size 8 is obese!"

"She has high public approval ratings. Would she wreck that by being the first Home Secretary to oversee an execution since 1964?"

"The Prime Minister will make sure she does. She could be a threat to his leadership, so the more hated she is, the better. The backbenchers love her, even if Cabinet members knife her."

"But isn't he terrified of a Welsh Independence Referendum, if a guillotining happens? Myfanwy Roberts has the backing of the Welsh National Assembly. Mayhew could go down in history as the Prime Minister who lost Wales!"

"The Welsh get lots of funding from the UK. They won't leave us!"

"Don't count on it. Remember Brexit, Gregory!"

Gregory sighed. "I won't relax till the blade has fallen."

"Of course you won't." Burstall smiled mockingly over his coffee cup.

"Did you get her old computer?"

"It was easy!"

"And where is it now?"

"Never you mind, Bishop. Relax!"

Peckham, 7th June

James Cardew shuffled uneasily as he arrived at Aidan and Miriam's house. Fervently hoping Miriam would be there, he was met by an edgy-looking Aidan.

"Hello James? This is a surprise."

"Sorry to trouble you. I've come to see Norma and Ceiba. I tried Bill Clinton towers. The neighbours said they're here."

"You'd better come in"

James and Aidan had hardly spoken at Tony's funeral, having called a truce out of respect for the family. But resentments still simmered.

Aidan showed him into the nappy-strewn lounge.

"How's Miriam?"

"She's out with Ceiba, Norma and the babies. They're at the Crematorium, taking flowers."

This would be painful. A tete-a-tete with Aidan.

"Can I get you a drink?"

There was temporary respite as Aidan disappeared into the kitchen, followed by an agonizing silence as they stared at mugs of tea.

"Any films coming up?"

"No. I'm resting, as they say in my profession."

"And, er... what do you do, when you're not acting?"

"What do you do, when you're not a Bishop?"

"Sorry, I'm not being intrusive. I just wanted to know what your interests are?"

"20th century classical music. Sibelius and Vaughan Williams. But not the choral stuff."

"Any family?"

"Not really. Just a stray ginger cat."

"So, you're into animals?

Aidan's heart sank. He'd said the wrong thing.
James sighed in exasperation.

"Once and for all, I've never had sex with a baboon!"

"I think we established that!"

"Yes, at Tony's deathbed."

"Look, I'm sorry my social media posts were a bit
harsh."

"Sorry I called you a…" James couldn't get the word
out.

"Any acting projects coming up?"

"No, my agent only gets me engagements for hen
parties, dressed as a traffic warden. Which I decline, you'll
be glad to hear."

Aidan burst out laughing.

"I had you down as a ladies' man!"

"I prefer the more intellectual ones!"

The ice had broken.

Orwell View B&B, Felixtowe, 22nd June

Evie had perfected the art of disguise.   In the
Felixtowe Guest House, she introduced herself as Janice.
She was recovering from a stroke and needed rest and
privacy. With a pale, scrubbed face, grey streaks in her
hair and stiffened left arm, she had also faked a droop in
her left jaw.

Evie inwardly thanked James for the occasions he had
brought her to Elstree Studios, to watch his pre-dawn
make up sessions. She had gazed in fascination as they
transformed him into a villain, hero, victor, space alien,
warrior or animal.   Her rapid elevation to high office had
ended those carefree times.

It had taken her weeks to identify this tiny,
anonymous, Suffolk B&B. Payment would be made from
one of her father's business accounts

She had meticulously covered every trace of her presence. Strolling along the windy promenade, the greyness of the North Sea, deserted shingle beach and biting wind felt wildly exhilarating. Far from Whitehall, the isolation gave a pleasurable thrill. All her electronic devices were left at home, after informing the Prime Minister, Style Hobbs and Home Office colleagues that she was bedridden with avian flu.

If a major incident occurred, which could not be handled by Home Office colleagues, she would be finished. This was the most reckless thing she had done and yet it was exhilarating.

Could she really fool Frank? But she sensed he would remain silent. For whatever motive, he was loyal and protective for now, though she dreaded the confrontation if he found out. His concern for her went beyond professional commitment.

Now she sat in a lovingly-furnished bedroom, drinking the generous supplies of Earl Grey tea which the elderly proprietor had provided. Old Mrs Cavendish would respect her privacy.

She sat on the bed, wearing plastic gloves. With tweezers and salad tongs she eased the photocopied documents into a plain brown envelope.

Photocopying had been a nightmare. Public facilities were few and far between and offered little privacy. Carbon emission policies had all but driven them out of existence. She eventually found a small library in Ipswich which still had an old copier, and where a noisy children's group had provided a welcome distraction from her presence.

She relished this moment. Sir Chawton Holland, the Secretary of State for Health, would soon be fighting for his political career. A major news story would cause an earthquake across the establishment and no-one would know she was behind it. She smirked, contemplating the media uproar which would erupt, just days before Prema Gupta's trial began. Gloria Baxter was about to receive the greatest gift in her professional life. The envelope burned in her hands. It was dynamite.

Evie gazed at the hundreds of names of deceased young men. Tony McCrief and other victims would now be avenged. Sophie Hammond and other women who had endured terror as they were strapped, sedated, anaesthetised and violated, had finally found a voice.

She was doing something totally unprofessional. She even wondered if Miriam and Aidan would call it a 'sin'. But somehow, this didn't feel ugly. Maybe there was an invisible being whose heart ached for these broken lives, even more than hers did?

Her political career would end if her actions were discovered. But this was a new type of fear. Not the oppressive terror she'd felt in recent months, but a sensation like diving from the highest board of a swimming pool.

Her heart pounded as she addressed the envelope: Erica Rayleigh, Editor, The Observian. A copy must go to her home.   She would not risk it being lost, recycled or intercepted at the The Observian's Head Office.

Meridian Birthing Centre, 29th June

Gregory Wilson had worked his entire shift on the women's labour ward. They were short-staffed, so he was forced to supervise the care of eight female clients.

It had been a lousy day. He detested pregnant women. This was partly because they reminded him that nature still had the upper hand. After all, a female death in childbirth was virtually unknown. But most of all, the women themselves made no secret of their contempt for him.

A raucous mother of four, delivering her fifth, had said sarcastically:

"'Ere, would you like a guided tour mate? I bet you haven't seen equipment like mine for pushing a kid out!"

As he left the birthing centre to go home, he got stuck in a revolving door and a young pregnant woman giggled:

"Hey, he doesn't know the right exit route!"

He hastily retreated to the deserted car park, promising himself a seafood risotto washed down with a bottle of Prosecco to drown his sorrows.

He did not see the black clad figure until the gleaming knife pressed against his throat.　Sudden terror and nausea rose in his throat, as the blade nicked his neck, drawing blood.　A familiar face leered into his as he felt himself being pressed against the wall.

"Gregory Wilson.　Useless waste of space.　So, how much did they offer you, you pathetic little runt?"

"Offer me?　For what?!!"

"Don't go all innocent with me, bonehead."

"I don't know what you mean!"

"Oh, don't tell me.　Prema Gupta's laptop took itself out for a walk, jumped onto a bus and decided to sell itself to the highest bidder?"

"No! I've kept it under lock and key!"

Vauxhall, 1st July

Towards midnight, Evie focused on her red box, staring at a spreadsheet of UK immigration figures until the lines blurred, with one statistic rolling into another.

She was becoming uneasy, as it was now ten days since she had posted the anonymous parcel to Erica Rayleigh.　The Observian loathed the Tory Independence Government.　She had given Erica the scoop of her life. Why hadn't she jumped at the bait?

By now, Westminster should have been in turmoil. Chawton Holland should have resigned or been sacked, while Prime Minister Orchard Mayhew should have been fighting for his political life.　She should have been waiting in the wings to seize high office, as a popular figure of stability.　But there was no earthquake in Whitehall and as each day passed, her frustration grew.

Erica had no clear reason to hold back the story. She might have bided her time, if an election had been a few months away, in to inflict maximum damage during an election campaign. The paper was strongly in favour of the Male Birth Incentive Scheme, but would Erica really miss the opportunity to attack a Tory Independence Government for releasing false statistics and serious health care failures?

And the paper fiercely opposed to the death penalty, even to the point of partnering with Amnesty International. They had regularly reported on Lucinda's campaigning and invited her to be a guest columnist. Any weakening of the Government would reduce the likelihood of executions being carried out.

So why the silence?

It was only six weeks until Prema's trial began. It would be illegal for the newspapers to release the story while the trial was in progress, as it would clearly prejudice the case. So maybe Erica and her colleagues were waiting until the week before the trial, to achieve maximum impact? Thus, Evie fought to comfort herself with excuses for Erica's delay. With a gulp of black coffee, she turned her attention to her new Community Policing Bill.

xi) Erica

Dalston, East London, 8th July

At 6.00am, Erica Rayleigh emerged from a small, fashionable development of flats and scuttled towards the London Overground station where early-morning tubes shuttled bleary-eyed commuters into the City. Most of them would be too weary to recognise a familiar face from a quality national newspaper, particularly with no makeup and straggly, unbrushed hair, instead of the French pleat which she would pin in place when she arrived at the Kings Cross office.

She was not in love. This was painfully brought home by the amorous young couple opposite her, who were oblivious to the jolting, clattering and jostling around them.

She refused to cry. To the world she was a powerful and assured woman. The Times had put her at number nine in their list of the hundred most influential people in the UK. Irritatingly, Evie Atherton was number three.

So why was she trapped in this relationship? It gave her no joy or security and it terrified her. Yet the danger she would face from dumping him was far worse than that of being stifled by him. Her career would be over. Maybe even her life.

She presented herself to the world as a champion of women's rights. Although he had supported the Male Birth Incentive Scheme, she had expressed concern that it could disempower women.

She was not a stereotypical aggressive feminist, having won almost universal respect by being more rounded than some of her hard-line predecessors. She proclaimed women's freedom to fulfil their dreams, while respecting the desire of men to do the same.

And here was a painful irony - while she declared that a woman needed no man to define her, her future destiny and safety was defined by the stranglehold of her menacing partner.

As she changed trains at Highbury and Islington, she turned her thoughts to Evie Atherton. The nation's third most influential woman, but she had no boyfriend. The tabloids picked the bones of her empty love life. Erica refused to stoop so low, preferring to attack Evie's policies. There would be no cheap shots. Besides, she had a sneaking respect for the feisty, raven-haired genius.

As the tube clattered along the Victoria Line, Erica remembered the parcel which had been delivered a week ago. Why did it have to arrive when he was there? He was so controlling that she could not even open her personal mail in private. She shuddered, remembering the tears and threats......

North Wales, 26th August

Father, daughter and 90-year-old great uncle enjoyed the view of Conwy Castle and Colwyn Bay, devouring pasties and cartons of juice, with the distant sea glistening a silvery yellow and the scorching midday sun warming the car.

Evie was in no mood to relax. She could not tear her thoughts away from Westminster and was also despondent about being thirty-five, single, childless and holidaying with elderly relatives.

By consolation, they were staying in the best hotel in Llandudno. The cascading water at Swallow Falls, the richly green, gentle heights of Snowdonia and the stroll across the Menai Bridge to the quiet privacy of Anglesey had been therapeutic.

The British holiday destination had been good for her public image as a down to earth, working class lass.

"Home Secretary does her bit for Welsh Tourism!" Proclaimed the mid-market papers read by Tory Independence housewives. Evie had smiled ironically at that. Orchard Mayhew was terrified at the prospect of a Welsh independence referendum. Here she was, shoring up Welsh relations and doing him a favour!

A visit to Albert Dock, in Liverpool had won the hearts of locals, even though the photo with her ice cream being snatched by a trans-species seagull was less than dignified.

But the looming horror made an overseas trip unthinkable. She had to remain near London. Today was the last day of Prema Gupta's trial and the Jury would be sent out this afternoon to consider their verdict.

As her father and Uncle Ron strolled to the sea, Evie sat in the stifling car, listening to the Old Bailey trial on her wrist phone.

For five days, she and her father had followed the proceedings in the hotel room, on the beach and even on the Blaenau Ffestiniog railway, with a silent veil of tension and fear disengaging them from Uncle Ron's war anecdotes and the babble of the carefree tourists.

The Judge summed up the case, presenting Prema as a mentally ill psychopath.

"Members of the Jury, you must consider whether you believe Gregory Wilson to be a reliable character witness. You should also remember the excellent character of Sir Ralph Hardcastle."

Evie was livid. Gregory Wilson was the darling of Daytime TV. How would any jury dare doubt him?

"You must also consider whether Sir Ralph Hardcastle had access to Prema Gupta's house with or without her knowledge? He had a full set of keys and some of his belongings were stored there, even after the divorce."

Evie sighed. What chance did she stand?

"Sir Ralph Hardcastle made a phone call to Gregory Wilson from Prema's home on 13th February. She denies all knowledge of him being there, but was she telling the truth? If he visited regularly, he was not an intruder. Although they were divorced, it would appear they still had contact."

"Your bias is sickening!" Shouted Evie at her wristphone.

"Members of the Jury, you cannot give a manslaughter verdict unless you believe Sir Ralph Hardcastle was violent, or could have been mistaken for a burglar. You must also bear in mind the character evidence given about Prema Gupta and her doctor's medical assessment.   She was described as aggressive and unstable."

"Aggressive and unstable, what planet are you on?" Cried Evie.

As the Judge sent the Jury out, stress and sunstroke sent a wave of nausea to her throat and she threw up on the grass verge.

The Old Bailey, London, 26th August

For five hours, Prema and Gloria had sat in a damp cell, under the Old Bailey. It was hot, stuffy and the smell of disinfectant mingled with vomit and urine from a previous occupant.

Prema was composed, but her face was haggard and drained, her eyes reflecting the anguish of lost hope and circled by dark lines from insomnia.

Gloria looked grim, as she flicked through a folder and stacked her papers. She sighed and glanced up.

"I won't lie to you."

"No need, Gloria. I know. I was so shocked that Ralph made a phone call from my house on 13th February. And he rang Gregory? But how often had he entered my house?

"And how did he get a key?"

"It was never his home. I bought it with the divorce money."

Prema sighed, gulped from a bottle of chilled water and tried not to retch, either from fear of the stench of the cell.

"The trial was a disaster."

"I wasn't prepared for the level of character assassination against you."

"That occasion when Ralph's bullying drove me to screaming fits was used by them as evidence of an unstable character. Then they said I was capable of violence!"

"You should have told me you used to take anti-depressants and sleeping pills. It looked bad when they found old drug supplies in your home. Your GP's testimony didn't help."

"I'm sorry Gloria, I didn't realise they'd use that. And it was awful when my work colleagues told the court about my depression three years ago, when I said: "I wish he was dead. I could kill the man"."

Gloria poured her a glass of water, with an almost gentle expression.

"You did your best. Gregory Wilson infuriated me, praising Ralph's character.   And as for Ralph calling you an unmanageable wife…."

"I was shocked at the words Gregory used, such as lazy, selfish, uncooperative, aggressive and unstable."

"Then he described Ralph as a loving husband and perfect gentleman."

"Ugh! He was a monster. Yes, he lavished a fortune on my clothes and jewellery. But I was a trophy.   When I went to Lewisham A&E in 2034 with a bruised and dislocated wrist, he had beaten me up. How dare Gregory claim Ralph had injured me when trying to stop me jumping out of a window."

"Gregory was infuriatingly slick under cross-examination. I've broken supergrasses, hardened police inspectors, pathologists and even a junior member of the Royal Family. But he was immovable."

"Gloria, I wish this had gone better, for your sake."

"You've coped so well. But I don't think it will help."

"Will they take long?"

"Twelve hours at least. The OJ Simpson case was nothing compared to this. This is the highest profile murder case in decades."

"The Judge will accept a majority verdict. That should speed things up."

"The Jury will want to look as if they've done a thorough job."

"Seven more hours of this.   If they find me guilty today, will the Judge sentence me immediately?"

"He could ask for medical reports and reconvene the Court next Tuesday. That gives me a window. If there's a guilty verdict, I'll demand a month to review your medical background. If I can prove you're of unsound mind...."

"I'm not mad."

"Diminished responsibility could save your neck. There are different types of mental illness, not just criminal insanity. I'll interview every doctor and counsellor, investigate the side effects of your drugs. A month's review would extend your life by thirty days!"

Gloria began to smell hope. Prema's sentence would be commuted to life imprisonment. She became distracted by a daydream of her own success...

Suddenly she jolted and her heart leapt as her wrist phone rang. Prema's questioning eyes met hers.

"The Jury has reached a verdict. They're bringing us back up."

North Wales, 26th August

Evie prepared for evening dinner, with her wet hair wrapped in warm towels. But her glamour routine had stalled and any appetite for enjoying champagne and seafood at an exclusive Llandudno restaurant had vanished.

Like around thirty-five million other British viewers, she was totally consumed by the events unfolding on the hologram TV in her hotel room. She was infuriated by the commentators and pundits filling the waiting hours with endless drivel, trying to predict the verdict.

Every illusion of being on holiday had evaporated this evening as she packed her cases to return to London. She aired a black, sombre dress and jacket to run the gauntlet of paparazzi.

She had expected the Jury to deliberate until Friday morning, giving her one more precious evening of respite. Now she must face the deluge of press conferences and public statements, as Home Office procedures were triggered by the first death sentence in Britain since 1964. Even on Sunday morning, they would drag her into the BBC studio for an 8.00am current affairs programme and interview with an aggressive presenter.

As the Old Bailey seats and gallery filled, Prema's Barrister, other lawyers and court officials murmured in clusters shuffling papers and smelling history. Evie scanned their faces for a clue to the outcome. Their voices rose as the frail, gaunt, Prema Gupta was led to the dock. She was as composed as ever, having carefully rearranged her hair and changed her blouse.

Evie felt an increasing admiration for this small, placid woman who had withstood a barrage of abuse from the Prosecution Counsel and successive hostile witnesses during the week. Devoid of hatred or anger, she had said very little for herself. This exquisite waif did not look like a hardened killer. Evie had always prided herself on her judgement of character.

Hearing a sharp rap on the door, Evie hastily pulled on a t-shirt and shorts.

"Dad!"

"Thought you might appreciate some company."

George squeezed his daughter's hand as the formidable hologram of the judge entered the court.

"Would the foreman of the Jury please rise? Have you reached a verdict?

"Yes."

"Is it the verdict of you all?"

"No."

Evie's pulse raced faster.

"What is your verdict?"

"Guilty, with the recommendation of the death penalty."

The courtroom erupted and above the gasps and cries, someone yelled.

"Yes! Kill the evil cow!!"

The only person who remained impassive, was Prema. As Gloria's complexion reddened and sweat beaded her forehead, she glanced anxiously at her client. But Prema only made brief eye contact and with a faint smile she withdrew into a world of her own.

"Silence in Court!!"

The noise and chaos subsided.

"Before I pass sentence, I will receive submissions from the Prosecution and Defence Counsel. I also request a mental health report. The court will reconvene on September 3rd."

"Objection, your honour! I request a month to obtain a full report."

"Your request is denied. All reports and medical assessments can be obtained in a couple of days. We're not living in the 1990s!"

Evie steadied her breath, straightened her shoulders and tightened her mouth. The fear was becoming a reality.

George placed an arm round her shoulder.

"I'm fine dad, we knew this would happen."

"Well, don't forget what I told you."

10 Downing Street, 26th August

Orchard Mayhew shook Evie's hand warmly, welcoming her into his office as an aide served coffee and a light supper. Ah, such hospitality towards a colleague whose political career was now as precarious as the pretty head on Prema Gupta's neck.

Evie squirmed. As Prime Minister, he exuded a tenuous charm which never hid his insecurity. The clammy-handed warmth could turn brittle and the media delighted in catching him off-guard, when the Cheshire cat smile dropped into a scowl. His speech makers gave him soundbites which were deftly shredded on Sunday morning and late night political shows, exposing his weakness, irritability and lack of charisma under fire.

Everyone knew he was the 'caretaker' leader of the Tory Independence Party until a more effective statesman emerged. The resignation of his predecessor had left a feeble pool of successors. Orchard had narrowly won the leadership contest. In the disastrous 2034 election, he had won a miserable 316 seats. With no overall majority, he struggled to sustain his party's confidence and supply arrangement with the Meccan Party. Cabinet Ministers with even less capability or charisma snapped at his heels.

His most serious threat was Evie. With sharp instincts and business acumen, she had shone as Secretary of State for Trade and Industry and was now an excellent Home Secretary. Her working-class appeal increased her majority in Warrington. Her Opinion Poll approval rating was 12% ahead of his.

But Orchard intended to enjoy tonight. Surely the guilty verdict would stall her meteoric rise? However much the public had called for the return of the death penalty, how would they react when faced with an actual beheading?

Millions had wept for Ralph Hardcastle, but public grief was such a fickle thing. Six months had passed since that February orgy of mourning. People had moved on with their lives. After a hot summer, a massive haul of medals at the Olympics and consistent economic growth, the national mood was upbeat. With bank holiday temperatures at 90f there would be little public appetite for the brutal killing of a young, frail, beautiful woman.

Orchard had made a public show of courtesy, arranging for a swift chopper to transport Evie from Llandudno to a Heliport in Battersea, where a ministerial car drove her to Downing Street.

Now he leaned forward, smiling and breathing garlic from the State Banquet he had attended earlier that day.

"Evie, I want you to know I have every confidence in you. Once the Defence and Prosecution Counsel have made their submissions, the Judge will issue the death sentence on Prema Gupta. You and your Department will do an excellent job, implementing the new Home Office procedures."

"It gives me no pleasure."

"But this is a historic moment. For the first time since 1964, this nation will show it's not afraid to impose the ultimate penalty for Murder. This is a new era for law and order."

"We don't know yet if she will be sentenced to death. Mental health reports and Counsel's submissions are done for a reason."

"A mere formality. It's highly unlikely they will diagnose her as having diminished responsibility."

"Gloria Baxter is good."

"She lost the case. This execution is the first test of our Government's strength. And we must show the Meccan party we're keeping our pact. They accepted a woman as Home Secretary!"

Evie refused to comment or drop eye contact. Orchard smiled nervously.

"The Lord Chief Justice, Judge Mayhew is a good man. He's my cousin and a loyal friend of my father.   I trust him to see this through."

The door opened behind them. Orchard gave a welcoming smile.

"Ah, come in, Style!"

Evie forced a smile.

"Style works for me, Orchard."

"He's working in my office now. I transferred him while you were on holiday. Oh, don't worry, I've found a suitable replacement and you'll be very pleased."

"I oversee my own appointments and decide whether they're suitable or not."

Orchard's blushed as he fidgeted with his handkerchief, wiping sweat from his hands.

"Your chauffeur's outside, to take you home."

As Evie left, Style was smirking. She hissed in his ear.

"Enjoy it while it lasts!"

Greenwich Holding Centre, 31st August

Prema was emotionally drained. Fantasy Rimmer, Consultant Psychotherapist and two Psychiatrists from West Kensington Hospital had grilled her for two hours.

The Judge wanted this assessment to be thorough. If he donned a black cap and became the first British judge to pass a death sentence for more than seventy years, everything must be above board. Yes, he wanted a peerage, but not at the cost of historic notoriety.

Gloria insisted on being present. Despite vehement protests from the doctors, The Judge had granted her request. Miriam was also there as an observer. But they were uneasy.

Miriam, with her pastoral experience, knew Prema showed no symptoms of trauma, PTSD, depression, or any other mental health condition.

Prema's calm, uncomplicated replies were exasperating. Why must she be so honest?

Gloria could no longer stay silent.

"But Prema, how did you feel in those weeks before Ralph's death? You went through that turbulent divorce. You were afraid of him."

"Be quiet. You're here to observe!" Snapped Fantasy. "And that was a leading question."

"Like some of yours!"

"We're acting in a professional capacity. Your interference is unprofessional."

Gloria was livid.

"My client could be dead in forty-two days."

"It must be traumatic for you too," cooed Fantasy patronizingly, "I hope you're getting some support."

Gloria went quiet but glared at Prema. She must try to help herself.

Miriam placed a calming hand on Gloria's shoulder.

"This is beyond our control, my love." She whispered.

But for the next hour, Prema showcased the most infuriating normality ever to frustrate the psychiatric profession.

Vauxhall, 4th September, 3.30am

Nightmares pursued Evie as a gnawing stomach pain intermingled with dark and chaotic dreams.

She was pursued along murky corridors by Oliver Bunton, now a fully-fledged parrot and driven into a grim, gaping cavern, lonely, yet full of isolated people with grey, transparent bodies. What was Sir Ralph Hardcastle doing here? He was dead. Fear gripped her stomach and the pain grew worse. Something about that cavern increased the agony.

She sunk into despair and tossed under a sheet tangled around her, dreaming that her legs were trapped. Suddenly Frank Southwold appeared, dressed in a white suit and gold tie. He looked much younger and a glow around his body dazzled the tormented people in the cave.

"Get me out of here!" She felt herself screaming.

Frank offered a tray containing white bread.

"Eat this bread and you will be free."

"No, my stomach hurts!"

Frank stepped aside. Behind him sat Judge Heywood presiding over Prema's trial at the Old Bailey. But he looked straight into her eyes, as he suddenly put on a black cap.

"I sentence you to be taken from this place to the Greenwich Holding Centre. From there you will be taken to the place of execution, where your head will be struck from your body by guillotine."

She felt herself crying as her agony intensified.

"Why didn't you say 'may God have mercy on your soul', like they usually do?" She asked.

"Because you refused mercy!"

As she was dragged away, Evie screamed and woke up.

In the grey, chilly dawn, she stared around with overwhelming relief that her bedroom was reality and the fading horror a dream.

But as she grabbed her remote control for the comfort of her hologram TV, memories from the day before flooded back and she realised some of the horror was real. She had an excruciating stomach bug. The repeated TV footage of Judge Heywood donning a black cap, made the truth inescapable. Prema Gupta was sentenced to death. The close-up of her face showed a calm demeanour, though she flinched slightly when the words of death were delivered.

When the Judge had asked if she had anything to say before sentence was passed, she had protested her innocence but then said:

"I accept the verdict of the jury and I forgive you. I thank the court for the time they've given to this case and I express particular thanks to my Defence Counsel. Your Honour, I forgive you for the sentence you're about to pass."

Peckham, 6th September

Evie was now a familiar presence in Aidan and Miriam's chaotic home.

Norma's verbal abuse had quietened to a sullen wariness over a haze of cigarette smoke. Evie took it stoically. This woman had been robbed of her son and home. She did not disclose her secret intervention with the Department of Work and Pensions to help them. For now, she endured the vitriolic remarks because they were understandable.

Ceiba had initially treated her with awestruck silence, but now asked what hairspray she used and even allowed her to cuddle baby Landscape.

With regurgitated milk stains on her silk shirt, Evie sat in the kitchen with Miriam.

"So, how's Prema?"

"Very calm, my love."

"Yes, she was, in court. But how is she really?"

"Resigned to the whole thing. Writing letters. She's more concerned about how others are taking it."

"But she still has three appeals to come!"

Miriam went silent, stared at the table, then glanced up at Evie uneasily.

"What?" Evie was agitated.

Miriam took a deep breath.

"She won't appeal."

"Won't appeal??!! Oh, don't be ridiculous, of course she will."

"I think she means it."

"I don't believe this. Why?!?"

"She thinks she'll lose anyway. She'd rather get it over with. As a notorious woman who's suffered an abusive, broken marriage, she believes her life amounts to nothing. And Lucinda's death devastated her."

Evie felt an inward pang as Lucinda's death was mentioned.

"I thought Prema was in the God squad like you?"

"She is, but some Christians don't see things as clearly as they should. And beneath that calm exterior, she's a broken, damaged soul, whatever useless ideas Fantasy Rimmer may have!"

"Well, maybe she's in shock. Tomorrow she'll realise that in five weeks, she faces the blade and the clock's ticking. That'll concentrate her mind."

"Evie, don't count on it."

"But she has to fight! I burned the midnight oil to get that appeal legislation through Parliament! I kicked dozens of backsides in Whitehall to fast track this. Have you any idea?"

Evie launched into a torrent of expletives and her outburst drew Aidan into the kitchen.

"Evie, you did your best. You gave her a way out. If she fails to take it, it's not your fault."

"But Aidan, I'll have to sign her death warrant. The Home Office oversees the process. After Lucinda, I refuse to have Prema's blood on my hands."

"You voted against the reintroduction of the death penalty. You didn't sentence Prema to death and you're not to blame for any of this."

"People will hate me. However much they hate Prema, they'll feel different when the guillotine goes into action."

"So, you're thinking of yourself?"

"Yes, I know that's selfish. But what about our nation? Wales will call for an independence referendum if we go through with this."

"That's their choice."

"Oh Aidan, stop being so matter-of-fact!"

Aidan calmly poured himself a coffee.

"Sorry Aidan, I didn't mean to jump down your throat, but there so few people I can talk to. The Prime Minister made me a sacrificial lamb when he promoted me as Home Secretary. And the Cabinet salivated at the prospect! They control my destiny."

She let rip a few more expletives. Miriam turned pink, but Aidan was unfazed.

"Evie, I know all about public hate and humiliation. You remember the names they called me when I joined the Anglican Evangelical Fellowship?"

"Fundamentalist and bigot were the politer terms."

"I was a target of lies and abuse. They even tried to prosecute me under Humanity legislation, though the case collapsed. And even now, you're nervous about associating with me. Admit it!"

"Yes, it's true, Aidan. And I'm sorry. But I've stayed loyal to you guys because I don't believe a word of it. I know how it is to be an outsider. The truth is, you're the one bit of goodness in my life right now."

"There are people who will believe in you. And Orchard and the Cabinet do not control your destiny. Someone much more important does, who once became a sacrificial lamb for you!"

"Oh no, not the God stuff. Not today, please!"

"Evie...."

"Aidan, save it!"

Greenwich Holding Centre, 11th October

A nurse had arrived to take her blood pressure, measure her height and weight, review her diet, nutrition and check her for any known allergies.

Prema found this absurdly pointless. On the 15th of October at 9.00am, her blood pressure would peak, then plummet to zero, her height would shrink by nine inches and her weight would drop by 10lb when a gleaming, sharp, electronically motored blade plummeted through her fragile neck at 200 miles per hour, with the refined, high-precision representing the best of British technology. The likelihood of her dying from an allergy in her white, clinical cell and cheating the executioner was as likely as her travelling to Mars.

The death of her tyrant husband had caused the greatest outpouring of national grief since England had lost the World Cup Final in 2032. Now she was a national scapegoat, not only for the death of the people's gynaecologist, but for every pain and frustration afflicting people's lives. The Sun, Mirror or Daily Mail would have blamed her for the recent floods in Southern England if they could.

The nurse, a young graduate, was distressed by the situation. She tried to be courteous and reassuring. But as she smiled, her eyes filled with tears. She swallowed and checked herself.

Prema tried to reassure her. "It's OK, I expected you and you have a job to do. Have you worked here long?"

The nurse shook her head as her cheeks reddened. The tension broke when a Prison Officer arrived with Miriam.

Miriam gave Prema a strong hug. She turned to the nurse.

"Sorry my love, have I interrupted you?"

The nurse shook her head and gathered her equipment. As she left, Miriam squeezed her hand.

Miriam turned back to Prema.

"How are they treating you, my love?"

"As well as can be expected. They give me a sleeping pill every night and lots of extra loo roll, which I've needed!"

"And your sister came yesterday?"

"Reeta comes every day."

"Oh, bless her"

"You will look after her, won't you, afterwards?"

"I promise. Have you read those books I gave you?"

"Total Forgiveness and Totally Forgiving Yourself, by R T Kendall?

"Yes, I've devoured them."

"What did you think?"

"They've really helped me. I've forgiven Ralph, the Judge, the Jury, the journalists and the public. I even forgave Gregory Wilson. I don't feel any anger or hatred towards them now. But there's one person I struggle with."

"Who?"

"Gloria, my lawyer! Even though she's on my side, she winds me up. Throughout my ordeal she's spoken to me like a misbehaved schoolgirl. It's weird, because her small put downs hurt more than all the abuse I've endured! Why?"

"Because the people nearest to you, hurt you the most."

"We've never been friends."

"But she's trawled through every detail of your life to save you. You've been vulnerable. That's laid you open to her."

"Well, at least I've forgiven everyone else."

"Prema, in a few hours, you will come face to face with Jesus. You must forgive Gloria now."

"I understand."

"Are you willing to try?"

"I'm willing to be made willing."

"That's a start."

Prema took a deep breath.

"OK. I…. I choose to forgive her. But Miriam, I can't like her."

"You took the first step."

"Can I renew my Baptismal vows?"

"Of course, my love!"

Miriam wrapped her arms around the slender shoulders as they read through liturgy. A new sense of peace flooded Prema. Her eyes almost seemed radiant, even with the tears and smeared mascara.

"I want to see it."

"See what, my love?"

"The execution room. The guillotine. I want to be brave and familiarise myself - practice kneeling down and...."

"It might make you more nervous."

"I'll be more prepared."

Romford, 11th October

You would never notice Ludo Cannock as he commuted from Harold Wood to Romford each day, to work at a small firm of quantity surveyors. But at sixty-five, he looked forward to an earlier retirement than his contemporaries.

He was small in stature with thinning grey hair, a moustache, mottled complexion and one shoulder sloped lower than the other. His beige shirt and brown jacket did little to enhance his appearance. But soon a lump sum of money and future windfalls would pay for smart clothes and exotic holidays. Who knows, he might even find a wife.

In his lunch hour, he strolled into a park. He distanced himself from the cyclists, joggers, runners and children gazing at birds in the aviary and settled on a park bench in the early autumn sun.

He swiped his finger across his wrist phone and an internet page (his favourite) appeared on his arm showing a detailed diagram of a state-of-the art piece of British machinery. He pulled a notepad from his pocket and intensively scribbled an algorithm. The mathematics were not strictly necessary. He could perform his task easily without it. But Ludo had a pathological obsession with detail and he wanted to know exactly how long it would take Prema Gupta to die, when he flicked the guillotine lever in four days' time.

No-one knew he had been appointed as the Executioner, apart from the Home Secretary and her closest staff, the Chief Commissioner of the Metropolitan Police, The Lord Chief Justice and the Governor of Greenwich Holding Centre. But Ludo had very few family or friends. He had taken a day's holiday from work, to perform his duty. His colleagues thought he was planning a liaison, as he'd laid a false trail of visits to a hologram dating site. It caused much ribald laughter in the office, while putting them off the scent.

Tonight, he would walk from Harold Wood Station to his semi-detached house which was overrun with collections of dead insects, butterflies, stuffed birds and stuffed squirrels. His walls were covered with historic photos and war memorabilia which were his pride and joy.

But favourite battle was the French Revolution. The gateway to enlightenment. A portrait of Robespierre gazed at him as he reheated yesterday's shepherd's pie. He felt sure the man would have approved....

Greenwich Holding Centre, 11th October

"Are you sure you want to do this?"

The Deputy Prison Governor had a grave, firm manner, but kinder eyes than Miriam expected anyone in his position to have. He looked more uneasy than either of the women.

"Are you really sure?" He repeated.

Prema nodded and squeezed Miriam's hand.

Miriam had a tightening knot in her throat, with a rising terror at what she would have to witness, next time she walked this route. She began to imagine how she would feel if she were being escorted, tightly gripped by two warders, into this death chamber.

The Governor touched a white button and on bio-sensory recognition, the wall before them slid aside. It was just a panel.

"I've been living beside my execution room all along?" Gasped Prema.

The ceiling was 5ft higher the other side of the wall. There were no windows and the smell of disinfectant from the bare floors hit Miriam's nose, then her stomach.

Prema took deep breaths and slowly acclimatised to what lay before her.

To the left, lay a white-clothed table with bibles and other religious books, phials of oil, white napkins and boxes of tissues. There was a large wooden cross and other religious artifacts and symbols including occult ones.

Before her were six rows of brand new white chairs. There was a 4ft aisle down the middle.

She stared down the aisle to a raised platform, with a microphone at the front. Then she saw the tall, rectangular, fibreglass construction in the middle, 2ft wide and 1ft deep, rising 15ft to the ceiling. At the front was a 6ft x 18-inch white bed, with a thin mattress and six rows of leather straps, leading to an 18-inch diameter tunnel, which tapered down to an eight-inch hole inside the machine. This was not the French guillotine she remembered from her history lessons. It was a sleek, sophisticated 21st century device. Had she not known it was an instrument of death, she might have mistaken it for a high-tech piece of hospital equipment.

"Where's the blade?"

"It's hidden inside the tower."

Prema slowly moved towards the guillotine, mentally rehearsing her final walk. When she reached the bed, she asked.

"Must they strap me in? It's so undignified. I don't need restraining."

"It's not up to us, it's official procedure. And you may feel differently on the day."

Prema shrugged and looked behind the guillotine.

"So, my head won't poke through? But once I'm in there I'll be utterly alone. I won't be able to see anything."

For the first time, there was a trace of fear in her voice.

"There's a viewing panel the other side so you can see through."

"And where will my head fall?"

"Inside the machine."

"So, no-one sees anything?"

The warder nodded.

"And where's the switch?"

"Its computer activated from a side room by the platform."

"Do I meet my executioner?"

"No."

"Who will attend?"

"The Prison Governor, a representative of the Home Office, your Lawyer, the Prison Officers who will escort you and strap you on the gurney, Ralph's Hardcastle's family, your own family, your spiritual adviser and ten journalists."

"Journalists??!! I don't want them there. How intrusive!"

Miriam put a hand on her shoulder.

"They can't hurt you any more, my love."

xii) The locksmith

Dulwich, 11th October

Extended Maternity leave was great! Amelia had enjoyed eight blissful months with no commuting to City Thameslink at 6.30am, no chilled 3D-printed sandwiches, twelve-hour days or managing other people's stress.

At seven months, Baby Perry was a lively, chubby catalyst of delight. Despite the sleepless nights and chaos, Amelia was besotted.

Aidan and Miriam lived one mile away and were perfect grandparents.

Amelia knelt in tattered jeans and a baggy t-shirt scrubbing out her kitchen cupboards, with the radio on at full blast. The joy of doing mundane tasks which working people were too exhausted to think about!

She dreaded this morning's visit. Her line manager was coming for Coffee.

"To have a catch up see how you're doing."

In other words:

"When are you coming back to work? The universe will implode without you."

Amelia was in no hurry to be sucked back into the whirlpool of deadlines. She liked her boss well enough, but…

As the bell rang her dirty, water-sodden jeans were badly soiled, but she couldn't be bothered to change or adjust her unkempt hair which was haphazardly scrunched into a top knot.

Gloria was five minutes early and infuriatingly punctual as ever.

"Hi Gloria!"

Gloria stoically endured the exuberant hug of dirty work clothes against her immaculate suit.

"Amelia, I've missed you!"

Some colleagues found Gloria's exacting standards difficult to work with. But the feisty, resilient, thick skinned Amelia relished the challenge. Her wicked sense of humour was the perfect foil to Gloria's serious professionalism.

"Well, I certainly haven't missed you! I've been far too busy!"

Amelia gave as good as she got. They made a perfect double act.

"You'll get bored soon enough!"

Gloria was dreading the possibility of Amelia becoming a stay at home mum and never returning.

"You're the best paralegal I've ever had, Amelia.   It's manic without you!"

Most of all, Amelia's loyal presence had reassured Gloria she was not totally dysfunctional, whatever colleagues might say about her.

Amelia gazed at her line manager for the first time in six months. The old sparring partner was back.

They drank two pots of black coffee, demolishing a mountain of biscuits.

"Are you well?"

"I had to go back into hospital for a bowel operation four months ago."

"So soon after the birth?"

"My consultant said it was vital."

"So how was the birth?"

"Try doing it yourself!   I drove Dave up the wall with my whingeing."

"Will you have any more?"

Amelia gazed at her baby wistfully.

"Sadly, I can't, not after my bowel surgery. She'll be an only child."

"I'm really sorry."

Amelia's face reddened. Then she composed herself and her chirpy manner returned.

"Anyway, the birth was no fun."

"Bad luck having Gregory Wilson as your midwife."

"He was pathetic, blubbing about Ralph Hardcastle."

"I heard his speech on the Hospital steps.

"And while my legs were in stirrups, he gossiped about your client, Prema.   They work on the same ward and live opposite each other."

"What a nightmare for her."

"He irritated me at the ante-natal appointments and then I bumped into him two days before I went into labour."

"Where?"

"In Dulwich, at the locksmiths, when I was getting spare keys cut for mum. He lectured me on my diet and…."

Gloria jolted her arm, spilling coffee over her skirt. But she didn't care….

"You saw Gregory in a locksmith's? When?"

"The 12th February."

"Where?"

"On Lordship Lane. So what?"

"Take me there now!"

Dulwich, 11th October

Phineas munched his sandwich and read the local paper, perched on a stool with his feet on the counter. He had closed the shop for fifteen minutes. Precious respite from key cutting and shoe mending.

As the buzzer rang, he sighed petulantly and peered through the window. But his mood changed when he saw the vivacious Amelia accompanied by a stylish redhead.

"Ladies, what can I do for you?"

"Gloria Baxter, from Baxter, Baxter & Hobbs. I represent Prema Gupta, who is due to be executed in four days' time. I understand you have vital evidence and may need to call you as a key witness."

"What, me?"

Amelia gave a flirtatious smile.

"Phineas, you're such a star, we can count on you!"

Energised by the winning combination of Amelia's charm and Gloria's cool elegance, Phineas cheerfully recalled the day he'd served Gregory Wilson.

"My first celebrity customer. I asked him about eating insects on that jungle programme! But I told him I would never get pregnant! Yes, it was 12th February and I rang my daughter to tell her."

"What sort of keys did you cut for him?"

"He wanted two sets of four! A latch key, a multipoint locking key and two five-lever deadlocks. He put them on a huge keyring with black and yellow bird. He said it was a souvenir from San Francisco."

"Anything else?"

"I mended his Size 11 Snow boots. 'Man at Roxanne' designer range, black with a white and purple stripe."

Gloria was seriously impressed as she gave him her business card.

"We will call you as a witness."

"But the papers say Prema Gupta won't appeal."

"Not yet!"

As they strolled back to Gloria's car, Amelia was jubilant.

"So, were they Prema's house keys?"

"I intend to find out. They work together and he could have removed the house keys from her locker and taken a copy while she worked her shift."

"But you must persuade Prema to appeal."

"I don't need to. If Gregory Wilson copied her keys two days before Hardcastle's death, he's potentially framing himself as Prema's accomplice in his murder. Or even the actual killer!"

"I don't understand."

"Think about it. He abandoned you for two hours during your labour, leaving you without gas and air. If he can't account for his movements that night, the Police have a case. Wilson's arrest would mean a long stay of execution for Prema. They'd need her as a witness for his trial!"

"But you don't believe Prema knowingly killed Ralph, or recognised him that night. So why would she have an accomplice?"

"The Jury found her guilty of deliberate murder, so that opens the possibility of an accomplice. Even if Wilson is cleared of any charge, I can buy Prema six months of life."

"But Gloria, you could send an innocent man to the guillotine. What was his motive in copying her keys?"

"I think he was Ralph's accomplice!"

"But what was Ralph planning to do?"

"Breaking into her house at night, with Gregory? I think they intended to kill her."

"And what about the boots?"

"I've said too much already."

Chelmsford, 12th October 2036

Accompanied by two Officers (from the Metropolitan and Essex Police), Gloria arrived at a white pebble dashed house on the edge of Chelmsford, a haven of tranquility with pond, patio and wilderness garden.

The homeowner's laid-back manner complemented her home. Gym toned, with a ponytail, perfect skin and no makeup, she gallantly defied her 47 years. Good-humouredly apologizing for the mess, she welcomed them into her lounge.

"We're sorry for this second intrusion at such a painful time. How are you since we last met?"

"I'm fine, thanks. My brother and I were never close. Ralph's only communication was his Christmas newsletters describing his exotic holidays in Puerto Rico, The Bahamas and New Zealand. We had little in common."

Indeed, Clare Hardcastle bore no physical resemblance to her famous brother.

"On the day Ralph died, when you identified his body, we understand you collected his personal effects from Lewisham Police Station."

"Yes, I did."

"We now need to re-examine those items."

"But I thought the case was done and dusted. Prema Gupta isn't appealing."

"We need to rule out a second suspect. A potential accomplice."

Clare retrieved the cardboard box of Ralph's belongings. Gloria craned her neck as the Police Officers examined the contents, wearing rubber gloves (ridiculous, as Clare had no doubt handled the items).

There was a wallet, credit cards, driving licence, a hospital staff ID pass, wrist phone, glasses, gloves and car keys. At the bottom was a set of four keys. Gloria held her breath as he turned over the key ring. It bore the image of a black and yellow bird.

"Mrs Hardcastle, we must take these items with us for forensic testing."

His words were music to Gloria's ears.

xiii) Gregory's choice

Lewisham Police Station, 13th October

He sat in the grim cell which Prema had occupied eight months before, with the words still ringing in his ears.

He buried his face in his hands, remembering the earlier police interview.

"Gregory Wilson, I'm arresting you on suspicion of the murder of Sir Ralph Hardcastle, acting in common purpose with Prema Gupta on the night of 14th February......"

"Impossible! I was on night shift at Meridian Birthing Centre."

"Who was your client?"

"Amelia Hammond."

"Anyone else?"

"No"

"According to Mrs Hammond's statement, you abandoned her for two hours without pain relief."

"But I never left the hospital that night. I took one coffee break. Her labour was normal."

"Hospital records show you failed to monitor her for three hours. Your swipe card records that you re-entered the ward at 3.00am.   And your DNA was found on Prema Gupta's house keys. How do you explain that?"

"I kept her spare keys for her. She was my neighbour."

"So how did they end up Ralph Hardcastle's pocket? Did you put them there after you and Prema killed him, to divert suspicion from yourself?"

"No, Prema must put the keys there."

"There's no trace of her DNA on them. How do you explain that?"

"I... I don't know."

"Perhaps you can explain why, on 12th February, you got those keys cut by a Dulwich locksmith?"

"No comment."

"I suggest that you and Prema had a close friendship. You knew Ralph was visiting her house that night. You had a pact to murder him. You abandoned your patient at the Meridian Birthing Centre. You live opposite Prema so you watched from your window until he arrived. You let yourself into the house and crept up behind him while Prema distracted him.

He resisted your attack from behind, so Prema hit him over the head with the picture frame."

"That's not true."

"So why is your DNA on Ralph Hardcastle's coat?"

"No comment."

Sydenham Hill, 14th October, 1.00am

As Gloria stared from her window at the distant lights of Canary Wharf and the Shard, unable to sleep. Gregory Wilson had been questioned by the Police for nearly thirty -six hours, but there was still no news.

In thirty-two hours, Prema would be led from her white room in the Greenwich Holding Centre for the last time. Twenty-four seconds later her life would end, and with it, Gloria's indomitable reputation.

She stared at Prema's newspaper photo.

"I always thought my nemesis would be a formidable hospital consultant, backed a vicious legal team," she mused "though I'm fearless against the most aggressive barristers and judges in England."

She reminded herself that she was revered and respected by her colleagues and could cut intrusive journalists to pieces which her sharp rebuttals.

"But now I face defeat from a quiet, understated young midwife with no force of personality, wit, intellect or even effective allies. I've been overcome by a woman with no fear of death, whose world weariness and unbelief in her own significance has made her more afraid of living."

Gloria began to realise that for Prema, death presented the opportunity of consequence and importance. She felt like a nobody and in dying courageously, she would become a heroine. Because, sooner or later, there would be a violent backlash against the guillotine and in years to come, the true character of Ralph Hardcastle would come to light. Besides, the first person to be executed on British soil in seventy-two years had a guaranteed place in the history books.

Gloria pondered on whether Prema's desire for significance was her one weakness? And could she exploit that?

She was clutching at straws. She had played her trump card in bringing about the arrest of Gregory Wilson. If that failed, her hand was empty. She had forgotten that providence, not skill, had led Amelia to tell her about Gregory's visit to the locksmiths. But divine intervention had never really featured in her worldview.

Vauxhall, 4.00am, 14th October

In any other circumstances, it would have been a joy to welcome Aidan and Miriam to her exclusive apartment, but the late evening dinner was a sombre affair. Even the choicest dishes from Evie's caterers did not whet their appetites.

Now, at 4.00am, as they huddled in the lounge over a fifth round of coffee, Evie was forced to plough through urgent papers in her red box which could not be neglected, however stressed she felt.

The Hologram TV chuntered in the background

"Still no news!" Groaned Aidan. "Surely the Police should charge Wilson by now? And if they think he conspired with Prema to murder her husband, they can't kill her!"

"Why hasn't Frank rung?" Sighed Evie.

Miriam fought her tears.

"She has twenty-nine hours to live."

Evie forced herself to stare at the Home Office execution procedures and updated timetable.

"They gave me the death warrant this afternoon."

"When must you sign it?" Asked Aidan.

"I have to sign, seal and despatch it at 3.00am tomorrow, if no appeal is lodged by Prema and her legal team. I have twenty-three hours left. I can't do it, Aidan."

"As I said before, Evie, none of this is your fault."

"When they arrested Wilson yesterday, I dared to hope. Now I feel powerless."

"None of us have any real power," said Aidan "but there is something we can do. Evie, I know you don't understand this, but we're not wrestling with human beings, but dark spiritual forces, as St Paul says."

"Oh, spare me the spook rubbish, please." Snapped Evie.

"Jesus Christ has defeated the powers that want to destroy Prema and glorify men like Ralph. We can pray."

"Stop getting religious on me, Aidan."

"I don't do religion. I'm talking reality. Prayers are not just nice words, but a weapon against the unseen forces."

"I never had you down as a sci-fi nerd."

"We should pray now. You needn't join in."

Evie sighed.

"OK, go ahead, but don't embarrass me!"

Evie tried to disengage herself as Aidan and Miriam paced around the room shouting their prayers ferociously. She inwardly squirmed. What had happened to this quiet dignified couple?

She tried to focus on her papers, but gradually, something stirred within her and a familiar sensation returned. Where had she felt this before?

A small spark of something ignited. Was it hope? Now they were praying for her.

"We pray you would fill Evie with peace and that she will not have to sign that death warrant tomorrow. Nothing is impossible with you."

Greenwich Holding Centre 14th October, 10.00am

    Her handwriting was beautiful, even as she frantically poured her heart onto the expensive, perfumed stationery, imparting everything remaining of herself in her final twenty-three hours on earth.

    No computerised typescript would do for the precious words to be treasured, preserved and wept over by closest family, friends and colleagues. Among the letters there were even conciliatory words for her enemies.

    Prema's sister had arrived at the Holding Centre at 6.00am and sat on the bed with her arms entwined around her, even as she was writing, desperately drinking in these final precious hours of her twin's company.

    "I'm fine, Reeta."

    Reeta sobbed uncontrollably.

    "But Prema, you could appeal, even now. You can stop this whole thing. Please, please don't leave me!"

    "You have Hardeep, you don't need me!"

    "I want my sister."

    "You should have thought of that before you abandoned me and went to Australia. You never skyped, emailed or texted me. You were so loved up, you betrayed me. It's your fault I married Ralph Hardcastle. You reduced me to that lonely, desperate state!   You've killed me!"

    "You married Ralph without Uncle Sanjay's permission. You brought shame on our family. You were selfish, reckless and unwise. You let your loneliness cloud your judgement and loyalty.   Our family is tainted by association with that wicked man."

    "That link will end when I die!"

    "How can you be so cruel? You're abandoning me, and the disgrace of your execution will be with us forever."

St Margaret's Church, Westminster, 14th October, 1.00pm

Lunch was impossible. The gloating and sympathetic glances from fellow MPs were intolerable.

Two hours before Prime Minister's question time (mercifully to be taken by Orchard himself), Evie sat discreetly behind a pillar in St Margaret's church. She was glad there were so few tourists, but she buried her face in her hands to avoid recognition. With twenty hours to the execution, there was still no news on whether Wilson would face charges. Prema steadfastly refused to appeal. The death warrant stared from her desk. There was nothing left.

She squirmed as she remembered Aidan and Miriam's loud and vocal intercessions. Yet their prayers for her to find peace had warmed something inside her.

As tomorrow loomed, an oppressive black cloud of terror was beginning to engulf her. Yet a beautiful, invisible something had pursued her for months. She had steadfastly resisted, yet still it drew her...... as though it wanted to enfold her in a loving embrace. So, what held her back? Was it pride? Maybe common sense or reason? Was she afraid of losing herself, even to that kindly voice which had become more persistent, reaching out to her through Miriam, Aidan, Frank and even the soldier with a sword in Westminster Abbey?

As her final walls of resistance crumbled and the rubble of self-sufficiency fell around her feet, she felt exposed and vulnerable, as if falling off a cliff, while knowing there was someone to catch her.

This was it. There was nowhere else to go. Every man-made effort had failed to deliver her from the political vice closing around her. With a supreme effort, she fell to her knees at the pew and whispered passionately, oblivious to anyone around her.

"Jesus, I think you must be real, so I hope you don't mind me bothering you. You seem to have been chasing me for months, so you've certainly bothered me! Don't give up easily, do you? I can't fight back anymore. I know I've done some pretty awful things. Miriam calls it sin, that's not a nice word, but I now accept she's right. I've never been spiritual and I've been so tough and ruthless.

I feel dreadful about the way I treated Lucinda. You must be appalled and I'm sorrier than you can even imagine. Miriam told me you died for me and can forgive anything. Please can you forgive me for that? For driving a good woman to her death?"

Tears began to roll down her cheeks and she fumbled in vain for a tissue.

"I want to let you into my life. You've been banging on the door long enough! And please, I desperately need your help. I can't face signing that death warrant, but what can I do if Prema won't appeal? Whatever her problem is, she can't be thinking straight. You were executed, so you understand how horrible it is. I don't want to subject her to that ordeal and I'm sure you don't either. So please give me a solution! You're supposed to be in charge of the world, so you must be able to sort it!

Thank you for listening. And if you have a lunch hour, I'm sorry for interrupting it."

As Evie stood up, a hideous weight seemed to evaporate from her shoulders and she felt strangely light. As she walked down the aisle, she almost felt carried and as she emerged into the early autumn sunlight, she knew she was a different woman from the one who had crept into the church twenty minutes earlier.

Lewisham Police Station, 14th October, 2.00pm

Gregory Wilson had been escorted to the Police interview room.

They had strangely ignored him during the morning, but the respite had given him quality time with Alan Wicklow, trusted lawyer and close friend of Bishop Burstall. He now felt more confident. The presence of his DNA on Ralph's coat and the keys may have been strong circumstantial evidence, but the delay had raised his hopes about reasonable doubts. In nineteen hours Prema, a crucial witness, would be dead and her pretty mouth would be silenced forever. He must hold his nerve.

The atmosphere in the interview room seemed more relaxed and Superintendent Vine's manner was almost cordial as he offered a fresh coffee.

Gregory gave a half-smile, anticipating release in the afternoon, invitations to TV chat shows to talk about his ordeal and lucrative offers from tabloids to recall his escape from the guillotine. Oh, how the plebs loved a human-interest story! Gregory's unabashed enjoyment of celebrity was only outweighed by his total contempt for the public who gave him so much adulation.

Chief Inspector Myles passed him a plate of chocolate biscuits and smiled almost compassionately.

"On TV, you appeared very distressed at Ralph Hardcastle's death. You seemed traumatised."

"Oh yes," replied Gregory, warming to the subject, "I was absolutely devastated. He was a fantastic colleague and mentor and so passionate about everything I stood for. It was a dreadful loss."

Superintendent Vine leaned forward.

"And what exactly was your relationship with Ralph?"

Gregory's body suddenly tensed, but he maintained his smile and composure.

"I told you, he was a respected and supportive colleague. I wouldn't be where I am without him."

"But all those tears? Perhaps your relationship went far beyond a professional level?"

"That's not true. We worked closely together, shared a common vision and occasionally socialised."

"I put it to you that had a close, intimate relationship."

Alan Wicklow interjected.

"You don't have to answer that."

"No comment."

Superintendent Vine went for the kill.

"You were lovers for many years, weren't you?"

"No! Of course not! He married Prema!" Cried Gregory, before his lawyer could stop him.

As Superintendent Vine suddenly pulled a handful of documents from a black folder, the colour drained from Gregory's face.

"If you weren't lovers, how do you explain these handwritten letters and scented cards found in Ralph Hardcastle's writing desk?"

"No comment."

"Do I need to embarrass you by reading out the contents?"

Gregory's lawyer objected.

"This is not relevant."

"It was a passionate, but very stormy relationship, wasn't it? He even punched you several times, according to the letters where you kissed and made up."

"No comment."

"Did you have a row on the night of Ralph's death? I suspect Prema must have hated him as much as you did. Did you both decide to kill him?"

"No! I keep telling you, I'm innocent."

"Or was something else going on? Did you and Ralph want to kill Prema and did the plan go horribly wrong? Did she know too much?"

"Too much about what?"

"You were a married man too, weren't you Gregory?"

The colour drained from Gregory's face as he struggled to hold down a chocolate digestive.

"You married Ralph Hardcastle three years after his wedding to Prema and long before he divorced her. It was a bigamous marriage, wasn't it? You married in Puerto Rico."

As Superintendent Vine pulled the marriage certificate from his folder, the biscuit made a hasty exit from Gregory's stomach onto the table.

Chief Inspector Myles adopted a gentler tone.

"You see, Ralph's sister in Chelmsford has been very helpful with our enquiries. She remembered that you and Ralph took a holiday together in Puerto Rico. She never knew the purpose of that trip, but we knew that Puerto Rico is a hotspot for weddings and our Interpol enquiries have traced the marriage registration records."

Gregory Wilson began to sob and gulp in sheer terror.

"I…. I didn't kill Ralph and I had no intention of killing Prema. I wasn't in the house. My DNA was on Ralph's coat because of our relationship."

"What about those house keys, which you had cut?"

"I wasn't in Prema's house that night!"

Superintendent Vine's grey eyes narrowed and bored into his.

"There are two more things."

He produced another keyring.

"These keys were found in your locker at the Meridian Birthing Centre. You had a second set of keys cut for Prema's house. And you entered her home again illegally on 14th April."

"I did not!"

"A neighbour saw someone entering the house wearing protective clothing."

Gregory rose to his feet angrily.

"The house was overrun with forensics!!"

"None of them went there on 14th April. And they always wore regulation white protective clothing, not the Meridian Birthing Centre blue scrubs worn by the intruder that day."

"I did not visit her house that day, or any other day!"

Chief Inspector Myles looked at him gently.

"Things will go better for you if you make a confession. You can't fight this anymore."

"No!"

"Then you give me no alternative."

Chief Inspector Myles pulled open a drawer from his side of the table and produced a crystal drinking glass.

"Gregory, have you seen this glass before?"

"Nooooo!"

"It was found in Prema Gupta's kitchen on the night Ralph Hardcastle was murdered. We didn't think it had any relevance as evidence, until we did a DNA test. But it wasn't Prema or Ralph's DNA. It was yours!!"

Gregory was now screaming and crying uncontrollably.

"So why did you and Ralph enter Prema's house illegally that night? I suggest there was an altercation, leading to Ralph's death. Did you kill him? Or did you and Ralph conspire to kill Prema that night, and did your plan backfire when Prema killed Ralph in self-defence?"

"No comment."

"Prema is about to die for murder. What have you to say to that?"

"No comment."

"Beheading! Nasty way to go! If she's innocent, could you live with yourself?"

"No comment."

"You have a choice. If you confess that you conspired to murder Prema, I will charge you accordingly. However, if you insist that you were not planning to kill her, I'll have no alternative but to charge you with the murder of Ralph Hardcastle."

Alan Wicklow had heard enough. "I wish to adjourn and speak with my client."

House of Commons, Home Secretary's Office, 14th October, 4.30pm

She had dreaded Prime Minister's Question Time, today of all days, seated on the front bench beside Orchard Mayhew, knowing the TV cameras were scrutinising her body language and every facial expression.

But as Orchard stood at the despatch box to take the inevitable questions about tomorrow's execution, something strange happened.

Instead of being terrified as she tried to keep her composure, an overwhelming sense of peace engulfed her. The green benches, braying members of the Opposition and smirking Cabinet rivals were less real than the warm arms which seemed to hold her. After decades of aching loneliness, she had come home. She would have endured those empty years a thousand times over to feel this overwhelming love.

And now she must snatch ten minutes to make that phone call, from her office.

"Hi Ceiba, can I speak to Miriam? Miriam is that you? Something's happened. No, there's no news about Prema or Wilson yet. It's about me. No, I haven't resigned or been sacked. And nothing's happened on the dating front. Are you sitting down? Don't faint or anything, but I think I think I've joined your team. I've become a Christian."

Evie held the receiver at a safe distance from her ear. The ecstatic screams were ear splitting.......

Lewisham Police Station, 14th October, 5.00pm

Gregory Wilson was hysterical, as Alan Wicklow vainly struggled to calm him.

"I don't want to die, I don't want to die!"

"Then confess to conspiracy to murder Prema Gupta. Because if you're charged with the murder of Ralph and found guilty, you'll face the guillotine."

At the mention of beheading, Gregory vomited on his trousers. With greasy dishevelled hair, sweat-drenched silk shirt, blotched, puffed and reddened complexion, he was reduced to a shadow of the suave TV personality adored by millions.

As he collapsed to the floor and punched the walls, there was a sharp rap on the door and he jerked his head round. Chief Inspector Myles had been expected, but even Alan's face blanched when he saw the menacing figure with him.

"I have a visitor for you both."

With grazed, bruised fists, Gregory gazed incredulously at the person he least expected or wanted to see.

"Good to see you again, Alan. Not your usual, stylish self, Gregory? Dear me!"

"Sir Chawton Holland!"

The Secretary of State for Health and his two bodyguards stepped over the pool of vomit and tried not to retch at the stench.

A dark heaviness filled the room. Chawton patted Gregory on the head in a patronising manner, then without warning sharply pulled him to his feet, viciously spraining his arm. His quiet, deep mocking voice purred.

"Well, Gregory, we are in a state!"

"Please... I don't want to die. They're threatening to charge me with the murder of Ralph."

"I've advised him to confess to conspiracy to kill Prema." Added Alan Wicklow.

"No, Alan, he will not confess the plan to murder that woman."

"Why not?"

"Are you totally brain dead? The Police, Crown Prosecution and Press will sniff around for Ralph and Gregory's motives to kill her. If they dig deeper than their pathetic love triangle, we're finished. They've overlooked us till now and we've carefully diverted them. But if our operation unravels, then Burstall, you and others will be guillotined!"

Alan tried to outstare him.

"Chawton, you'll face the chop before any of us. You're the one with more blood on your hands, you...."

Alan staggered against the wall as one of Chawton's bodyguards struck him across the face.

"Leave him, Callum! But Alan, if you dare speak to me like that again, you will feel his boots on your windpipe!"

Alan regained his balance, clutching his jaw.

"Then what's the alternative? How should Gregory plead?"

"Gregory will be tried for Ralph's murder."

"Noooo!"

"Oh, don't worry, my friend, we won't let them chop off your pretty little head!

As a senior Cabinet member, I can pull strings long before they serve your final meal. I'll make sure your Defence Counsel finds plenty of mitigating factors. I know an excellent Consultant Psychotherapist to testify that you're of unsound mind. If the jury decides it was a crime of passion you'll get a light sentence.

On the other hand, if they find you criminally insane, you'll get a stretch in Broadmoor, but I hear their accommodation is pretty comfortable, these days! The alternative is beheading for at least six of us!"

Alan nervously touched the back of his neck, as though he could already feel the blade tickling against the edge of his collar. Why had he ever got involved with these people? He put a reassuring hand on Gregory's arm.

"Gregory, there's no alternative. Let's get this over and done with. I'll call Superintendent Vine and you can tell him your decision. If he charges you with Ralph's murder today, at least Prema gets an immediate stay of execution."

Sir Chawton Holland wrenched Gregory into an excruciating armlock, twisting his matted hair until he whimpered in pain.

"No!! You'll keep your pathetic little mouth shut for now! We will demand Police give you a further twenty-four hours to make your choice. You will not be charged for either offence today.   I'll see to that!   Prema Gupta dies first! I want her silenced for good!"

xiv) Betrayal

Peckham, 14th October, 5.30pm

Miriam had to conceal her joy for now and repress an overwhelming urge to tear into the garden and scream to the world that her second greatest prayer had been answered.

Never mind the arthritic knees! Evie had passed from death to life and was now a new creation, belonging to the same kingdom as herself, Aidan and centuries of saints before them.

But her other prayer hovered perilously in the balance, as a heavenly battle raged over the life of Prema. She had fasted the whole day, rarely leaving her bedroom. Beyond exhaustion, she had barely slept all week.

As she knelt, sighed and groaned before heaven, her spirit sensed an insidious evil, even more malevolent than the wicked forces in the public domain. Deep in her heart, she recognised that beloved voice, warning her there was no breakthrough yet. It has taken her years to learn to discern God's voice and separate that inner prompting from all the other thoughts and wishful thinking cluttering her mind. There was a hidden force, as yet unknown, which must be defeated and destroyed.

A major prayer battle must be won. If not, Prema would meet her maker tomorrow. The first execution on British soil for over seventy years would be the shameful butchering of an innocent woman, but where were the intercessors? Was God raising up anyone apart from herself and Aidan? There must be others out there?

And frustratingly. Ceiba chose this very moment to interrupt her.

Miriam forced a smile. Ceiba deserved that much.

"What is it, Ceiba?"

"It's nana. She's crying again and won't stop, I've tried everything."

Norma's grieving process had been long, arduous and emotionally draining for all of them over the last seven months.

Ever since Tony's death, her moods had swung from shortness of temper, to aggressive control, silence, withdrawal or catatonic heart-wrenching weeping which resounded through the house. They had walked this journey with her. Some days they supported her willingly, but at other times they felt themselves being drawn into the tunnel of despair which sucked the life out of them.

As a trained counsellor, Miriam spent long hours with her, but her patience was wearing thin. It was one thing to counsel a client for a one hour a week. But Norma was there night and day and almost controlled the household with her behaviour.

"She's driving me nuts, Miriam!"

Now, even feisty, resilient little Ceiba was at her wits end, even though she was eighteen going on forty.

"I know you've been good with her Ceiba. I'll see to her later. I'm on my way out."

With limited life experience, Ceiba had borne the traumas of recent months with a courage and maturity that belied her years. Miriam had grown to admire this sturdy, faithful teenager and regretted her earlier prejudices against the blonde streaked hair, body piercings and nail extensions.

"Please Miriam, I need you now. I wouldn't normally make demands on you, but she's cracking me up!"

Miriam sighed. At eighteen, Ceiba had lost her beloved brother, her home and had nursed two babies and a broken grandmother while lodging in the house of two relative strangers. But she never complained or uttered a word of self-pity. She just got on with it.

"OK, Ceiba, I'm coming."

Miriam struggled to her feet, grabbing Ceiba as pain shot through her knee. When she reached the chaotic lounge, Norma's howling had woken baby Lakeside, whose angry cries added to the appalling racket.

Miriam wrapped her arms around Norma until the sobbing subsided, grabbing tissues to wipe the mucus, which oozed down her face and onto her newly-washed jumper.

"Norma, we want to support you, but you've been like this for months now. I want to get you extra help."

"I ain't going to any doctor!"

Tony's death had deepened Norma's terror of drugs and medical intervention.

"Norma, you need proper therapy."

"You're a counsellor, innit! And what use are you?"

Miriam was impervious to her torrent of expletives.

"You need someone more specialised than me, to help you move forward."

"Why did this happen, why?? You useless Bishop's wife!!"

Ceiba put a reassuring hand on Miriam's shoulder.

"Take no notice of her, Miriam."

Ceiba and Miriam sat in silence, staring at the floor as Norma's sobs and swearing subsided.

"I've heard you use a posh word, 'closure'. There is a way we close this. Then Nana can get better and live again."

"How, Ceiba?"

"You remember Tony's dying request to find his baby's mother. We must try. It would give Nana some answers. I keep thinking about it myself. Who is she? Why did she do it?"

"Its data protected, my love. Only the Government and the relevant Health Trust will know."

"What about Evie? She's in the Government! And she owes you one. She drops round here whenever she likes! It's payback time!"

"Evie's our friend and I won't take advantage of her. Do you realise what it's like being a politician? Everyone tries to use them.   She's lonely, but we love her unconditionally."

"Miriam, are you soft in the head? She's as hard as nails, stinking rich and can take care of herself. You're just the flavor of the month to her. She'll find other mates when it suits her!"

"Ceiba, that is not true! She's a human being! And she's now a Christian!"

"A Christian?! She's having you on!! I know women like her. Whether they're in Peckham or Parliament, they're all the same. Do a reality check, Miriam!"

"Ceiba, whatever you feel, Evie's the Home Secretary, not the Health Minister. She won't have access to records and I can't ask her to break the law."

"I no longer care about the law. All that matters are Tony, nana and our kids.   I've got a mate in Bill Clinton towers. He hacks computers and……."

"Ceiba, no dodgy business, please! I can't think about this now!"

Miriam's patience finally snapped.

"I'm visiting Prema tonight. Tony died in his bed. She's about to die in a vicious contraption that will butcher her, as blood spurts from her arteries! Other people are suffering, as well as you and Norma. Do you know how stressed I am right now? This is the worst thing I've ever had to do!"

And with that, she grabbed her coat, bag, car keys and slammed the door behind her.

Greenwich Holding Centre, 14th October 7.00pm

Prema prepared for her last night on earth. Soon, Miriam would join her to keep vigil. She would be there overnight, to give her the last rites and accompany her to the execution chamber.

She also expected Gloria, who would be at her side, working frantically through the night in last-ditch attempt to secure a reprieve.

Her eyes were red and her face was puffy and swollen from the gut-wrenching final farewell to her sister. Sniffing and occasionally catching her breath, she slowly regained her composure as she sat on her bed and tried to read her Bible. Until yesterday, she had felt surprisingly little fear, but now impending death was no longer a distant precipice appearing as haze on the horizon. It was clearly and swiftly sweeping into focus as a terrifying jagged cliff edge with the mist obscuring what lay beyond. She could no longer be in denial.

They would come for her at 8.58am. She had been granted special permission to make a speech (ninety seconds), but she would be dead at 9.00am. During her tedious months in prison, she had survived by meticulously planning each day and sticking to an hourly routine. Wake up, wash and dress at 7.00am, breakfast at 7.30am, Bible reading at 8.00am, arrange and pin her hair immaculately at 8.30am, apply her nail varnish at 9.00am, then at 9.30am……

But now, she must acclimatise herself to the fact that there would be no 9.30am. A violent shutter would wrench her from every known point of reference and from bodily consciousness itself.

There would be a new reality, in the arms of the one who had loved her from the womb and had never forsaken her, even when she had made disastrous choices to fill the void in her life. But the grim portal through which she must tread to reach that place of peace, moved relentlessly towards her, second by second, minute by minute, hour by hour.

Her life in Greenwich Holding Centre had been marked and measured by the hourly BBC news bulletins. Now the sound of the pips and the familiar signature tune at the top of each hour twisted a knot of fear in her stomach. fifteen, fourteen, thirteen more news bulletins to go…….

And with each hour grew her fear of sudden, excruciating pain. The prison staff all reassured her she would feel nothing. The high precision electronic blade, they reminded her, would sever her spinal cord in 1/100th of a second, making it impossible for her nervous system to register or send any message to her brain. But what if they were wrong? She was the first human to be killed with this new technology.   The ape didn't count. (Though she had the dubious honour of appearing in numerous articles about Rochdale Engineering in commercial publications).

She now dreaded the utter loneliness – the gawping faces of journalists, Government officials and Ralph's relatives. Her sister would be there, but she would not make eye contact because it would weaken her and she was determined to keep her composure.   And Gloria would be there, her mission having failed. She thought about those final seconds, tightly strapped to a trolley, her head and shoulders positioned in the dark box. Those tense last seconds, waiting…. waiting…. waiting. Miriam would walk with her tomorrow, into the cold, sterile execution chamber.   The last sound she'd hear would be Miriam's prayers. But Miriam could not accompany her through the ordeal and into the safe eternal harbour which lay the other side.

A thought was germinating in her mind. She made a superhuman effort to push it back, before it reached the stage where her brain could articulate it into words. She must not think it or even acknowledge it as a potential thought.

Battling to distract herself, she switched on the hologram TV and tried to lose herself in a nature documentary. As the camera zoomed in on exotic birds in the Australian outback, she felt a sense of wonder as those beautiful, perfectly created, intricate creatures soared in the sky, fearless and free. The cloudless skies above the rich 3D greenery of the jungle lifted her spirit and gave her a longing to fly herself, away from the white walls around her, out of Greenwich, beyond London to wherever….?

She stood up, reached out and tried to stand in that virtual sky, letting her fingertips touch the sun…. her heart was soaring, but she realised with alarm that the flame in her spirit was now catching her emotions, and that her emotions were rising from her stomach to her throat. She pulled herself back to the bed.

"I mustn't…… I must stop this!"

The door opened and she wheeled round as an ashen faced Miriam swept her up in a maternal embrace.

"Oh, how are you my love?"

"I don't want to die! I don't want to die!! Help me. Help me!!!"

Convulsive sobs shook her body.

The battle of her will had been lost.

Vauxhall, 14th October, 7.30pm

The death warrant stared at her, splattered with the dark, syrupy coffee, which Evie had been chain-drinking all day.

Her phone had stayed eerily silent all evening.

The BBC, ITV and Sky news coverage was totally unyielding. They were having the biggest media frenzy since England had reached the World Cup Final in 2032. Who cared if Prema Gupta lived or died, as long as they won the ratings war? While delivering little comment on the arrest of Gregory Wilson, the channels spewed out relentless coverage and footage of the impending execution. Surely, they were trying to torment her?

Every hour they repeated the same recorded items - an eccentric, wild-haired historian re-told the stories of famous executions in the 1950's and 60's: Timothy Evans (who had been innocent), Derek Bentley (who had been a teenager) and Ruth Ellis (who had been the last woman to be hanged in Britain). Of course, many journalists had highlighted the parallels. Ruth Ellis had murdered her lover and Prema had been found guilty of killing her husband.

Every channel produced a rolling parade of pundits including doctors, scientists and engineers to explain how the guillotine worked, what happened to the human body when decapitated and when the heart, lungs and brain would cease to function. They speculated on how much pain the victim would suffer. The same gruesome computer graphics and diagrams were shown hour by hour.

They wheeled out an assortment of religious leaders to debate the morality of capital punishment and express their views on how Prema should prepare for death.

Food and fashion pundits speculated on her final meal, what she would wear and how her hair would be styled for its final outing.

Even more infuriatingly, a self-important Consultant Psychotherapist, Fantasy Rimmer, had given an interview on how Prema would be feeling at this moment, how she might be coming to terms with death and what her mental condition would be. Evie reflected on how this stupid waffle would fill Sunday newspaper reviews for weeks, months and years to come.

And there was the live coverage outside the Greenwich Holding Centre. It was a warm evening, but the reporter wore a heavy overcoat and hat, for effect and gravitas no doubt. Behind him were hordes of demonstrators and a line of Policemen controlled the crowd. Frank had his work cut out tonight. An angry mob screamed:

"Behead the murderess!!"

But several abolitionists stood with candles and one of them held a placard with the words:

"Evie Atherton MURDERESS!"

Evie stared back at the death warrant. It would not go away. Her isolation intensified as the night closed in. No-one in the world could help her now.

She curled up on the sofa, desperately seeking solace against her favourite cushion, as she tried to tune out the relentless ticking of the clock. Suddenly, from nowhere, a thought dropped into her mind. *"You are not alone."* Had she imagined it? Another thought formed in her head. *"I will never leave you nor forsake you."*

And then she realised. Her life had changed in St Margaret's Church earlier in the day. She was no longer facing this alone.

She rose from the sofa and dropped to her knees.

"Lord? Hello, it's me again. Sorry to bother you. I know your hands are full today, with the Middle East crisis, the US Presidential candidate who's a trans-species mongoose and that Scottish Bishop who wants to baptise his guinea pig. But I desperately need your help. I really don't want to sign Prema Gupta's death warrant. Please can you stop this? "

She remained silent for a moment, but felt a slight unease in her spirit. What was wrong?

"Please Lord, what's the problem?"

And then she heard the small, still voice in her heart.

"Why do you want to stop this, Evie?"

"Because everyone will hate me?"

"So, you only want to save yourself? Because you're scared about what people think of you?"

Evie was feeling a new sensation. Was this shame? Conviction?

"Please Lord, I'm sorry. I'm being selfish. But what about my political career?"

Then it dawned on her. She had handed over the steering wheel of her life after thirty-five years of being in control. What if He had other plans and didn't want her to be a politician? Could she still trust God, even if her cherished ambitions collapsed around her? How would she endure the humiliation of ridicule from the testosterone filled incumbents of the House of Commons who longed for her downfall? Could she still be significant?

Fears and insecurities jostled and crowded in her head. Life without Roxanne fashion, status, power, influence, or her face in the daily papers?

"OK God, this is difficult, but I've made a choice now. It's not about me. I accept the consequences, whatever happens. It all goes with the territory, I guess. Look, this is way out of my comfort zone, but I have to accept you know best."

Her sense of peace returned.

"And by the way, Lord, Prema seems a decent woman. Bit of a waif, but I actually think she's braver than me. I'd be doing my nut in her situation. Sorry I haven't taken much interest in her. I just regarded her as a political football. I apologise for that. But anyway, she's a human being and the poor lass had a vile husband. I don't think she deserves any of this."

Cardiff, 14th October, 8.00pm

The makeup artist made finishing touches. Myfanwy Roberts, First Minister for Wales, demanded perfection.

"Go easy on the blusher. Darker eyeliner, please, I need gravitas."

In the National Assembly Debating Chamber, cameramen shuffled into position. Under the stifling heat of studio lighting, Welsh National Assembly members had gathered. Cyclists for Justice supporters, students and members of public squeezed into the tightly packed gallery. Massive crowds gathered along the Cardiff Waterfront.

Myfanwy emerged on the platform wearing a bright red suit, to tumultuous applause and cheers, as she gave a triumphant smile and signalled for calm. Her statement was expected and had briefly diverted news coverage from the Greenwich Holding Centre.

"At 9.00am tomorrow morning, Prema Gupta is sentenced to die by guillotine. If the execution proceeds, this barbaric act will shame our nation throughout the world. The British nation, once known for its compassion and humanity will plummet into a new dark age, even as this woman's head falls into the basket.

The Criminal Justice Reform Act to reintroduce the death penalty became law in January this year. We made it clear to the Government that if anyone is guillotined, The National Assembly for Wales will demand a Welsh Independence Referendum so that our people can decide whether they want to be part of a United Kingdom which no longer holds humanitarian values.

We have continued to hope the Government will reconsider its position, while making preparation for a referendum by March 2037. If Wales chooses independence, we will negotiate the terms of our secession for two years, enabling us to be a fully independent nation by March 2039.

We will take this vote, whether or not the Government agrees to it.

Prime Minister Orchard Mayhew and Home Secretary Evie Atherton stand at a crossroads tonight. Will they be responsible for losing Wales?"

Her final sentence was drowned by a huge roar of approval and thunderous applause, not only from the chamber, but also from the crowds along the waterfront. Then applause gave way to one of the loudest spontaneous renditions of the Welsh National Anthem in its history.

Lewisham Police Station, 14th October, 10.30pm

A trail of blood oozed onto the crumpled bedding, as a dishevelled Gregory Wilson curled in foetal position, with soiled, clenched fists, catching his breath between sobs.

A further beating from Sir Chawton Holland and one of his henchmen an hour ago had dislodged a front tooth, split his lip and bruised his cheeks so that the slick, groomed, camera-ready, smiling features, once so popular on daytime TV, were now barely recognisable.

Throughout the evening, the Police had almost ignored, or at least seemed to have quietly acquiesced with the comings and goings of Holland and his vicious cohorts.

Gregory faced the terrifying realisation that the power of the Secretary of State for Health extended far beyond his department, the Health Trusts, major pharmaceutical companies or even the corrupt machinations in which he himself had become entangled. So, senior police officers bowed and scraped to him? He quietly wondered what Home Secretary Evie Atherton would think about that. But he quickly dismissed the thought. Let that pathetic, fat, tarty woman deal with her own difficulties. He faced enough horrors of his own.

He was a dead man now, whatever choice he made. If he confessed to the murder of Sir Ralph Hardcastle in common purpose with Prema Gupta, then he would become the first man to be executed on British soil since 1964. If he admitted to conspiracy to murder Prema Gupta, he would get off with a prison sentence, maybe less than 10 years if the Judge was lenient and he would then get remission for good conduct.

For most people, it would be a no-brainer. In his mid-forties, he would still have time to begin his life afresh. But this was different. Holland had threatened him that if he went to jail, he would be dead within six months and suffer a far more terrifying and painful death than the swift dispatch of the high-speed precision blade.

And who knows what might be exposed if he was tried for conspiracy to murder Prema? The horror of public vilification was worse death itself.

So for him, then, death either way.

But for Prema? His choice would be the difference between her death tomorrow, a conventional lifespan, or may a few months of extra life while he faced trial.

Ah, Prema! That weak, pathetic, needy little waif who was so naively ignorant of the reality around her. She had been an unwanted gooseberry and a total encumbrance to Ralph and himself, but an inconvenient necessity. So, he had tiptoed around her, appeased her, lived a lie and kept her compliant.

Gregory had played the role of sympathetic work colleague with consummate skill.

On the Labour Ward, Prema was an outstanding professional. She was skilled, calm, measured, trusted and totally in control of her emotions. She was a reassuring rock, even when handling the most hair-raising complications which childbirth could throw at her patients, often with little warning and limited back up. He was quietly jealous, because she was a better midwife than him.

But in her lunch breaks Prema's guard had dropped, as she had cried on his shoulder before drying her eyes, rearranging her hair and returning to her patients.

"Ralph just ignores me. Our physical relationship is non-existent. Sometimes I don't see him for a whole week. And when I see him, he's angry and belligerent."

Gregory had an endless store of platitudes. He reminded her that Ralph's absence was due to long shifts and work commitments. The poor man was stressed and exhausted. She must learn to support him. And yes, of course Ralph loved her.

But in reality, as Ralph spent more time with Gregory, politicians, members of the Royal Family and less reputable individuals who would have destroyed his public reputation, his repertoire of excuses had run embarrassingly low. Prema's intrusive questions had triggered outbursts of ferocious anger and violence, spiralling their relationship down into a cesspool of emotional and physical abuse.

Nine months ago, Ralph had wanted her dead. She was a dangerous liability. Once divorced and independent from Ralph, she owed him nothing. It was a relief that she was no longer a clinging, suffocating, unwitting encumbrance, but she now posed a far more serious threat.

Prema had always been in the way and now she stood between the prospect of a quick death or a slow, lingering agony. At a second trial Prema might talk, especially from the safe seclusion of the Greenwich Holding Centre. It was a cruel irony that the deadly fortress was a secure hideaway. But had any threats penetrated those grim, white walls? So far, she had remained silent.

As his blood congealed on the pillow and coagulated around his lip, shock, fear and nausea began to give way to extreme fatigue. He tried to focus on the cracked, green, peeling walls, desperately struggling to process the choices before him. But sleep closed in on him, not as a welcoming angel bringing respite, but as a deathly soporific demon assigned to subdue his mind and will to a temporary oblivion, for the tense hours when Prema's future hovered between earth and eternity.

Greenwich Holding Centre, 15th October, 12.30am

Gloria and Miriam were still with her.

Miriam had adamantly refused to leave Prema alone in her cell. Two prison warders had arrived at 11.00pm to escort her and Gloria out. They had been courteous enough.

"We must follow the new Home Office execution procedure manual to the letter. Section 11a says the condemned person must spend their final night in seclusion, accompanied by two warders and monitored hourly by a nurse."

Miriam had exploded with rage.

"You're adding insult to injury. What was Evie Atherton thinking of when she had signed off this drivel? I don't care what the Home Office says. You're not turfing me out and I refuse to go anywhere!"

Prema had never realised that this gentle, Godly woman could be so feisty.

"Prema will not spend her final hours without her friends. Are you women totally inhuman? Stuff your stupid protocols, and this whole vile process! Over my dead body! I don't care what you do to me. I've a good mind to tell the press how you're treating her. Anyway, she'll be dead in ten hours and Gloria and I will be out of your hair. So, what have you to lose?"

"And I refused to abandon my client," snapped Gloria "she's entitled to full representation to the end!"

The two young warders were extremely nervous despite their professional veneer. Nothing like this had happened in their lifetime and they were beginning to realise their rigorous training had not prepared them for the reality of killing a 'client'. They yielded very quickly, reluctant to find their names in the papers for cruelty to a dying woman.

Gloria had refused to sleep for twenty-four hours and would stay awake the whole night.   As the BBC News had sounded the midnight hour, her final, threadbare comfort blanket had been ripped away. The day before was 'not quite yet' and a fragile cushion of time before 15th October reared its terrifying head. But this was execution day. The day she either miraculously saved or irrevocably lost her client.

Gloria's hand shook as she made endless frantic phone calls, to the office of the Lord Chief Justice, the Home Office and her Press Officer who received updates before they were broadcast on the news.

As social media traffic, TV channels' coverage and street protests accelerated into a frenzy, it seemed that London refused to sleep on this historic night. But no waking soul offered a crumb of hope for Prema Gupta.

The Observian Newspaper, Kings Cross, 15th October, 2.00am

An eighteen-hour day was nothing new for Erica Rayleigh. But tonight was different.

The editorial floors were a hive of activity and even more frantic than the mayhem of a General Election. The proprietors salivated at the prospect of an explosion of catatonic liberal outrage. The execution of Prema Gupta would send their readership through the roof. Of course, officially, the newspaper was vehemently opposed to the death penalty. But in reality, the rolling of Prema's head would launch the most powerful editorial that their heavyweights had ever unleashed. This was their moment.

Erica surveyed the scene from the glass panelled office built especially for her. She had insisted on this luxury, not from delusions of grandeur, but from a desperate yearning for the solitude and privacy she rarely found at home. She would cheerfully have slept in that office. Indeed, she often worked later than necessary, just to avoid the company Chawton Holland.

And tonight, she must be alone. She flashed a smile of comradeship to every colleague scurrying past her window. But if her actions succeeded, she would dash the hopes of every hungry journalist sharpening their claws on the case of Prema Gupta.

She turned to her computer screen and clicked on the scanned images she had stealthily uploaded at home. It had been a slow, painstaking and frightening process, snatching the hours when Chawton was least likely to come home. But she had finally scanned an electronic copy of the precious parcel of documents which had been anonymously posted to her. Chawton had locked them in a cabinet in his study. Did that wretched man really think a woman was incapable of unscrewing and reassembling a piece of flat pack furniture?

She would not go home tonight, but would catch the Gatwick Express for a 6.00am flight to Cyprus, to meet her brother. But she would not feel safe until he had smuggled her across the sea and over the border of Israel with a new identity. Mercifully his contacts could transport her via routes avoiding passport control and biometric data inspections.

She would resign as Editor of The Observian citing ill-health and exhaustion as the reason. By the time they discovered the truth she would be untraceable. The thought of leaving England forever terrified her, but there was no alternative. Holland (or one of his henchmen) would kill her if she remained in the country.

She clicked her email account and hesitated. If she acted now, would she remain safe until 3.00am?

She waited another thirty minutes. It was 2.30am.
She stared around the office and bit her lip. No tears!
She almost loved this place. The journalists could be
utterly infuriating and at times almost impossible to
manage. They were intense, irascible and high-
maintenance, yet they inspired and energised her. Kings
Cross was drab and grimy but its dreariness now almost
seemed homely. She would even miss the cold, damp and
pollution of North London. *"Erica, pull yourself together!"*

She took a final look around the Editorial floor, then
turned back to her computer, gritted her teeth and
composed the email to the Prime Minister, copied to his
Communications Office. Orchard Mayhew was about to
learn that The Observian had a story which could destroy
his Government. She would give him the opportunity to
'come clean', otherwise they would publish.

Of course, Orchard had no idea that in twenty
minutes, she would leave London forever and would never
read his response. But it would take him several days to
realise she had disappeared and by then he would have
acted on the assumption that The Observian was about to
wreak total havoc. Indeed, her successor might well carry
out her threat, but she would be past caring.

She clicked the 'send' button, frantically cleared her
desk and gathered her coat. She would collect her
suitcase at the left luggage office at Kings Cross Station,
because bringing it to the office would have aroused
suspicion. She left her family photographs and personal
possessions behind, because for now, everyone must think
she was coming back.

She gave her Deputy Editor a quick ten-minute
briefing and left him in charge until the morning. She
shouted "good night" to her colleagues as she scuttled
through the open-plan office to the lifts, mentally
photographing each face to hold as a treasured memory of
this season of her life.

She stepped into the damp, freezing night air and walked briskly towards the station. A group of nightclubbers staggered past her. She slipped on a pool of drunken vomit as she glanced nervously over her shoulder. She steadied herself against a shop window as the damp fog caught the back of her throat.

She drew deep breaths and urged herself forward. She must hold her nerve for the next three hours. This was the beginning of her escape from the control, bullying, undermining and physical abuse she had endured for many months. And whatever might happen to her tonight, a young woman in Greenwich must be in an even worse state of terror. If only she could save Prema Gupta, whatever her own fate might be.

Vauxhall, 15th October, 3.30am

Evie had fallen into a fitful sleep, sprawled over scattered sofa cushions. The TV mercilessly chuntered coverage from the Greenwich Holding Centre.

The death warrant lay on the table, unsigned.

As the phone rang and disrupted her chaotic dreams, Evie pulled herself up and glanced at the clock. Five hours to go.

"Prime Minister?"

"Evie, have you signed the death warrant yet? Greenwich Holding Centre have been chasing all night for it. What are you playing at? They're going mad. They even had the nerve to contact my office. It's your responsibility and they should be pestering your department!"

"Sorry, no, I haven't yet. I er… I was doing a final check of the paperwork"

"Just do it now!"

"What about Gregory Wilson?"

"Nothing's happening there. This execution goes ahead."

"But what if…."

"Look, just get on with it. Hang on, I've got to go. I have an urgent phone call from my Press Office. What do they want this time of the morning? Bye!"

Evie sighed and slumped on the sofa. Supposing she didn't sign the warrant and just sat on it until 9.00am tomorrow. What could they do?

Gatwick Airport, 15th October, 4.00am

The one-hour journey from Kings Cross to Gatwick was an excruciating eternity.

Once safely beyond East Croydon, Erica had relaxed slightly. But every stop through central London posed a new danger, if Chawton Holland was alerted to her actions and contacted one of his cohorts.

Her adrenaline levels were still stabilising after a false alarm at Blackfriars when a police officer had joined the train and stared at her incessantly. He alighted at London Bridge, but after that, every carriage occupant was a potential assassin.

Erica rushed off the train at Gatwick Station. A few passengers stood on the platform, mainly returning holidaymakers heading south. As she approached the escalator to the South Terminal, she glanced over her shoulder.

A young man with a rucksack, no older than twenty-five, from among the waiting passengers, was now following her along the platform. She could feel her bowels turning to liquid. She scuttled up the escalator, through the ticket barrier and across the South Terminal concourse. He was still behind her.

She raced across to Passport Control and Security and stood in the slow-moving queue. He joined the queue three places behind her. No-one could harm her here, surely? Not in view of security staff? And surely any weapon would be detected and removed? But even so, she would have an hour's wait in the departure lounge.

The queue moved forward faster and she was soon safely beyond the metal detectors and grim looking woman who frisked her.

She hastily zigzagged through the waiting passengers. Bruising her ankle painfully against a suitcase, she hobbled to a coffee shop which was full of family groups and couples. The young man with the rucksack had disappeared. She grabbed a cappuccino and pastry. A very frail elderly lady asked to join her table and Erica gave her a welcoming smile.

She raced to the toilet as the pain in her bowels intensified, then returned to the table to sip her coffee. Once she boarded the plane, she would be almost safe. She suddenly felt overwhelmingly tired. Maybe it was the sheer sense of relief? But why was she so exhausted? She could barely keep her eyes open….

Greenwich Holding Centre, 15th October, 6.00am

Prema had not slept. Gloria dozed in the armchair, overcome with exhaustion, while Miriam stirred on the bed beside her.

When there was a sharp knock on the door, everyone was suddenly alert. Gloria rose sharply to her feet and Prema and Miriam sat up, their hearts pounding.

A portly woman marched into the room escorted by two male prison warders. She wore a black suit and black court shoes, and her grey hair was swept into a French pleat. Her face was lined and heavily powdered, with lips pursed in a grim expression. She extended her hand to Gloria.

"Good morning. Margaret Wilton, the Governor of Greenwich Holding Centre."

"It's not time yet, is it? My client was told 9.00am!"

"That's correct. Prema Gupta?"

Prema rose to her feet, fighting to compose herself.

"Ms Gupta, it is my painful duty to inform you that your death warrant has now been signed. There is no further avenue of appeal and you must therefore prepare yourself to face execution at 9.00am this morning.

The Prison doctor will examine you at 6.30am to confirm that you are physically fit to be guillotined and to fit a monitoring device to measure your heart-rate, blood-gas levels, oxygenation and other biometric data during the process. Your spiritual adviser and lawyer can remain with you and accompany you to the execution chamber. Do you have any questions?"

"Yes, I do. Can you confirm I will be allowed to make a ninety-second speech?"

"That is correct."

"Will I be handcuffed or blindfolded?"

"You will be handcuffed when the execution party arrives to escort you to the guillotine. You will be blindfolded before being strapped onto the trolley."

"I don't want to be blindfolded, I can face this. And please don't handcuff me. I will cooperate in every way and I want to enter that room with dignity. I won't give you any trouble and anyway, I'm sure your guards are strong enough to restrain me."

"I make no promise, but I'll see what can be done."

"Will the executioner escort me to the chamber? I haven't met him yet."

"Your executioner is not present in this building."

"You mean, he's late?"

"He's not coming here at all. He will activate the guillotine remotely."

"Guillotine me remotely? But how?"

"The executioner has access to our intranet system and has been issued with the operating codes which are directly transmitted to the electronic system controlling the guillotine."

"But where will he be?"

"In his own home."

Vauxhall, 15th October, 6.30am

The door buzzer rang, jangling discordantly into the delirious turmoil engulfing Evie's head as she slept fitfully on the sofa. She woke with a start and grabbed the entry phone with a thudding heart. Now what? An overwhelming sense of relief flooded her at the sound of a familiar voice.

"Aidan? Aidan!! Do come up."

Aidan emerged from the lift with a piping-hot takeaway breakfast and fresh coffee.

"There's nothing I can do for Miriam at the moment, so I thought I'd better help you!"

"Aidan, you're a saint."

"Oh, I'm just a Bishop thrown on the rubbish heap! But I hear you've now joined the company of saints!"

"I'm a beginner. Wearing 'L' plates. I'm not as holy as you, yet!"

"But you've been washed clean, by the blood of the Lamb and you're wearing new robes, so you're every bit as holy as me."

"Any news from Miriam?"

"She's been at Greenwich Holding Centre all night. I have the strongest, bravest, kindest wife in the world. She's often sat with dying people, but never in these circumstances."

Evie dived into the hash browns and scrambled egg, placing the greasy bag on the coffee table.

"Evie, what's that document you've just stained?"

"It's the death warrant and frankly, I don't care!"

"Evie, are you sure about this?"

"I made a life changing decision yesterday. I used to get the odd murmuring of conscience in the old days, but now it sounds like a megaphone in my head. I don't think God will be happy with me if I sign that document. Do you agree, Aidan?"

"I think so. But it's not for me to tell you what to do. I don't want to influence you, because it's not my career which is at stake."

"Dear old Aidan, trying to be wise and impartial! You're still so very Anglican, aren't you! It's true, I'm scared. I've lived, eaten and breathed politics for more than 10 years. Being a constituency MP is the most fulfilling thing I've ever done. I thrive on the cut and thrust of being in the cabinet (even if I detest every chauvinist in it,) and ….and…"

Her voice trembled.

"What Evie?"

"I wanted to be Prime Minister. And don't you dare breath a word of that to anyone! Everyone round that Cabinet table is hungry for it. And anyone who denies it is a liar!"

"My lips are sealed. And I'd be proud to see you at Number 10."

"But I can't sign that warrant with a clear conscience and I refuse to pursue my career with blood on my hands."

"I know. But Evie, make sure you really have counted the cost before you make a stand. I was once in your shoes. I told God I was willing to sacrifice my post as Bishop, rather than compromise with the ungodly standards of this nation.

I stood firm, but then I had to face the consequences. I was suddenly out in the cold, banished from the House of Lords, out of Angelica House and excluded from my charmed circle of friends, no longer one of the 'great and good.' I had to read vitriolic articles about myself in the press. It's been a sore and lonely road. Yes, you must do the right thing, but ask God to strengthen you for the path ahead."

"My nightmares torment me with the cold reality. Orchard will sack me. I'll face life in the wilderness as a backbencher and then deselection at the next General Election. Oh, I could go back to Roxanne and the fashion industry, but I'm an ageing, overweight middle-aged spinster, so that wouldn't last forever."

"But don't forget, God has a hope and a future for you. His plans are better than anything we could hope for, even if it means a total change of direction."

"Well at least for now, things have gone quiet. Since 4.00am, no-one has chased me for the death warrant. Orchard gave me an ear bashing during the night, but after that nothing."

"Let's put the on the TV on see what's happening."

The BBC news showed footage of utter chaos around the Greenwich Holding Centre and all the roads and public transport leading there. Police resources were stretched to control the crowds. St John's Ambulance treated people who were injured, or had fainted in the crush. It was total mayhem.

Then the coverage went back to the studio, with a newsflash.

"We have just been informed that the death warrant for Prema Gupta has been signed by the Home Secretary and has now arrived at Greenwich Holding Centre."

Evie gave a piercing scream and gripped Aidan's arm, digging her fingers into his flesh and making him yelp in pain.

"WHAT???!!! Are they crazy? I haven't signed anything. The warrant is here!"

"Calm down. There must be some terrible mistake!"

"Or more skulduggery! They're lying. They're lying!!"

Evie gave vent to a torrent of expletives. Aidan winced, but said nothing. She was only a very new believer, after all!

"Someone has fixed this! Orchard Mayhew and Chawton Holland! I always knew those creeps would do anything to destroy me."

"But your signature?"

"Yes, someone must have forged it. They've no doubt produced a second original. With the seal of the Lord Chief Justice. So, he must be in this! I'M GOING TO BE THE MOST HATED WOMAN IN THE COUNTRY!!!!"

As Evie began to make angry, frantic calls, Aidan sighed, checked his own wrist phone and tried to contact Miriam.

Miriam decided she was a useless hairdresser.

Either that, or utterly overwhelmed by the circumstances in which she was learning to plait and weave the dark locks which had remained beautiful and lustrous, even after months of incarceration. Her hands shook as she held the sparkling hairpins and either dropped or carelessly misplaced them, so that locks of Prema's hair cascaded untidily back to her shoulders.

Prema smiled.

"Don't worry Miriam, you're doing your best. Just plait a few strands and coil them round my head."

Finally, Gloria sighed and came to the mirror. Hairdressing was not her talent either, but this was the last thing she would do for her client. She helped Miriam to braid the glossy tresses of hair, twisting white ribbon in the plaits and securing them with pins and combs. She felt uneasy as her hand caught the warmth of Prema's neck.

That warmth reminded her that in two hours' time, the arteries which pumped into her pulsating neck would expel a gushing torrent of blood and the slender body would become cold and lifeless. Bile began to rise in her stomach and she forced it back.

The professional horror of losing a client had been totally eclipsed by her revulsion at the butchery of this sweet but unorthodox stubborn young woman, who had exasperated her, but finally won her grudging respect.

As Miriam stared at Prema's reflection, she saw that her face was composed and peaceful. She could almost have been a bride preparing for her wedding day, if Miriam had not sensed that the composure was driven by willpower.

Prema was spiritually prepared, but there was no disguising the inner battle to brace her flesh for the chasm she must cross this morning and to fiercely cling to her belief in what lay the other side.

Miriam struggled to control her emotions as Prema drew deep breaths, involuntarily clenched her fist and continued to remain calm. Miriam bit her lip, but tears welled up and her face reddened and she sniffled as she wiped them away. But she was losing the battle as she tried to stifle the sobs and began to catch her breath.

"Miriam, please don't cry."

But Miriam wept uncontrollably.

Vauxhall, 15ᵗʰ October, 6.45 am

Evie was still shaking with fury. In a torrent of rage, she had called the Prime Minister's office, the Home Office, the Lord Chief Justice and Greenwich Holding Centre - only to vent her indignation on private secretaries and administrative staff. Everyone who mattered stonewalled her and it had been impossible to get hold of anyone who truly merited her wrath.

Adrian endeavoured to calm her.

"They're all in it. The whole despicable crew!"

Aidan flinched once again at the language which followed.

"Evie, when you joined God's team yesterday, you declared an allegiance. You immediately became a target for the evil one. But remember this. The Bible says: 'Many are the troubles of the righteous, but the Lord delivereth him out of them all'. Whatever these 'expletive' politicians may do to you, you must believe that God is bigger. Put not your trust in princes!"

"OK, Mr Perfect, so you've never had a pity party? What state were you in, when they dumped you as a Bishop? Smiling serenely, were you?"

"Of course not. But I have a new life now.   Just think, I'm supporting you this morning, while Miriam looks after Prema. That would never have happened if our lives hadn't changed so radically. I'll make you another coffee and let's watch the news again."

"Oh, give me a break," she growled "I've seen enough coverage! I don't want any more newsflashes or nasty surprises."

Aidan calmly ignored her and switched on the television.

They were now using tear gas and water cannons to control the stampeding demonstrators outside Greenwich holding centre. One person had been killed and several taken to hospital.

The braying mob who hated Prema had also turned violent and had broken through the Police cordon, to attack the demonstrators.

Suddenly the coverage reverted to the studio for a further newsflash. Evie's blood ran cold.

"We have just received confirmation from Downing Street that Sir Chawton Holland, the Secretary of State for Health resigned from office, in the early hours of this morning. We await further information."

Evie felt the blood rush to her face.

"Holland resigned?! But why now?"

"I don't know, Evie. But he's gone."

"But in my weakest hour? I've never been more vulnerable. And his position was never stronger. All he had to do was sit and wait for the vultures to eat me alive. What's he playing at"

"As I told you Evie, God is bigger!"

Evie slumped into the sofa, struggling to take everything in. There was no greater ecstasy, after having her worst fears realised, than suddenly discovering that her secret wish had been fulfilled.

Lewisham Police Station, 15ᵗʰ October, 7.00am

Chief Inspector Myles had not slept for 36 hours. But events from 3.30am had given him a new lease of energy. He was not a man to be easily intimidated, but for most of the night he had struggled to maintain some semblance of authority in the presence of Holland and his henchmen, with their power to either have him removed from office or beaten to a pulp.

But how things had changed! In the early hours, Holland had been summoned to the Prime Minister's office and his thugs had left with him. He had not seemed unduly perturbed by unearthly hour of the call. He had even seemed smug, attributing it to his own importance and indispensability. He had left the Police Station with a series of vicious threats.

But now Myles had seen the news on the small hologram TV in his office. Chawton Holland had resigned! Whatever had passed between him and the Prime Minister had resulted in his removal from office. So now he was back in control of his own ship.

And after a brief conversation with Superintendent Vine, the way forward was clear….

In a semi-consciousness state, Gregory Wilson was tormented by a nightmare of strangulation and suffocation, surrounded by interrogators. Chawton Holland, the police and even his friend Bishop Burstall. But they spoke in riddles he could not decipher and his airways tightened the more his memory failed him…

A sharp rap on the cell door woke him. He realised the congealed blood in his nasal passages had constricted his breathing. He lifted his head from the soiled pillow as Chief Inspector Myles, Superintendent Vine and his lawyer, Alan Wicklow entered the room. Still semi-comatose, he was not yet lucid enough to register the sombre expression on their faces. He tried to force a smile.

"Gregory Wilson, I am charging you with the murder of Ralph Hardcastle, in common purpose with Prema Gupta. You do not have to say anything, but …"

The rest of his words were drowned by a piercing scream from Gregory.

xv) Knife edge

Home Office, Marsham Street, 15th October, 7.30am

The city stirred in the damp mist and drizzle, as the first early-morning commuters shuffled along Horseferry Road and Victoria Embankment. A chauffeur-driven car arrived at the Home Office. Wrapped protectively in a heavy grey coat, but wearing minimal makeup or jewellery, a flint-faced Evie emerged clutching a black briefcase. Mercifully there was only a small cluster of journalists. Most of the paparazzi anticipated richer pickings in Greenwich.

Aidan had followed on foot, ensuring that he did not draw attention to his association with Evie, particularly as his wife ministered to Prema in her final moments.

With mixed emotions, Evie battled to remain inscrutable. Her fury at the signing of the death warrant was tempered by a massive sense of triumph at Chawton Holland's resignation. Amidst the horror, there was something to play for. With her fist clenched and her eyes boring into the middle distance, Evie strode towards the front entrance, blanking the photographers.

Then suddenly, she paused and stopped. All her political life, she had firmly stonewalled reporters, except when she chose to make a sharp, humorous quip, or on the very rare occasions when the press could be of use to her. Now was such a time.

She slowly walked towards the poised microphones.

"Home Secretary! Home Secretary! How did you feel when you signed that death warrant this morning? How does it feel to be taking the life of another human being?"

She drew a deep breath and looked directly at the cameras.

"Good morning. I would like to make it clear that have not signed Prema Gupta's death warrant today. There has been a serious miscommunication and I arrived at the Home Office this morning to rectify the situation and instigate a full enquiry, to determine how this grave error has arisen."

"But will you be signing her death warrant this morning?"

"There has been a serious breach in Home Office procedure. Until that matter has been resolved and addressed, no death warrant will be signed. An execution cannot be lawful unless the correct process has been followed.

I would like to take this opportunity to apologise to the families of Prema Gupta and Ralph Hardcastle, for the anguish this must be causing them, at a very distressing time."

"So, if you didn't sign the death warrant, who did?"

"I will be making further enquiries and we will make a statement and publish a press release in due course. Thank you."

She stormed into the building, glaring at the security staff and daring them to check her ID.

"Give me a list of every person who has entered the building since 6.00pm last night." She snapped.

She was determined to eliminate everyone at the Home Office. Surely the culprit was from Downing Street? A security woman frantically hammered at the keys of her computer, and brought to the screen a list of everyone who had swiped their card into the building overnight.

"I've transferred the records to your computer, ma'am."

Evie forced a half-smile, realising she had abandoned her Northern charm this morning. She peered at the name badge. "Thank you being so prompt…… Sapling".

Too impatient to await the lift, she breathlessly tackled five flights of stairs. Bursting into her office, she activated her IT system. On the voice recognition screen, she frantically dictated messages and gave them her electronic Home Office seal and code number. The first was to the Governor of Greenwich Holding Centre.

"I hereby give immediate notice to suspend the execution of Prema Gupta. The stay of execution takes effect at 7.25am. Please stop all preparatory procedures and await further instruction. The Death Warrant you received is a suspected forgery and must be treated as null and void."

She printed three hard copies of the message, sealed it and summoned three Home Office bike couriers, ordering them to take the messages to Prime Minister Orchard Mayhew, the Lord Chief Justice and The Governor of Greenwich Holding Centre.

Then she frantically dictated a press release, to inform the world's media of the stay of execution and the forged warrant signature. She refused to trust her Communications staff. At the click of a button, the press release winged its way to every major news agency in the country.

She clicked onto the webpage of Thomson Reuters to check their coverage of the execution. A newsflash appeared on the homepage. A wild hope rose within her. Was this about her statement to the waiting journalists, fifteen minutes ago?

"Midwife Gregory Wilson has been charged with the murder of Ralph Hardcastle, acting in common purpose with Prema Gupta. Wilson faces the guillotine if convicted. Will Prema Gupta be given a stay of execution to be called as a witness?"

Her heart thudded. Where was her statement to those journalists? Surely, they had told their news agencies immediately? Why did Reuters say nothing about her announcement of a stay of execution, the forged signature or the breach of Home Office procedure?

So, the whole world still believed that she had signed the death warrant and that only Gregory Wilson's arrest could offer Prema a reprieve? The media would call her 'the Wicked Witch of the West', even if Prema survived!

Dazed, exhausted and engulfed by unbearable loneliness she staggered towards the kitchen. And where was Aidan? She had told the Reception staff to expect him. She noticed a lone figure in the coffee breakout area, a tall, skinny man. At that moment, almost any human face would have been welcome......

"Hello?"

As the man turned, she froze.

"Style? Style Hobbs? What are you doing here?   I thought you were working in the Prime Minister's office now?"

"I... I..."

"Oh, please don't tell me that he's sacked you and dumped you back at the Home Office?"

"No, no, I......"

"Then what are you doing here??!!"

Flight BA 0663 to Larnaca, 15ᵗʰ October, 7.45am

Usually, she hated turbulence, but today the sensation filled her with gratitude. It was a miracle she had boarded the plane.

Erica's head throbbed as she drank another black coffee.

In an hour, she would reach Cyprus and comparative safety.

At Gatwick, she had collapsed before recovering to semi-consciousness. The airport doctor had examined her and advised her not to fly. Somehow, she had found the strength to protest. A kindly young couple, called Apricot and Loom, with three daughters had offered to take care of her. If she hadn't been an atheist, she would have believed they were heaven-sent.

So now she slouched in the aisle seat, pumping caffeine into her system to stay awake. The three little girls adored her, despite her dishevelled state and the four-year-old rested her head on Erica's shoulder.

It was obvious she had been drugged. But by whom and why had it not been a fatal dose? For some reason, Chawton and his cohorts had not used a toxic nerve agent or a weapon of mass destruction. One drop on her skin would have killed her.

Grateful to be alive, she found herself praying she would arrive in Larnaca without further incident, to meet her brother and disappear into obscurity for the rest of her life. And then she checked herself. She was supposed to be an atheist, wasn't she?

She glanced up at the BBC News screen and was suddenly jolted wide awake.

Chawton had resigned, but Prema's death warrant had still been signed. Her heart sank. She had done enough to ruin her tormentor, but not to abort the execution. The death warrant was the point of no return and even if The Observian carried out her threat to publish the scandalous information they held, only a miracle could bring a reprieve now.

Greenwich Holding Centre, 15th October, 8.00am

This was the defining moment in her career. Margaret Wilton, Governor of Greenwich Holding Centre greeted representatives from the Home Office, Police, Judiciary and Press as they cleared security checks and were escorted to their seats in the execution chamber. With a further layer of powder applied to her face and her French pleat tighter and more severe than ever, she presided over the biggest event since Ralph Hardcastle's funeral.

Her wrist phone buzzed incessantly, but she chose to ignore it. She was too important to take calls or read messages today.

Suddenly, her red faced personal assistant burst through the assembled throng. "Mrs Wilton…. Mrs Wilton."

"Not now, Maple."

"But there's a message from the Home Office, on your computer and wrist phone. Didn't you read it?"

"Maple, we have important guests. This is totally inappropriate."

"But… but…"

A good-looking, grey-haired, uniformed man joined them.

"Forgive me for eavesdropping Mrs Wilton, but if you have a message from the Home Office, it is vital you check it, today of all days."

As Mrs Wilton found herself staring into the blue eyes of Frank Southwold, she simpered like a teenage schoolgirl.

"Oh, Frank darling, of course. Let's read it."

Her face reddened as she opened the email.

Maple became impatient.

"Shall I tell everyone? We're running out of time."

"Shup up Maple, certainly not. Er…this message does not have a valid Home Office security code. I'm issuing instructions to override it. Excuse me, Mr Southwold. Come along, Maple."

She dragged her bewildered assistant into her office.

"Maple, how dare you!"

Maple was in floods of tears.

"But it's a reprieve!"

"It's an unauthorised message with no valid electronic seal. You will delete it now. And don't you ever dare embarrass me before distinguished company again."

"But it must be from Evie Atherton. Gregory Wilson has been charged, it's on BBC News. There's a clear reason to stop this wretched business."

"You're being hysterical and unprofessional. The warrant is signed, there will be an execution this morning and you must learn to cope with it. I'm sending you home for the day on sick leave."

Maple ran from the room, sobbing.

Margaret deleted Evie's message. Then she re-read the earlier email she had received from Orchard Mayhew. She knew where her loyalties lay....

The Home Office, 15th October, 8.15am

Aidan had arrived at the Home Office and now struggled to keep the peace, as Evie's angry eyes flashed at Style Hobbs.

As she lashed out, Aidan forcibly restrained her. Evie was astounded that the gentlemanly ex-Bishop had such an iron grip, and she unleashed some choice expletives at him. But his hold tightened, the harder she fought.

"It was you, wasn't it!!" She screamed "You forged my signature. You used my seal. Do not even try to deny it! You pathetic, obsequious little creep!"

"I don't know what you're talking about."

"Then what have you been doing here all night, Style?"

She pulled her left arm free from Aidan's grip and thrust her wrist in Style's face.

"Look at the Reception security list on my wrist phone! It clearly says that you arrived in this building at 1.00am this morning. How do you explain that? You work at 10 Downing Street, not here!!"

Style's quiet, self-assured façade was slipping away and Aidan could see the fear in his eyes.

"Evie, remember who he works for. Who do you think masterminded this? Style isn't your real adversary."

Evie stopped to recover her breath and stared at Style with a mix of pity and disdain. The corridors of Whitehall had reduced this once idealistic graduate to the lowest form of sycophancy.

"Style," she said, almost gently "what kind of lowlife have they turned you into? When you were a student, you supported Amnesty International. You demonstrated against torture and the death penalty. And now you've forged the execution warrant of a 34-year-old woman."

He could no longer look her in the eye.

"Style, if you have any shred of decency left in your being, tell me who put you up to this. Was it Orchard?"

After an almost eternal pause, Style gave a faint nod. As he stared at the floor and bit his lip, Evie knew he was fighting back tears.

Evie felt a new sensation. A shred of compassion for an enemy? Could she really have changed that much in less than twenty-four hours?

"I forgive you Style. But you will face the consequences. You've committed a serious crime. The legal system must take its course. Orchard cannot protect you forever."

"Put not your trust in princes." Added Aidan.

Evie sighed.

"Style, I have more important things than you to worry about this morning. I have forty minutes to save the life of Prema Gupta. The Prime Minister, Lord Chief Justice and Governor of Greenwich Holding Centre are stonewalling my stay of execution."

Style nodded. "I know"

"And they're gagging the UK media and international networks. I might have guessed."

"Orchard has a reciprocal agreement with the US and CNN and other networks," added Style "so they've put a lid on it too."

"Style, you once worked for me. When I was in a hole, you always came up trumps. Please think of something now! You've got me into this mess".

Style began to regain his composure. Burning ambition pushed back against the flicker of conscience which had reared its head. Evie sensed the internal battle.

"If Prema dies this morning, your forged warrant has killed her. You'll face trial and your name will be dragged through the press. Her survival could make things easier for you."

His once-boyish features now registered his plight. Self-preservation, rather than conscience won the day. He shut his eyes and tightened his lips, collecting his thoughts.

"OK. There are three options. Number one, we issue an order to the Governor of Greenwich Holding Centre."

"Which hasn't worked."

"Number two, we give the Ministry of Defence the arming codes to launch a missile on the Holding Centre?"

"You mean you could blow the place to kingdom come?" Aidan was stunned. "I thought only the Prime Minister had that power.

"Yes, but it would kill most people in the building. The missile's a secret weapon, to be used if international Terrorists break into the Greenwich Holding Centre, or if they themselves become the focus of a rescue attempt from death row."

Evie sighed.

"Option two is not tempting. So, what's option three?"

Style paused. His old self-assurance was returning, but Evie sensed his discomfort.

"We can sabotage the execution."

"Don't be absurd. We're in Westminster and the executioner, a certain Mr Ludo Cannock, is in Greenwich, rubbing his grubby little hands together and waiting to pull the lever."

"No, he's not. He's at home in Harold Wood, sitting at his computer."

"His computer? What do you mean?"

"He's doing the execution remotely. He's been given the Guillotine operation codes on Greenwich Holding Centre's intranet site."

"Doing the execution remotely?! But I'm the Home Secretary! I never knew such a thing existed! Why wasn't I told?"

Style sounded irritatingly smug.

"There are certain things the Home Secretary doesn't need to know. The responsibilities of high office give you no time to concern yourself with the minutiae of execution technology. We've taken care of it in Whitehall"

"It wasn't even in the procedure manual I signed off. But you knew about this?"

"Yes."

He glanced nervously into Evie's ferocious green eyes.

"I.... I set the codes."

"While you worked for me?!"

"Yes."

Evie's loathing of Style was only outweighed by her desperation to save Prema.

"You're a man of hidden talents."

"But I can change the codes, if you'll give me access the Home Office intranet system."

Before Aidan could stop her, Evie suddenly lunged, grabbed Style by the scruff of the neck and frogmarched him into her office, like a miserable schoolboy in the grip of a terrifying headmistress.

"Access!? You've already hacked into my system to get my seal code for the death warrant! Get your miserable little carcass to that computer and change those guillotine codes NOW!!!!!"

Style tried to maintain some final vestiges of dignity, as Evie logged into the system. She was stunned as he navigated to hidden drives.

Suddenly, he turned on Aidan.

"Get that ex-Bishop out of here. He hasn't signed the Official Secrets Act."

"Leave him alone, your officious little worm!" Cried Evie. "After your behaviour last night, you've forfeited any right to uphold the law!"

His failed attack on Aidan and the sharp verbal slap from Evie left him squirming, as he frantically fumbled through a maze of sub-sites.

"I can't get to the code-setting page."

"You'd better find a way or I'll hang you out to dry, in every newspaper in the country!"

Greenwich Holding Centre, 15th October, 8.30am

Miriam tried to keep her voice steady as she read the Anglican Communion Liturgy, broke chunks of bread and poured wine into a plastic mug.   Her eyes were red and puffy from earlier tears, but she now remained self-possessed. Prema knelt, her lips moving silently in prayer.

Gloria looked on uncomfortably. She didn't do religion, but for some strange reason the words of the liturgy awoke feelings she preferred to ignore. As emotions surfaced, she could barely wait for the Eucharist to end, so she could return to the safety blanket of cerebral detachment, (threadbare though it had now become) and harden herself for the horror ahead.

Gloria was used to handling painful events by drawing on her repository of resilience and intellect. But there was no precedent for this. Sure-footed in most situations, she now struggled into unchartered territory, emotionally and professionally. The word 'spiritually' also crossed her mind, but she hastily pushed it away. She could not handle any more new concepts today.

The sudden, sharp knock on the door jolted everyone's nerves.

A doctor entered with two prison warders. The pained expression on his face gave way to anguish and he struggled to maintain his professional demeanour, as he saw the frail woman kneeling against the bed.

"Ms Gupta? I'm so sorry to interrupt you…. I've come to do your medical checks and attach your monitoring device."

Prema looked up and forced a faint smile.

"It's OK. I know what you have to do."

He gently checked her heartbeat, blood pressure and then carefully strapped an electronic contraption around her forearm.

"I'll…. I'll hide this under your sleeve, so it won't spoil your dress."

"Thank you."

He pulled a syringe from his bag.

"I'm giving you a sedative now. This will make you a little drowsy."

Prema blinked back tears, but kept her voice steady.

"No. I don't need drugs."

"Are you sure? You might change your mind when…."

"I can do this."

"OK. And just to reassure you, it will all be very quick. You won't feel anything."

Prema smiled gently.

"That's just what I used to tell my patients!"

Miriam stepped forward and clasped his hand.

"Thank you, doctor, you've been very kind."

As he left the room, Miriam and Gloria sat beside Prema on the floor. Miriam looked gently into her eyes.

"Stop looking at me like that, the pair of you!"

"What do you mean?" Said Gloria.

"As if you're expecting something from me, like famous last words. It's not like that. Get real! Dying people don't always come out with pearls of wisdom. I'm a nurse, so I should know! Their final words are often something nondescript like 'I want to go to the toilet'.

Maybe I just want a mundane last few minutes on earth? I've said all I want to say to you. Miriam, you know how I feel about your friendship. Gloria, we've talked about all that's happened in the past few months."

"But how are you feeling, my love?"

"As though I'm walking on a tightrope. The narrowest possible wire across a canyon, with peace on one side and total abject fear on the other. The slightest wobble in my emotions and I'll lose my grip and be engulfed in an abyss of terror. I have a few precious minutes left with you. I just need warmth and physical contact, to stop me going over that precipice. Hold me, please…."

Gloria slumped onto the floor and slowly, tentatively, wrapped her arms around her. The surfacing memory was excruciating, but compared to Prema's anguish it was nothing. Her comfort zone no longer mattered. Anguish flooded back from the night she'd held her brother through his final agonies of labour and felt his dying breath on her cheek, as his life ebbed away.

She clutched Prema tighter and buried her head in her shoulder to hide her tears.

"They're murdering you because you destroyed the evil monster who killed my brother!

Prema knew that in her last minutes, she had finally met the real Gloria.

The Home Office, 15th October, 8.45am

"I can't change the operation sequence! The site's frozen!"

With clammy and shaking hands, Style still battled to change the Guillotine access codes.

"Get out of that chair, let me do it!" Snapped Evie.

"But you don't know how!" Sighed Aidan.

The gathering hysteria on BBC News 24 only forced their adrenaline levels higher.

"Evie, sit down. There's nothing more you can do, except pray."

"How can you be so infuriatingly calm?" She retorted.

"Evie, if you have no further power over a situation, what's the point of winding yourself up? Unless a miracle occurs, Prema's life is over and all you can do is commend her to God and place your own future in His hands too."

Evie collapsed into a swivel office chair and steadied her breath. The anger in her eyes subsided to sadness.

"I've come to the end. I've had it."

"That's how I felt a few months ago. Maybe it's the best place to be. At the end of your own strength, power and resources. You've put up a brave fight. You amended the law to let Prema appeal. She refused to fight her sentence. You didn't sign the death warrant. And remember, it was the actions of cowardly men that manoeuvred you into the Home Office."

"I wish I'd fought harder, Aidan."

"Let's pray, now."

Style squirmed as Aidan prayed fervently, with Evie tentatively joining him. An invisible presence seemed to fill the office and everything inside him wanted to flee the room, the building and even West London, to escape that powerful something pervading the space around him.

Greenwich Holding Centre, 15th October, 8.55am

Prema, Gloria and Miriam huddled on the floor, feeling almost suspended in time and space.

They were jolted into final reality with another sharp rap at the door, as Margaret Wilton, the Governor, marched into the room with two prison warders. Prema drew deep breaths, to control the vicious knot tightening in her stomach.

"Ms Gupta, are you ready?"

Gloria leapt to her feet.

"My client has three more minutes. It's not time yet!"

"It's time to prepare the prisoner, before she's escorted to the execution chamber. Ms Gupta, please stand up?"

Miriam helped Prema to her feet, as she tried to remain steady.

"Give me your full name and date of birth, please."

"Prema Sameera Gupta, 27th February 2004."

"Have you stored and handed over all of your personal effects?"

Prema pointed to a box in the corner of the room.

"My Chaplain has been given custody of all my personal belongings."

"Please remove all jewellery and personal adornments."

Gloria was livid.

"What??!!"

"This is a routine health, safety and security procedure. Please remove your jewellery and hairpins."

"Her hair has been pinned up so it doesn't impede the guillotine. Your colleague gave permission. Your request has nothing to do with health and safety, it's just a cruel humiliation!"

"Very well, but the jewellery must come off now!"

Struggling to keep her hands steady, Prema removed her earrings and bracelets, giving them to Gloria. "I want you to have these."

"Secure and restrain the prisoner!"

With a lightning movement, one of the warders twisted a plastic handcuff strap around Prema's wrists. Her eyes watered as the sharp plastic edge cut into her flesh.

"Stop! You're hurting her!" Shouted Miriam.

"And I don't want to be handcuffed," added Prema "I... I want to walk unrestrained."

"It's in the procedure manual, signed by the Home Secretary." Retorted Margaret Wilton, briskly.

"I know Evie Atherton and she would want Prema treated with dignity!" Snapped Miriam.

Suddenly, Miriam ripped off her dog collar and lifted her shirt over her head.

"Miriam, what are you doing?" Gasped Prema.

"If they won't treat you with respect, I refuse to act with decorum"

Gloria looked at her watch.

"Miriam, there's no time for a protest. Please get your clothes back on."

But Miriam had now removed her trousers and was wearing nothing but pants, long-johns, bra and a corset which barely contained her size 18 figure.

One of the warders lunged towards Miriam, but only succeeded in knocking a cup of cold coffee over Gloria's suit and blouse.

"Take the prisoner into the chamber, now!" Snapped Margaret Wilson.

"Miriam, get dressed!" Cried Gloria.

But at the press of a button, the wall of Prema's bedroom slid back and opened into the execution room.

The Home Office, 15th October, 8.57am

Beyond exhaustion, Aidan and Evie gazed at the horror unfolding on the Hologram TV screen, as Style still struggled to change the Guillotine codes.

As the scene descended into total anarchy, smoke bombs were let off outside the Greenwich Holding Centre, looking almost too real as the TV rays projected the grey swirling mist into the room. Trampled bodies and scenes of arrest intermingled with intense jets of icy water cannon, which made Evie shiver in the draughty room, even though her clothes were bone dry.

At least five police officers and twenty protestors were reported dead and Evie's thoughts turned to Frank. His carefully-masterminded strategy to ensure order and safety had miscarried horrendously. But Evie guessed that the pandemonium was not driven by genuine protesters. It was no doubt coordinated by some anarchists, who cared nothing for Prema Gupta, but were driven by their ambition to destabilise the Government.

The reporter, from the safety of a rampart in the Holding Centre, gave a running commentary.

"We understand the Governor and Warders have now arrived at Prema's cell and are preparing to lead her to the execution room."

Glamourised for the occasion with a designer black suit, glistening brooch and bouffant hair, the reporter continued with banal speculation on what Prema would be thinking in her final moments and what her last words would be.

Greenwich Holding Centre, 15th October, 8.58am

As the execution party entered the room, the assembled police, prison officers, journalists and members of the judiciary were subjected to the sight of Prema flanked by an angry Margaret Wilton and two disgruntled warders, followed by a coffee-drenched lawyer and a Chaplain wearing nothing but her bra, long johns and ill-fitting corset.

Prema was let to a microphone at the front platform.

"Ms Gupta, do you have anything to say before sentence is carried out."

Prema gazed at the sea of faces in front of her.

So, this is my final view of the world? All these people feel safe in their seats. But one day they'll tread this road. It won't be the guillotine, but maybe cancer, heart attacks, strokes or road accidents will carry them into eternity, perhaps when they least expect it, with no chance to prepare their souls as I've done.

She drew a deep breath and her beautiful, clear voice resonated across the room.

"I would like to thank the staff of Greenwich Holding Centre for treating me with consideration during my time here. I forgive the executioner and those who were involved in my prosecution and sentencing. I also forgive Home Secretary Evie Atherton who, I understand, signed my death warrant.

I give my love to my family and close friends. You know who you are, but I particularly acknowledge Miriam my chaplain, Gloria my lawyer and my beloved sister, Reeta.

I would like to reiterate that I did not deliberately murder Ralph Hardcastle. I acted in self-defence on the night he broke into my home and attacked me. I also wish to declare that Gregory Wilson was not involved in his death.

I have committed my life to Jesus and I now commend my soul into His hands. If you have not already received Him as your Saviour and repented of your sins, I urge you to do so without delay, because none of you know when you will meet your maker. God bless each and every one of you. Goodbye."

She turned to the guillotine. Her throat was dry and she struggled to swallow. This was it.

Six warders suddenly seized her and forced her onto the trolley. She felt straps tighten around her. She had known they would do this to her, but was still shocked at the speed and ferocity with which they worked. In less than 10 seconds she was trussed and pinioned to the narrow, plastic gurney. She was conscious of Miriam repeating Psalm 121 and tried to turn her head, but she was bound so tightly bound she could barely move and could only see a faint image of ill-fitting underwear, before she was thrust into darkness......

The Home Office, 15th October, 8.59am

Aidan and Evie knelt on the floor, not only in prayer, but as the only way they could pay their respects as the nation held its breath, waiting for the electronic blade to fall.

Evie clenched her fists, refusing to cry in front of the two men.

Greenwich Holding Centre, 15th October, 8.59am

In the dark tube, Prema felt as though time and space had been suspended. She braced every inch of her body for sudden, excruciating pain and the unknowable and unfathomable beyond it. She quietly cried out to God to receive her and pull her across the chasm between Earth and Heaven, safely into his arms.

A strange sensation surrounded her as the tube flooded with warmth and light. Yet still, no blade fell. Was she already dead? Had she passed into eternity without noticing? Loving arms seemed to enfold her, bathing her in overwhelming bliss.

The Home Office, 15th October, 8.59am

Evie could not bear to look at the TV screen and buried her head in her hands. The camera focused on the noticeboard outside the Holding Centre door. She did not want to see the moment when Prema's death was confirmed.

Suddenly, Style gave a shout.

"I'm there! I've got into the page!"

"Do we still have time?"

Evie leapt to the computer.

"Navigate to the codes, NOW!!! We only have seconds to spare!"

"OK, I'm there!"

"Move it!"

"I'm doing! I've changed the 'standby code'... I'm changing the 'execute' code."

"It's 8.59 and fifty-seven seconds. Are we definitely still in time?"

"Yes, we've done it!! The 'standby' code was entered by Ludo Cannock five seconds ago, but he hasn't activated the 'execute' code."

Evie collapsed to the floor again, emotionally spent.

For several moments, no-one could speak.

"Prema lives, for now," sighed Aidan "and I'm so relieved for her and for you"

He shook hands with Style and clasped him round the shoulder. But then he slumped wearily into a chair, his face was troubled.

"What is it, Aidan?"

"So many other people have died today. It's a bloodbath. How can I rejoice? The guillotine has plummeted this nation to new depths. Violence, hatred, greed in the media and a ghoulish public appetite for every vile aspect of the whole process. I'm ashamed to be British."

"You're right Aidan. Unless I use my power to drag my beloved country out of this vile cesspool, I've achieved nothing of real value. And I may have bought Prema some time, but unless her sentence is overturned, I've only given her breathing space until 'they' discover our sabotage. My real job hasn't even begun."

"Catch your breath for a few minutes, old girl!"

Greenwich Holding Centre, 15th October, 9.00am

Prema was still bathed in the cloud of warmth and light around her, when she suddenly felt the strange sensation of reversing. She was going backwards. Had decapitation disoriented her? Was this how it felt?

Suddenly the execution room reappeared. The straps around her body were being loosened. She could hear Miriam's excited voice.

"Prema! Prema my love!"

She tried to lift her shoulders, as her upper torso was released and then felt Miriam's arms pulling her up and embracing her. She turned to see a red-faced Margaret Wilton on the phone and several agitated wardens. The tension had broken in the rows of spectators and there was now a tumult of excitement and conversation.

"Prema my love, there's been a stay of execution! Margaret Wilton has just been told!"

Flight BA 0663 to Larnaca, 15th October, 9.05am

As the flight made its final descent into Larnaca, Apricot offered Erica a moist wipe and some perfume.

"Would you like to freshen up?"

"No thanks, Apricot." Erica preferred to remain dishevelled. She would be less recognisable.

"Are you sure you'll be OK?"

"I'll be fine when I meet my brother."

"Someone drugged you. Is there any risk they're still around? Or might they have contacts in Larnaca?"

"I don't know."

"This may sound a bit forward, but why don't you stay in our villa for a couple of nights. It's just... I sense that you might be safer doing that."

"What do you mean, you sense I might be safer?"

"I feel a bit weird saying this, but I er.... I prayed about it. And my husband felt the same. Sometimes God speaks to us."

"Frankly, it does sound weird. And how do I know you guys are safe? I'm not being funny, but I hardly know you. You might stick a knife in my back."

Apricot looked slightly hurt, but then nodded in acknowledgement.

"It's OK, I understand. In your shoes, I wouldn't trust anyone. But even if you don't come with us, please do something unpredictable. Meeting your brother is obvious behaviour and someone could be watching his movements. There's another party on the plane I could introduce you to, if you want to hide with them. The Retired Journalists' Beer Tasting Association are here for their autumn conference. If you want to stay anonymous, you can be sure they'll never remember you."

"Heaven preserve me, I think I'd be safer with you!"

The Home Office, 15th October, 9.10am

Evie could have easily drifted asleep on the floor, except for yet another newsflash. Orchard Mayhew was about to make a statement.

She smirked. Did he already know the guillotine had failed? How would he dig himself out of this hole?

The coverage shifted to 10 Downing Street, as Mayhew emerged from the door to flashing cameras and walked to the microphone.

"I would like to announce that Prema Gupta will not be executed by guillotine this morning. I have ordered a six-month stay of execution, pending the trial of Gregory Wilson, who, early this morning, was charged with joint responsibility for the murder of Sir Ralph Hardcastle.

As you will be aware, the Home Secretary signed her death warrant this morning, but I had no alternative but to revoke the execution order. Prema Gupta deserves to have her case reviewed, if the trial of Gregory Wilson uncovers any material evidence giving rise to a reasonable doubt about her level of complicity and involvement in the death of Sir Ralph Hardcastle.

While the Home Office followed due process and the letter of the law, I felt that mercy is a much higher priority and the exercise of fairness and justice must be above question.

When I became Prime Minister, I promised a new style of Government, putting integrity above process or bureaucracy. Today I have kept my word.

I appreciate this stay of execution will be distressing to Sir Ralph Hardcastle's family, friends and all who loved him. The murder of the People's Gynaecologist, was a cruel and wicked deed and I promise that our judicial system will resolve this case. Thank you."

Evie screamed angrily at the TV

"HOW DARE HE! How dare he undermine me!!"

She threw her expensive, designer stiletto at the screen.

"Evie, calm down!"

She pushed Aidan out of the way with her elbow, shaking with rage.

"He blocked my stay of execution and now he's issued his own reprieve! Now the whole world thinks I'm a faceless, merciless bureaucrat who wanted to execute her, while he presents himself as the hero who spared her! The dirty little baby-faced rat!!"

"Evie, pull yourself together and look at the bright side. His six-month reprieve will give you a lot of breathing space!"

"We deactivated that guillotine. Now no-one will ever know."

"If Prema's reprieve had depended on our sabotage, it would not have bought her much time. You'd have faced the same scenario again, within days, or even hours!"

Aidan's calm logic pressed all the wrong buttons and triggered increasingly angry responses from Evie until he quietly gave up, letting her vent her frustration to her heart's content.

A damaged hologram TV was a small price to pay.

Greenwich Holding Centre, 15th October 9.10am

As Prema struggled to stand, the room swam before her eyes. Miriam and Gloria caught her arms.

Amidst the turmoil in the execution room, a tall, grey haired man from the front row stepped forward, gently led her to his seat and wrapped a blanket around her.

"It's OK, you'll be fine. Let me get you a drink, Prema."

Within two minutes he returned with a cup of hot sugary tea and a glass of brandy.

"Get that down you and I'll get you some food. Those warders should be doing this, but they seem to have forgotten you!"

Prema focused on his grey blue eyes, which, amid the turmoil, seemed the only stable thing in the room.

"Thanks... you're... you're very kind. What's your name?

"Frank Southwold, Chief Commissioner of the Metropolitan Police."

He shouted frantic instructions on his wrist phone.

"Sorry, it's chaos out there. I have to go."

As he raced from the room, he yelled at the warders, "Give her something to eat. Look after her! What's the matter with you?!!"

Home Office, 15th October, 9.15am

Style had left the room promptly, once Orchard Mayhew had strengthened his position. His own danger was receding now Prema was reprieved. No-one need ever know about his forged death warrant.

Aidan and Evie ignored him.

"An amoral, time serving young man," mused Aidan "who has sold his soul to the highest bidder."

Risking further wrath, he renewed his attempts to pacify Evie.

"If Orchard's afraid to proceed with this execution, there's every likelihood he'll chicken out of future ones. He has the threat of a Welsh referendum hanging over him. He may even want the legislation revoked. Your problems could be over!"

Evie sighed.

"Maybe you're right. But I'm furious at how this happened. I'm sorry Aidan, I should be happy for Prema today. She gets to live, at least for 6 months."

"The right outcome has been achieved."

"And I apologise for the unedifying language I've used in the last few hours. What, with me in the God squad and you a man of the cloth!"

"No worries, it was understandable."

Aidan turned back to the news screen to watch the chaos in the execution room. Having cancelled the guillotining, the Governor had allowed cameras into the chamber.

"It's chaos in there. Someone's wrapped Prema in a blanket and she's eating breakfast. Wait a minute!! That's my wife next to her, in her underwear!!"

xvi) Into the wilderness

Portcullis House, 15th October, 2.00pm

Evie and Frank faced each other across a narrow desk in a small, formal, sterile, pastel-coloured office.

"I guess you're relieved, Evie. Even though Mayhew knifed you?"

"My problems are only just beginning. It's been a horrific day for others."

"That's why I'm here. It was a bloodbath at the Greenwich Holding Centre. Thirty-five dead. My men should have controlled things. I take full responsibility. I'm therefore offering my resignation."

"Resign? No, Frank!"

"I insist."

Evie tossed back her dark, glossy mane, folded her arms and reared up to her full height, her flashing eyes burrowing into his.

"I refuse to accept your resignation!"

Frank was taken aback. Evie could be formidable, but had never been so assertive with him.

"Frank, the area around the Greenwich Holding Centre was not built to hold the thousands who arrived last night. My predecessor authorised the designs. It was a deathtrap. And the Welsh Nationalists and Cyclists for Justice collaborated with anarchists who are on the radar of M15. I carry some responsibility for this. And the media are also culpable. Their hype was totally irresponsible."

"It was still my job to contain things."

"You're staying. You're the best chief the force has ever had. And you've been a rock to me. This is best for London and for you! Wait a fortnight at least, before you decide! Try praying about it."

"Really, Miss Cynical? Since when did prayer matter to you?"

"Something's happened to me. I joined your 'team' yesterday. Probably Aidan and Miriam's influence. But I think you played a part!"

"That's the best news in the world, Evie. Tell me your whole story, when I'm less exhausted!"

They were silent for a few moments, both struggling to stay awake after 24 hours without sleep.

Then Frank nervously cleared his throat.

"Evie, there's something else I want to ask you."

"Fire away."

"I.... I'm plucking up courage to say this, but I care very deeply about you."

Evie suddenly felt a knot forming in her stomach.

"Whatever you have to say Frank, I'm too tired for this sort of conversation."

"Please hear me out. I may lose my nerve when I'm more awake! We have a close friendship. We're a part of each other's lives, now. I've thought about asking you to be my girlfriend, but I can't be doing with all that courting nonsense."

"What a relief! My views exactly!"

Evie relaxed slightly.

"So instead, I.... I want you to be my wife. Will you marry me?"

"Marry you??!!"

Evie's blood pressure soared higher than it had been all night.

"Is the idea so horrendous? I want to share my life with you."

"Frank, I'm in shock. I must digest this and I'm in no fit state to think about it now. We're shattered. Give me two weeks and I'll give you an answer."

"Is that all you can say? At least tell me how you feel about me."

"I.... I don't know. I like you. I enjoy your company. I need time to think."

10 Downing Street, 16th October

Evie's chauffeur driven car drew up to the entrance of 10 Downing Street. She emerged in a scarlet suit and matching lipstick, with her hair lacquered to the most defiant perfection her deftly manicured hands could achieve. She held her head high.

Orchard Mayhew received her, slouched across his desk, with his face earnestly upturned and fingers pressed together. He reminded Evie of the consultant who had broken the news of Uncle Ron's impending demise. Except the consultant did not have the face of an overfed hamster and a wet clammy handshake. Neither did he permeate the room with a stench of garlic.

"Evie, how are you? It's been a gruelling 48 hours."

"You haven't called me here for therapy. Just get down to business."

"Evie, your achievements at the Home Office this year are exceptional. You've empowered community policing. A record number of graduates are joining the Police Force. Your investment in MI5 technology has made us the envy of the West. Your streamlined prosecution procedures have reduced the number of prisoners held on remand. Your 'Stay Safe' scheme for senior citizens is a resounding success...."

"But...." Interrupted Evie.

"As I said, your community success......"

"There's a 'but' isn't there? Stop dithering and get to the point."

Sweat appeared on Orchard's forehead.

"I'm waiting, Orchard."

"Despite your good work, Evie, I have serious concerns about your effectiveness and loyalty to this administration."

"I only voted against the Party Whip once."

"Yes, when you opposed the reintroduction of capital punishment. And that has been your weakness."

"Despite that, you made me Home Secretary."

"Yes. Because of your efficiency, talent and drive. I thought you'd have the sense to put your personal views aside, in the interests of this party's unity. We have a minority Government. I assumed you'd want us to stay in power."

"I took the post because you gave me little option."

"And look how you've betrayed me! You sat on that death warrant all night, causing utter chaos."

"So, you asked Style Hobbs to forge my signature!"

"While you sabotaged the guillotine, and bullied him into hacking the Home Office execution portal."

"He'd already hacked into it! He's soiled goods, Orchard, just like you!"

"Your disloyalty, Evie, is compounded by your lack of effectiveness."

"Lack of effectiveness??!!"

"Thirty-five people died in the riots at the Greenwich Holding Centre, including five police officers."

"A horrific tragedy, but I'm not directly responsible, though I acknowledge MI5 should have monitored those anarchists more closely."

"The Chief Commissioner of the Metropolitan Police, Frank Southwold, was directly responsible and he's accountable to you!"

"How dare you blame Frank or me! You dumped us in a nightmare situation. The first execution in over seventy years, with political chaos and Wales threatening independence.

You let the media hype up the execution, generating the biggest public frenzy since Princess Diana's death. And the London Mayor, your best buddy Will Lambert, offered free tube travel and extra trains for half a million spectators going to the Greenwich Holding Centre! He even waived the congestion charge so more people could go!"

Orchard was visibly shaken, as he rubbed his clammy fingers together. Then his agitated features slowly regrouped to a faint smile.

"Cyclists for Justice were among those agitators Evie."

"Of course, they were." There was a split second before Evie realised her danger.

"A generously-funded organisation, even since the lovely Lucinda died. I often wonder where their money came from..."

Evie remained silent.

"We'll say nothing more Evie. But I would like your letter of resignation please. You can mention your unavoidable family commitments, your elderly dad and dying uncle. But you are warmly grateful for the opportunity I gave you and remain unswervingly loyal to the Government."

"I know how to write a letter."

"I want you to perform one final duty."

"If it's about Prema Gupta's case, you can sort it yourself!"

"You will revoke the citizenship of Oliver Bunton, before he's taken into quarantine! A Speaker who's chosen to become a parrot is an even bigger disgrace to Parliament than you are!

"Well, so much for your so-called liberal, tolerant, metropolitan ideals." Snapped Evie.

Buckhurst Hill, Essex, 23rd October

Oliver Bunton was surrounded by suitcases, boxes and carrier bags.

On his table lay a document to certify that he was no longer a British citizen, but now classed as a "trans-species hybrid human in pre-mutation quarantine."

Tomorrow morning, a van would collect and transport him to the Pre-Mutation Orientation Centre, a secure unit in Battersea, where he would spend his final six weeks as a human being. He would be kept in custody until his operation, further quarantine and transportation to Australia.

The Government had ruled that transmutants must be detained for forty-two days before surgery, to prevent resistance or withdrawal of consent.

He remembered the scathing lecture, which Sir Chawton Holland had given him.

"Having spent taxpayers' money on transitional drugs and therapy, we don't want the embarrassment of patients like you cancelling. And we don't want to be left with hybrids. Those half-baked wretches need long term care and cannot be restored to their human state."

There had been many cancellations in the early days. Shortly before surgery, some clients had been overcome with fear. In horror, grief or in some cases, fear for their souls, they had pulled from the brink of the abyss.

Transmutants were now slowly sedated and brainwashed for six weeks, so they had neither the physical capacity nor desire to resist the operation.

The necessities of Oliver's human life were packed, cleaned, labelled and catalogued, ready for distribution to his estranged wife, family, friends, charity shops, recycling stations or the refuse tip.

He reflected on the strangeness of things you associate with being human. Plates, cutlery, crockery, tablecloths, napkins. The very concept of etiquette was meaningless to a parrot. The sanitary practice of a man such as soap, after-shave, deodorant, toilet roll. Personal hygiene would never be his concern again.

His watch would be meaningless. What would time matter, except to note the rising and setting of the sun as he slept with his head under his wing? Books, magazines and papers? How much energy did humans devote to processing the ideas of others? He would bid farewell to politics, philosophy, ideologies and poetry. His genetically grown, transplanted brain would have no capacity for intellect, emotion or spirituality. He would fly freely, gathering food and avoiding predators, with no accountability to man or beast.

A bar of chocolate lay on the table. A brand he had loved since childhood. The memory of the taste and aroma stirred a tide of memories which threatened to flood his emotions. He realised that in six weeks, he would be unable to enjoy it. He fiercely repressed the thought. He must not weaken.

His shoe was becoming tight and hurting his toes. He pulled it off and flinched as he carefully removed his sock, to identify the source of pain. He curled his foot and stared at his three smallest toes. Gone were the nails and the soft, pink skin. Hideous grey, scaly claws curled into the pink sole of his foot, causing red, swollen weals.

As Oliver's eyes moistened, he tried to convince himself that he was not weeping for the toenails he would never see again....

Greenwich Holding Centre, 23rdth October

Prema, Miriam and Gloria enjoyed afternoon tea, on silver platters.

There was little space to sit, with the half-packed cases and clothes strewn across the bed, but who cared?

"My last day here!"

The staff at the Greenwich Holding Centre had been surprisingly generous, lavishing a farewell tea on the prisoner whose exemplary behaviour, in the face of execution and subsequent reprieve had won their respect. Even the warder who had so painfully strapped her wrists gave her a sheepish smile and enquired after her well-being.

They were moving Prema back to the Epping Holding Centre. She would still be in a solitary room and secure unit, but no longer on death row. She would be allowed a daily walk in the garden and was relishing the prospect of some greenery.

Gloria carefully kept her new batch of legal paperwork away from the jam and cream.

"Prema, we can't enjoy the honeymoon period for long. The six-month clock is now ticking and don't take that cushion for granted! I don't trust the Government and Orchard Mayhew will reinstate your sentence tomorrow, if it suits him!

In the meantime, when Gregory Wilson is brought to trial, you'll be called as a witness. We must start working now."

"Yes, I know. And I'll co-operate. I really want to live now! I've been given my life back and it's so precious!"

"We must prove you did not cause Ralph's death and that Gregory must have killed him."

"But he didn't!"

"Gregory broke into your house that night. The Crown Prosecution believes there is a case."

"But I hit Ralph with that frame. I didn't even know Gregory was there!"

"They were both there, probably to kill you. But it backfired. So maybe Gregory attacked Ralph? Perhaps the blow you inflicted was not the fatal one?"

"But why would Gregory would want to kill him."

Gloria drew a deep breath. Was this the right time to break the news?

"Prema, there's some evidence I haven't shared with you. It helped to secure your reprieve, but it may be painful for you to hear."

"What?" Prema braced herself.

Three years ago, Ralph was unfaithful to you.

"That doesn't entirely surprise me. Our marriage a mess."

"The identity of his lover may come as a shock. He had an affair with Gregory."

"With Gregory?!"

"Yes, and he secretly married him in Puerto Rico."

"He committed bigamy?!"

Prema leaned back in her chair to digest the news.

"Are you OK, Prema?"

"I... I'm shocked but in a way, almost relieved. He constantly tormented me about my so-called inadequacies. Now I know was something else going on...."

"Ralph's relationship with Gregory was passionate but tempestuous. Ralph was angry, aggressive and violent with him, too. Occasionally Gregory fought back, but overall, he came off worst. So, you can see, Gregory had a motive. It's possible Ralph's behaviour pushed him over the edge."

"I don't know whether to hate Gregory or feel sorry for him. But I cannot give evidence to send him to the guillotine when there's still a possibility I inflicted the fatal head injury."

"Prema, if you stand up in court and say Gregory is innocent, you will be in the execution chamber again in six months, this time with no reprieve!"

"Gloria, I don't care. I can't say that Gregory did it. I'd be perjuring myself. Anyway, in my execution speech I exonerated him."

"We can argue you were under extreme stress. People say all sorts of things when they're about to be killed. Anyway, I thought you wanted to live!"

"I do. But I cannot lie!"

Miriam broke her silence.

"I agree with her Gloria. She cannot send an innocent man to his death."

Everyone had lost interest in the cream tea.

"I killed Ralph in self-defence. Let's re-visit that argument. I refused to appeal before, but this time I'll appeal as often as I'm allowed to. I fully believe Ralph intended to kill me."

The smallest flicker of hope registered on Gloria's face.

"Prema, why are you so convinced of his murderous intentions?"

Prema was silent.

"If I am to defend you on grounds of self-defence I must know everything. You cannot hold anything back."

Prema's unease permeated the room. Miriam took her hand.

"Prema my love, can you confide in me?"

Gloria continued to probe.

"What about Gregory? Did he have a motive to kill you?"

Prema looked very agitated now.

"I don't want to talk any more, for now."

"Gloria, give her a break!" Urged Miriam. "She's been through enough for one week."

Warrington, 24th October, 8.30am

"Well, Dad, how does it feel to have a lowly backbencher staying with you?"

"I would never describe you as lowly."

As he piled a hearty cooked breakfast onto Evie's plate, George Atherton enjoyed the unexpected pleasure of her company, despite the sacking which had driven her home.

"It's been a humiliating week. Wall to wall coverage of my exit from the Cabinet. The papers don't believe I resigned for family reasons!"

"He's shot himself in the foot, love. You were the only popular Minister."

"But they all think he sacked me because he wanted to save Prema and I didn't. It's a lie!"

"Look on the bright side. You're a free woman! You can criticise the Government and the guillotine now. They'll deselect you at the next election. You've nothing to lose!"

"True. But the Almighty is teaching me a tough lesson in humility!"

"You don't do God."

"I do, since last week."

"This time my lass really has flipped!"

xvii) Find the mother

Leytonstone, East London, 24th October, 11.00am

The road was grim, with shabby Victorian terraced houses divided into flats, neglected gardens, overflowing bins, fly-tipped furniture and unlicensed cars abandoned along the road.

Ceiba struggled through the drizzle, driving wind and puddles with a pushchair and two restless, fractious babies. Struggling to keep the hood of her parka over her head, her bedraggled blonde hair was saturated. Her jeans were drenched by a car speeding through a kerbside puddle.

But she was doing this for Tony. It had taken just a week to trace this address, after more than eighty hours trawling through social networks.

She was visiting the man she had never wanted to see again. Callum changed his address more often than most people change their socks. He was an easy person to lose. But he was the only tenuous link to those who knew the mother of Tony's baby.

As she rang the bell, her hand dislodged peeling paint and chipped woodwork. She braced herself.

"Ceiba? Look what the cat dragged in. How did you find me?"

"I need to talk to you."

"I kept tellin'ya, that baby ain't mine!"

"It's about someone else's baby."

"I ain't made no-one else pregnant."

"This ain't about you."

Callum's obsession with body building had not improved his appearance. Steroid-pumped, oiled muscles bulged from his soiled, torn vest and unwashed jeans. His slanted mouth drew on a rolled-up cigarette and his cold, dark eyes scrutinised her under thick, untamed eyebrows which met in the middle.

"You'd better come in."

Ceiba did not feel safe and fervently hoped the presence of two babies offered her some protection.

She tried not to retch, as the smell of decaying refuse and stale, congealed, cooking oil caught the back of her throat.

"How are you doing Callum?"

"Lost my job, innit! I worked for that Chawton Holland and he's been fired."

"Yeah, I realised you worked for him, when I saw you on the telly. You must have seen some sights, being one of his bodyguards?"

"Ha! Gave me a few laughs. I met that Midwife Gregory Wilson a week ago. What a wimp!"

"Callum, I need to talk about Tony."

"What's he up to, these days? In trouble, is he?"

"Tony died, giving birth."

Ceiba paused for effect, but Callum's sullen face showed no flicker of emotion.

"When he passed away, he asked me to find the mother of his child. You spent loads of time with that Health Minister, can you help?"

"Get real, I was only security staff."

"But you must know the people around him, who could help me?"

Callum drew on his cigarette and his eyebrows pulled closer together with the effort of getting his brain to churn. Ceiba fidgeted and tried to conceal her anxiety and revulsion.

"He had a bird, Erica Rayleigh. She did a runner, just before he was sacked, so I reckon she shopped'im!"

"But where is she now?"

"My mates found out she took a flight to Larnaca. Then she disappeared. I reckon she's in Cyprus somewhere. But he'll get her!"

"Anyone else?"

"There was another bird he fell out with. A parrot!"

"A parrot? Don't be daft."

"That Speaker bloke, Oliver Bunton, Olly Beak! They hated each other. I'm sure Bunton would have helped you, but…."

"But what?"

"He was taken into custody this morning, ain't you read the papers?"

"Arrested?"

"Nah! It's what they do with 'em transmutants, they lock 'em up six weeks before their final operation. They don't want them chickening out!"

"So how can I reach him?"

"Special security visiting pass. Only the Home Secretary can give it, and you'd need a good reason!"

"I know Evie Atherton, but she's been sacked!"

Callum smiled sardonically.

"You know 'er? Well miss hoity toity, you 've gone up in the world!"

"She won't help me. She's signed the Official Secrets Act."

"She might change her mind, now Orchard's sacked her!"

"Is there nothing else?"

"Gimme your mobile number and I'll call you if I think of anything."

Callum leered and moved towards her. Ceiba edged the buggy towards the hallway and the front door.

"You're looking good, Ceiba."

Ceiba shouted her mobile number as she pulled the buggy through the front door. There were people on the pavement.

He wouldn't dare cause her any trouble.

Warrington, 24th October, 2.00pm

Evie was back in Uncle Ron's house.

Oliver Bunton had given her the best parting gift imaginable. On removal of his citizenship, he had given her a crystal decanter, gold napkin rings and, best of all his old computer, topped up with £200 of 'pay as you go' access (having closed his bank account).

MI5 did not expect him to use it again. It would not be monitored!

She hid in the bedroom, while Uncle Ron immersed himself in the horse racing at Newmarket and Doncaster.

With plastic gloves, she opened the brown envelope and spread the contents across the bed. Scanning hundreds of names on fifty pages of photocopied spreadsheets, she found Tony McCrief. So, who was Sophie Hammond, the mother of his baby, whose date of birth was 15th April 2010? There was no other data apart from her NHS number.

She searched the internet and trawled the main social networks. Dozens of Sophie Hammonds, born when female names had still been allowed.

She navigated to the Somerset House site. Had the new Home Secretary disabled her privileged access yet? She clicked on Births, Marriages and Deaths and drilled down. Yes, she still had permissions to the restricted areas!

But there were no Sophie Hammonds born on 15th April 2010.

Supposing Sophie was married and Hammond was not her maiden name?

She did a further search, this time only for the name Sophie. Eight were born on 15th April 2010. She drilled down to the old NHS number of each one. There was a Sophie who matched!

Evie's heart thudded as she extracted Sophie's personal data. She was born in Manchester. Her two middle names looked strangely familiar. A coincidence, surely? But when she clicked the birth certificate to read the identity of her parents, her blood ran cold……

Peckham, 24th October, 2.30pm

James enjoyed his regular visits to Aidan and Miriam. Miriam's lemon drizzle cake and even the nappy strewn chaos gave him a desperately longed-for taste of reality.

His relationship with Aidan had mellowed from their previous, hostile encounters on social media. Aidan's reproaches about baboons and 'A Parking Ticket to Africa' had long ceased.

Aidan did not endorse James's films, but avoided the subject.   Through evenings of real ale and Colombian roast coffee, he learned that James's first love was the theatre and that he loathed the film industry.

"I'm auditioning for Richard III at the National Theatre, tomorrow."

"But you're too nice, my love!" Exclaimed Miriam.

James immediately transformed himself into a snarling hunchback and Miriam squealed with laughter as he lunged towards her.

Aidan applauded.

"Excellent!"

James reverted to himself and slumped on the sofa.

"It's great to relax. You need a life as well as a career."

"What d'you mean, Aidan?"

"You live alone with a cat."

"It's my escape. I'm perfectly content."

"Don't you want a girlfriend?"

"You can be so blunt, at times!"

"I'm only thinking of your best interests! I know Lucinda's rejection and then her death was devastating. But there are other women out there."

"I wasn't as heartbroken as you think."

Miriam was taken aback.

"What do you mean?"

"I wasn't in love with her."

"Really? But what about Evie? Do you ever think about her?"

"Sometimes. But our lives are so different now. Her world is politics."

"Not now. She's feeling pretty dejected. She'd be glad of some company. She can't hide in Warrington forever."

Warrington, 24th October, 2.30pm

Evie was in turmoil. The revelation of Sophie's identity would cause unimaginable pain.

"I can't face carrying this knowledge in silence," she sighed, "but the Official Secrets Act bans me from telling a living soul."

Communication must be anonymous and untraceable. She grabbed a notepad and scrawled the words:

"DO YOU KNOW SOPHIE HAMMOND"

She tore off the sheet, shoved it into an envelope and addressed it to Ceiba McCrief.   Aidan and Jennifer had told her of that feisty girl's dogged determination to discover the truth.

"So, let's see how sharp you are young madam," murmured Evie "and whether you're astute enough to take this as a hint?"

She checked the train times on her wristphone and frantically grabbed her coat.

"I must to avoid a Warrington postmark!"

Twenty minutes later, she was on a train to Birmingham, to catch the 5.00pm post.

Epping Holding Centre, 24th October, 5.00pm

The fiery furnace of trauma had refined Prema.

She now had a new sense of authority and was at ease with herself and comfortable in her own skin. This poised serenity had replaced the brittle, resolved self-possession she had displayed during her earlier months of imprisonment.

For the first time, Miriam engaged with an equal, as she gazed into those bright brown eyes which reflected a new confidence.

"Do you really want to live, Prema?"

"Of course! I was miraculously given my life back. There must be a reason. I'll leave this earth in God's own time and not before."

"Then tell Gloria everything. You owe her that much."

"Of course."

"Even the painful stuff about Ralph. However bad it was, you're stronger now."

"There's no need for soul-baring. I'll just give her the facts."

"But are you withholding any information, Prema?"

"Leave this to me! And stop the schoolmarm act!"

Miriam's headmistressy retort was interrupted by a rap on the door.

As Frank Southwold entered, Prema extended her hand and smiled at the man who had comforted her with brandy and blankets on execution day.

"Mr Southwold, how good to see you."

"I'm checking up on you, after your ordeal."

"You've been very kind."

"You look amazing, after such a trauma."

"The grace of God, I think!"

Miriam clasped his hand.

"Mr Southwold, no-one's introduced us. But I've heard all about you, through Evie of course. I know you are best mates! "

"Ah, she's a good woman!"

"We love her. Still a bit of a spinster, mind you, but Aidan and I are on her case!"

"Really?" Frank struggled to remain inscrutable.

"Oh yes. We know her ex-boyfriend. James Cardew's a lovely lad and single again! She's lost her job, poor love. She needs a bit of romance! I know she misses him and I think he's pining for her! Watch this space!"

Frank shuffled uneasily. Prema squirmed. She swept across to the kettle, swishing her batik skirt and wafting jasmine perfume. She retrieved a china teapot.

"Earl Grey, Mr Southwold?"

Peckham, 25th October

Post was a rarity in this electronic age.

Gulping a bacon sandwich, with a wriggling baby under one arm, Ceiba was intrigued as she stared at the Birmingham postmark.

"It's not my birthday, or Valentine's day!"

Miriam was preparing baby food. "What's up my love?"

Ceiba tore at the envelope.

"Huh! A piece of blank paper. A sick joke?"

Scrawled across the page were the words:

"DO YOU KNOW SOPHIE HAMMOND?

"Nothing exciting?"

Ceiba shrugged and stuffed the paper into her tracksuit pocket.

"No, a bit of junk mail."

She wandered into the hallway, distracted.

"If Callum has sent this," she muttered "he's got my address!"

She hissed an expletive. An anonymous note was typical of his intimidating behaviour.

"But if it's from Callum," she murmured, "is it about Tony's baby mother? Why else would he write? But who's Sophie Hammond?"

She held baby Landscape closer, breathing the comforting warmth of his soft, shampooed hair. A disturbing thought jolted her.

"Of course, I know a 'Hammond'! But she's not called Sophie."

Ceiba felt sick to the stomach.

"I must check this out," she whispered to the baby "but I can't tell anyone close to her. If she's your mum, Landscape, they'll be wrecked by the news. So, who can help? They'd have to be as desperate to know as I am."

Her brain was addled from sleepless nights and two wakeful toddlers. She gulped her coffee. Another tiring day lay ahead. She never complained about the treadmill her life had become, but she had no energy to think about that message now.

She switched the TV to a channel combining serious news with chit-chat and recipes. She watched an interview with James Cardew, indulging her crush on him, as she remembered the smell of his aftershave.

She had almost fallen asleep, when the news coverage shifted to Gregory Wilson and Prema Gupta. Prema's lawyer was making a statement outside the Greenwich Holding Centre.

"Prema has been given a six-month reprieve and we will fight to clear her name. I can confirm she will stand as a witness at Gregory's trial. She will also be appealing against her own conviction and sentence."

"Of course!! Gloria Baxter!!!"

Ceiba frantically searched the address of Baxter, Baxter & Hobbs, LLB on her wristphone.

Epping Holding Centre, 27th October

Prema was out of sorts this morning.

The euphoria of reprieve had evaporated, as well-wishers dispersed and bouquets of flowers wilted and died, leaving her only with regular visits from Miriam, Gloria and Reeta.

The grey routine of the Epping Holding Centre had closed in on her. Breakfast, exercise, cell, lunch and infuriatingly, the post 'execution' psychotherapy sessions with Fantasy Rimmer.   Fantasy now sported blue-dyed hair, massive pink glasses and half the antique jewellery from Portobello Road Market, thanks to massive fees from the BBC for broadcasting Prema's pre-execution state of mind.

As the countdown to Gregory's trial began and all that lay ahead was either years of incarceration or the execution chamber.

In recent days, a chesty cough had sapped her energy and her mood was further dampened with by a dull stomach ache and the irritable bloatedness of PMT. Her skirt stretched across her bulging waistline. She found herself secretly praying that neither Frank Southwold or any other male visitor would arrive today. Then she hastily banished the thought. Why would she even pray such a thing?

By 11.00am the pain had intensified, twisting sharply into her lower abdomen, as waves of nausea engulfed her.

Was this delayed shock? Her body was allowed to live, so now it had permission to be ill?

She curled up and struggled to distract herself by watching an old movie, The Hunger Games. The heroine, Katniss Everdeen, survived death against all the odds. But each scene seemed to increase the agony radiating through her abdomen.

When had she last been in such torment? She banished harrowing memories, as a rising fever blurred her mind.   She began to cry as red-hot pokers stabbed their way through her intestines. Through delirium she screamed:

"He's dead! He can't hurt me now!"

In utter desperation, she pressed the emergency help button....

Baxter, Baxter & Hobbs, LLB Holborn, 27th October

Ceiba re-applied her pink lipstick and waited in the tastefully refurbished reception at Baxter, Baxter & Hobbs, LLB, her stilettos sinking into the plush carpet. She was determined to look credible. Her eyeliner was black, smudged and heavy, but her blonde hair extensions were tamed into a neat chignon and the black dress from Tony's funeral was appropriate for the ambience.

She tried to look self-assured, as slick lawyers and secretaries strutted around her.

"Ceiba McCrief?"

Gloria Baxter was even more sophisticated than she had imagined. Ceiba was struck by the understated impact of her style. Her neatly tailored grey shift and jacket were complemented with an emerald brooch, diamond stud earrings, designer court shoes and Chanel perfume. Her immaculately cut chestnut hair was expensively coloured and conditioned.

In those few seconds, Ceiba became painfully aware of all she wanted to be, and everything she wasn't. An uncomfortable thought jabbed at her. Surely, the James Cardews of this world preferred women like this?

Gloria surveyed the feisty, weathered creature before her with chapped hands and black hungry eyes with dark, sleepless circles betraying fatigue and survival. Ceiba gazed back at Gloria's perfect skin and steely green eyes. Let business commence.

Gloria ushered her into an oasis of soft, green-leathered upholstery, original watercolour paintings and a water fountain bubbling over multicoloured stones and shards of glass.

"You have some evidence to help me with the case of Prema Gupta?"

"Yeah. If you want to incriminate Ralph Hardcastle!" Ceiba added a few expletives.

Gloria remained impassive. "Ralph Hardcastle's dead."

"Or incriminate the people who worked with him?"

Gloria nodded.

Ceiba handed the scrawled scrap of paper to Gloria.

"So, who is Sophie Hammond?"

Gloria stared at the handwriting.

"Where did you get this?"

"Someone posted it to me anonymously. My brother died in childbirth. I'm trying to find out who his mother is. I think someone wants to tell me it's Sophie Hammond. But who is she?"

Gloria froze as she stared at the name. A knot formed in her stomach. Surely, surely not?

Ceiba began to feel ignored as Gloria turned away in a silence, angry tears pricking her eyes.

"Hardcastle killed my brother!" She shouted.

Gloria's eyes slowly met hers.

"He killed mine, too."

The tension was broken by the ringing of Gloria's wrist phone, accompanied by a red emergency flash.

Gloria answered through her earpiece.

"What? Prema Gupta?? Where is she now?

She glanced back at Ceiba.

"Leave this to me.   I have a major emergency. I must go now!"

Princess Alexandra's Hospital, Harlow, 27th October, 4.00pm

The hospital canteen was a heaving, chaotic nightmare of bad-tempered staff, anxious relatives, crying children, spilled drinks and discarded half-eaten junk food.

As Gloria arrived, Miriam battled to comfort Reeta, while supervising Ceiba's toddlers.

"Appendicitis and peritonitis??"

"She's in a dreadful state poor love. She's in the theatre now. And they've handcuffed her even under anaesthetic!"

Reeta clenched her fist angrily.

"How could they do this to my sister?"

"No client of mine is handcuffed while undergoing surgery!" Cried Gloria.

"She's got blood poisoning and major internal damage. Her insides are a mess. They're not sure she'll make it…."

There was fire in Reeta's eyes.

"She survived the Guillotine. She can't die now!"

"She's due out at 5.00, we must go soon."

Warrington Bank Quay Station, 27th October, 5.30pm

Evie boarded a London train packed with passengers from Glasgow, Carlisle and Preston. There was little privacy, even in First-Class.

Self-pity had been effaced by a ferocious resolve to face life again and return to Parliament.

She glanced at her wrist phone to check the headlines. So, Prema Gupta had been rushed to Harlow Hospital under tight guard? Why had no-one told her? Then she remembered.   She was no longer Home Secretary with a right to know.

The brown envelope lay buried in her case like hidden dynamite.   Whoever had smuggled the data into her red box had now irrevocably changed the life of Sophie Hammond and her loved ones.

The anonymous messenger had also handed her the ammunition to cause a political earthquake and wreak havoc on the establishment.   What had she said to Aidan?

"Unless I do my part to pull my beloved country from this cesspool, I've achieved nothing."

Dared she launch the missile?

She began to relish her secret power, then suddenly felt self-conscious. An elderly lady in the carriage recognised her. Evie smiled politely, then buried herself in a book to avoid conversation as the train pulled away from the safe cocoon of Warrington.

Memories surfaced as night fell on the fields and suburbs of Cheshire flickering past the windows. The clocks had gone back and winter was looming.

Her tightly-fit navy suit reminded her of her old school uniform, when she had been a gauche 11-year-old sent to boarding school for the first time, frightened, vulnerable and waving goodbye to dad on the platform. Tears pricked her eyes. But why such emotion twenty-four years later?

Then she remembered. In 2016 Lucinda had been there to look after her. Who would support her now?

She rebuked herself for feeling so needy. She was tough, talented, resourceful and fully intended to turn her recent downfall to her advantage. She would mine the depth of her being for the reserves she needed.

But she painfully realised her self-made repository of resilience was not enough. A gentle, inaudible voice planted a thought in her mind.

"Pray."

Princess Alexandra's Hospital, Harlow, 27th October, 6.00pm

They huddled together in the cramped relatives room, as the ashen-faced surgeon gazed compassionately at Reeta.

"Your sister is out of the theatre and in intensive care. She has appendicitis, peritonitis and evidence of serious internal injuries inflicted in recent years. She also has sepsis and a very severe chest infection. We've put her on very high doses of antibiotics, but I cannot promise...... you need to prepare yourself. I'm sorry."

Reeta took a deep breath.

"The second time in two weeks! What evil is trying to destroy my sister? They will not succeed!"

Miriam nodded.

"I think you understand, Reeta. *For our struggle is not against flesh and blood, but against the rulers, against the authorities, against the powers of this dark world and against the spiritual forces in the heavenly realms.*"

Gloria and the surgeon looked bemused.

"Where have I heard those words before?" Asked Reeta.

"At Sunday school, maybe? Ephesians Chapter 6."

"We do have a battle on our hands," acknowledged Gloria "even if I don't agree with all your supernatural stuff. Prema must live. If she dies, the truth goes with her."

House of Commons, 28th October

Evie sat resolutely in the House of Commons bar, refusing to be fazed by the mocking or even sympathetic looks of fellow MPs.

She sipped a diet coke and focused on her papers. It was only 12 noon, three hours before Question Time. A man shuffled into the seat opposite her. She kept her head down.

"Mind if I join you?"

The smell of pipe tobacco was familiar. It was Vernon Stack, Leader of the Opposition.

Evie shrugged and gave a half smile.

"To what do I owe this pleasure, Vernon?"

Vernon placed two huge glasses of red wine on the table.

"I thought you might enjoy something stronger."

Evie sipped appreciatively.

"A lady never refuses a fine Chianti, even from her fiercest opponent!"

"I'll skip the 'how are you' claptrap and cut to the chase. Orchard Mayhew has shot himself in the foot!"

"I'm in the wilderness, Vernon. Enjoying it, are you?"

"I miss our exchanges at the Despatch Box, though your departure makes life easier for me! Frankly, you were always more fearsome than him!"

"A compliment indeed, from my adversary!"

"I'm not doing myself any favours by telling you this, but you realise you could bring him down?"

"There's the small matter of getting the Tory Independence party on the side of a lame duck!"

"They're supporting a lame duck Prime Minister. The miserable lot need you! You're the best of that motley crew, though I despise everything you stand for. Your minority Government has lost two seats, following the Parrot nonsense of Oliver Bunton and the death of old Madge Ridley."

"So, you smell blood? A vote of No Confidence in the Government? You'd love that, wouldn't you Vernon? A snap election and Labour almost certainly back in power?"

"But wouldn't you love it, too, Evie? The fall of Orchard Mayhew? A party leadership election? And you a prime candidate, with your popularity ratings?"

"Chancellor David Reefe will throw his hat in the ring. And I'd be up against Chawton Holland, if he decides to fight from the back benches and come back to power! He's even more unscrupulous than you!"

"Forget that loathsome toad"

Evie savoured the expensive wine, as it warmed through her.

"You would need a convincing reason to propose a Vote of No Confidence."

"Have you asked yourself why Chawton Holland suddenly crashed out of the Cabinet?"

"You know something, Vernon?"

"What do you know, Evie?"

Evie's thoughts turned to the brown envelope.

Do business with her adversary? There were worse allies than Vernon Stack....

Princess Alexandra's Hospital, Harlow, 28th October, 3.00pm

Prema's eyes registered recognition as Reeta and Miriam clasped her hands. Her matted hair had soaked the pillow and her grey complexion was beaded with perspiration. She was sprawled in a tangle of tubes and saline drip.

As her white blood cell count soared, she hovered between life and death.

There was no privacy. Warders sat either side of the bed and a Police officer stood by the door. The handcuffs had been removed and Reeta constantly glared at the three intruders, daring them to impose any kind of restraint.

10 Downing Street, 28th October, 5.00pm

The tension was unbearable.

"Any more news, Style?"

Orchard Mayhew was flushed, sweaty, agitated and irritable. When the Prime Minister was in this kind of mood, Style Hobbs began to wish he still worked for his old mistress.

"Nothing Prime Minister."

"I didn't expect Evie back in London so soon. I thought she'd stay up north till Christmas, licking her wounds. Instead, she's swanning round Westminster. If we're not careful, disgruntled backbenchers will start sniffing around her. She'll be setting up court with her own entourage."

"Evie's yesterday's news. You're in a better position now. No execution and your public approval ratings are up. The threat of a Welsh Referendum has receded."

Orchard refused to be placated.

"And is Prema Gupta still alive? She's been lingering in intensive care since yesterday. I'll have one less headache when she's gone."

"But you reprieved her, Prime Minister."

Orchard was silent for a moment, then a cruel smirk registered on his bloated, boyish face.

"Yes, Style, funny you should mention that. I reprieved her. And why do you think that was?"

"To stop the Welsh Independence Referendum, hide the embarrassment of a so-called 'technical hitch' and convince the public that you're more merciful than Evie Atherton."

"So that's your understanding, Style? Are you sure?"

Something in Orchard's manner suddenly made him extremely uneasy.

"Of course. Why else?"

Orchard sank back into his chair and stared at Style in silence for a full minute. Style struggled to hold his gaze.

"Let's revisit the morning of the execution, when you gained unauthorised access to the Home Office intranet system and changed the Guillotine authorisation codes?"

Style felt his stomach lurch.

"I told you before. She bullied me. She was very aggressive."

"Were you really so scared of her? Perhaps you were keeping your options open, by doing a favour to your old mistress?"

"I've already told you, I…."

"You have a habit of hacking into computer systems, don't you Style?"

"What do you mean?"

"Someone has tampered with a very confidential area of the Secretary of State for Health's restricted intranet site."

"I've never touched it!"

The door clicked open. Out of the corner of his eye, Style saw two security men enter the room.

"It was nothing to do with me!" He shouted.

"Clear your desk now, hand in your security pass and leave this office forever by 5.30pm."

Lewisham, 29th October

A dying summer sun refracted final shards of golden light through the almost-bare oak, pear and chestnut trees. Amelia had been blowing dead leaves from the path, pruning branches for a bonfire and mowing the lawn one last time before the oppressive grey smog of winter closed in on South East London.

Amelia had not returned to work after maternity leave. Dave's lucrative Government salary for 'classified' rehabilitation work allowed her to enjoy motherhood away from the relentless treadmill at Baxter, Baxter & Hobbs, LLB in Holborn.

Gloria had been painfully disappointed to begin with, facing isolation among hard-headed colleagues with whom she had little in common. But outside work, their friendship had matured from office banter to a solid sisterhood.

With Amelia, she never had to pretend. Such safe transparency was a precious rarity since the death of her brother. Indeed, the vivacious, uncomplicated, straight-talking Amelia never allowed her to dissemble.

Amelia emptied the mowed grass onto the compost heap, as she heard the familiar clacking of Gloria's heels on the footpath.

"Hi Gloria, my old mucker. What's eating you? You've got a face like a camel."

Gloria was pensive and unusually pale.

"Gloria, put your briefcase down, kick off your shoes and fix us some coffee."

Gloria was in no mood for levity.

"I need to talk."

"Yeah, sorry mate. I know you've had a rough couple of days. Any more news on Prema?"

"Slight improvement today, but she's not looking good."

Amelia scraped two rusty garden chairs onto the patio.

"Gloria, you did your bit to save her."

"But if she dies now, the truth will go with her. And people like Ralph Hardcastle will carry on killing men and women."

"Women? I thought he got men pregnant. Hundreds of them, by the sound of it!"

"The Surgeon told me Prema has even worse problems than peritonitis. There were dozens of old injuries in her abdomen. Her body's a time bomb. I'm surprised she survived the rigours of trial and prison."

"Old abdominal injuries?"

"And I suspect she's not the only woman. A young man died in childbirth earlier this year, you remember Tony McCrief?"

"Ceiba's brother. That was awful."

"Someone's anonymously given me the name of the baby's mother"

"And Prema must survive, so you can talk to her?"

There was a strange look in Gloria's eyes.

"No, Amelia I need to talk to you."

A terror began to rise in Amelia's throat.

"Or maybe I should use your full name - Amelia Miriam Sophie Hammond?"

Amelia froze in her chair.

"How long have you known?"

"Just a few days."

"And how much information do you have?"

"Only that you were the egg donor. But there's more, isn't there?"

Amelia nodded silently, fiercely fighting back her tears.

"Please take your time. But we've never had any secrets, have we, apart from this?"

In a total daze, Amelia staggered into the kitchen, to make a black coffee. Gloria followed her.

Amelia sank into the sofa, armed with caffeine.

"Dave and I were desperate for kids. For two years I struggled to get pregnant. We went for tests. We were frantically saving for surgery on my fallopian tubes and fertility drugs, now the Health Trust no longer provide them. We had no private insurance and no company would treat a pre-existing condition.

Then I met Midwife Gregory Wilson at the fertility clinic. He said he knew someone who could help me. He introduced me to Ralph Hardcastle. They promised me free fertility treatment, in return for...."

Amelia struggled to compose herself.

"In return for what?" Probed Gloria, as gently as she could.

"I had to sign a contract allowing them to harvest my eggs for a year, at first. For the Government Male Pregnancy scheme. And they did other experiments and took tissue from my ovaries, fallopian tubes and uterus. A year of relentless hormone treatment and surgery. But at the end of the contract, they asked me to extend it for another two years. And when I refused...."

"They forced you?"

"And they blackmailed me and threatened to disclose Dave's transspecies rehabilitation job to my dad."

"They pretended to relent. They gave me an appointment to repair my fallopian tubes, but when I came for my pre-surgical clinical appointment, they drugged me up, they......"

Amelia buried her face in the cushion.

"Amelia, you had a bowel operation four months ago, after you'd had your baby."

"They took my uterus. I signed away my womb. It was part of the deal. That's why I can't have any more children."

Gloria wrapped her arms around her, interspersing words of comfort with furious expletives.

xviii) Bring him down

Portcullis House, Westminster, 1st November

The Adjournment Restaurant at Portcullis House offered exquisite cuisine and polished waiter service. Only the best would do for today's piece of networking.

As the lamb shanks and petits pois arrived, Evie eyed up her quarry.

Her guest was Veracity Dunmore, MP for Basildon, Essex, a marginal Tory Independence seat. A petite, vivacious, blonde rising star with a down-to earth Thames Estuary twang, a common touch and a sharp mind. Four years younger than Evie, she was beginning to make her mark, though she was still unrefined and as yet, lacked the gravitas of a stateswoman.

Veracity was also the former Parliamentary Under Secretary of State for Health. Following Chawton Holland's fall, she had been reshuffled to the post of Under Secretary for Education.

In a year or two, she would be a serious thorn in Evie's side, but for now Evie intended to maintain control. It was time to bluff.

"Veracity, I know exactly why Chawton Holland resigned so quickly."

Veracity was silent as she poured the redcurrant sauce over her meat. Evie held her breath. Would this baby snapper in the pool bite?

Veracity sighed.

"Yes. The Observian story was about to break."

"So, putting it crudely, the Editor had Orchard Mayhew by the….!"

"Yes, Erica Rayleigh blackmailed Orchard, the night before Prema Gupta's scheduled execution. She pushed for a stay of execution and also demanded that either Holland resigned, or she would publish the entire scandal. And she proved she had all the documents. The entire dirty linen basket of Orchard and Chawton's involvement."

"So, she demanded Chawton Holland's head on a plate and Prema's reprieve buried some very damaging news?"

"Oh yes, his resignation was totally eclipsed by the stay of execution. The headlines were focused on Orchard's merciful decision and Britain's escape from a Welsh referendum! The Observian played ball, of course! Even though Erica Rayleigh now appears to have resigned and vanished into thin air!"

"It would seem the world remains ignorant that Orchard Mayhew sanctioned Chawton's involvement in the kidnapping, drugging and butchering of hundreds of women. Some of them were criminals hoping for a shorter sentence, some of those poor wretches were promised housing and benefits...."

".... And others were lured by their desperation for fertility treatment." Added Veracity.

Evie pushed a chunk of sauté potato around her plate and gazed intently into Veracity's kohl-lined grey eyes.

"Orchard has to go. This Government must go. And it has to be done by us. By our party."

"Exposure? Scandal? A vote of No Confidence?"

"Yes."

"That would mean a snap election. Political suicide. We could lose. And I have a marginal seat, it's OK for you, you're sitting on an 8,000 majority!"

"If we do nothing and stand by him, we'll be tainted by association. Now that would be real political suicide, especially for you, Veracity. You were Chawton's Under-Secretary. You knew about it."

"I was not directly involved. And I hated every minute of working with him."

"The public won't believe that, unless you make a stand and disassociate yourself. Your career depends on it."

"But how can you persuade The Observian to let the cat out of the bag? Orchard delayed the execution, giving them what they want for now. They'll await a better occasion, to suit their own agenda and timing."

"Other papers may be sympathetic. The time is ripe. Labour's shifting to the right. The Times is wearying of Orchard's obsession with media and youth culture. Vernon Stack has been wooing the Financial Services sector with a very aggressive champagne offensive. They're starting to like his views on investment in declining industrial communities. And we can always rely on the Daily Mirror to throw a grenade at us!"

"And who will launch this nuclear missile?"

A slow smile spread across Evie's face.

"I'm not stupid, Evie. I know full well you'll stand for the party leadership. What's in it for me?

"Education Secretary."

"I'll only be Shadow Education Secretary if it goes belly-up."

"Take it or leave it. I'm giving you a chance to disassociate yourself from Chawton Holland. So, are you with me?"

"I guess so. Your only serious rivals are Harper Sykes, now he's replaced you at the Home Office and David Reefe, the Chancellor. But I won't be joining him. There's the small matter of Treasury funds hemorrhaging into the Male Birth Programme through the back door. Now if that could be leaked into the public domain...!"

Evie was laughing now. Veracity Dunmore was singing like a bird!

Baxter, Baxter & Hobbs, 2nd November

Gloria had taken control of the situation.

Baby Landscape's biological origin must be disclosed on neutral territory.

"Amelia, your privacy is protected by law. You're not obliged to say anything to Ceiba, Aidan or Miriam. Under the Official Secrets Act and Data Protection law, you're not even supposed to know yourself. The information came to Ceiba and me illegally. Only DNA testing can officially confirm the truth, though in reality we know."

"I want to face the music myself." Amelia had insisted.

"I'm not afraid of Ceiba. Well OK, actually I'm terrified, but determined to do it anyway. And I must tell mum and dad that Landscape is their grandson."

"Amelia, this matter will be covered by family law, once DNA testing gives official proof. You're all entitled to legal representation, even if you don't choose me. I'm not a family lawyer, but I can, in the simplest terms, give you basic information on your rights."

So now, Amelia and Dave braced themselves in Gloria's office, awaiting the arrival of the others.

Ceiba strode purposefully into the room first, with baby Lakeside. As soon as she clocked Amelia, she glanced at Gloria and nodded

"Yeah. I knew it." She refused to look at Amelia, as they sat in chilling silence. Dave wrapped a protective arm round his wife.

Ten minutes later, Aidan and Miriam arrived.

"Ceiba, Amelia and Dave! What are you doing here?" Cried Miriam.

"I thought this was about Prema's case," added Aidan "what's up?"

"The information I'm about to give you is linked to Prema's appeal," acknowledged Gloria, "but there are other developments closer to home. You must prepare yourselves for some difficult news."

She drew a deep breath.

****

Aidan held Amelia tightly in his arms.

"You nearly died, two years ago, when you had Sepsis. And I never knew why you became so ill."

"Dave and I were afraid to tell you."

"But we would have helped and sent you to a private clinic. We've got savings. We'd do anything for you. Why, did you do this? You've betrayed everything we stood for. "

"You were struggling to buy the house in Peckham," sobbed Amelia, "you'd lost your Bishopric and you were going through a dreadful time. I couldn't make things worse for you."

"You didn't have to put yourself in the hands of Ralph Hardcastle and his cronies."

"In the end, they forced and blackmailed me."

Dave gave her a warning glare, terrified she would blurt out his occupation.

"I can't discuss why, but I became more and more trapped."

"They could have killed you."

"I know. And if I'd breathed a word, they would have murdered me."

"Ralph Hardcastle would have murdered my daughter. I'm glad he's dead! Let him rot, him and his filthy crew!!"

"Dad, please forgive me...... for everything."

"It's them I blame, not you. You're safe with me now, Amelia. I never want to let go of you again. But I wish I could have protected you. Why didn't you let me? My little girl...."

"I wanted to give you a grandchild."

"But not at such a price!"

Amelia was silent for a few moments, buried in her father's arms.

"Dad, from now on, I'll do whatever it takes to destroy these people."

Then she turned to Ceiba.

"Ceiba, I know you hate my guts right now. But I hope, one day, you can forgive me for my part in Tony's death."

Ceiba scowled ferociously.

"You ain't having Lakeside, ever! I don't want him anywhere near you! He's mine! Mine and Norma's! I don't care what those DNA tests say. I'll fight you through every court in the country. And Aidan and Miriam – you ain't having him either!"

Amelia sighed.

"Ceiba, this isn't about custody. I don't want Lakeside. Or any of the other babies I've been forced to mother. Dozens, probably."

"I don't know how you sleep at night!" Snarled Ceiba.

"I don't sleep Ceiba, if it makes you feel any better. I'm on sleeping tablets, anti-depressants, beta-blockers, every chemical to block my brain from the dead fathers and motherless orphans I've helped to create."

"Poor you!" Said Ceiba sarcastically.

"And then there's the daily torment of acting normal," cried Amelia, "playing the loving, happy daughter! Being a vivacious, lively friend and even a jokey, up-together ex colleague. Yes Gloria, I've even put on an act around you!"

Miriam turned to Ceiba.

"You desperately wanted the truth, Ceiba, my love. Unfortunately, if we get what we want, we don't always like it."

"But now I have to live with this horror and with you, knowing that Lakeside is your flesh and blood!"

"We don't want to take him away from you. You're his mum. You've fed, clothed and nursed him from birth. And he's Norma's grandson."

Gloria gazed compassionately at the exhausted Amelia.

"This won't be a custody case. We've done enough for today, so let's finish for now. But Amelia, there's another matter Miriam and I want to discuss with you."

**Princess Alexandra's Hospital, Harlow,
3rd November, 3.00pm**

A wheelchair clattered along the bustling hospital corridor.

Prema was almost unrecognisable. Still in danger and on a high-dependency ward, her broken body shivered through the draughty passageway. With a grey, bloated complexion and lank hair, she was wrapped in warm pullovers and a thermally-padded bath robe over a hospital gown and furry slippers.

A nurse carried the IV drip as Miriam pushed the chair to the pastel-furnished visitor's room.

The consultant had insisted Prema was far too ill for this meeting, but Gloria was terrified that if she died, every hope of this conversation would vanish forever. She had also convinced the consultant that Prema's defence case depended on it.

"Both you and I are fighting to save her life," she had insisted, "and I do not trust Mayhew's six-month stay of execution. They could reinstate her death sentence at any moment, especially if she survives this illness!"

Aidan, Amelia and Gloria waited for them. Two warders and a policeman were stationed outside the room.

"Prema my love, meet my husband Aidan."

Aidan gently took her hand.

"It's an honour to meet you at last."

But he was shocked by her appearance and immediately wrapped his anorak around her shoulders.

Prema noticed how tightly Miriam clasped Amelia's arm.

"And this is my daughter, Amelia."

Amelia was tense and ashen-faced, but her uncomplicated warmth and spirit still radiated out of her vibrant, blue eyes as she gripped Prema's clammy hand. Prema felt an immediate trust and bond with her.

"Prema, I think you're the bravest woman in the world. Straight up. I can't believe those idiots wanted to kill you. I could never have faced that Guillotine, I'd have been a screaming wreck. Respect to you!"

Prema smiled faintly and her chest rattled as she gave a croaking whisper.

"Didn't enjoy the experience myself!"

"And I'm sorry about your dreadful illness. What a nightmare, eh? I'm glad you're on the mend."

"It's been grim. I'm still very rough."

Amelia moved to pull her chair beside Prema.

"Prema, I desperately need to talk to you. I've suffered the same way as you. Sepsis and all the other stuff, two years ago. Some evil people did terrible things to me and I think you've been through the same. Please can we talk? I... I think it would help us both."

Gloria discreetly led Miriam and Aidan out of the room.

Crystal Palace Park, 5th November, 4.30pm

A swirl of dark brown leaves caught around their legs, as they strolled through the damp fog. At 4.30 on Bonfire Night, dusk approached and they heard the distant explosion of early fireworks.

James and Evie had intended to meet, ever since Miriam had insisted on reuniting them. Her incessant 'heart to hearts' with each of them, had finally broken their resistance and the fear, pride and vulnerability underpinning it. James took the first step. Partly to silence Miriam but driven by an almost unbearable desperation. For months, he had mentally rehearsed ways to contact her – then berated himself for procrastination.

He contrived to make the phone call light-hearted.

"Let's catch up while I'm still unemployed!"

In a coffee shop in Crystal Palace, they kept the banter flowing, despite initial nerves. Old jokes were resurrected.

"I'll never forget that day Oliver Bunton laid a Parrot egg!"

They laughed raucously, disturbing customers around them.

"Evie you'll get both of us carted off in a Humanity arrest van!!"

James's mirth made him splutter his coffee, as Evie's giggling fits held their deeper issues at bay.

"I've read the rumours about you in The Times and Daily Mail!" Chuckled James.

"Rumours, dear friend?!"

"Apparently, you're schmoozing with Tory Independence backbenchers, these days!"

"Schmoozing is for showbiz, James, that's your department!"

"But the Daily Mail reckon you'll stage a coup and go for the Party Leadership!"

"Little old me? Don't believe all you read in the right-wing tabloids! I'm a defunct backbencher, now! A political has-been!"

"What about the Opinion Poll in the Telegraph? 60% of voters think you'd make a better Prime Minister than Orchard Mayhew!"

"Oh, typical midterm blues! Orchard's safe. He got a standing ovation at the Party Conference in October. I only got a polite ripple of applause!"

"You're plotting something Evie. I know you! I recognise that twinkle in your eyes when you're scheming. You never say die. There's a fire in your belly and it will burn in Westminster for decades to come!"

"Plotting, James?!"

"It is Guy Fawkes night! The gunpowder plot! What kind of explosion are you planning?"

"So, what's your next film?" Laughed Evie, changing the subject. "Will we see you as a trans-species reindeer, romancing Santa in a Christmas special?"

As the café manager glared at them, they left to take a stroll and James sensed their repertoire of superficial conversation was exhausted.

They walked into Crystal Palace Park past the Stadium and the ready-made arena, where spectators were arriving for a huge firework display.

As Evie slipped on the brown sludge of fallen leaves on the muddy pathway, James swiftly caught her. She quickly regained her balance, but he hesitated before disengaging his arm from her waist.

There was a long, pregnant silence before he drew deep breath.

"I've found life really strange without you. It's been a long time."

"Me too."

Another pause.

"This is the best afternoon I've had in months. We must do it again soon and...."

"Yes. As mates."

"As mates?" His tone was wounded.

Evie sighed.

"James, it's no good. You chose Lucinda and she dumped you. "

"But......"

"It's only four months since she died. You must grieve properly and taking up with your ex is not the way to do it. We're close friends. I can even be a shoulder to cry on. But I won't let you chew me up and spit me out again."

"But Evie, it's all lies. She didn't dump me, I dumped her!"

"But I thought she broke your heart."

"I let people think that because she insisted, and to spare her feelings I went along with it."

"You really dumped her? Why?"

"We had nothing in common. After six weeks, I realised it was physical attraction and nothing else. We soon exhausted that and had little else to talk about. She was the warmest, kindest person on this planet. But she wasn't brain of Britain. Oh, she was so confident. She could impress anyone. But there was nothing if you scratched below the surface."

"And that's what you thought of her?"

"All her campaigning and demonstrating was the adolescent posturing of a rebel without a cause. But when I probed and questioned her beliefs, I realised just how shallow and inconsistent her ideas were. She hated it when I challenged her, because I exposed the narrow-minded bigotry behind her so-called humanitarian views. We fell out several times, before we split."

"I see. There was no meeting of minds?"

"She wasn't my soulmate. It just made me appreciate what I had with you. She made me realise I can do without sex appeal, good looks, skinny figure, charm, elegance and good breeding."

Anger suddenly burned inside Evie and her green, heavily made-up eyes flashed with rage, as she cried.

"So that's what you think of me? A woman with no beauty, charm, elegance or breeding?"

"Of course not! I think I love you."

"You think you love me? While insulting me in every possible way? How dare you!"

"But I didn't mean it like that, what I'm saying is I don't need...."

"You've said enough. I don't need a pathetic excuse of a man who sees me as a compromise. I haven't sat there like some needy wimp hankering after you, these past months. I don't need you."

"Evie, please...."

"Sort out your own life, face your own issues. Don't come whingeing after me, because I don't want to see you again. Goodbye."

And with that, she stomped into the dusk and descending mist, until James stood alone under the damp, icy dripping of a gnarled tree shedding its dead leaves, as dusk turned to darkness and the smell of gunpowder and explosions of fireworks enjoyed by families, lovers and friends intensified the pain of his isolation.

He didn't move for an hour. The cold gnawed into his bones, his jacket became saturated and he didn't care. He wanted to feel cold discomfort and the inertia of his frozen, sterile life.

Where was there to go? He had scaled the heights his acting ambition and found it vacuous, fickle and meaningless. As for that Bafta, he just wanted to smash it to pieces.

He had loved two of the most famous, beautiful and talented women in England. Now his life was empty. Let him get pneumonia, nothing mattered.

Suddenly, he jumped as something rubbed against his legs. The moonlight picked out green eyes and red fur. He tensed, sensing a presumptuous or even aggressive fox. Then a familiar meow pushed out a repressed tear, as the soft ginger coat and purr signalled that a devoted little cat had found him half a mile from his home.

Harlow Hospital, 5th November, 6.00pm

"Do these warders never leave?" Snapped Amelia.

"I'm a dangerous prisoner," whispered Prema with a wry smile "so I've got used to it."

Amelia opened a vacuum-bag and pulled out a Chinese takeaway.

"You need some serious grub!"

"Thanks! I need a serious makeover too. I'm ashamed of the state I'm in!"

"You're no oil painting, but I looked a worse mess than you, two years ago."

As Amelia served the food, they exchanged glances, each seeing mirrored in the eyes of the other, the shadows of unspeakable trauma. With steroid-induced hunger pangs, Prema devoured her chow mein.

As Amelia wrestled with her chopsticks, Prema noticed a small scar across the back of her hand.

"Did they hold you down and drug you?"

"Yes."

"And they did experiments and tissue removal, as well as the eggs?

"Yes."

"Ralph and his cohorts, I take it?"

"Of course. And they forced me to sign away my uterus, ovaries, everything…. I went through the operation a few months after my baby was born. They blackmailed me into silence, of course. I take it they did the same to you?

Prema hesitated, then nodded.

"Why did you say nothing at the trial, Prema?"

"The shame and the fear. I thought they'd kill me even before the guillotine, if I dared speak out. I didn't care if I died. But I was frightened about the manner of my death. Their associates have access anywhere and they're capable of anything."

Vauxhall, 5th November, 7.00pm

Evie channeled her anger into furious activity, as she hammered out electronic messages and scrawled her way through papers in her Red Box.

Her fury was mostly at herself, for daring to hope.

She had weakened this afternoon. It would not happen again. She would now focus on the one constant bedrock in her life.   Like the Mersey tide it would ebb and flow, rise and fall, but it was in her veins and her hunger for power would rage long after James, or any other man, ceased to matter.

Another ghost had begun to surface. As her feelings of remorse faded, the Leviathan of hatred for Lucinda had broken its chains and surged in her being once again, intent on overturning and extinguishing the forgiveness she had chosen two weeks before.

So, Lucinda had died a pathetic wreck? She would become the greatest stateswoman in British history!

A Bible still lay on her coffee table, but the coffee-stained notes dated 28th October remained unturned since the last day she had prayed.

She refilled a glass of whiskey to deaden her emotions and power her through the long night ahead. It was bonfire night. Let the Palace of Westminster be afraid!

When the silence was rudely shattered by her intercom buzzer, she slammed down her papers angrily and dragged herself to the entry phone.

"Aidan?"

She would have sent anyone else packing, even Frank. But Aidan's quiet authority trumped even that of her drinking companion.

"To what do I owe the pleasure?"

"I've interrupted your Jack Daniels and paperwork, so I assume it's not a pleasure! Miriam will join us later – she's with Prema. We don't want to neglect you!"

"So, I'm a pastoral case now, am I Bishop?"

"We keep an eye on you, young lady!   I'll have a coffee, by the way."

"Sorry Aidan, I'm a useless host. Pressure of work!"

"Pressure? I thought you'd retired to constituency affairs! Unless the rumours are true?"

"Rumours?"

"The Radio 4 Politics Show think you're trying to topple Orchard Mayhew! And the gossip columns tell of your wining, dining and scheming in Westminster!"

"I'm surprised you trust those rags, ex-Bishop!"

"I don't underestimate you, Evie"

Aidan's clear grey eyes seemed to pierce her very soul.

"Orchard is an incompetent lowlife who became PM with the help of his Etonian cronies. He's on his way out, Aidan, with or without my help!"

"Two weeks ago, you told me of your longing for the top job."

Evie's cheeks burned and she felt the blotches rising on her neck. Aidan was deceptively mild mannered and yet he could deliver a lethal blow with pinpoint accuracy.

"So I did."

"And now your scarlet, manicured fingers are stretching for the prize!"

"Would you blame me?"

"No, but if your hunger for power eclipses the first flush of your love for God, I'll start to worry about you."

"Don't worry your holy head. I'm still on regular speaking terms with the Almighty!"

"Regular, young lady? Your last conversation with Him was on 28th October!"

"Are you psychic?"

"No, I looked at your coffee table."

"I don't need this heavy stuff!"

"Can I speak frankly with you? You're a very young believer and alone in a dangerous environment. If you wade into the quagmire of power without God, the piranha pool of Westminster will corrupt, swallow and destroy you."

"I can look after myself, Aidan, I'm not a little choir girl."

"You're not just dealing with human beings, Evie. There are dark, invisible forces stalking the corridors of power.

If you take one step at a time, obeying God and listening to the Holy Spirit, I know you'll be in a good place. But if you step outside God's covering and walk in selfishness, disobedience and hardness of heart, you'll lay yourself open to powers you cannot deal with alone."

Evie leapt up angrily.

"How dare you lecture me, you pompous old dinosaur! I don't need a sermon! You have come uninvited this evening and now you lay this stuff on me!"

"I'm sorry if I sounded heavy, Evie. I may be an old relic, but I want the best for you and hold you in high esteem.

When we first met you, I realised you're a remarkable woman. I believe you could be one of the greatest people England's ever produced and a powerful influence for good in this decaying nation."

"Well you've never said that before."

"I mean it. But I also see how vulnerable that makes you. If God raises you up, it will not go unchallenged by the enemy of your soul.

Remember David in the Old Testament. He was a great King, but he committed adultery with a woman called Bathsheba and the consequences affected his nation for many generations."

Evie fidgeted and swirled the whiskey around her glass.

"And I don't want you to suffer the way I did. If you stand up for what's right, you'll need to be totally dependent on God. I experienced the lion's den first hand, in the House of Lords.

I was besieged with people who knifed and backstabbed me. They wanted to break and destroy me. I became paralyzed by fear, loneliness, self-doubt, loss of confidence and I thought I was going mad.

I was surrounded by sycophants and false friends. Everyone seems to love you, except Orchard and his cronies. But sooner or later they'll turn against you."

"So, what do I do?"

"Each day is a fresh battle. Submit your plans to God. Ask for His guidance. And keep listening to the promptings of the Holy Spirit. Don't take your eyes off Jesus and continually check your heart and attitudes. Never let grudges take root in your heart. And most of all, remember you're a public servant whose decisions affect millions of people. Stay focused on serving others, not yourself."

Evie quietly nodded, quietly lost in thought as she made coffee.

Many years later, she would repeat Aidan's words at his funeral, when giving his eulogy. This was a conversation she would never forget.

"And how are Miriam and family?"

Aidan drew a deep breath.

"That's the other thing I need to talk to you about."

Battersea, 5th November, 8.00pm

Oliver Bunton, the former Speaker of the House of Commons, now known as 'Pickles the Parrot', was a miserable, wretched sight.

In Transmutation Unit 65, a high-security, windowless concrete block in Battersea, he sat in a massive iron cage with plastic toys, bells, a seed tray and cuttlefish, struggling to keep his balance with claw-like hands on a soiled wooden perch.

Green and red feathers sprouted from his neck, hair and stubbled face, intermingled with the moustache and beard which his human DNA was still growing. His eyebrows and eyelashes had disappeared and his eyes had grown larger and bulged over his shrunken nose and mouth which was gradually transforming into an orange beak.

The final DNA transfer would take place in 4 weeks' time, but he was now receiving intensive genetic, drug and hormone treatment and his body changes had accelerated over the last 12 days.

At this stage, he was mildly sedated – enough to make him pliable and stress-free, but the dosage was increasing daily and he would be almost comatose the week before his final surgery.

He had an unwelcome visitor. Fantasy Rimmer, Consultant Psychotherapist, sat beside him on a specially constructed seat on the perch.

Her bright orange smock, long patterned skirt and huge purple-rimmed glasses made a colourful compliment to her strange client. But she was totally ill-at-ease at being locked with 'Pickles' in the stinking, dingy cage.

In her mid-Atlantic drawl, she struggled to delve into the soul which would soon cease to exist.

"So, Pickles, when did you first begin to realise you were a Parrot trapped in a human body?"

She flinched as Pickles responded with an aggressive screech, irate at being asked the same infuriating questions he'd answered months ago.

"I tellya before!! Squawk!! Gwadually!"

"Gradually? But how did it start?"

"My mother and father! They had a parrot! Screech!"

"So, you looked at that parrot and recognised your true identity?"

"No!! Waaaak!!! My mother and father didn't love me! Didn't want me. I was their fifth child!"

"Ah, childhood rejection."

Pickles screeched in exasperation, wondering how this shallow woman had ever become a consultant with such entry-level observations.

"But they loved the parrot! Waaaak! Adored it! Parrot was given everything! I always wanted to be that parrot!"

"So, your parents loved their parrot more than you. To them, that parrot was their true child. Do you know what that means? Your parents were parrots themselves. Repressed parrots, who never admitted their true identity.

You're therefore the offspring of two parrots, making you in every sense, a parrot. But you're braver than your mother and father were. You have the courage to shed your false human body and live as your true species."

"Squaawk!"

"Let's have a high five to celebrate your courage!"

But in lifting the scaly claws twisted around gnarled fingers, Pickles collapsed from his perch and into the seed tray. An angry flurry of matted, feathered limbs scattered the seed.

"Squaawk! Aarrk!! Could murder a curry! I want a curry!"

"Pickles, you can't have a curry. That's a false human craving. Embrace the seed as your true food!"

Vauxhall, 5th November, 8.30pm

Evie shook her head in horror. Miriam poured a strong coffee, as Aidan broke down and wept bitterly.

"They did this to our daughter! My little girl!"

"Why did neither of you tell me before?"

"We've only just found out!"

For the last half hour, with a breaking voice, Aidan had shared the horror of Amelia's ordeal. Miriam was beyond tears, having channeled all her emotional energy into being strong for Amelia. But Aidan was still utterly tormented by his failure to protect his child, albeit unknowingly.

The colour drained from Evie's face, as she registered the pain, humiliation, fear and trauma which Amelia had endured, along with Prema and hundreds of other women. Volunteers supposedly helping with 'pioneering treatment', struggling students, convicted prisoners hoping for a shorter sentence and women desperate for fertility treatment which a financially stretched Health Trust no longer paid for.

For months that ominous brown envelope had glowered at her from among her papers. Now the victims were no longer names on spreadsheets, but living, breathing, broken human beings, with scars, ongoing pain and recurrent nightmares.

Now she faced the brutal, visceral reality of Ralph Hardcastle's practice, under the regime of Chawton Holland and with the collusion of Orchard.

"Evie, this must remain in strictest confidence."

"Of course, Miriam, but I feel sick! I'm so sorry, I don't know what to say. And all this time, your biological grandson has lived in your house?"

"And he has my nose. How could I not recognise I'm his grandmother?"

"Aidan, I'm sorry for being stroppy earlier. I had no idea what you've both been going through."

Aidan's sobbing subsided, but now trembled with rage.

"I always loathed Ralph Hardcastle. Now I want to kill him with my bare hands! But he's dead and I can't! I'm sorry Evie, I feel a hypocrite. There I am preaching about not having grudges or bitterness. Yet I'm a seething mass of hate!"

"I'm ashamed to be part of the Government that sanctions this. I always quietly halted the Male Birth Incentive Scheme, but now......."

"But surely my love, your Government had no idea what Hardcastle was really up to?

Evie looked nervously at Miriam. But a quiet prompting in her heart urged her to speak.

"I need to say something in strictest confidence."

"Is it worse than we thought?"

"I knew nothing till recently. But someone's given me evidence that the Prime Minister knew."

Aidan's grey eyes burned into Evie's

"Bring him down! Him and this vile, evil Government! With my blessing! But whatever you do, stay accountable to God!"

Battersea, 5th November, 8.45pm

Fantasy Rimmer was desperate to escape the filthy, dingy, cage and the company of her hideous, cantankerous client.

Blood streamed down her hand from the ferocious peck Oliver Bunton (or Pickles) had given her earlier. She scribbled a reminder on her notepad to a) get a tetanus jab and b) recommend that Pickles received stronger sedation.

As her usual breathing and mindfulness techniques failed her, she strongly resisted the urge to press the 'help' button before the psychotherapy session ended. But fear of displaying weakness or professional incompetence kept her seated firmly on the perch.

She was unspeakably relieved when a warder, accompanied by two Police Officers arrived with jangling keys.

"Sorry to interrupt your session, Ms Rimmer."

"No worries Warder, we're done!"

"The Police need to speak with Mr Bunton."

"Pickles the Parrot, if you don't mind!"

With that prim rebuke, she hastily jumped from the perch, gathered her briefcase and made a hasty exit.

The two Police Officers entered the cage, trying not to retch at the stench on the sanded floor.

"Mr Bunton, I'm Chief Inspector Rayleigh. Enjoying your new accommodation?"

He received an unintelligible squawk for a reply.

"Speak English, Bunton. You can understand it and you still have a tongue and teeth!"

"Whaddayou want?"

"I need to question you about the theft of a brown envelope of documents and a computer memory stick containing data from the office of Chawton Holland, during his time as Secretary of State for Health."

"Aaarkk! Dunno what you're on about!"

"Some classified and extremely sensitive documents fell into the hands of Erica Rayleigh, the former editor of The Observian. Did you hack the Department of Health IT system, steal data, remove those items from Chawton's office and send them to her?"

Pickles jerked his head sharply from side to side in an agitated birdlike frenzy.

"Squawk! Nothing to do with me!"

"We've done a thorough search of Chawton's office. Can you explain why a red feather was found in his files and a green feather in his drawer?"

As Bunton agitatedly squawked and flapped his wings, a foul-smelling deposit fell to the floor of the cage.

"Nervous are we, Bunton?"

Bunton screeched.

"You had a quarrel with Mr Holland. He refused funding for the treatment you are now getting. Here's a copy of the emails you exchanged. Have you anything to say about that?"

"Squawk! Didn't do it!"

"And you knew a man called Dave Hammond! At Roehampton Rehabilitation Centre."

"Aarrkk!!"

"His wife, Amelia, took part in the Male Pregnancy Incentive Scheme and she became seriously ill. David confided in you, didn't he?"

"Noooo!"

"Yes, he did, when you went for a drink. The landlord was deaf, but he could lip-read your conversations. He was most helpful. You always sat at the same table near the bar, and he had so few daytime customers that it kept him entertained. Dave had a grudge against Ralph Hardcastle and you hated Chawton Holland."

"Aark!"

Sergeant Wade chimed in with a more sympathetic approach. It was time to play 'nice cop'.

"You felt sorry for David, didn't you, when Amelia was critically ill?   Did you want to avenge them, as well as getting revenge for yourself?"

"Oliver Bunton, I am arresting you on suspicion of the theft of..."

"Can't! I'm no longer British Citizen!"

"You're not a parrot yet!"

As Sergeant Wade deposited the former Speaker in a Police van, a young constable handcuffed his feet together and grinned.

"Who's a pretty boy now then?"

xix) A coke can ring

Vauxhall, 5th November, 9.00pm

With Aidan's blessing, Evie would launch her missile tonight. But as she battled to focus on her work, emotions surfaced, clamouring for her attention.

Two Evie's had fought a gruelling war, head locked in ferocious combat.

Pragmatic, political Evie threw vicious punches at her gentler, inner self, reminding her that Frank Southwold had offered her security, affection and a family.

Marriage to a respectable professional man would improve her appeal to voters and chances of holding to the highest office in the land. Would Margaret Thatcher or Theresa May have entered Number 10 unmarried? Did the age of so-called equality really stretch to single women, even in 2036?

Frank was toned, athletic, fitter than many men half his age and great company, with a heart of gold. Most of all, he shared her faith. At thirty-five, was this the best offer she would receive?

But the deep core of Evie struggled back. Thrown against the ropes by a perceived second rejection from James, she nursed a faint hope which refused to die, however much cold water hard headed Evie threw upon it. But then she mentally replayed his words in her head.

"How dare he!" She bellowed at her paperwork.

As she burned with anger, she struggled to regain her self-control and channel her pent-up energy into the task ahead.

As she switched on Oliver Bunton's computer, the documents from the memory stick and scanned contents of the brown envelope flickered before her. She clicked the addresses of the editors of the Daily Telegraph, The Times and Daily Mail.

It was time to light the blue touch paper. She pressed 'send'.

Wandsworth Prison, 6th November, 5.30am

In a cramped, solitary cell, Gregory Wilson tossed and turned under a foul-smelling blanket. The relentless banging, whizzing and popping of fireworks and faint smell of gunpowder (which even permeated the prison walls), were a painful reminder of the social pleasures he no longer enjoyed.

Instead, he endured the raw loneliness of long, terrifying nights, punctuated by the sound of clanging doors, echoing footsteps, fights, quarrelling and the screams of inmates suffering from nightmares or the pangs of drug withdrawal.

His grief was still raw and even after nine months, the memory of Ralph Hardcastle's face, voice and mannerisms, the smell of his designer shirts, tobacco and even his hoarse laugh could send him plummeting into an abyss of searing pain.

The privilege of a miniature hologram TV was the only bolt hole for his tormented mind. He had flicked through the tacky programmes in the 'graveyard' slot between 1.00 and 5.00am and then switched to the mundane comfort of the rolling news.

At 5.30 he was almost asleep, when a red strapline of breaking news jolted him awake.

As he sat up sharply, images of Ralph, Chawton Holland and Orchard Mayhew leapt on the screen sending a sharp stab of terror through him.

A seeping realisation of his own dispensability began to engulf him....

Portcullis House, 6th November, 7.00am

She needed carbohydrates for the daunting task ahead and she had two important matters to settle.

Evie had invited Frank to enjoy the heartiest breakfast Portcullis House could provide. Bacon, eggs, sausages, bubble and squeak, lard-saturated fried bread and mushrooms, totally smothered in HP Sauce.

"Evie, are you savouring this morning's headlines? With Orchard and Chawton implicated in medical malpractice, and the butchery and abduction of hundreds of women? Removal of eggs, uterus, ovaries, reproductive tissues, often without their consent?"

Evie assumed her most prim and solemn expression.

"I am appalled if these allegations are true, but am not at liberty to comment."

"Your disapproving schoolmarm act cuts no ice with me! The papers say a certain Junior Minister can testify against them. Veracity Dunmore? Ally of yours, is she?"

"Frank, the workings of Westminster are my domain. The safety of London is yours. Have you decided whether you will be staying in your post?"

"No, Evie. I'm still resigning. Sorry"

"I'm disappointed."

"I'm moving to Sussex. It means a demotion, but there's no guillotine in Bognor Regis. Better place for my kids. They're my priority now."

"I fully understand. Your kids come first and I love Sussex! I'm grateful for your excellent work. You're leaving the Met in good shape, with 15 years of impeccable service."

Frank smiled in acknowledgement.

"You've been the best boss!"

"Thanks. And I want to answer your question."

Evie leaned forward and took his hand.

"Frank, I will marry you! I love you very much. You're fantastic and you'll make me so happy. I want to live in Bognor and I can split my time between there and Westminster and……"

Frank began to look agitated and interrupted.

"But Evie…."

"I adore your kids and I'll be the best step mum in the world……"

"Evie, stop!!"

"What's the matter?"

"It's no good."

"What? You proposed and I've said yes."

"You don't love me. I can't do this."

"I do love you."

"For a politician, you're a useless liar. You love two things more than me. Your political career and James Cardew.

Evie's neck and cheeks reddened with blotches.

"Nonsense!"

"Then why did you spend yesterday with James, having that very emotional conversation."

A dreadful realisation hit Evie.

"Your men were spying on me?!!"

"I'd asked two of my officers to shadow you for your own safety. They followed you from Vauxhall. Once again, you were utterly careless about your personal security. An amateur disguise with a beanie hat and sunglasses in November! As an ex-Home Secretary, did you really think that would fool a terrorist?"

"I'm no longer Home Secretary. This is totally inappropriate!"

"You're still a high-profile figure. I don't want to scare you, but MI5 is monitoring people who want to kill you. I don't know who you've rattled, but I'm determined to keep you alive, for personal and professional reasons!"

"I'm not scared. Every politician worth their salt has enemies! I'd feel a failure, otherwise!"

"Well, last night, you were your own worst enemy."

"What do you mean?"

"You let your pride ruin your chance of happiness."

"So, your men heard every word I said and then told you? How dare they!"

"You were having a row. They reassured me it was a lover's tiff and you weren't at risk."

"We're not an item."

"You clearly wish you were."

Evie's eyes conceded defeat.

"If you can't be honest with me, Evie, at least be truthful with yourself."

Evie sighed.

"Your still love James. And he's besotted, mooning like a lost puppy after you walked off in a huff.   Sort it! That's an order! Once again, I'm saving you from yourself, at my expense.   I'd gladly take a bullet for you. But this hurts more."

"I'm sorry Frank. I haven't been fair on either of us. You're the best mate in the world and you deserve better."

She smiled sheepishly.

"I screwed this one up."

"Good luck Evie. Just don't screw the country up! And stay safe. I'll keep a distant eye on you from Bognor."

Angelica House, Hertfordshire, 10ᵗʰ November, 11.00am

Harper Sykes, the new Home Secretary, was a welcoming host to his predecessor.

Evie had been a favourite colleague.

Anyway, her sharp, witty, hilarious observations of the Home Office were invaluable. Even after her short tenure as Secretary of State, she had a thorough knowledge of the department and piercing insight into the strengths and weaknesses of key staff.

"Don't re-employ Style Hobbs, whatever you do!"

"I have enough on my hands with Oliver Bunton under arrest," laughed Harper, "how do I deal with an ex-Speaker who's neither a British Citizen, human, animal, vegetable or mineral?"

Evie adopted her most innocent tone.

"I hear he stole sensitive documents?"

"They're now all over the tabloids!   Well, if the PM's involved, he deserves to go down."

"If there's a vote of No Confidence, will you support it?"

"Yes, Evie, even if it triggers an election."

"And if Orchard resigns, will you stand for the leadership?"

"No. The timing's wrong. Angora's pregnant. She's had four miscarriages. She doesn't need the stress. If you throw your hat in the ring, I'll back you."

"That's a relief Harper, you'd have been a serious threat!"

"In five years, watch out! For now, I'd rather serve under you."

"Understood. And thanks for letting me to bring a guest."

"James? He's great company. He's so down-to-earth. Nothing luvvy'ish about him. Are you back together?"

"No, but watch this space. I like the privacy away from London. We'll take a stroll before lunch – and leave you and Angora in peace!"

St Albans 10th November, 11.45am

A vicious wind blasted through the bare trees which offered no protection against the gnawing chill. As her feet froze in wellingtons, Evie realised Heartwood Forest was better enjoyed through a heated car window.

The traffic on the M1 droned in the distance as she and James strolled towards St Albans, avoiding the main roads. It was too cold to enjoy the muddy trek and her designer raincoat offered no warmth. She was quietly willing James to put an arm round her.

"Thanks for coming all this way, especially after my tantrum on Bonfire night. I hope the grace-and-favour luxury's a peace offering!"

"Luxury, Evie? Angelica House is a shabby, mouse-infested dump!"

Evie exploded with laughter.

"Blunt as ever! Thanks for putting up with Harper and Angora, too! You're no fan of politicians!"

"They're OK, but we've had no privacy."

"James, I need to say something before I lose my nerve."

She glanced around the forest. No snooping police would hear this time. It was as silent as the grave.

"I'm sorry I lost my rag last week. You're the most tactless man I ever met and you were unforgivably rude. But that's why I always liked you. You've no idea how to charm or flatter anyone. You can't even pretend! Ironic, for a top actor!"

"I make no excuse. I'm useless with words and socially inept. I don't fit in with the Hampstead set, or anywhere else! You should have seen me at Tony McCrief's funeral, I didn't know where to put myself."

"And yet you got him to hospital and stayed at his bedside. A total stranger. Few men would have done that."

"Aidan says God saw it, though I didn't know God then. Thought I was just doing the decent thing."

"You mean you know God now?"

"Yes. Aidan helped on that one."

Evie smiled and digested this piece of news.

"I see. So, it seems we've been on the same journey. Aidan and Miriam have been midwives to us both. They get no fame or credit, yet they've set both of us on a new road!"

"Evie, I don't want to travel that road alone."

"Look out, mind your foot...!!!"

As James tripped over a branch he tumbled into the dead leaves, saturating his trousers with icy mud. Evie squealed with laughter.

"Ugh!! Look at the state of you!!"

James made no attempt to get up, but with a sheepish expression, stayed kneeling in the squelching peat. Evie tried to pull him up, giggling helplessly. Clouds had gathered and icy rain began to spit.

"Come on! You can't stay down there, you're soaking!"

"Evie, let me stay down here. It's utterly unglamorous, but that's my life from now on. Hollywood actors can keep their spray tans, waxed bodies and designer clothes! I don't want the limelight. I'd rather help someone else to shine..."

"If you're having an identity crisis, please do it back at Angelica House in the warm!"

"Let me continue before I lose my nerve...... Evie, you're truly great. You don't need stupid scripts or agents. You're out there making a real difference, with all the sweat, cut and thrust of political mayhem."

"Just get up, you'll freeze your bits off down there!"

"Evie, I want to be in the shadows while you dazzle. I'll be Dennis to your Margaret Thatcher, Philip to your Teresa. James the unknown, but your rock, encourager and champion. I cringe when I remember what an idiot I was last year, but now I'm totally sure what I want. Please marry me."

Evie's squeal resounded through the forest. The trees rustled, a deer scuttled away and crows fluttered, as the rain turned to heavy drizzle. She sank to her knees, no longer caring about her filthy raincoat. As she gathered him in her arms, they slid to the ground laughing hysterically, covered in brown mouldy leaves and decaying twigs.

"Yes!! Of course, I will!"

As they embraced, they ignored the continuous high-pitched ringing on James's wrist phone.

"That must be Harper and Angora chasing us for lunch! Let them wait!"

James gently pulled her up, brushing her dark, soaking locks from her tear-stained face.

"Come on, let's get back and share the good news, or we'll catch pneumonia!"

He picked up a ring from a discarded Coke can on the ground.

"That's all I can give you for now, Mrs Cardew!"

"So that's how you bid farewell to showbiz glamour!"

As he slipped the soiled ring on her finger, it occurred to Evie, through her haze of euphoria, that litter meant the presence of other walkers.

The thought had barely lodged in her mind, when James yelled an unintelligible warning and threw himself violently in front of her, hurling her to the ground.

A vicious, excruciating pain ripped through her arm and shoulder as gunshots shattered the stillness of the woods. In a sea of agony and streaming blood, she became aware that James lay crumpled in his face.

It was only a few seconds, but it seemed like an eternity before her brain registered the life slipping from his pale, drained, features.

Three further gunshots blasted through the freezing air, as a man fled through the trees, pursued by a uniformed officer.

Though her intense pain she glanced back at James as his shallow breathing ceased, yielding into eternity the precious soul that had touched hers.

The cruel vice of devastation began to claw her emotions, but then her head swam with a vile cocktail of nausea, confusion and shock, as blood spurted from her wounds. Strong arms enfolded her and she heard a reassuring voice calling her name, before she lost consciousness.

Epping Holding Centre, 11th November

Aidan wept unashamedly in front of Prema and Gloria. In their few previous meetings, Miriam had done most of the talking. Today she was otherwise engaged.

The Hologram TV churned out tributes, interviews, film footage and speculation on the identity of the murderer.

"I'm so sorry Aidan. Miriam told me you and James were such close friends."

Prema slipped her cool, manicured hand into his. The warm, brown eyes which had once comforted women and men in the throes of labour, now coaxed him through his searing loss.

"He was only 37. I hated him to begin with, but he became the best mate ever. I'll never have a pint with him again."

Aidan fell silent, biting back his emotions.

"Let me make you a chamomile tea."

"No Prema. You're still very frail."

"The hospital discharged her too soon," added Gloria "they're irresponsible!"

"I've faced death twice now, Gloria, I'm not afraid."

Prema's serenity rang alarm bells.

"There won't be any third time, Prema!"

"I'll appeal, if Gregory's case goes against me. And my surgeon will give evidence of the damage Ralph inflicted on me."

"Any more news on Evie after her three-hour operation, Aidan? "

"She's conscious, stable and on morphine. They removed bullets from her arm, shoulder and collarbone. The ones meant for her heart killed James."

"He threw himself in front of her."

Gloria sighed wearily.

"But why did someone try to assassinate Evie? And why now?"

"The papers were full of rumours about her leadership bid. Of course, she has enemies!"

Watford General Hospital, 12th November

As the blissful cloud of morphine-induced sleep dispersed, the pain made its presence felt.

First, she felt a menacing discomfort, which steadily increased to a gnawing ache, radiating through her arm and shoulder with growing intensity. And with the physical agony returned a gut-wrenching pit in her stomach. Oblivion and fading dreams gave way to searing grief. Drugs had offered a temporary separation from the nightmare, but as the ceiling lights dazzled her eyes, she uttered an anguished groan and unintelligible plea to the pretty nurse leaning over her. Evie noticed tears in her warm grey eyes as she gently took her hand.

"Evie, how are you? You have a visitor."

"Is...is it Miriam or Dad?"

"No, they've both gone back to Miriam's, to get a few hours' sleep."

"I can't face seeing anyone else. Who is it?"

"It's Vernon Stack."

"Vernon Stack?!!"

Evie jerked forward, wincing in pain. She was suddenly wider awake. Why was the Leader of His Majesty's Opposition visiting her so soon? But nothing made sense or mattered any more. She was trapped in a hideous parallel universe. If this was merely another part of a horrific dream, so what?

"I'll see him, but please give me another shot of morphine."

"I'll top up the drugs and do your hair and lipstick."

She fiercely fought the tears which welled up at the nurse's kindness. Vernon Stack must not see any weakness.

He was more unkempt than ever, in a food-stained roll-necked jumper and corduroy trousers.

"Sorry about my appearance. I've been looking after the grandchildren."

"I apologise for mine too."

Evie smiled weakly, pointing to the layers of bandages across her chest and shoulder.

"I hope my early visit isn't an intrusion. I am utterly sorry for your terrible loss. And I've come to offer the condolences of my wife, my family and my party. We sit on opposite sides of the house, but this is a dreadful tragedy and wicked crime, against you and the Parliament we both serve. "

"Thanks, Vernon. It's ironic that the Leader of the Opposition's visiting me, but there's no sign of Orchard Mayhew!"

"Let him stay in his bunker. We MPs have a common bond. You serve with distinction, mingling with the public to serve the community. You daily face that risk."

"I wasn't attacked in a public place."

"You deserved to walk in safety. How are they looking after you here?"

"Excellent. I feel so groggy though. They got the bullets out. But they couldn't save……he was dead on arrival…."

She bit her lip and fought savagely to maintain her dignity.

"Always the fighter, aren't you Evie?"

"Not any longer. Vernon, I'm finished. I'm standing down as an MP."

"Standing down? No!"

"Yes. So, I'm handling you victory on a plate. A Government in chaos and a Vote of No Confidence looming. Oblivion for the Tory Independence Party, with no credible leader in sight."

"I won't hear of it."

"I thought you'd be delighted."

"People like you thrive in the House and you're it's lifeblood. If they make you party leader, you'll be a thorn in my side. But frankly, bring it on! I'm not afraid of you. The opinion polls give me a 25% lead, so I can still win the next election, even if you make a tiny dent in my landslide!"

"Have your Labour Socialist landslide, Vernon. I won't stand for the leadership. I'm past caring. Nothing matters any more."

"Evie, you're in shock, pain and grief right now. It won't pass any time soon, you know me, no false promises! But you will get your hunger and vision back.

I may disagree with your ideas, but strangely, you thrive on them. And if you suddenly lose your constituency, as well as the man you loved so dearly, the vacuum in your life will be intolerable."

"I can't feel worse than I do now."

"Well, don't make a hasty decision. Parliament is desperately short of committed, decent people like you. And don't let your assassin win. You owe that to all of us in the House! Stand firm and show these evil blighters what we're made of!"

Evie struggled to remain alert as the fresh dose of Morphine took hold.

"What will you do now, Vernon?"

"Call for a Vote of No Confidence in December. If we win, I guess Parliament will be dissolved before Christmas. No-one wants an election campaign over the festive period, so Polling Day is likely to be on Thursday 30th January. Giving you eleven weeks to get your act together, young lady!"

"It won't happen Vernon, get used to it. But thanks for the heads-up!"

"Evie, you're a gifted politician."

"And my high profile killed the only man I ever loved. You have the support of a wife, Vernon."

"I never cease to be grateful. Shirley was so upset at the news. She was a huge fan of James. Downloaded every box-set of his TV dramas and films! A lesser man than me would be jealous!"

Evie smiled weakly. He handed her a prettily-wrapped tin.

"A gift from Shirley, she thought you'd like this."

"A home-made fruit cake? That's so kind of her."

As a wave of emotion flooded her, she closed her eyes. Sleep was less embarrassing than tears.

She was asleep again, as her father returned, utterly bemused to meet Vernon Stack.

Larnaca, Cyprus, 12th November, 11.45pm local time

A small private plane descended in a deserted, disused airfield, a few miles from Larnaca. Bitterly cold for an autumn Mediterranean night, a biting wind whipped across the field, as the passengers disembarked.

A bulky figure faltered down the step and staggered to the cover of nearby shrubs. Clinging to the wild hope of 'disappearing', the former Secretary of State for Health acclimatised to his status as a fugitive. His short stay in Cyprus was on borrowed time, given the Cypriot extradition treaty with the UK. But there was unfinished business to settle.

Chawton Holland had company. An unkempt, oiled, muscular figure emerged from the cabin. Callum had more realistic hopes of achieving anonymity and a future on nightclub doors. His recently-renewed employment with Chawton would end, after one final act of service.

They stumbled into the back a waiting van which sped away into the cloudy, starless night. Comfort must be sacrificed to concealment, as the driver lurched and jolted around hairpin bends to a secure gated house, twenty miles along the coast and dubious hospitality.

Chawton tried to banter amicably with Callum, striving to preserve his last vestiges of loyalty. While his bodyguard offered protection, his services carried a risk. As Callum's cigarette lighter cast an orange light on his cold, sullen features, Chawton pondered on the wisdom of terminating his contract, with a creeping fear that Callum would betray him for a price. But Callum was a worse liability as part of his entourage. After being on camera with him in London, his presence increased the likelihood of recognition. And Callum had enough enemies of his own, to draw unwelcome attention.

Callum's mouth twisted lopsidedly around his roll-up, as smoke billowed in stuffy confines of the van and mingled with the sickly smell of his stale sweat.

"Do you seriously think she's still here, guv?"

"I'm paying you to find out."

"And then what?"

"Need you even ask?"

Watford General Hospital, 15th November

"Ouch! Mind that step, you clumsy oaf!"

Aidan wheeled Evie along the corridor, as Miriam supported her IV drip.

"And stop jolting! My shoulder's in agony and my stitches are pulling. As if that physiotherapist hasn't hurt me enough! Honestly Aidan I can't believe you were once a volunteer for a local disability group."

Aidan kept calm and exchanged glances with Miriam. After five days, they were getting used to Evie's mood swings, which ranged from floods of inconsolable tears to savage outbursts of rage, with occasional spells of quiet, numb withdrawal.

Evie sighed.

"Sorry, I didn't mean to take it out on you."

Aidan pushed the wheelchair into the private bedroom, while Miriam ordered tea.

Evie eased herself onto the bed, flinching in pain as she transferred her weight from the chair. Aidan gazed at her drained complexion, hollow tear-reddened eyes framed with dark circles and the tangle of perspiration-drenched dark locks, lank and dulled by a combination of anaesthetic, drugs, sparse eating and loss of interest in personal grooming. The professional veneer had been wiped away to reveal the lost, lonely, vulnerable young woman underneath.

Miriam poured the tea.

"Honestly my love, I can't believe Vernon Stack visited you. What a nerve."

Evie shrugged.

"I can handle him. Anyway, I don't care anymore."

"So, you're definitely standing down?"

"Yes, Aidan and no lectures or pep talks, please!"

"Only you can decide. I support you either way."

"My fame killed James. That and my pig-headed stupidity. I risked that walk in the woods without a private detective."

"Don't beat yourself up, my love. There were three police officers shadowing you. Someone put them there."

"Miriam, I want to attend the post-mortem hearing."

"Are up to it my love?"

"Apart from the funeral, it's the last thing I can do for him."

The mention of the funeral caught at Aidan's throat and he bit his lip, drawing deep breaths.

"This hurts me too, Evie."

"I know."

"We're not just here to comfort you. We're here because…."

Aidan struggled to finish the sentence.

"Because your friendship is a comfort to us."

"Even when I act like a total toe rag?"

"Yes. This year we've lost Tony and now James. You're like our second daughter.   Right now, you just need to know how loved you are."

xx) Flying retribution

10 Downing Street, 15th November

Orchard's clammy fingers slid nervously around a glass of port.

Lord Chief Justice Henry Mayhew was unruffled, as he reclined in a black leather chair, surveying the disintegration of his younger cousin.

"Calm yourself, Orchard."

"I understand the documents flying around the media are now being reviewed by the Crown Prosecution Service. What do I do, Henry?"

"Well frankly, barring miracles, they have enough to proceed against you. You were crazy to get involved."

"We had a UN target to reach. We've reached that goal. This country is now a global role model, thanks to the success of the Male Birth Incentive Scheme over the last 5 years."

"You mean *was* a role model. The criminal malpractice unravelling in the public domain will make this country into an international pariah."

"If things go badly for me, I could face jail. What can save me?"

"Well Chawton's done a runner, but of course, when you became PM they took away your passport and inserted a microchip tracker in your backside! So, a private jet is of no help! Start building your defence case now."

"Prema Gupta will appeal. She stayed silent before, but this time she'll have all guns blazing. She'll reveal everything."

"Hardcastle's own wife? You don't mean to tell me he…"

"He stopped at nothing."

"And you and Chawton didn't stop him? You never considered the possibility of a marriage break-up and the anger of a woman scorned?"

"I didn't know till I saw the files. Other women had good reason to stay silent. She was always our main risk, after the divorce."

"So, what did happen on 14th February? You know, don't you Orchard?"

Orchard remained silent, as his face reddened and sweat poured.

Henry's eyes bored into those of his disintegrating cousin.

"Self-defence, was it? Prema intercepted her would-be killer, didn't she?"

As Orchard's hand shook, the glass of port cracked on the table and red liqueur mingled with his papers.

"You can't link me to that night. You've got nothing on me, if you're suggesting I was an accessory or joined a conspiracy to murder."

"No wonder you wanted that execution to go ahead. That face-saving reprieve must have stuck in your throat! The botched guillotining was your worst nightmare! And as for her six-month stay of execution, I guess you hoped a re-trial might rid you of Gregory Wilson too! You'd kill two birds with one stone!"

"Yes, the sooner Wilson is out of the picture, the better!"

For a moment, Henry was gazing at the sweet, indulged, five-year-old cousin playing hide-and-seek in the Norfolk mansion, erring into forbidden rooms, crying piteously when he got lost. And then his 2036 lens refocused on the cowering, full grown monster before him."

"Please help me Henry. Please…. I'll do whatever you ask," pleaded the five-year-old, "I'll resign."

"No, you won't. That would be seen as an admission of guilt."

"Can you help me?"

"Leave it to me."

Regent's Park Hybrid Custodial Centre, 16th November

Regent's Park Zoo had a surprising number of visitors for late autumn. The mild weather drew hordes of families, school parties, tourists and students through the gates.

But as they enjoyed the newborn polar bear, the genetically recreated dodo and other recent attractions they, like the rest of the public, remained oblivious to a grim secret lying two metres below their feet.

Dank and devoid of sunlight, illuminated by strip lighting reflected against white, tiled walls, Regent's Park Hybrid Custodial Centre was the dungeon which concealed the most macabre failures of modern medicine and genetic technology from the public eye.

This morning, a high-profile guest received a guided tour.

"This is our fourth storey basement, Your Honour. Over there, you can see we've incarcerated a cloned hybrid sabre-toothed tiger, whose ancient DNA was merged with that of a famous 2012 British Olympic medalist. We keep him alive for research."

Five iron fences separated the vile two-legged monster from the nervous warden. Even Lord Chief Justice Mayhew shuddered as he gazed at the fangs, twisted, misshapen torso, splayed legs and tormented eyes which were still clearly human.

The second storey held long corridors of pitiful wrecks who had survived botched transspecies surgery, but could never be returned to society.

"The Government keeps the public ignorant of the failures. Only the PM and a chosen handful of people know. "

"He's even kept me ignorant!" cried Mayhew. "My own cousin! And I'm surprised our courts aren't overrun with legal cases from their families?"

"Their families are told they're dead. It's kinder that way, I guess."

"Kinder? To be abandoned without hope? And no-one fighting for you?"

"Shh! Some of these inmates still understand English!"

But someone had heard. From a musty locked cave came the hideous sobbing of a small, hairless, striped creature with long blonde hair was all that remained of a young woman who had pursued her dream of becoming a zebra.

Further along the corridor was cramped, dingy 4ft by 4ft cage with a tree-branch across the middle and an old bucket of stale water on the floor.

"Here he is, guvnor!"

Henry Mayhew strode up to the bars.

"Oliver Bunton! Or do you prefer to be called Pickles the Parrot these days?"

"Waarrk! Gemme outta here!!"

Mayhew waved the warden away, in a bid for privacy.

He leaned closer to the cage and lowered his voice. "I'm here to help you."

The green, feathered face, with a growing beak but still recognisably human features tilted to one side.

"You have a choice. You can either remain in this dark, stinking dungeon until you die, or I can find you a place with natural light, suitable care and human company."

Bunton's gnarled, twisted feet scurried across the branch and he came to the cage bars, face to face with Mayhew.

"Your level of co-operation now determines where you spend the rest of your life."

"Waark! Whaddo I do?"

"You stole documents from Chawton Holland's office, didn't you?"

The green and red-feathered head jerked up and down in a nod.

"Who did you give them to?"

There was a long silence.

"I'm waiting. Do you want to die here?"

The residual conscience in Oliver Bunton's brain knew that the lives of others depended on his response. The cynical part of his brain thought they might kill him anyway. Memories of his human life flashed across his mind. The House of Commons, Amelia and Dave Hammond, Evie Atherton and the laptop he had given her....

As he lied to Mayhew, his atheistic mind frantically prayed that Evie had used his old laptop and had not betrayed her possession of that brown envelope.

"Papers......Aark! Editors.... Waark! Emailed 'em to the Mail, Telegraph and Observian! Before I was taken into quarantine!"

"So, you sent them to the editors of national newspapers and no-one else?"

"Waark! No-one else!"

"Where's the missing memory stick?"

"Destroyed!"

"If I ever find out you've lied, I will have you destroyed."

"Whenndo I geddout?"

"All in good time. Leave it to me!"

Watford General Hospital, 16th November

Evie longed for her Vauxhall apartment. Oh, to shut the world out and grieve on her own sofa.

She was weary of 6.00am breakfasts, regular SATS monitoring, the IV drip, physiotherapy and DVT-prevention injections.

This morning she was responding to the mountain of condolence messages on her table. But her injured shoulder ached and the line in her vein pulled painfully, as she typed with one hand.

Her face fell as Frank arrived. She had dreaded this.

"Evie! How are you? Is that sling your latest Roxanne fashion?"

"I'll be glad to see the back of it!"

He pulled up a chair beside her.

"I'm so sorry about James. I don't know what to say. This was a wicked crime, but…"

"Go on, say 'I told you so'. Yes, I was crazy, walking with James unguarded."

"Actually, you had three officers shadowing you. They called for the air ambulance."

"No prize for guessing who sent them. I owe you my life, Frank."

"I'm sorry they failed to spot your assailant till it was too late. And the bunglers let him get away."

"I'm to blame for James's death."

"No Evie, it's my fault you were there. I told you to reconcile with him. You agreed to marry me and I ungraciously rejected you."

"With good reason. If we'd got engaged, we'd have a different set of regrets. Don't you dare feel guilty. That's an order!"

Frank pulled two lagers and greasily-wrapped paninis from his rucksack.

"For old times' sake. Drink up! What will you do now?"

"Attend James's funeral, then slip into obscurity."

"Obscurity? But you're a national heroine."

"For getting shot?"

"You have the world's sympathy. Hundreds of cards. The hospital garden is overrun with the flowers from politicians, celebrities, the public, even the King. You're more powerful now than ever!"

"And yet, like you Frank, I'm choosing the quiet life!"

"You're not finished yet. How do you know God hasn't raised you up for such a time as this?"

Epping Holding Centre, 18th November, 8.00am

Prema carefully twisted her glossy braids of hair around her head, she inserted sparkling pins, then she applied eyeliner and pink lipstick.   Style was a matter of breeding and etiquette, even when her only companions were Miriam, Gloria and Reeta.

Frank had visited, to check how she was. Such concern was an honour, because for most of her life she had felt invisible. No-one put themselves out for her, but she always went the extra mile for others.

Her nail polish was drying as a young prison guard brought her breakfast. Prema's eye widened at the sumptuous spread on a beautiful tray.

"Strawberries and passion fruit? Bucks Fizz? Earl Grey tea? Smoked salmon? What's this in aid of?"

The Guard smiled and tears pricked her eyes.

"It's your very last morning and...we wanted to give you a good send-off. We.... we've grown to like you. You're a lovely person. You've never been any trouble."

A knife twisted in Prema's stomach, as her adrenaline surged, accelerating the blood through her veins and arteries. A cold sweat broke on her face. She clutched a chair gasping breath.

"Last day? What's going on? I thought...."

"Oh, I'm so sorry," whispered the Guard, "I thought your lawyer had already warned you. There's been a decision from the Lord Chief Justice during the night."

Prema's voice was hoarse, as the white walls seemed to sway before her.

"How long have I got?"

"About 45 minutes. I apologise you have so little time to prepare. And I'm sorry to break it to you like this. The Prison Governor will see you shortly."

"Please.... please find Gloria. I'm so frightened."

Panic rose in Prema's stomach.

"She's already on her way – but I'll ring her mobile."

"You're very kind. Thanks."

"You're...finally going where you belong."

"Yes, yes, I believe Jesus has prepared a place for me. But it's still a shock."

The Guard scurried from the room. Terror tightened around her chest in a vice-like grip. For months, she had longed for death and embraced the prospect. But since her reprieve, hope and a new hunger for life had flourished as she had begun to embrace the possibility of a future.

Angry sobs erupted, as she hurled her tray of food across the room. The bone china crockery shattered, as food and drink splattered across the white cell.

She pulled at her beautifully-styled hair and tore at her shirt. Who cared what she looked like now?

"Please God, why?! Why now?!"

A guillotining without warning? Was this some twisted act of misguided mercy?

She frantically switched on the BBC News Channel. Mundane headlines on the economy and interest rates, geriatric hooliganism and a trans-species terrapin. Media silence?

She threw herself on the bed weeping uncontrollably, clutching the pillows to her stomach, as though such primal comfort could shield her from the horror to come.

The door quietly opened.

"Prema? Prema! What's up with you? I have some important news. You need to prepare yourself."

As Gloria tried to pull her from the bed, Prema scratched, punched and screamed with every trace or air in her lungs.

"WHY DIDN'T YOU TELL ME???" WHY!!?? WHY??!! YOU LIED TO ME AND I HATE YOU!!!! I NEVER WANTED THIS! I THOUGHT IT WOULD NEVER HAPPEN!!!"

"What do you think you're doing! Stop scratching me! I thought you'd be pleased."

"I might have been once. But now? And to spring it on me like this! How cruel can you get?!"

"You're the most impossible client I've ever had."

"Please…. I don't want to die…. not this morning! Nooo!""

"Die?? Who said anything about dying?"

"The warder who gave me my last breakfast. Crying her eyes out, she was."

"Prema, what planet are you on? Of course, she's upset. It's the last time she'll see you. But you're not going to die. You're being released this morning!"

Prema's head swam as the vicious grip of fear evaporated and she clutched the wash basin to steady herself."

"Released?? I'm not being executed?"

"No! Lord Chief Justice Mayhew reviewed your case early this morning. He's ruled your murder conviction is unsafe."

"But why?"

"He believes you killed Ralph Hardcastle in self-defence and that he and Gregory entered your home illegally."

Gloria caught Prema by the waist as she fainted.

As she regained consciousness, through blurred vision she stuttered. "But... but how?... I haven't even appealed."

"All I care about is at 9.00am you're a free woman. The Police will take you to a safe house."

"I.... I'm under house arrest?"

"Only for two weeks. There's a press embargo until 2nd December. After that, you'll go home to Lewisham, accompanied by a police officer 24/7. The public now hate Ralph Hardcastle, but you're still at risk."

"This...this has to be a miracle. We have an amazing God......."

"And a terrified Prime Minister!"

"Hence the media silence?"

Vauxhall, 24th November

The queue to Evie's toilet was infuriatingly long, as the mourners assembled.

Aidan, Miriam, Ceiba, Norma, James's 93-year-old grandfather, five cousins and friends from the world of TV, film and theatre. James had no surviving parents.

Organising the troops was a temporary diversion from her searing grief.

"Babies and grandparents to the loo first!" She hollered.

Fear of being late for Southwark Cathedral and dread of the TV cameras was eclipsed by annoyance at the luvvies wearing sunglasses indoors, while guzzling her sherry and brandy.

Ceiba jetted a final blast of hairspray onto Evie's back-combed up-do. Evie squeezed her hand.

"You've done a great job!"

Ceiba smiled shyly.

"How's your shoulder?"

"Can't lift my arm. Please will you hold my Order of Service, when we get to the Cathedral?"

Aidan turned from the window.

"The cortege and police escort are nearly here!"

As reality hit home, Evie tensed. Miriam gently took her arm."

"I'm OK Miriam. I'm glad they released his body for burial so soon. But I don't understand."

"None of us understand it, my love."

"I've become a Christian yet I've had the worse five weeks of my life. I've lost my job, my man…."

Tears welled as she gazed at the coke can ring on her finger.

"Evie, when you chose Jesus, you joined his side. You're a casualty of war. But out of the worst evil can come the greatest good. For now, just take things gently, one step at a time. Let's just get through today, my love."

Cyprus, 25th November

Callum scowled and stood over Chawton as he transferred money into his bank account.

"£20,000 is a generous severance payment. You never found Erica and you totally botched up that other big job Hertfordshire!"

"You employed me as a bodyguard, not a hitman! Yet I've killed dozens for you!"

As Callum spewed his choicest expletives, even Chawton blushed.

"Control yourself. You'll find other politicians to fleece!"

"I want cash. I'm keeping my head down, so I ain't using my bank account."

"£5,000 cash. And you leave tonight. Is that a deal?"

"Done!"

Chawton turned to unlock his safe. As the heavy door opened, sudden excruciating pain ripped through his arm and shoulder blade, as Callum swung him round in a vice-like grip, then forced him to the floor.

It briefly occurred to him that Callum was wearing plastic gloves, before the snapping of his neck banished him into eternity.

Callum relaxed his grip and spat on the earthly remains of his employer.

"A measly £5,000," he hissed into the ear of Chawton's lifeless body, "don't make me laugh!"

He pulled a gold ring from Chawton's finger.

"You were gullible enough to trust me alone. So much easier than the job you gave me at Heartwood Forest. Stalking that pathetic woman and her lover boy. And look what happened when I opened fire!!"

Callum cursed at the memory.

"A huge soldier with a sword appeared beside her! He must have been 8ft tall and had a dazzling light round him. You never warned me she had a bodyguard. The bullets never reached her.

And here's another weird thing - James Cardew was in two places at once. Dead on the ground, but standing, laughing and talking with the soldier. Was I on LSD? Then he leaned over and kissed his girlfriend. Even weirder, he and the soldier flew into the sky and vanished. But I didn't take any drugs that day!"

He rolled Chawton's lifeless body over and ripped a gold chain from the neck.

"So now you're dead and that fat tart's still alive! But I'll kill Evie Atherton one day. I ain't being outdone by a squaddie with a medieval sword!   Anyway, I outran the other three 'normal' police officers, they were useless."

Callum swiftly emptied the contents of the safe into his rucksack, cash, cards, gold watches and cufflinks.

"I'll kill Erica Rayleigh too! Others will pay me!"

He locked front door of the rented villa and disappeared into the night.

Wandsworth Prison, 25th November

Gregory Wilson splashed his face with freezing water, waiting to be escorted to the Governor's office.

"Pull yourself together man!"

"Why have they summoned me?"

Alan Wicklow tried not to retch at the smell of his client's vomit.

"The Crown Prosecution have fast-tracked your case, after recent developments. The Lord Chief Justice has reviewed it. I'll object to the lack of notice in the strongest possible terms."

As Gregory threw up in the sink, thoughts of Orchard Mayhew's disgrace tortured his brain and corkscrewed through to his bowels. The Prime Minister was fighting for his political life. The People's Midwife was dispensable.

"The PM wants me dead!"

He mentally rehearsed the searing agony of the blade slicing through his neck. Another wave of nausea surfaced.

As buzz of the electronic lock signalled the warder's arrival, he wiped his mouth on a soiled sleeve. Panting, he struggled to mine his old celebrity skills and maintain some dignity.

He staggered along the clanging corridor and even in that short journey, believed it was better to travel than to arrive.

A blast of warmth hit him, as he was led into a massive, centrally-heated, oak-panelled, newly refurbished office. The first shock was to see a young, pretty Governor, with blonde highlighted hair, welcoming manner and public-school accent.

He was ushered to white leather chair. The comfortable squeaking would have been pleasurable in other circumstances.

"Mr Mayhew, I'm Cayenne Forbes and this is Barrister Trellis Fisher, representing the Crown Prosecution Service."

So, this was it. Trellis Fisher cracked his knuckles and gathered his papers. At 6'3 he peered down at Gregory as though he were already a cadaver.

"How long have I got?" Croaked Gregory, with a parched throat.

"Mr Wilson, I wish to inform you that Prema Gupta has been cleared of the charge of murder and released from prison."

"What happens to me?"

"The Lord Chief Justice has ruled that she committed manslaughter in self-defence. The Crown Prosecution has therefore withdrawn the murder charge against you."

Gregory staggered to his feet but collapsed into the opulent folds of his chair, as Ian Wicklow caught his arm.

"Is my client free to go?"

"We could still charge him with the lesser offence breaking and entering Prema's home and release him on bail. But the Crown Prosecution will drop the case, if he cooperates."

"Cooperates?"

Gregory jolted forward again.

"How?"

"Sign the enclosed document and also the Official Secrets Act."

Ian snatched the papers and scanned them.

"Gregory, are you willing to swear to secrecy about the events of 14th February and all circumstances relating to them?"

Gregory was on his feet.

"Give me a pen!"

Crystal Palace, 26th November

Frank's six-seated Asteroid Galaxy hurtled from Hastings along the A21, to the din of screaming toddlers and chaos of fizzy drinks, sweet wrappers and baby-vomit, overpowered by the stench of fish and chips.

Ceiba and Norma were buoyant. Even Evie almost resembled her old self, despite her weight loss. Her eyes were still hollow from insomnia and thick dressings protruded from her shirt. But their bracing walk had restored some colour to her cheeks.

"So, are you and Frank an item now?" Shouted Norma from the back seat.

"No," laughed Evie, "he's just our chauffeur for today!"

At dusk, Frank battled through heavy South London traffic.

Ceiba was rattled, as he headed away from Peckham.

"Why are we going towards Crystal Palace? I'm busting for the loo!"

Crystal Palace Tower flickered against the sunset, as Frank pulled up Westow Hill and drew outside a smart three-storey Victorian house with a panoramic view of London.

"Everyone out!" Ordered Evie. "I want to show you something!"

"Wot 'ere?"

Norma struggled from the car grumbling, as Ceiba gathered two hot, sticky children from the back seat. Evie led them up the driveway and pulled a set of keys from her bag.

Evie took them into a spacious, parquet-floored hallway.

"Ceiba and Norma, this is your new home."

Ceiba laughed scornfully.

"What? Don't make me laugh! Bit posh, innit?"

Evie ushered them into the lounge.

"She's flipped!" Snapped Norma.

Tears welled up in Evie's eyes, as the familiar smell of polish mingled with dusty books, aftershave and cat litter caught at her throat. She struggled to compose herself.

"I haven't flipped, guys. This house belonged to James. I'm his Executor. He left me nearly everything in his will. I'd like you to live here."

"We can't afford the rent," gasped Ceiba, "because we're on benefits!"

"You can stay here rent free on a twelve-month lease and I'll review it annually. You'll only pay gas and electricity."

Norma's hand trembled as she clasped Evie's arm. Joy and gratitude shone out of the dark, grief-weary eyes.

Ceiba let out an expletive and raced to the bathroom.

Frank chuckled.

"She's making herself at home already!"

Evie pottered around the lounge, watering the wilting plants and tidying a pile of coffee stained, dog eared scripts. Totally speechless, Norma sleepwalked around the room, muttering and stroking the cushions, like an old tabby cat depositing her scent upon a new territory.

Evie hugged James's discarded sweatshirt which lay strewn across the sofa, allowing a wave of pain to engulf her. She gazed at the laughing toddlers whom Ceiba had deposited on the Afghan rug.

"Out of the greatest evil can come the greatest good."

Maybe.

Battersea Transition Centre, 29th November, 8.00am

His beak made a filthy mess as he ate curry for breakfast. Congealed lumps of Madras flew around his cage.

"Morning Oliver, or Pickles? How do you like your new home?"

Judge Mayhew entered the cage. Pickles spluttered on a poppadom.

"Waark! Good! Daylight at last!"

"We've reviewed your case. We can't remove your human brain, as your knowledge is too valuable to the Police, MI5 and Government. You must therefore remain a hybrid."

"Waark! Not going back to the dungeon!"

"We won't return you to Regent's Park. It's becoming impossible for the Government to stay silent about hybrids. Too many of you to hide these days. Sooner or later, a paper will make an embarrassing leak.

It will be better to break the news to the public in a controlled way. Taxpayers' money will have to be spent on proper care and people won't like it!

I doubt my cousin will be at Number 10 much longer, but other ministers and indeed, Vernon Stack (if he wins the next election,) are sympathetic. By February this will all go public. Before then, we face the thorny problem of telling families that their 'dead' relatives are alive."

"Whaddya gonna do to me?"

"I'm setting up a trust to care for hybrids. I'll grant money to local authorities. For now, you and others like you can live here in Battersea, and you can eat human food if your transitory digestive system allows it, watch TV and enjoy some of your former comforts. What do you say?"

In a flutter of excitement, huge lumps of curry sauce landed on Mayhew's shirt.

"I've brought you today's Times, to reintroduce you to civilisation!"

Judge Mayhew left in a Madras-sodden hurry, forgetting to shut the cage door.

Pickles seized the paper with his claws and gazed at the headline.

"Chawton Holland found murdered in Cyprus"

So, Holland had fled and now lay dead. The former Speaker of the House of Commons screeched in triumph. His revenge was complete. The brown envelope had wreaked more havoc than he had ever dared hope.

He read the next heading:

Vote of Confidence. Mayhew in peril.
Orchard's fate would be decided today? For the first time since renouncing his citizenship, Pickles suddenly missed Parliament.

House of Commons dining room, 29th November, 1.00pm

She was poised and elegant, suppressing her nerves. In a royal blue suit, her hair was swept into a French pleat. Today she would carry herself as a stateswoman and leave politics with style and gravitas.

Harper Sykes swooped across the Commons dining room as Evie eased stiffly into a chair.

"Don't worry Harper, I'm only here for the No Confidence vote!"

"Join the club! We're Turkeys voting for Christmas - we'll all lose our seats in the snap election!"

"I don't care, I'm standing down!"

"Why, Evie? You have a majority of 8,000. Orchard's crumbling. The leadership door's wide open!"

"I might have wanted it a month ago, but my life's in turmoil."

"I'm sorry."

"So Chawton's dead after fleeing to Cyprus?"

"He had an empire, which will now crumble. Heaven knows how many skeletons we will find in his cupboard."

"There's enough scandal already, but no-one's arrested Orchard yet. The evidence is overwhelming. Why, Harper?"

"The Police are unusually slow. Orchard has friends in high places."

"His head must roll today. With five hours of debate, we may finish him off before the Division Bell!"

"You're sharpening your teeth! You'll be sorely missed, Evie."

Peckham, 29th November, 2.00pm

Aidan struggled to pacify Miriam.

"Ceiba, Norma and the babies are going! She's taking our lodgers!"

"Evie's grieving and she's confused, Jen. Anyway, they don't pay rent. It's no loss!"

"We'll be lonely without them. And Lakeside's our grandson. The DNA test proved it. They can't manage alone."

"Ceiba's very capable."

"Prema's being released," she blurted out, "so I'm losing everyone."

"Released?!"

"Oh, sorry my love, I was sworn to secrecy."

"How?"

"Her murder conviction's quashed. She's in a safe house."

"No retrial? Praise God! I'm over the moon! This is fantastic news!!!"

"She won't need me anymore."

"Is that all you can think about? She's free, Miriam. Your prayers have been answered! Anyway, we've got Evie."

"She'll go back to Warrington."

Aidan mopped up another flood of tears. This was no time for a lecture on co-dependency.

House of Commons, 29th November, 5.00pm

For three hours, verbal cross-fire ricocheted across the Despatch Box, from both sides of the House, drawing heat, sweat and tension in the densely-packed chamber.

The Vote of No Confidence loomed. The Government majority was wafer-thin. Every vote counted, dead or alive.

MPs had been summoned from honeymoons, sick-beds and one wore a surgical gown, having been called from an operating table. A 95-year-old Scottish Nationalist MP was dead on arrival from Edinburgh, but his intrepid party leader demanded to know if his corpse could be carried through with the 'ayes' when the division bell rang.

The Opposition party members had systematically pulverised Orchard Mayhew. His clumsy reintroduction of capital punishment, the trade deficit, the slowing growth rate, the increase of geriatric delinquency, the number of people below the poverty line….

At 5.00pm, Harper Sykes rose to his feet.

"I was appalled at the dreadful anarchy on the day Prema Gupta was due to be executed at Greenwich Holding Centre. The loss of life was horrific and this Government must bear responsibility for the failure of the Metropolitan Police."

Vernon Stack and his Labour colleagues roared in agreement.

Evie scowled. This was a double-edged missile against Orchard and herself. Why was Harper attacking her? She glared across at his slim, athletic figure, lightly tanned face and designer tailoring. His long fingers swept back his stylishly-cut hair. He was dressed to impress.

Had he lied? Would he really wait for 5 years to make his bid for power?"

She refocused on the debate. Backbenchers demanded budget figures for the Male Pregnancy Incentive Scheme.

Vernon stepped up to the Despatch Box.

"The media have documents implicating the senior Government Ministers in the abduction of 50 women and the coercion of hundreds more to donate their reproductive organs. I put it to you that the Prime Minister knew exactly what his colleagues were doing, yet he shamelessly refuses to resign! He is a disgrace to this House and to this country!"

Evie's heart thudded. This was it. Her face reddened and she quietly prayed. Her body was flooded with a gentle warmth and sense of peace as she rose to her feet.

"Members of the House, despite my recent loss, I feel compelled to be here today, in the national interest. I love this country, this House, our democracy and every value of common decency held by so many of my constituents.

Ten years ago, the Government introduced the Male Pregnancy Incentive Scheme with colonic interface surgery, causing the death of hundreds of young men and their babies. It is an insult to our national sovereignty that we bowed to the UN demand to meet their 5% quota. And the man responsible for that decision is the Prime Minister.

The violation of thousands of young women is even more scandalous. The forcible harvesting their eggs and removal their reproductive tissues and organs. They did not only do this to volunteers, or women cooperating for IVF treatment, but also to prisoners hoping for a reduced sentence.

This was all done with the knowledge Orchard Mayhew."

Orchard's veins throbbed on his beetroot complexion, as he screeched across the chamber.

"That's a lie!!"

"But members of the House," continued Evie, "there is something even more wicked. This year alone, over fifty women have gone missing. We have speculated about a serial killer. But I suggest that these victims met a different fate. I have in my hand, the Department of Health documents which were leaked to the press."

Orchard's complexion faded to a sickly green and his cowering, flabby figure shrank into the bench. Harper Sykes, seated beside him, pursed his lips and turned his head in the opposite direction, signalling his disapproval to the TV cameras.

Evie adopted her most commanding pose.

"These papers include the names of the women who were manipulated or coerced into donating eggs, reproductive organs and tissues. Their organs were either transplanted or used in laboratories for multiple-cloning. But fifty are not named! They merely have a four-digit code.

My Right Honourable colleague Veracity Dunmore will now share her recent findings with the House."

Veracity rose to her feet, tossing her sun-bleached, highlighted hair.

The strident, Thames-basin accent of the Basildon MP resounded across the Chamber, nearly devoid of 'h's', but still asserting a new authority. The plough of tumult had churned up a rising star.

"Members of the 'ouse, my department 'ave checked the four-digit codes for over fifty nameless women against 'ealth Trust databases. We have found a corresponding database which holds both their codes and their 'ealth Trust numbers. I can reveal they are the missing women."

Pandemonium erupted, as the Speaker vainly hollered:

"Order! Order! Order!"

As Evie's voice thundered across the Chamber, the noise subsided to a murmur.

"These women were abducted, restrained, forcefully anaesthetised, butchered under the scalpel, abused, violated, mutilated and MURDERED! I suggest that the Prime Minister himself allowed the abductions, to meet the UN male birth quota, because there were not enough prisoners or volunteers to be bullied or manipulated! They were killed to silence them forever!

Losing all control, Orchard screamed his denial with vile expletives and was silenced by the Speaker.

Evie pointed at the front bench.

"This Government is debased, wicked and totally unfit to govern. While arrogantly parading itself as a flagship for humanity it has plummeted to levels of depravity not seen since ancient Rome!

I therefore support the No Confidence motion. I once loved my party, but I now love God much more and it is His name that I call upon every one of you to vote with me today. If you have any fear of God and if indeed you love your country, then you must end this abomination! As the Division Bell rings, hear the cry of those women from their graves!"

The fire still pumped through her veins as she collapsed into her seat. Pain and fatigue took their toll, but the power flowing through her spirit had no earthly source. She was caught up in another dimension between heaven and earth.

Then her eyes focused across the House to the Visitor's Gallery. Could it really be??!!

The tall, shining army officer with the flaming sword from Westminster Abbey stood at the back. Engulfed in a bright light, he was taller than any man. But as she stood and pointed, he dissolved into a radiant cloud, faded and vanished.

She barely registered the tumultuous applause and cheering which resounded across the House and colleagues clasping her hand. Their hugs and embraces barely hurt her shoulder. Today she had fought back.

Suffolk, 29th November

Prema clapped and cheered around the room.

"Brave woman! I love her! Evie Atherton has spoken for me and hundreds of women!"

The young police officer seated beside her became agitated.

"Be quiet and shut that window!"

"But we're miles from anywhere, Cloud!"

"You must be careful Prema," added Frank, "I always thought you were a quiet woman!"

Prema tilted her head and smiled.

"Only on limited acquaintance! But I'm grateful you've come."

"To make sure they look after you properly. You're a vindicated woman."

"I could happily stay here. Clean air, country cottage, views across the River Orwell. Why go back to Lewisham?"

"You'd really leave London?"

"Nothing there, but sickening memories."

House of Commons, 29th November

Animated crowds stood outside the Houses of Parliament, chanting, singing and savouring the drama within, relayed on a massive hologram TV. With a colourful array of slogans, banners and placards they braved the drizzle, their discomfort outweighed by a sense of history.

Suddenly, everyone screamed and ducked as a spine-chilling screech resounded above the police sirens.

A hideous red and green figure swooped through the air across the river and over the gathered multitudes, its sharp claws narrowly missing people's heads as it clumsily wheeled round and dived into the entrance of Parliament, knocking a policeman to the ground.

The Division Bell rang and MPs sprang to their feet, filing out of the chamber. With a blood-curdling scream, the bulky 5ft green and red monster hurtled though the entrance.

With huge blue bulging eyes, a semi-human face, vicious beak, cruel talons and massive wing span, but recognisably human arms and legs, it circled and dived towards Orchard. He shielded his face and rolled to the floor, as vicious pecks drew blood through his suit and matted hair.

Five police officers charged in behind the creature shouting:

"Everyone get down! On the floor!"

But the MPs ignored them, in their frantic exodus to the 'Ayes' and 'Noes' rooms. The creature dug its claws into the quivering Prime Minister who lay in a heap on the carpet. The words tumbling from its mouth were human, but the voice was unmistakably that of a parrot. "Waark!! Traitor!! Murderer!! Waark!

An SAS officer tore Pickles the Parrot away from a sobbing Orchard, who was taken to St Thomas's Hospital as the MPs sealed his political fate.

Dulwich, 29th November

Dave and Amelia were riveted by the commentary on BBC News 24.

"Pickles the Parrot, the former Speaker of the House of Commons has now been restrained and the paramedics are taking the Prime Minister to a waiting ambulance outside. We understand that Oliver Bunton was taken to the Battersea Transition Centre in October. His final operation has not been carried out so he is still legally human, though no longer a British Citizen."

Amelia sighed.

"He's finally denounced Orchard, whatever state he's in. I only wish he'd done it sooner."

Dave put an arm round her shoulder.

"Evie spoke for you and many other women today."

"I won't be happy till I see the result of this vote, Dave."

"The Prime Minister's finished love. I don't know what they'll do to Oliver Bunton, but I hope they don't operate on him. The human part of him had the guts to speak out though he was so violent, I hope they sedate him. I'm chuffed, I finally taught him to fly!"

"But do you still want to work at Roehampton?"

"I've had doubts for ages, Amelia. I bond with my clients then lose them forever. I never get used to it. The money's lousy and anyway, I hate deceiving Aidan and Miriam about what I really do."

"I just hope they never find out."

"The people who blackmailed us are finished - well, most of them. We'll never feel completely safe, but I don't care."

"A fresh start, then?"

"Yeah!"

xxi) For such a time as this

Peckham, 30th November

"Best headlines in years!"

Aidan punched the air.

"*613 votes to 38. Unfit to Govern! Snap election January.* And look at the Daily Mail – *Traitor! Murderer!*"

"And the Sun," laughed Miriam, "who say *Gotcha! PM Savaged by Atherton and Parrot.*"

"Here's the Telegraph editorial," chuckled Aidan, "*Evie Atherton's speech yesterday is worthy of the hall of fame shared by Churchill, Macmillan, Margaret Thatcher and Sir Geoffrey Howe.*

Yesterday, Orchard Mayhew was mauled by a lioness. Atherton displayed gravitas, authority and eloquence as she lambasted his corrupt, self-indulgent and amoral administration.

If she stands down in December, we will lose a flourishing stateswoman. There is only one place for her if the Tory Independence Party is to survive – party leader."

Miriam turned to Evie.

"How are you my love? You look so pensive. We're proud of you!"

"I can't return to high office, whatever the Telegraph says."

"Evie, don't go into exile. You're a woman of God! You must be in a place of influence. And I still believe He will raise you to great heights."

"Forget it, Aidan. I've had my fingers burned and my heart broken. I'll keep my head below the parapet. But I realised yesterday how much I'll miss Parliament. So, I've decided to stand for re-election in January. But only as a backbench MP, so don't get your hopes up."

"Just a backbencher?"

Tears welled up in her eyes.

"I'll lose my seat anyway, Aidan. Our party will be slaughtered. The opening Opinion Poll gives the Labour Socialists a 20% lead!

Anyway, I don't feel like a lioness. When I got home last night, I felt empty and flat. When James first died, I was wrapped in a bubble of love and sympathy, but now I only have wilting flowers for company. I miss him so desperately.... I want him back......"

Evie flung herself across the sofa in floods tears and it was several minutes before her convulsive sobbing subsided.

"We're always here, my love."

"I've decided to live with my dad in Warrington, at weekends. But my flat's so lonely. I wondered, please can I move in with you on weekdays? Until I get back on my feet?

Miriam's shriek of ecstasy resounded through the thin terrace walls.

Cardiff, 1st December

Ten thousand angry people gathered outside the Welsh Assembly buildings and the Waterfront was blockaded by hundreds of bicycles. A volatile melting pot of students, anarchists, Cyclists for Justice protesters and irate members of public.

Myfanwy stepped up to a hastily-erected podium to address the gathering.

"Good morning everyone. Like so many demonstrators around the country, we are here today to express our anger and outrage at the murderous and tyrannical government which has abducted and killed innocent women. I am now certain that Wales can no longer be a part of the United Kingdom and I am calling for a referendum at the earliest opportunity, in March."

Cheers erupted and pedestrians and cyclists surged forward. As violent explosions ripped across the crowd, pillars of fire and smoke engulfed the area. Screams pierced the air as crash barriers collapsed, fighting broke out and bodies were crushed under the stampeding masses.

BBC News 24 coverage moved to Birmingham, Manchester, Newcastle, Sheffield, Bristol and other major cities as similar scenes unfolded....

Honor Oak Crematorium, 3rd December

As Gloria drove through the congested roads of Dulwich, the setting winter sun yielded to the homely Christmas lights in shop windows and extrovert house displays.

At Honor Oak Crematorium, dusk approached. The gates were still open as she clutched a prickly Advent wreath and walked to the memorial plaques, searching in the fading light for the name of Daniel Baxter 1998-2032.

She knelt on the gravel and gently laid her wreath on the damp turf.

"Dan, I miss you," she whispered, "and I'm still battling for you with every case I fight. And someone else has spoken up for you."

She pulled a newspaper cutting from her handbag and laid it under the wreath. The words "PM savaged by Atherton" were still visible.

"I wish you'd lived to see it. Sleep tight, bruv."

Suffolk, 3rd December

Prema carved slices of gammon for Frank and her police escort.

"One more week here!"

"Then Lewisham?"

"Until I move to Australia with Reeta, but that'll take weeks to organise. I dread going back to my old house."

"There's another possibility, if you're interested? I've moved to Bognor. I haven't sold my Dulwich house yet. You could stay there while you make plans."

"You're very kind. I'll take you up on the offer."

Frank's wrist phone suddenly rang.

"What? Today? You mean immediately?"

He turned to Prema.

"It's the Home Office! The Acting Prime Minister is announcing your release to the press now. We're taking you back to London."

"Why so soon?"

"They kept your release quiet to save Orchard's skin. But he's gone now, so they may as well go public."

Prema's heart sank. Now she must face London with all its memories and dangers.

House of Commons Bar, 6th December

A glass of Italian red wine appeared on Evie's table. She recognised the familiar tobacco-pipe smell behind her.

"Vernon? A parting gift before my demise?"

"Merely an end-of term celebratory drink as Parliament is dissolved."

"I congratulate you on winning the vote. Everything's going your way, including the anarchy riots and death and carnage across the UK.   They're all looking to you as their hero and saviour! Lucky coincidence for you, that these anarchists are kicking off now."

"You think I engineered these riots?"

"I wouldn't put it past you."

"You think I'd risk losing Wales on my watch?"

"A small price to pay, for you to reach Number 10."

"Every MP has their price to reach Number 10. I'm sorry you've lost your ambition. I'd have relished the pleasure of such a worthy opponent."

"Your party's triumph will wipe us all out of Westminster. And I value my soul more than the highest office."

Greenwich Holding Centre, 1st January 2037, midnight

A glassy-eyed Orchard Mayhew watched his hologram TV as the Big Ben chimes and massive firework display along the Thames ushered in the last year of his life.

He would not live to see 2038.

The Old Bailey trial for his role in dozens of abductions and serial killings would commence in May.

He was certain that Vernon Stack would abolish the guillotine if he won the election on 29th January, but not until the precision-built device had been used for one special prisoner, himself.

"You had this machine built," Vernon had sneered, during a special visit to his cell, "so it is only fitting that, if you are found guilty, you should die on it. I will make sure of that, when I get to Number 10!"

In any case, Orchard knew that the anarchists would not tolerate clemency.

Chris Evans Community Centre Warrington, 30th January, 3.00am, election night.

The cavernous community hall echoed with the murmur of election officials, tellers, party members and a crowd smelling an imminent declaration.

Evie awaited her result in Warrington South, resigned to defeat with a 20% swing to the Labour Socialists and catastrophic losses to her party throughout the night.

She hadn't really tried. After a miserable, wretched Christmas when the festivities and sentimental TV adverts had intensified her pain and grief, she had invested minimal effort in her election campaign.

Her social media communication was at an all-time low. Dragging her boots through snow and ice to knock on doors, every hustings and community event had drained the life out of her as she battled 'flu, depression and post-traumatic stress.

And yet, three days before the election, the reality of losing her seat had hit home. After weeks of indifference, she had suddenly begun to care.

"Have Labour gained Oxford?"

A political nightmare unfolded before her eyes, but she could not tear herself away.

"This bloodbath will easily erase my 8,000 majority and I'm rehearsing my loser's smile!"

She grinned ruefully at a fellow party worker.

"I'm fine, Jim! There's life after politics!"

"Like what?"

"I'll go back to Roxanne Fashions.   And er...there's my faith. I'm a Christian now. Maybe God's planned something else. Perhaps I'll go to a remote Scottish island and open a retreat centre for burnt-out, washed-up politicians!"

"An island?! You'll need half of Scotland!"

"Shh!! The BBC are at Finchley North for Harper's declaration! I can't believe he's Acting Prime Minister. He's sitting on a 12,500 majority, creep!"

The camera zoomed on the candidates with a rainbow of rosettes. The Mayor stepped to the microphone.

"......... *Harper Chesterton Sykes, Tory Independence Party, 22,352*"

Evie shrugged.

"He's done it. Huh!"

"*Almond Isles, Labour Socialist candidate, 26,897*

"Harper's out!" She shrieked.

But as she quietly repented of gloating, an official called her to a back room with her rival candidates.

She berated herself for being afraid.   A vicious bullet had ripped the most precious thing from her life. Nothing could hurt her again. Yet her wrist phone showed a pulse rate of 140.

She gave a polite nod to her opponents.

"Good morning. This is your briefing before the public declaration."

The Labour candidate had an irritating smirk on his face. Evie braced herself.

"I can confirm... a Tory Independence hold. Evie Atherton retains her seat!"

Evie staggered back and caught a chair.

"What?? I've won?? By how much?"

"By a majority of 5,129."

Lewisham, 1st February

Gregory Wilson sprawled across the pine floor, as he spoke to Bishop Burstall on his wrist phone.

"I'm so depressed. I know I should be grateful. Two months' freedom. No murder charge or guillotine. I've had a £1 million advance to write my biography and yet...."

"Oh, snap out of it Gregory. You got off lightly. A terrified Prime Minister with friends in high places. You've signed the gagging clause. Just get on with your life."

"Got off lightly? I'll never work again. I've lost my TV career and hospital job. Everyone knows I was in Prema Gupta's house the night of 14th February, though they've never proved why. You're still a Bishop."

"Stop whingeing."

"You still have your Radio 4 slot and House of Lords seat, as you manipulate Episcopalian churchgoers into accepting Ralph's brave new world. Well carry on spreading your poison. I'm no longer a part of it. I hate colonic deliveries, screaming men and I hate you!"

"You're hysterical. If you cause trouble, I can make one call and have you silenced for good. I can't listen to you all day, have a toddler to feed."

The line went dead.

Gregory groaned. He was free and alive, but for how long? Chawton was gone, but who else wanted him dead? His home was a fortress of locks and alarms.

He racked with pain and grief for Ralph. Not for his death, but the relationship which died years ago.

He threw Ralph's photo to the floor, smashing the frame.

"You tormented me! I hate you! First came the passion, then came your violence! Prema felt neglected and I thought you loved me more. But you pushed me out too! You controlled everything. We were both your victims.

You bullied me into becoming an accessory to her attempted murder. But you're dead and I'll suffer the consequences forever.

Thank you for wrecking my life!"

Bognor Regis, 1st February, 12.30pm

As Evie's car hurtled along the A27, the view of Chichester was obscured by a driving blizzard. Today she looked forward to a leisurely lunch with Frank, chilled conversation and a revival of their warm friendship.

Frank waited on the doorstep as she pulled into the driveway of a white bungalow on the sea front.

"Short notice, but roast beef's ready as ever!"

"Same old Frank!"

The cosy familiarity of fresh coffee, an open fire and the company of three stroppy teenagers almost banished the horrors of November.

"Evie, congratulations! A five-thousand majority!"

"I was shocked."

"You had so much public sympathy and your currency shot up when you attacked Orchard Mayhew! I was cheering."

"Loyal as ever. I've really missed you , Frank. How's life by the sea? Much crime in Bognor?"

"Work's fine, but so much has happened since New Year."

"Indeed?"

"Evie, I have some major news. I've got engaged."

The news smacked into her like another bullet. Reeling, she struggled to compose herself and gave him a warm embrace.

"You? Engaged?! Frank, congratulations! But how come? You dark horse, that's quick work! We only turned each other down three months ago!"

"Is it such a shock, that I've found someone else? It all happened over Christmas. Whirlwind romance, but we both knew immediately."

Frank, I'm really pleased for you. It's just a bit sudden, that's all."

"My fiancée is here and having lunch with us."

Frank called across to the kitchen.

"Darling, come and meet Evie."

Evie gulped her coffee, struggling to fill the pit in her stomach, as every complacent anticipation of the day evaporated. She turned her head, as expensive perfume wafted into the room.

A dark, beautiful, svelte, elegant young woman with massive brown eyes stood before her. With a navy cashmere jumper, gold jewellery and a beaded skirt swirling to her ankles, she epitomised style and taste. Evie suddenly felt frumpy, but the biggest shock of all was that her pretty features were all too familiar.

"Prema? Prema Gupta?"

Prema stepped forward and embraced her. But this was an assured and radiant woman, not the pallid, repressed creature Evie had seen on TV.

"Evie, I'm so honoured to meet you at last."

Evie squirmed as Prema gushed effusively.

"I admire you so much…. You made that amazing speech in Parliament. You spoke up for all of us. And it was you who saved my life on the day of my execution. Frank has told me everything.   I can never thank you enough. "

"I'm honoured to meet you too. You were incredibly brave. I wish I'd saved you sooner. I'm sorry you suffered such a long ordeal."

Frank wrapped his arm around Prema's waist.

"Hasn't God blessed me with a beautiful woman?"

Evie laughed nervously.

"He certainly has. Well, er, congratulations both of you!"

Bognor Regis, 1st February, 5.00pm

As dusk fell, Evie drove blindly though the drizzle. She felt nothing for Frank. So why was this excruciating?

Throughout lunch, Prema had gazed at him, utterly besotted. And Frank was clearly smitten.

She poured out her heart to the voice recognition diary on her wrist phone.

"Prema deserves all the happiness in the world after her ordeal. Frank has rightly moved on, but the speed of his change of heart has really hurt me! I enjoyed his attention and having him to myself!

They excluded me during lunch. I hoped to rekindle Frank's friendship, but instead he ambushed me with his news and behaved like a lovestruck teenager.

I had to endure Prema's endless prattling about their Christmas romance and Easter wedding plans. She kept flashing her huge ruby engagement ring."

Evie sadly gazed at the coke can ring on her own finger.

"She's clearly a gentle, thoughtful woman, so why did she offer no condolences on James's death? She didn't even acknowledge it. Can love really make a kind-hearted person so insensitive?"

I had no appetite for that roast dinner as it grew colder on my plate.

And I desperately wanted quality time with her, but Frank monopolised her. We needed to talk - about the months of torment we both shared, the miscarriage of justice which had changed both our lives forever. I often imagined meeting her, but today's introduction was a total anti-climax. I hope we meet again, without Frank whispering sweet nothings in her ear."

Prema's life has changed from pain to joy. God, did you use her suffering to bring Frank into her life?"

She stared down the motorway as a fierce gale whipped against the side of her car.

"Dear Lord, I feel so alone...."

Blinded by tears, she pulled into a lay-by.

"Lord what now? Everyone else has moved on.... Prema, Frank, Ceiba, Norma. James has been murdered. Lucinda's dead. I can't live with Aidan and Miriam forever. Dear God, if ever I needed to hear from you, it's now."

A feeling of warmth began to surround her. She felt slightly better as her tears subsided. The heaviness gradually lifted. She shut her eyes as the torrential rain continued and cars droned past in the twilight.

She was almost asleep when the shrill, ringing of her wrist phone jolted her awake.

"Hello? Veracity?"

Veracity Dunmore's high-pitched Essex accent squawked her ears.

"Evie, where are you? The Party's in turmoil. At Tory Independence HQ, they're running around like headless chickens. Once and for all, will you stand for the leadership?"

"No. You know exactly how I feel, Veracity. I've had enough!"

"But there ain't no-one else! The public love you. We're in a total mess. You're our only hope! Anyway, you promised me, remember? Shadow Education Secretary."

"I can't think about it now.   This is a really bad time."

"Well don't navel-gaze too long! We need to give Vernon Stack a run for his money!"

"Veracity, stop hassling me. Just go away! I need time to pray."

"Look Evie, I don't do God. But maybe your God has put you here for such a time as this? Orchard's left this country in an utter mess. We have no Opposition leader. If you won't do this, who will?"

"Just leave me alone!"

Jerusalem, 4th February

A pretty barista prepared a double expresso, chatting to her clients in the draughty café.

She had forgotten how wet and chilly Israel could become in February, although the landscape became delightfully greener. She pulled her thick, shabby thick cardigan around her shoulders and shuffled over to a table in slouchy suede boots.

"Thank you, Gita!"

She remembered to smile at her customer, acknowledging her new name. Another relaxing day in her new 'career'.

But as she glanced across to a corner table, her heart suddenly seemed to stop. A hulking figure slouched over his coffee, with oily muscles, thick brows and a torn t-shirt. His surly mouth twisted around a roll-up.

Mercifully, he gave no indication of recognising her. Her throat grew dry, as she tried to keep her tray steady.

With an Italian accent, clanging chunky jewellery, a deep tan, dark eyeliner and black-dyed hair, Erica Rayleigh, the former Editor of The Observian, was almost beyond recognition.

But even three months later, she carefully eyed every client who came through the door. This was her nightmare come true.

As Callum drained his cup and left without a backward glance, she dared to hope her disguise had worked, for now.

But as soon as he was out of sight, she grabbed her bag and took the rest of the day off sick.

She would never return to that café.

She would always be on the move.

Peckham, 4th February

Miriam had a new role, as Prema's wedding-planner.

"Prema, you must invite Evie," she murmured, checking the guest list, "she's a close friend of Frank's."

"Of course! She had lunch with us on Sunday. She's lovely, but so pale and withdrawn. Not at all like her public image.

Aidan looked at her reproachfully.

"She's suffered horrendously."

"Sorry, I forgot."

Miriam picked up baby Lakeside, as he whimpered.

"Will you start a family?"

"Not after what Ralph did to me …. but I'll have three stepchildren and we're adopting!"

"A baby?"

"No, we're adopting a hybrid!"

"A hybrid?!"

"Yes, Miriam, from Battersea. They've opened a care centre for failed transspecies patients, with long-term special needs. We've been screened and approved as carers. We already have a hybrid selected for us."

Aidan was aghast.

"Are you crazy?"

"You already know him. He's so sweet. He's called Pickles the Parrot and he used to be Oliver Bunton, the Speaker of the House of Commons!"

"Let me get this straight, Prema, you're having that monstrosity in your house?"

"I know it's a big undertaking, Aidan, but I've faced the guillotine and Frank was in charge of the Metropolitan Police. If anyone can cope, we can. Besides, I want to do something meaningful. I'll never go back to midwifery, but I want to serve in some way.

"Anyway," added Miriam, "the Government no longer allows Evangelical Christians to adopt babies, so what else can they do?"

Aidan shook his head.

"But think of the filth, the mess and the physical and mental demands he will place on you. And look how viciously he attacked Orchard Mayhew!"

"Mayhew deserved everything he got. Anyway, Pickles is on tranquillisers and having therapy. I know he'll behave. He likes us. The Social Services and RSPCA are adapting our home for him and Judge Mayhew's giving us a grant from his trust fund."

"Well, good luck with that one."

Westminster, House of Commons, State Opening of Parliament 14th February

Thousands assembled outside the Houses of Parliament awaiting the arrival of the His Majesty the King at the Sovereign's Entrance for the State Opening of Parliament. With camp beds, portable tents, gas stoves, sleeping bags and thermal mountain-wear, multitudes braved the vicious February blizzard for a glimpse of the Royal Family.

In the House of Commons, the MPs waited to be summoned to the House of Lords.

Evie straightened her black suit and adjusted her silk scarf and ruby brooch. Veracity leaned across and whispered in her ear.

"You can't wear a coke can ring on your finger today!"

"Don't you ever dare say that to me again. I owe James my life. I'll wear this forever."

"I'm sorry. Are you nervous?"

"Ask a silly question! Who wouldn't be. But I'm determined go through with this."

With three sharp raps on the door, Black Rod summoned the MPs to the Upper House and the presence of His Majesty the King.

Prime Minister Vernon Stack, a staunch republican, audibly made his feelings know.

"Blooming parasite, let him come to us!"

Evie checked her posture as everyone prepared to cross the Lobby, to be seated behind the ermine-clad Peers of the Realm. Undaunted by the splendour, she was determined to carry herself with authority.

Vernon Stack glanced at her with a wry half smile and murmured:

"Are you ready, lioness?"

The smile faded as he assumed a commanding demeanour as the new Prime Minister with a massive majority, poised to hear the delivery of his first King's Speech.

Evie gave a courteous nod and walked beside him at the front of the MPs' procession, as newly-elected Leader of His Majesty's Opposition.

She turned to the battered remnant of Tory Independence MPs behind her.

"Stand tall everyone," she commanded, "our fight-back begins!"

Some of the troops were respected and talented individuals, but others were reprobates tainted with the corrupt rule of Orchard Mayhew. She would root them out.

And as her own broken life began to rise from the ashes of grief and despair, she quietly prayed:

"Dear God, I'm terrified, but I'm doing this anyway. Your word says that when I walk through the fire, you will be with me. I'll try to reform this party and serve everyone in this country. You've raised me to this position of influence. Help me to honour you. In the name of Jesus Christ my King."

As she stepped forward, peace began to flow into her heart, even amid the searing ache for her beloved James. Her bullet-battered body remained fragile and her heart was still raw in the early stages of grief, but as she crossed the lobby, she sensed that an invisible angel with a flaming sword was guarding her.

Evie took another glance at Vernon Stack and the other 600 MPs with their myriad of ambitions, passions, convictions, talents, vices and virtues. In such colourful, vibrant surroundings, a small seed of zest for life began to germinate within her.

Let battle commence!